D1179404

ROUND ABOUT
THE CHRISTMAS TREE

ROUND ABOUT
THE CHRISTMAS TREE

Edited by
BECKY BROWN

With an introduction by
NED HALLEY

With illustrations by
ALICE ERCLE HUNT

MACMILLAN COLLECTOR'S LIBRARY

This collection first published by Macmillan Collector's Library 2018
an imprint of Pan Macmillan
20 New Wharf Road, London N1 9RR
Associated companies throughout the world
www.panmacmillan.com

ISBN 978-1-5098-6656-4

1 3 5 7 9 8 6 4 2

A CIP catalogue record for this book is available from the British Library.

Casing design and endpaper pattern by Andrew Davidson
Printed and bound in China by Imago

Visit www.panmacmillan.com to read more about all our books
and to buy them. You will also find features, author interviews and
news of any author events, and you can sign up for e-newsletters
so that you're always first to hear about our new releases.

Contents

Introduction

NED HALLEY

Comfort and joy. These are the precious gifts brought to us in the best of Christmas stories. And the twenty-two tales in this seasonal selection deliver generously. All are from great writers of the nineteenth and early twentieth centuries – the golden age of storytelling, and, judging by these accounts, of the festival of Christmas too.

It's tempting, of course, to imagine that Christmases past were more spiritual and authentic than our own Christmases present, tarnished as they might be by twenty-first-century commercialism and superficial sentiment. But authors of the calibre of William Makepeace Thackeray, Charles Dickens and Louisa May Alcott rejoiced as much in the calamities of Christmas as they did in all the goodwill. They found Christmas uplifting, benevolent and funny.

Thackeray (1811–63), whose 'Round About the Christmas Tree' takes pole position in this collection, evokes a familiar seasonal theme: the cost of it all. The story, one of a series written for the *Cornhill Magazine* in the early 1860s, delights in the scene of a family's younger members plucking sweetmeats and bonbons from the tree, and ruefully reflects that for 'the elderly . . . in the packets which WE pick off the boughs, we find enclosed Mr. Carnifex's review of the quarter's meat, Mr. Sartor's compliments and little statement for self and the young gentlemen; and Madame de Sainte-Crinoline's respects to the young ladies, who encloses her account, and will send on Saturday, please'.

In his inimitable style, here featuring his trademark genius for the comically apt professional name, the author of *Vanity Fair* summons up one of the great constants of Christmas with reassuring good cheer. The story moves on to atmospheric descriptions of festive London at the time, including a ludicrous pantomime based on *Hamlet* with some sensational special effects, and a visit to the zoo to see 'our fellow creatures in the monkey room' – a topical tilt at Charles Darwin's *On the Origin of Species*, published in 1859.

Thackeray was a shrewd observer of human folly, but he loved Christmas just the same, and wrote a hugely popular series of stories for children, *Christmas Books*, in 1854. At the height of his fame, aged fifty-two, he died following a stroke on Christmas Eve 1863. Seven thousand mourners came to his funeral.

'The Adventure of the Blue Carbuncle' by Sir Arthur Conan Doyle (1859–1930) first appeared in the January 1892 edition of the *Strand Magazine*, and was among the twelve stories later included in *The Adventures of Sherlock Holmes*. The great detective investigates the theft of a fabled sapphire swallowed by a Christmas goose. Holmes, of course, unravels the mystery, and shows more than a little festive goodwill in doing so.

Hans Christian Andersen (1805–1875), originator of the modern fairy tale and pioneer of writing for children, knew the kind of hardship depicted in 'The Little Match Girl', his New Year's tale of 1845. An only child aged eleven when his father died, Hans had to work to support himself at the local charity school in Odense, Denmark. The fairy-tale success of his later life – Andersen's works have been translated into more than

100 languages – never dimmed his compassion for the poor, and particularly for their children.

Andersen demonstrates his talent for animating every kind of entity in the moral fable 'The Fir-tree', first published in Copenhagen at Christmas in 1844. The tale was republished in Danish at several subsequent Christmases during its author's lifetime, and has been prolifically translated and reinterpreted ever since. It is a compelling caution to readers of every age: Live every day in the moment. Do not pine away dreaming of future glories, Christmas included.

Washington Irving, author of immortal tales including 'Rip Van Winkle' and 'The Legend of Sleepy Hollow', was born to British parents in New York in April 1783, within days of the end of the American War of Independence. He was named in honour of George Washington and became the first American writer to win equal fame on both sides of the Atlantic. He lived in Europe for seventeen years, and served as US ambassador to Spain.

'Christmas Eve' is a fragment from *Bracebridge Hall*, an episodic novel written by Irving while living in England. The splendid central character of Squire Bracebridge, with his old-fashioned ideas and 'singular mix of whim and benevolence', is probably inspired by the fictional Sir Roger de Coverley, a foolish but kindly old Tory gentleman featured in the *Spectator* in 1711.

'Christmas at Thompson Hall' by Anthony Trollope (1815–1882) is a surreal comedy of manners by one of the great Victorian originators of psychological story-telling. As with his great Barchester and Palliser novels, Trollope shows his mastery of female characters in this Christmas classic. The mortifications of the formidably strong-minded Mrs. Mary Brown, caught up in a deliciously tortuous series of misapprehensions, are a joy indeed.

Canadian Lucy Maud Montgomery (1874–1942) won immortality with her masterpiece *Anne of Green Gables*, and was the author, too, of twenty further novels and more than 500 short stories. 'A Christmas Inspiration', written in 1901, is a heartwarming tale of festive kindness in a city boarding house.

'Christmas at Red Butte', a late L. M. Montgomery tale, tackles the dilemma of an impoverished widow unable to afford Christmas gifts for her young children, and in the very best of the sentimental, uplifting traditions of the season, it's her sixteen-year-old adopted daughter, Theodora, who saves the day.

'The Flying Stars' is one of the fifty-three Father Brown short stories written by G. K. Chesterton between 1910 and 1936, the year the author died. London-born Chesterton, well-known as an Anglican journalist and novelist, is said to have based the character of Brown on his friend Father John O'Connor, the parish priest who later inducted the writer into the Catholic faith.

Father Brown's intuitive skills are on full display in the Christmas setting of 'The Flying Stars'. It is a key story in the series, in which arch-villain Hercule Flambeau, Father Brown's antagonist in most of the fifty-three mysteries, is caught in the midst of a fiendish crime, is confounded by an irresistible moral plea, and finally renounces his life of transgression.

Sir Henry Fielding Dickens (1849–1933), eighth of Charles Dickens's ten children, wrote in a fond memoir of family Christmases that they were 'a great time, a really jovial time, and my father was always at his best, a splendid host, bright and jolly as a boy and throwing his heart and soul into everything that was going on'.

For the author who has done more than any other to define the festival as it is understood today in Britain and around the world, depicting Christmas was a personal mission as well as a creative one. His story of 1835, 'A Christmas Dinner', written when he was just twenty-two, was among his first essays and was reprinted the following year in his first book, *Sketches by Boz*. Dickens had begun his writing life as a lawcourt reporter and was an exacting observer as well as an inspired narrator.

'A Christmas Dinner' is a magical depiction and a rich slice of social history, forever fresh in imagery and in its understanding of the conflicting sentiments all of us inevitably feel about the festival. 'A Christmas Tree', written for his own magazine *Household Words* in 1850, seven years after his sensational novella *A Christmas Carol*, is an autobiographical story. The author, still in his thirties, looks back with an old man's nostalgia on long-past seasons, focusing on what was then a recent innovation, 'that pretty German toy' first popularized in Britain by Queen Victoria's new consort Prince Albert in 1840.

The recollections are unreliable. There were no Christmas trees in the time of Dickens's childhood, and we know this famous author had an insecure and sometimes impoverished upbringing. The festive tree of his imagining was 'brilliantly lighted . . . and everywhere sparkled and glittered' in its towering heights, but in its lower branches harboured darker emblems: a horrible frog, a hideous mask and an 'infernal snuff-box out of which there sprang a demoniacal Counsellor in a black gown'.

Is the story a plea for a better understanding of the childhood mind in the midst of the festive wonder? Ghostly, abstract and notably devout, this is a contemplative work of enduring mystery.

O. Henry, author of 'The Gift of the Magi', was the pen name of one of America's favourite storytellers, William Sydney Porter. His life, like his stories, was marked by twists and turns. The son of a North Carolina doctor, he showed early promise in both writing and art, but at nineteen began work as a pharmacist. He left home for Texas, where well-connected new friends helped him find better-paid work as a bank teller. He met and married an heiress, Athol Estes, in 1887. Her family had not consented to the union, as Athol suffered from tuberculosis, but the couple's only surviving child, Margaret, was born two years later.

All the while, William was writing stories in his own time. He started his own magazine, interestingly called *The Rolling Stone*. But in 1894 came a turn. He was accused of embezzlement by the bank, was sacked, and then arrested a year later. In a moment of madness the day before his trial, he jumped bail and fled to Honduras in Central America, where he continued to write, selling stories under pseudonyms including Oliver Henry.

After six months he travelled home to see his seriously ill daughter and at once turned himself in to the police. Athol died before the trial, at which he was found guilty and sentenced to five years' imprisonment. On his release, he moved to New York.

From this rackety life arose nearly 300 much-loved American stories. 'The Gift of the Magi' is from a 1906 collection of tales of New York called *The Four Million*. The title was inspired by the author's anger at a snobbish canard of the day that there were only 400 people among the city's four million who were worth notice. In the short tale of an ordinary young couple anxious to show their love for each other at Christmas, this flawed but formidable writer offers us a profoundly moral fable with a famous twist.

L. Frank Baum (1856–1919) is another great American popular writer, best remembered for *The Wizard of Oz*, and one of the most imaginative of authors for children in any era. One of nine children of a father born of German stock (*Baum* is the German word for tree) and a British mother, Frank grew up in a happy, prosperous home in New York state, where Christmas was celebrated in exuberant style.

'A Kidnapped Santa Claus' was published as a short story in 1904, two years after Frank's inventive novel *The Life and Adventures of Santa Claus* presented the great Christmas benefactor as a fairy-tale character. Story and novel share the same setting of the Laughing Valley, Santa's home, but this kidnapping exploit is a one-off adventure, also with a moral message.

'The Ghost of Christmas Eve' by J. M. Barrie (1860–1937) is from the novel *My Lady Nicotine* of 1890, written fourteen years before *Peter Pan*. The novel concerns the dilemma of an avid smoker whose fiancée tells him he must quit tobacco before they can marry. This fragment is an intriguing piece of Christmas whimsy by an author famous for his enjoyment of the festive season, his aptitude for supernatural themes, and his ambivalent fondness for smoking.

'A Country Christmas' by Louisa May Alcott (1832–1888) is a lively romantic tale from *Kitty's Class Day and Other Stories*, a collection for young readers published in 1868, the same year that *Little Women* made this much-loved American author very famous indeed. Alcott came from a large New England family headed by the philosopher-educationalist Amos Bronson Alcott, who founded his own school in Boston and moved in an intellectual circle that included Ralph Waldo Emerson and Nathaniel Hawthorne, but failed to make a proper living.

Louisa's animated home life undoubtedly inspired much of her writing for both adults and children. A firm feminist and abolitionist, her success owed much to her compassionate sense of humour, which saw her through tragedies that befell her family, her own disappointments (she never married) and the bitter years of the American Civil War of 1861–1865, which is referenced in much of her later work. In 'A Country Christmas', she fully exploits the potential of encounter, as homely and wise Aunt Plumy welcomes a fashionable young party from the big city to her farmhouse in Vermont.

London-born Edith Nesbit (1858–1924), originator of the children's adventure story and best known for *The Railway Children*, had an extraordinary family life. A committed Marxist and co-founder of the socialist Fabian Society, she had five children with her notoriously faithless husband and wrote some forty novels and story collections for children as well as numerous books for adults. 'The Conscience-Pudding' is a comedy-adventure Christmas tale with a positive moral purpose.

Thomas Hardy (1840–1928) wrote a dozen novels, several of them masterpieces, eight volumes of poetry including some of the most moving in the language, and more than fifty short stories – few of which have enjoyed the reputation they deserve.

'The Thieves Who Couldn't Help Sneezing' (1877) is

a comic yarn with a Christmas theme set in the familiar surroundings of Hardy's Wessex. On Christmas Eve night, young hero Hubert is robbed of his horse, but exacts an ingenious revenge with the aid of the local gentry.

'Christmas Every Day' by William Dean Howells (1837–1920) is a cautionary tale, a pioneering warning to keep Christmas within bounds. Howells, who has been called the leading American man of letters of his day, was a brilliantly versatile writer of many romances, dramas and stories. He was editor of the national magazine the *Atlantic Monthly*, spoke several languages, was US consul in Venice for a time and a leading proponent of social realism in literature. His 1885 novel *The Rise of Silas Lapham* is an American classic.

Saki is the pen name of Hector Hugh Munro (1870–1916), a true son of the British Empire. He was born in Burma, his father a senior colonial officer, his mother the daughter of an admiral. She died when Hector was only two and he was sent to live with two aunts in Devon. In 1887, his father retired, and took Hector on extensive travels through Europe. The young man drew on his experiences and sold stories to leading newspapers such as the *Daily Express* before becoming a foreign correspondent for the *Morning Post*. For his fictional work, both novels and short stories, often satirical or comical and sometimes supernatural, he adopted the name Saki (he never revealed its origin) and gained a vast following. 'Bertie's Christmas Eve' was among a collection entitled *Toys of Peace*, published posthumously in 1919. Hector, although too old to be enlisted, had joined up on the outbreak of the First World War in 1914, and was killed in France two years later.

Harriet Beecher, born into a deeply religious and learned Connecticut family in 1813, was working as a teacher in Cincinnati when she married Calvin Ellis Stowe, a professor of theology and zealous campaigner against slavery, in 1836. They had seven children. She wrote articles and robustly moral but good-humoured short stories from an early age. 'Christmas; Or, The Good Fairy' appeared on the front page of Washington's *National Era* newspaper on Boxing Day 1850. In the following year, the same paper began to serialize Mrs. Stowe's sensational anti-slavery novel *Uncle Tom's Cabin*.

Nathaniel Hawthorne (1804–1864) was directly descended from America's first Puritan settlers, one of whom persecuted the so-called witches of Salem in 1692–1693. Hawthorne, born in Salem, made it his life's work to write about the conflicting effects of religious doctrine, in the process producing some of the greatest novels and stories – most notably *The Scarlet Letter* – in American literature.

'The Snow-Image', published 1852, is a beautifully inventive fantasy of compelling realism in which an imaginary friend lovingly created by children in the snow is extinguished by the linear will of a kindly Puritan paterfamilias. It perfectly illustrates Hawthorne's own reality–belief paradox: 'a neutral territory, somewhere between the real world and fairy-land, where the Actual and the Imaginary may meet, and each imbues itself with nature of the other'.

'A Christmas Tree and a Wedding' by Fyodor Dostoevsky (1821–1881) is a chilling tale of festive bonhomie masking greed and the theft of innocence. The great Russian prose stylist wrote the story in 1848, just months before his four-year imprisonment in Siberia and forced military service for membership of a socialist organization. It was a decade before he wrote again, producing masterpieces including his novels *Crime and Punishment* and *The Idiot*. This early Christmas story, in which a children's party in St Petersburg turns out to have a sinister purpose, demonstrates that Dostoevsky already had a dark side, but also that he had a fully developed genius for storytelling.

W. M. Thackeray

Round About the Christmas Tree

The kindly Christmas tree, from which I trust every gentle reader has pulled out a bonbon or two, is yet all aflame whilst I am writing, and sparkles with the sweet fruits of its season. You young ladies, may you have plucked pretty giftlings from it; and out of the cracker sugar-plum which you have split with the captain or the sweet young curate may you have read one of those delicious conundrums which the confectioners introduce into the sweetmeats, and which apply to the cunning passion of love. Those riddles are to be read at *your* age, when I daresay they are amusing. As for Dolly, Merry, and Bell, who are standing at the tree, they don't care about the love-riddle part, but understand the sweet-almond portion very well. They are four, five, six years old. Patience, little people! A dozen merry Christmases more, and you will be reading those wonderful love-conundrums, too. As for us elderly folks, we watch the babies at their sport, and the young people pulling at the branches: and instead of finding bonbons or sweeties in the packets which *we* pluck off the boughs, we find enclosed Mr. Carnifex's review of the quarter's meat; Mr. Sartor's compliments, and little statement for self and the young gentlemen; and Madame de Sainte-Crinoline's respects to the young ladies, who encloses her account, and will send on Saturday, please; or we stretch our hand out to the educational branch of the Christmas tree, and there find a lively and amusing article from the Rev. Henry Holyshade, containing our dear Tommy's exceedingly moderate account for the last term's school expenses.

The tree yet sparkles, I say. I am writing on the day before Twelfth Day, if you must know; but already ever so many of the fruits have been pulled, and the Christmas lights have gone out. Bobby Miseltow, who has been staying with us for a week (and who has been sleeping mysteriously in the bath-room), comes to say he is going away to spend the rest of the holidays with his grandmother—and I brush away the manly tear of regret as I part with the dear child. "Well, Bob, good-by, since you *will* go. Compliments to grandmamma. Thank her for the turkey. Here's—"*(A slight pecuniary transaction takes place at this juncture, and Bob nods and winks, and juts his hand in his waistcoat pocket.)* "You have had a pleasant week?"

BOB.—"Haven't I!" *(And exit, anxious to know the amount of the coin which has just changed hands.)*

He is gone, and as the dear boy vanishes through the door (behind which I see him perfectly), I too cast up a little account of our past Christmas week. When Bob's holidays are over, and the printer has sent me back this manuscript, I know Christmas will be an old story. All the fruit will be off the Christmas tree then; the crackers will have cracked off; the almonds will have been crunched; and the sweet-bitter riddles will have been read; the lights will have perished off the dark green boughs; the toys growing on them will have been distributed, fought for, cherished, neglected, broken. Ferdinand and Fidelia will each keep out of it (be still, my gushing heart!) the remembrance of a riddle read together, of a double almond munched together and the moiety of an exploded cracker ... The maids, I say, will have taken down all that holly stuff and nonsense about the clocks lamps, and looking-glasses, the dear boys will be back at school, fondly thinking of the pantomime fairies whom they have seen; whose gaudy gossamer wings are battered by this time; and whose pink cotton (or silk is it?) lower extremities are all dingy and dusty. Yet but a few days, Bob, and flakes of paint will have cracked off the fairy flower-bowers, and the revolving temples of adamantine luster will be as shabby as the city of Pekin. When you read this, will Clown still be going on lolling his tongue out of his mouth, and saying, "How are you to-morrow?" To-morrow, indeed! He must be almost ashamed of himself (if that cheek is still capable of the blush of shame) for asking the absurd question. To-morrow, indeed! To-morrow the diffugient snows will give place to Spring; the snowdrops will lift their heads; Ladyday may be expected, and the pecuniary duties peculiar to that feast; in place of bonbons, trees will have an eruption of light green knobs; the whitebait season will bloom ... as if one need go on describing these vernal phenomena, when Christmas is still here though ending, and the subject of my discourse!

We have all admired the illustrated papers, and noted how boisterously jolly they become at Christmas time. What wassail-bowls, robin-redbreasts, waits, snow landscapes, bursts of Christmas song!

And then to think that these festivities are prepared months before—that these Christmas pieces are prophetic! How kind of artists and poets to devise the festivities beforehand, and serve them pat at the proper time! We ought to be grateful to them, as to the cook who gets up at midnight and sets the pudding a-boiling, which is to feast us at six o'clock. I often think with gratitude of the famous Mr. Nelson Lee—the author of I don't know how many hundred glorious pantomimes—walking by the summer wave at Margate, or Brighton perhaps, revolving in his mind the idea of some new gorgeous spectacle of faery, which the winter shall see complete. He is like cook at midnight (*si parva licet*). He watches and thinks. He pounds the sparkling sugar of benevolence, the plums of fancy, the sweetmeats of fun, the figs of—well, the figs of fairy fiction, let us say, and pops the whole in the seething cauldron of imagination, and at due season serves up THE PANTOMIME.

Very few men in the course of nature can expect to see *all* the pantomimes in one season, but I hope to the end of my life I shall never forego reading about them in that delicious sheet of *The Times* which appears on the morning after Boxing-day. Perhaps reading is even better than seeing. The best way, I think, is to say you are ill, lie in bed, and have the paper for two hours, reading all the way down from Drury Lane to the Britannia at Hoxton. Bob and I went to two pantomimes. One was at the Theatre of Fancy, and the other at the Fairy Opera, and I don't know which we liked the best.

At the Fancy, we saw "Harlequin Hamlet, or Daddy's Ghost and Nunky's Pison," which is all very well—but, gentlemen, if you don't respect Shakespeare, to whom will you be civil? The palace and ramparts of Elsinore by moon and snowlight is one of Loutherbourg's finest efforts. The banqueting hall of the palace is illuminated: the peaks and gables glitter with the snow: the sentinels march blowing their fingers with the cold—the freezing of the nose of one of them is very neatly and dexterously arranged: the snow-storm rises: the winds howl awfully along the battlements: the waves come curling, leaping, foaming to shore. Hamlet's umbrella is whirled away in the storm. He and his two friends stamp on each other's toes to keep them warm. The storm-spirits rise in the air, and are whirled howling round the palace and the rocks. My eyes! what tiles and chimney-pots fly hurtling through the air! As the storm reaches its height (here the wind instruments come in with prodigious effect, and I compliment Mr. Brumby and the violoncellos)—as the snow-storm rises, (queek, queek, queek, go the fiddles, and then thrumpty thrump comes a pizzicato movement in Bob Major, which sends a shiver into your very boot-soles,) the thunder-clouds deepen (bong, bong, bong, from the violoncellos). The forked lightening quivers through the clouds in a zig-zag scream of violins—and look, look, look! as the frothing, roaring waves come rushing up the battlements, and over the reeling parapet each hissing wave becomes a ghost, sends the gun-carriages rolling over the platform, and plunges howling into the water again.

Hamlet's mother comes onto the battlements to look for her son. The storm whips her umbrella out of her hands, and she retires screaming in pattens.

The cabs on the stand in the market-place at Elsinore are seen to drive off, and several people are drowned. The gas-lamps along the street are wrenched from their foundations, and shoot through the troubled air. Whist, rush, hish! how the rain roars and pours! The darkness becomes awful, always deepened by the power of the music—and see—in the midst of a rush, and a whirl, and scream of spirits of air and wave—what is that ghastly figure moving hither? It becomes bigger, bigger as it advances down the platform—more ghastly, more horrible, enormous! It is as tall as the whole stage. It seems to be advancing on the stalls and pit, and the whole house screams with terror, as the GHOST OF THE LATE HAMLET comes in, and begins to speak. Several people faint, and the light-fingered gentry pick pockets furiously in the darkness.

In the pitchy darkness, this awful figure throwing his eyes about, the gas boxes shuddering out of sight, and the wind-instruments bugling the most horrible wails, the boldest spectator must have felt frightened. But hark! what is that silver shimmer of the fiddles! Is it—can it be—the grey dawn peeping in the stormy east? The ghost's eyes look blankly towards it, and roll a ghastly agony. Quicker, quicker ply the violins of Phœbus Apollo. Redder, redder grow the orient clouds. Cockadoodledoo! crows the great cock which has just come out on the roof of the palace. And now the round sun himself pops up from behind the waves of night. Where is the ghost? He is gone! Purple shadows of the morn "slant o'er the snowy sward," the city wakes up in life and sunshine, and we confess we are very much relieved at the disappearance of the ghost. We don't like those dark scenes in pantomimes.

After the usual business, that Ophelia should be turned into Columbine was to be expected; but I confess I was a little shocked when Hamlet's mother became Pantaloon, and was instantly knocked down by Clown Claudius. Grimaldi is getting a little old now, but for real humour there are few clowns like him. Mr.

Shutter, as the gravedigger, was chaste and comic, as he always is, and the scene-painters surpassed themselves.

"Harlequin Conqueror and the Field of Hastings," at the other house, is very pleasant too. The irascible William is acted with great vigour by Snoxal, and the battle of Hastings is a good piece of burlesque. Some trifling liberties are taken with history, but what liberties will not the merry genius of pantomime permit himself? At the battle of Hastings, William is on the point of being defeated by the Sussex volunteers, very elegantly led by the always pretty Miss Waddy (as Haco Sharpshooter), when a shot from the Normans kills Harold. The fairy Edith hereupon comes forward, and finds his body, which straightaway leaps up a live harlequin, whilst the Conqueror makes an excellent clown, and the Archbishop of Bayeux a diverting pantaloon, &c. &c. &c.

Perhaps these are not the pantomimes we really saw; but one description will do as well as another. The plots, you see, are a little intricate and difficult to understand in pantomimes; and I may have mixed up one with another. That I was at the theatre on Boxing-night is certain—but the pit was so full that I could only see fairy legs glittering in the distance, as I stood at the door. And as if I was badly off, I think there was a young gentleman behind me worse off still. I own that he has a good reason (though others have not) to speak ill of me behind my back, and hereby beg his pardon.

Likewise to the gentleman who picked up a party in Piccadilly, who had slipped and fallen in the snow and was there on his back, uttering energetic expressions: that party begs to offer thanks, and compliments of the season.

Bob's behaviour on New Year's day, I can assure Dr. Holyshade, was highly creditable to the boy. He had expressed a determination to partake of every dish which was put on the table; but after soup, fish, roast-beef, and roast-goose, he retired from active business until the pudding and mince pies made their appearance, of which he partook liberally, but not too freely. And he greatly advanced in my good opinion by praising the punch, which was of my own manufacture, and which some gentlemen present (Mr. O'M—g—n, amongst others) pronounced to be too weak. Too weak! A bottle of rum, a bottle of Madeira, half a bottle of brandy, and two bottles and a half of water—*can* this mixture be said to be too weak for any mortal? Our young friend amused the company during the evening, by exhibiting a two-shilling magic-lantern, which he had purchased, and likewise by singing "Sally, come up!" a quaint, but rather monotonous melody, which I am told is sung by the poor negro on the banks of the broad Mississippi.

What other enjoyments did we proffer for the child's amusement during the Christmas week? A great philosopher was giving a lecture to young folks at the British Institution. But when this diversion was proposed to our young friend Bob, he said, "Lecture? No, thank you. Not as I knows on," and made sarcastic signals on his nose. Perhaps he is of Dr. Johnson's opinion about lectures: "Lectures sir! what man would go to hear that imperfectly at a lecture, which he can read at leisure in a book?" *I* never went, of my own choice, to a lecture, that I can vow. As for sermons, they are different; I delight in them, and they cannot, of course, be too long.

Well, we partook of yet other Christmas delights besides pantomime, pudding, and pie. One glorious, one delightful, one most unlucky and pleasant day, we drove in a brougham, with a famous horse, which carried us more quickly and briskly than any of your vulgar railways, over Battersea Bridge, on which the horse's hoofs rung as if it had been iron; through suburban villages, plum-caked with snow; under a leaden sky, in which the sun hung like a red-hot warming-pan; by pond after pond, where not only men and boys, but scores of women and girls, were sliding, and roaring, and clapping their lean old sides with laughter, as they tumbled down, and their hobnailed shoes flew up in the air; the air frosty with a lilac haze, through which villas, and commons, and churches, and plantations glimmered. We drive up the hill, Bob and I; we make the last two miles in eleven minutes; we pass that poor, armless man who sits there in the cold, following you with his eyes. I don't give anything, and Bob looks disappointed. We are set down neatly at the gate, and a horse-holder opens the brougham door. I don't give anything; again disappointment on Bob's part. I pay a shilling a piece, and we enter into the glorious building, which is decorated for Christmas, and straightway forgetfulness on Bob's part of everything but that magnificent scene. The enormous edifice is all decorated for Bob and Christmas. The stalls, the columns, the fountains, courts, statues, splendours, are all crowned for Christmas. The delicious negro is singing his Alabama choruses for Christmas and Bob. He has scarcely done, when, Tootarootatoo! Mr. Punch is performing his surprising actions, and hanging the beadle. The stalls are decorated. The refreshment-tables are piled with good things; at many fountains "MULLED CLARET" is written up in appetizing capitals. "Mulled Claret—oh, jolly! How cold it is!" says Bob; I pass on. "It's only three o'clock," says Bob. "No, only three," I say, meekly.

"We dine at seven," sighs Bob, "and it's so-o-o coo-old."
I still would take no hints. No claret, no refreshment,
no sandwiches, no sausage-rolls for Bob. At last I am
obliged to tell him all. Just before we left home, a little
Christmas bill popped in at the door and emptied my
purse at the threshold. I forgot all about the transaction, and had to borrow half-a-crown from John
Coachman to pay for our entrance into the palace of
delight. *Now* you see, Bob, why I could not treat you on
that second of January when we drove to the palace
together; when the girls and boys were sliding on the
ponds at Dulwich; when the darkling river was full of
floating ice, and the sun was like a warming-pan in the
leaden sky.

One more Christmas sight we had, of course; and
that sight I think I like as well as Bob himself at Christmas, and at all seasons. We went to a certain garden of
delight, where, whatever your cares are, I think you can
manage to forget some of them, and muse, and be not
unhappy; to a garden beginning with a Z, which is as
lively as Noah's ark; where the fox has brought his
brush, and the cock has brought his comb, and the
elephant has brought his trunk, and the kangaroo has
brought his bag, and the condor his old white wig and
black satin hood. On this day it was so cold that the
white bears winked their pink eyes, as they plapped up
and down by their pool, and seemed to say, "ha, this
weather reminds us of dear home!" "Cold! bah! I have
got such a warm coat," says brother Bruin, "I don't
mind;" and he laughs on his pole, and clucks down a
bun. The squealing hyenas gnashed their teeth and
laughed at us quite refreshingly at their window; and,
cold as it was, Tiger, Tiger, burning bright, glared at us
red-hot through his bars, and snorted blasts of hell. The

woolly camel leered at us quite kindly as he paced round his ring on his silent pads. We went to our favourite places. Our dear wambat came up, and had himself scratched very affably. Our fellow-creatures in the monkey-room held out their little black hands, and piteously asked us for Christmas alms. Those darling alligators on their rock winked at us in the most friendly way. The solemn eagles sat alone, and scowled at us from their peaks; whilst little Tom Ratel tumbled over head and heels for us in his usual diverting manner. If I have cares in my mind, I come to the Zoo, and fancy they don't pass the gate. I recognize my friends, my enemies, in countless cages. I entertained the eagle, the vulture, the old billy-goat, and the black-pated, crimson-necked, blear-eyed, baggy, hook-beaked old marabou stork yesterday at dinner; and when Bob's aunt came to tea in the evening, and asked him what he had seen, he stepped up to her gravely, and said—

> "First I saw the white bear, then I saw the black,
> Then I saw the camel with a hump upon his back.
>
> (Chorus of Children.)
> — Then I saw the camel with a HUMP upon his back!
>
> Then I saw the grey wolf, with mutton in his maw.
> Then I saw the wambat waddle in the straw;
> Then I saw the elephant with his waving trunk,
> Then I saw the monkeys—mercy, how unpleasantly
>   they—smelt!"

There. No one can beat that piece of wit can he Bob? And so it is all over; but we had a jolly time, whilst you were with us, hadn't we? Present my respects to the doctor; and I hope my boy, we may spend another merry Christmas next year.

ARTHUR CONAN DOYLE

The Adventure of the Blue Carbuncle

I had called upon my friend Sherlock Holmes upon the second morning after Christmas, with the intention of wishing him the compliments of the season. He was lounging upon the sofa in a purple dressing-gown, a pipe-rack within his reach upon the right, and a pile of crumpled morning papers, evidently newly studied, near at hand. Beside the couch was a wooden chair, and on the angle of the back hung a very seedy and disreputable hard-felt hat, much the worse for wear, and cracked in several places. A lens and a forceps lying upon the seat of the chair suggested that the hat had been suspended in this manner for the purpose of examination.

"You are engaged," said I; "perhaps I interrupt you."

"Not at all. I am glad to have a friend with whom I can discuss my results. The matter is a perfectly trivial one"—he jerked his thumb in the direction of the old hat—"but there are points in connection with it which are not entirely devoid of interest and even of instruction."

I seated myself in his armchair and warmed my hands before his crackling fire, for a sharp frost had set in, and the windows were thick with the ice crystals. "I suppose," I remarked, "that, homely as it looks, this thing has some deadly story linked on to it—that it is the clue which will guide you in the solution of some mystery and the punishment of some crime."

"No, no. No crime," said Sherlock Holmes, laughing. "Only one of those whimsical little incidents which will happen when you have four million human beings all jostling each other within the space of a few square miles. Amid the action and reaction of so dense a swarm of humanity, every possible combination of events may be expected to take place, and many a little problem will be presented which may be striking and bizarre without being criminal. We have already had experience of such."

"So much so," I remarked, "that of the last six cases which I have added to my notes, three have been entirely free of any legal crime."

"Precisely. You allude to my attempt to recover the Irene Adler papers, to the singular case of Miss Mary Sutherland, and to the adventure of the man with the twisted lip. Well, I have no doubt that this small matter will fall into the same innocent category. You know Peterson, the commissionaire?"

"Yes."

"It is to him that this trophy belongs."

"It is his hat."

"No, no; he found it. Its owner is unknown. I beg that you will look upon it not as a battered billycock but as an intellectual problem. And, first, as to how it came here. It arrived upon Christmas morning, in company with a good fat goose, which is, I have no doubt, roasting at this moment in front of Peterson's fire. The facts are these: about four o'clock on Christmas morning, Peterson, who, as you know, is a very honest fellow, was returning from some small jollification and was making his way homeward down Tottenham Court Road. In front of him he saw, in the gaslight, a tallish man, walking with a slight stagger, and carrying a white goose slung over his shoulder. As he reached the corner of Goodge Street, a row broke out between this stranger and a little knot of roughs. One of the latter knocked off the man's hat, on which he raised his stick to defend himself and, swinging it over his head, smashed the shop window behind him. Peterson had rushed forward to protect the stranger from his assailants; but the man, shocked at having broken the window, and seeing an official-looking person in uniform rushing towards him, dropped his goose, took to his heels, and vanished amid the labyrinth of small streets which lie at the back of Tottenham Court Road. The roughs had also fled at the appearance of Peterson, so that he was left in possession of the field of battle, and also of the spoils of victory in the shape of this battered hat and a most unimpeachable Christmas goose."

"Which surely he restored to their owner?"

"My dear fellow, there lies the problem. It is true that 'For Mrs. Henry Baker' was printed upon a small card which was tied to the bird's left leg, and it is also true that the initials 'H.B.' are legible upon the lining of this hat; but as there are some thousands of Bakers, and some hundreds of Henry Bakers in this city of ours, it is not easy to restore lost property to any of them."

"What, then, did Peterson do?"

"He brought round both hat and goose to me on Christmas morning, knowing that even the smallest problems are of interest to me. The goose we retained until this morning, when there were signs that, in spite of the slight frost, it would be well that it should be eaten without unnecessary delay. Its finder has carried it off, therefore, to fulfil the ultimate destiny of a goose, while I continue to retain the hat of the unknown gentleman who lost his Christmas dinner."

"Did he not advertise?"

"No."

"Then, what clue could you have as to his identity?"

"Only as much as we can deduce."

"From his hat?"

"Precisely."

"But you are joking. What can you gather from this old battered felt?"

"Here is my lens. You know my methods. What can you gather yourself as to the individuality of the man who has worn this article?"

I took the tattered object in my hands and turned it over rather ruefully. It was a very ordinary black hat of the usual round shape, hard and much the worse for wear. The lining had been of red silk, but was a good deal discoloured. There was no maker's name; but, as Holmes had remarked, the initials "H.B." were scrawled upon one side. It was pierced in the brim for a hat-securer, but the elastic was missing. For the rest, it was cracked, exceedingly dusty, and spotted in several places, although there seemed to have been some attempt to hide the discoloured patches by smearing them with ink.

"I can see nothing," said I, handing it back to my friend.

"On the contrary, Watson, you can see everything.

You fail, however, to reason from what you see. You are too timid in drawing your inferences."

"Then, pray tell me what it is that you can infer from this hat?"

He picked it up and gazed at it in the peculiar introspective fashion which was characteristic of him. "It is perhaps less suggestive than it might have been," he remarked, "and yet there are a few inferences which are very distinct, and a few others which represent at least a strong balance of probability. That the man was highly intellectual is of course obvious upon the face of it, and also that he was fairly well-to-do within the last three years, although he has now fallen upon evil days. He had foresight, but has less now than formerly, pointing to a moral retrogression, which, when taken with the decline of his fortunes, seems to indicate some evil influence, probably drink, at work upon him. This may account also for the obvious fact that his wife has ceased to love him."

"My dear Holmes!"

"He has, however, retained some degree of self-respect," he continued, disregarding my remonstrance. "He is a man who leads a sedentary life, goes out little, is out of training entirely, is middle-aged, has grizzled hair which he has had cut within the last few days, and which he anoints with lime-cream. These are the more patent facts which are to be deduced from his hat. Also, by the way, that it is extremely improbable that he has gas laid on in his house."

"You are certainly joking, Holmes."

"Not in the least. Is it possible that even now, when I give you these results, you are unable to see how they are attained?"

"I have no doubt that I am very stupid, but I must confess that I am unable to follow you. For example, how did you deduce that this man was intellectual?"

For answer Holmes clapped the hat upon his head. It came right over the forehead and settled upon the bridge of his nose. "It is a question of cubic capacity," said he; "a man with so large a brain must have something in it."

"The decline of his fortunes, then?"

"This hat is three years old. These flat brims curled at the edge came in then. It is a hat of the very best quality. Look at the band of ribbed silk and the excellent lining. If this man could afford to buy so expensive a hat three years ago, and has had no hat since, then he has assuredly gone down in the world."

"Well, that is clear enough, certainly. But how about the foresight and the moral retrogression?"

Sherlock Holmes laughed. "Here is the foresight," said he, putting his finger upon the little disc and loop of the hat-securer. "They are never sold upon hats. If this man ordered one, it is a sign of a certain amount of foresight, since he went out of his way to take this precaution against the wind. But since we see that he has broken the elastic and has not troubled to replace it, it is obvious that he has less foresight now than formerly, which is a distinct proof of a weakening nature. On the other hand, he has endeavoured to conceal some of these stains upon the felt by daubing them with ink, which is a sign that he has not entirely lost his self-respect."

"Your reasoning is certainly plausible."

"The further points, that he is middle-aged, that his hair is grizzled, that it has been recently cut, and that he uses lime-cream, are all to be gathered from a close examination of the lower part of the lining. The lens discloses a large number of hair-ends, clean cut by the scissors of the barber. They all appear to be adhesive, and there is a distinct odour of lime-cream. This dust, you will observe, is not the gritty, gray dust of the street but the fluffy brown dust of the house, showing that it has been hung up indoors most of the time; while the marks of moisture upon the inside are proof positive that the wearer perspired very freely, and could therefore, hardly be in the best of training."

"But his wife—you said that she had ceased to love him."

"This hat has not been brushed for weeks. When I see you, my dear Watson, with a week's accumulation of dust upon your hat, and when your wife allows you to go out in such a state, I shall fear that you also have been unfortunate enough to lose your wife's affection."

"But he might be a bachelor."

"Nay, he was bringing home the goose as a peace-offering to his wife. Remember the card upon the bird's leg."

"You have an answer to everything. But how on earth do you deduce that the gas is not laid on in his house?"

"One tallow stain, or even two, might come by chance; but when I see no less than five, I think that there can be little doubt that the individual must be brought into frequent contact with burning tallow-walks upstairs at night probably with his hat in one hand and a guttering candle in the other. Anyhow, he never got tallow-stains from a gas-jet. Are you satisfied?"

"Well, it is very ingenious," said I, laughing; "but since, as you said just now, there has been no crime committed, and no harm done save the loss of a goose, all this seems to be rather a waste of energy."

Sherlock Holmes had opened his mouth to reply, when the door flew open, and Peterson, the commissionaire, rushed into the apartment with flushed cheeks and the face of a man who is dazed with astonishment.

"The goose, Mr. Holmes! The goose, sir!" he gasped.

"Eh? What of it, then? Has it returned to life and flapped off through the kitchen window?" Holmes twisted himself round upon the sofa to get a fairer view of the man's excited face.

"See here, sir! See what my wife found in its crop!" He held out his hand and displayed upon the center of the palm a brilliantly scintillating blue stone, rather smaller than a bean in size, but of such purity and radiance that it twinkled like an electric point in the dark hollow of his hand. Sherlock Holmes sat up with a whistle. "By Jove, Peterson!" said he, "this is treasure trove indeed. I suppose you know what you have got?"

"A diamond, sir? A precious stone. It cuts into glass as though it were putty."

"It's more than a precious stone. It is *the* precious stone."

"Not the Countess of Morcar's blue carbuncle!" I ejaculated.

"Precisely so. I ought to know its size and shape, seeing that I have read the advertisement about it in *The Times* every day lately. It is absolutely unique, and its value can only be conjectured, but the reward offered of £1000 is certainly not within a twentieth part of the market price."

"A thousand pounds! Great Lord of mercy!" The commissionaire plumped down into a chair and stared from one to the other of us.

"That is the reward, and I have reason to know that there are sentimental considerations in the background which would induce the Countess to part with half her fortune if she could but recover the gem."

"It was lost, if I remember aright, at the Hotel Cosmopolitan," I remarked.

"Precisely so, on December 22nd, just five days ago. John Horner, a plumber, was accused of having abstracted it from the lady's jewel-case. The evidence against him was so strong that the case has been referred to the Assizes. I have some account of the matter here, I believe." He rummaged amid his newspapers, glancing over the dates, until at last he smoothed one out, doubled it over, and read the following paragraph:

'Hotel Cosmopolitan Jewel Robbery. John Horner, 26, plumber, was brought up upon the charge of having upon the 22d inst., abstracted from the jewel-case of the Countess of Morcar the valuable gem known as the blue carbuncle. James Ryder, upper-attendant at the hotel, gave his evidence to the effect that he had shown Horner up to the dressing-room of the Countess of Morcar upon the day of the robbery in order that he might solder the second bar of the grate, which was loose. He had remained with Horner some little time, but had finally been called away. On returning, he found that Horner had disappeared, that the bureau had been forced open, and that the small morocco casket in which, as it afterwards transpired, the Countess was accustomed to keep her jewel, was lying empty upon the dressing-table. Ryder instantly gave the alarm, and Horner was arrested the same evening; but the stone could not be found either upon his person or in his rooms. Catherine Cusack, maid to the Countess, deposed to having heard Ryder's cry of dismay on discovering the robbery, and to having rushed into the room, where she found matters as described by the last witness. Inspector Bradstreet, B division, gave evidence as to the arrest of Horner, who struggled frantically, and protested his innocence in the strongest terms. Evidence of a previous conviction for robbery having been given against the prisoner, the magistrate refused to deal summarily with the offence, but referred it to the Assizes. Horner, who had shown signs of intense emotion during the proceedings, fainted away at the conclusion and was carried out of court.

"Hum! So much for the police-court," said Holmes thoughtfully, tossing aside the paper. "The question for us now to solve is the sequence of events leading from a rifled jewel-case at one end to the crop of a goose in Tottenham Court Road at the other. You see, Watson, our little deductions have suddenly assumed a much more important and less innocent aspect. Here is the stone; the stone came from the goose, and the goose came from Mr. Henry Baker, the gentleman with the bad hat and all the other characteristics with which I have bored you. So now we must set ourselves very seriously to finding this gentleman and ascertaining what part he has played in this little mystery. To do this, we must try the simplest means first, and these lie undoubtedly in an advertisement in all the evening papers. If this fails, I shall have recourse to other methods."

"What will you say?"

"Give me a pencil and that slip of paper. Now, then:

Found at the corner of Goodge Street, a goose and a black felt hat. Mr. Henry Baker can have the same by applying at 6:30 this evening at 221B Baker Street.

That is clear and concise."

"Very. But will he see it?"

"Well, he is sure to keep an eye on the papers, since, to a poor man, the loss was a heavy one. He was clearly so scared by his mischance in breaking the window and by the approach of Peterson that he thought of nothing but flight, but since then he must have bitterly regretted the impulse which caused him to drop his bird. Then, again, the introduction of his name will cause him to see it, for everyone who knows him will direct his attention to it. Here you are, Peterson, run down to the advertising agency and have this put in the evening papers."

"In which, sir?"

"Oh, in the *Globe, Star, Pall Mall, St. James's, Evening News Standard, Echo*, and any others that occur to you."

"Very well, sir. And this stone?"

"Ah, yes, I shall keep the stone. Thank you. And, I say, Peterson, just buy a goose on your way back and leave it here with me, for we must have one to give to this gentleman in place of the one which your family is now devouring."

When the commissionaire had gone, Holmes took up the stone and held it against the light. "It's a bonny thing," said he. "Just see how it glints and sparkles. Of course it is a nucleus and focus of crime. Every good stone is. They are the devil's pet baits. In the larger and older jewels every facet may stand for a bloody deed. This stone is not yet twenty years old. It was found in the banks of the Amoy River in southern China and is remarkable in having every characteristic of the carbuncle, save that it is blue in shade instead of ruby red. In spite of its youth, it has already a sinister history. There have been two murders, a vitriol-throwing, a suicide, and several robberies brought about for the sake of this forty-grain weight of crystallized charcoal. Who would think that so pretty a toy would be a purveyor to the gallows and the prison? I'll lock it up in my strong box now and drop a line to the Countess to say that we have it."

"Do you think that this man Horner is innocent?"

"I cannot tell."

"Well, then, do you imagine that this other one, Henry Baker, had anything to do with the matter?"

"It is, I think, much more likely that Henry Baker is an absolutely innocent man, who had no idea that the bird which he was carrying was of considerably more value than if it were made of solid gold. That, however, I shall determine by a very simple test if we have an answer to our advertisement."

"And you can do nothing until then?"

"Nothing."

"In that case I shall continue my professional round. But I shall come back in the evening at the hour you have mentioned, for I should like to see the solution of so tangled a business."

"Very glad to see you. I dine at seven. There is a wood cock, I believe. By the way, in view of recent occurrences, perhaps I ought to ask Mrs. Hudson to examine its crop."

I had been delayed at a case, and it was a little after half-past six when I found myself in Baker Street once more. As I approached the house I saw a tall man in a Scotch bonnet with a coat which was buttoned up to his chin waiting outside in the bright semicircle which was thrown from the fanlight. Just as I arrived the door was opened, and we were shown up together to Holmes's room.

"Mr. Henry Baker, I believe," said he, rising from his armchair and greeting his visitor with the easy air of geniality which he could so readily assume. "Pray take this chair by the fire, Mr. Baker. It is a cold night, and I observe that your circulation is more adapted for summer than for winter. Ah, Watson, you have just come at the right time. Is that your hat, Mr. Baker?"

"Yes, sir, that is undoubtedly my hat."

He was a large man with rounded shoulders, a massive head, and a broad, intelligent face, sloping down to a pointed beard of grizzled brown. A touch of red in nose and cheeks, with a slight tremor of his extended hand, recalled Holmes's surmise as to his habits. His rusty black frock-coat was buttoned right up in front, with the collar turned up, and his lank wrists protruded from his sleeves without a sign of cuff or shirt. He spoke in a slow staccato fashion, choosing his words with care, and gave the impression generally of a man of learning and letters who had had ill-usage at the hands of fortune.

"We have retained these things for some days," said Holmes, "because we expected to see an advertisement from you giving your address. I am at a loss to know now why you did not advertise."

Our visitor gave a rather shamefaced laugh. "Shillings have not been so plentiful with me as they once were," he remarked. "I had no doubt that the gang of roughs who assaulted me had carried off both my hat and the bird. I did not care to spend more money in a hopeless attempt at recovering them."

"Very naturally. By the way, about the bird, we were compelled to eat it."

"To eat it!" Our visitor half rose from his chair in his excitement.

"Yes, it would have been of no use to anyone had we not done so. But I presume that this other goose upon the sideboard, which is about the same weight and perfectly fresh, will answer your purpose equally well?"

"Oh, certainly, certainly," answered Mr. Baker with a sigh of relief.

"Of course, we still have the feathers, legs, crop, and so on of your own bird, so if you wish—"

The man burst into a hearty laugh. "They might be useful to me as relics of my adventure," said he, "but beyond that I can hardly see what use the *disjecta membra* of my late acquaintance are going to be to me. No, sir, I think that, with your permission, I will confine my attentions to the excellent bird which I perceive upon the sideboard."

Sherlock Holmes glanced sharply across at me with a slight shrug of his shoulders.

"There is your hat, then, and there your bird," said he. "By the way, would it bore you to tell me where you got the other one from? I am somewhat of a fowl fancier, and I have seldom seen a better grown goose."

"Certainly, sir," said Baker, who had risen and tucked his newly gained property under his arm. "There are a few of us who frequent the Alpha Inn, near the Museum—we are to be found in the Museum itself during the day, you understand. This year our good host, Windigate by name, instituted a goose club, by which, on consideration of some few pence every week, we were each to receive a bird at Christmas. My pence were duly paid, and the rest is familiar to you. I am much indebted to you, sir, for a Scotch bonnet is fitted neither to my years nor my gravity." With a comical pomposity of manner he bowed solemnly to both of us and strode off upon his way.

"So much for Mr. Henry Baker," said Holmes when he had closed the door behind him. "It is quite certain that he knows nothing whatever about the matter. Are you hungry, Watson?"

"Not particularly."

"Then I suggest that we turn our dinner into a supper and follow up this clue while it is still hot."

"By all means."

It was a bitter night, so we drew on our ulsters and wrapped cravats about our throats. Outside, the stars were shining coldly in a cloudless sky, and the breath of the passers-by blew out into smoke like so many pistol shots. Our footfalls rang out crisply and loudly as we swung through the doctors' quarter, Wimpole Street, Harley Street, and so through Wigmore Street into Oxford Street. In a quarter of an hour we were in Bloomsbury at the Alpha Inn, which is a small public-house at the corner of one of the streets which runs down into Holborn. Holmes pushed open the door of the private bar and ordered two glasses of beer from the ruddy-faced, white-aproned landlord.

"Your beer should be excellent if it is as good as your geese," said he.

"My geese!" The man seemed surprised.

"Yes. I was speaking only half an hour ago to Mr. Henry Baker, who was a member of your goose club."

"Ah! yes, I see. But you see, sir, them's not *our* geese."

"Indeed! Whose, then?"

"Well, I got the two dozen from a salesman in Covent Garden."

"Indeed? I know some of them. Which was it?"

"Breckinridge is his name."

"Ah! I don't know him. Well, here's your good health, landlord, and prosperity to your house. Good-night.

"Now for Mr. Breckinridge," he continued, buttoning up his coat as we came out into the frosty air. "Remember, Watson, that though we have so homely a thing as a goose at one end of this chain, we have at the other a man who will certainly get seven years' penal servitude unless we can establish his innocence. It is possible that our inquiry may but confirm his guilt; but, in any case, we have a line of investigation which has been missed by the police, and which a singular chance has placed in our hands. Let us follow it out to the bitter end. Faces to the south, then, and quick march!"

We passed across Holborn, down Endell Street, and so through a zigzag of slums to Covent Garden Market. One of the largest stalls bore the name of Breckinridge upon it, and the proprietor, a horsy-looking man, with a sharp face and trim side-whiskers, was helping a boy to put up the shutters.

"Good-evening. It's a cold night," said Holmes.

The salesman nodded and shot a questioning glance at my companion. "Sold out of geese, I see," continued Holmes, pointing at the bare slabs of marble.

"Let you have five hundred to-morrow morning."

"That's no good."

"Well, there are some on the stall with the gas-flare."

"Ah, but I was recommended to you."

"Who by?"

"The landlord of the Alpha."

"Oh, yes; I sent him a couple of dozen."

"Fine birds they were, too. Now where did you get them from?"

To my surprise the question provoked a burst of anger from the salesman.

"Now, then, mister," said he, with his head cocked and his arms akimbo, "what are you driving at? Let's have it straight, now."

"It is straight enough. I should like to know who sold you the geese which you supplied to the Alpha."

"Well, then, I shan't tell you. So now!"

"Oh, it is a matter of no importance; but I don't know why you should be so warm over such a trifle."

"Warm! You'd be as warm, maybe, if you were as pestered as I am. When I pay good money for a good article there should be an end of the business; but it's 'Where are the geese?' and 'Who did you sell the geese to?' and 'What will you take for the geese?' One would think they were the only geese in the world, to hear the fuss that is made over them."

"Well, I have no connection with any other people who have been making inquiries," said Holmes carelessly. "If you won't tell us the bet is off, that is all. But I'm always ready to back my opinion on a matter of fowls, and I have a fiver on it that the bird I ate is country bred."

"Well, then, you've lost your fiver, for it's town bred," snapped the salesman.

"It's nothing of the kind."

"I say it is."

"I don't believe it."

"D'you think you know more about fowls than I, who have handled them ever since I was a nipper? I tell you, all those birds that went to the Alpha were town bred."

28

"You'll never persuade me to believe that."

"Will you bet, then?"

"It's merely taking your money, for I know that I am right. But I'll have a sovereign on with you, just to teach you not to be obstinate."

The salesman chuckled grimly. "Bring me the books, Bill," said he.

The small boy brought round a small thin volume and a great greasy-backed one, laying them out together beneath the hanging lamp.

"Now then, Mr. Cocksure," said the salesman, "I thought that I was out of geese, but before I finish you'll find that there is still one left in my shop. You see this little book?"

"Well?"

"That's the list of the folk from whom I buy. D'you see? Well, then, here on this page are the country folk, and the numbers after their names are where their accounts are in the big ledger. Now, then! You see this other page in red ink? Well, that is a list of my town suppliers. Now, look at that third name. Just read it out to me."

"Mrs. Oakshott, 117, Brixton Road—249," read Holmes.

"Quite so. Now turn that up in the ledger."

Holmes turned to the page indicated. "Here you are, 'Mrs. Oakshott, 117 Brixton Road, egg and poultry supplier.'"

"Now, then, what's the last entry?"

"'December 22nd. Twenty-four geese at 7s. 6d.'"

"Quite so. There you are. And underneath?"

"'Sold to Mr. Windigate of the Alpha, at 12s.'"

"What have you to say now?"

Sherlock Holmes looked deeply chagrined. He drew

a sovereign from his pocket and threw it down upon the slab, turning away with the air of a man whose disgust is too deep for words. A few yards off he stopped under a lamp-post and laughed in the hearty, noiseless fashion which was peculiar to him.

"When you see a man with whiskers of that cut and the 'Pink 'un' protruding out of his pocket, you can always draw him by a bet," said he. "I daresay that if I had put £100 down in front of him, that man would not have given me such complete information as was drawn from him by the idea that he was doing me on a wager. Well, Watson, we are, I fancy, nearing the end of our quest, and the only point which remains to be determined is whether we should go on to this Mrs. Oakshott to-night, or whether we should reserve it for to-morrow. It is clear from what that surly fellow said that there are others besides ourselves who are anxious about the matter, and I should—"

His remarks were suddenly cut short by a loud hubbub which broke out from the stall which we had just left. Turning round we saw a little rat-faced fellow standing in the centre of the circle of yellow light which was thrown by the swinging lamp, while Breckinridge, the salesman, framed in the door of his stall, was shaking his fists fiercely at the cringing figure.

"I've had enough of you and your geese," he shouted. "I wish you were all at the devil together. If you come pestering me any more with your silly talk I'll set the dog at you. You bring Mrs. Oakshott here and I'll answer her, but what have you to do with it? Did I buy the geese off you?"

"No; but one of them was mine all the same," whined the little man. "Well, then, ask Mrs. Oakshott for it."

"She told me to ask you."

"Well, you can ask the King of Proosia, for all I care. I've had enough of it. Get out of this!" He rushed fiercely forward, and the inquirer flitted away into the darkness.

"Ha! this may save us a visit to Brixton Road," whispered Holmes. "Come with me, and we will see what is to be made of this fellow." Striding through the scattered knots of people who lounged round the flaring stalls, my companion speedily overtook the little man and touched him upon the shoulder. He sprang round, and I could see in the gas-light that every vestige of colour had been driven from his face.

"Who are you, then? What do you want?" he asked in a quavering voice.

"You will excuse me," said Holmes blandly, "but I could not help overhearing the questions which you put to the salesman just now. I think that I could be of assistance to you."

"You? Who are you? How could you know anything of the matter?"

"My name is Sherlock Holmes. It is my business to know what other people don't know."

"But you can know nothing of this?"

"Excuse me, I know everything of it. You are endeavouring to trace some geese which were sold by Mrs. Oakshott, of Brixton Road, to a salesman named Breckinridge, by him in turn to Mr. Windigate, of the Alpha, and by him to his club, of which Mr. Henry Baker is a member."

"Oh, sir, you are the very man whom I have longed to meet," cried the little fellow with outstretched hands and quivering fingers. "I can hardly explain to you how interested I am in this matter."

Sherlock Holmes hailed a four-wheeler which was

passing. "In that case we had better discuss it in a cosy room rather than in this wind-swept market-place," said he. "But pray tell me, before we go farther, who it is that I have the pleasure of assisting."

The man hesitated for an instant. "My name is John Robinson," he answered with a sidelong glance.

"No, no; the real name," said Holmes sweetly. "It is always awkward doing business with an alias."

A flush sprang to the white cheeks of the stranger. "Well, then," said he, "my real name is James Ryder."

"Precisely so. Head attendant at the Hotel Cosmopolitan. Pray step in to the cab, and I shall soon be able to tell you everything which you would wish to know."

The little man stood glancing from one to the other of us with half-frightened, half-hopeful eyes, as one who is not sure whether he is on the verge of a windfall or of a catastrophe. Then he stepped into the cab, and in half an hour we were back in the sitting-room at Baker Street. Nothing had been said during our drive, but the high, thin breathing of our new companion, and the claspings and unclaspings of his hands, spoke of the nervous tension within him.

"Here we are!" said Holmes cheerily as we filed into the room. "The fire looks very seasonable in this weather. You look cold, Mr. Ryder. Pray take the basket-chair. I will just put on my slippers before we settle this little matter of yours. Now, then! You want to know what became of those geese?"

"Yes, sir."

"Or rather, I fancy, of that goose. It was one bird, I imagine, in which you were interested—white, with a black bar across the tail."

Ryder quivered with emotion. "Oh, sir," he cried, "can you tell me where it went to?"

"It came here."

"Here?"

"Yes, and a most remarkable bird it proved. I don't wonder that you should take an interest in it. It laid an egg after it was dead—the bonniest, brightest little blue egg that ever was seen. I have it here in my museum."

Our visitor staggered to his feet and clutched the mantelpiece with his right hand. Holmes unlocked his strongbox and held up the blue carbuncle, which shone out like a star, with a cold, brilliant, many-pointed radiance. Ryder stood glaring with a drawn face, uncertain whether to claim or to disown it.

"The game's up, Ryder," said Holmes quietly. "Hold up, man, or you'll be into the fire! Give him an arm back into his chair, Watson. He's not got blood enough to go in for felony with impunity. Give him a dash of brandy. So! Now he looks a little more human. What a shrimp it is, to be sure!"

For a moment he had staggered and nearly fallen, but the brandy brought a tinge of colour into his cheeks, and he sat staring with frightened eyes at his accuser.

"I have almost every link in my hands, and all the proofs which I could possibly need, so there is little which you need tell me. Still, that little may as well be cleared up to make the case complete. You had heard, Ryder, of this blue stone of the Countess of Morcar's?"

"It was Catherine Cusack who told me of it," said he in a crackling voice.

"I see—her ladyship's waiting-maid. Well, the temptation of sudden wealth so easily acquired was too much for you, as it has been for better men before you; but you were not very scrupulous in the means you used. It seems to me, Ryder, that there is the making of

33

a very pretty villain in you. You knew that this man Horner, the plumber, had been concerned in some such matter before, and that suspicion would rest the more readily upon him. What did you do, then? You made some small job in my lady's room—you and your confederate Cusack—and you managed that he should be the man sent for. Then, when he had left, you rifled the jewel case, raised the alarm, and had this unfortunate man arrested. You then—"

Ryder threw himself down suddenly upon the rug and clutched at my companion's knees. "For God's sake, have mercy!" he shrieked. "Think of my father! of my mother! It would break their hearts. I never went wrong before! I never will again. I swear it. I'll swear it on a Bible. Oh, don't bring it into court! For Christ's sake, don't!"

"Get back into your chair!" said Holmes sternly. "It is very well to cringe and crawl now, but you thought little enough of this poor Horner in the dock for a crime of which he knew nothing."

"I will fly, Mr. Holmes. I will leave the country, sir. Then the charge against him will break down."

"Hum! We will talk about that. And now let us hear a true account of the next act. How came the stone into the goose, and how came the goose into the open market? Tell us the truth, for there lies your only hope of safety."

Ryder passed his tongue over his parched lips. "I will tell you it just as it happened, sir," said he. "When Horner had been arrested, it seemed to me that it would be best for me to get away with the stone at once, for I did not know at what moment the police might not take it into their heads to search me and my room. There was no place about the hotel where it

34

would be safe. I went out, as if on some commission, and I made for my sister's house. She had married a man named Oakshott, and lived in Brixton Road, where she fattened fowls for the market. All the way there every man I met seemed to me to be a policeman or a detective; and, for all that it was a cold night, the sweat was pouring down my face before I came to the Brixton Road. My sister asked me what was the matter, and why I was so pale; but I told her that I had been upset by the jewel robbery at the hotel. Then I went into the back yard and smoked a pipe, and wondered what it would be best to do.

"I had a friend once called Maudsley, who went to the bad, and has just been serving his time in Pentonville. One day he had met me, and fell into talk about the ways of thieves, and how they could get rid of what they stole. I knew that he would be true to me, for I knew one or two things about him; so I made up my mind to go right on to Kilburn, where he lived, and take him into my confidence. He would show me how to turn the stone into money. But how to get to him in safety? I thought of the agonies I had gone through in coming from the hotel. I might at any moment be seized and searched, and there would be the stone in my waistcoat pocket. I was leaning against the wall at the time and looking at the geese which were waddling about round my feet, and suddenly an idea came into my head which showed me how I could beat the best detective that ever lived.

"My sister had told me some weeks before that I might have the pick of her geese for a Christmas present, and I knew that she was always as good as her word. I would take my goose now, and in it I would carry my stone to Kilburn. There was a little shed in the yard, and behind this I drove one of the birds—a fine big one, white, with a barred tail. I caught it, and, prying its bill open, I thrust the stone down its throat as far as my finger could reach. The bird gave a gulp, and I felt the stone pass along its gullet and down into its crop. But the creature flapped and struggled, and out came my sister to know what was the matter. As I turned to speak to her the brute broke loose and fluttered off among the others.

"'Whatever were you doing with that bird, Jem?' says she.

"'Well,' said I, 'you said you'd give me one for Christmas, and I was feeling which was the fattest.'

"'Oh,' says she, 'we've set yours aside for you—Jem's bird, we call it. It's the big white one over yonder. There's twenty-six of them, which makes one for you, and one for us, and two dozen for the market.'

"'Thank you, Maggie,' says I; 'but if it is all the same to you, I'd rather have that one I was handling just now.'

"'The other is a good three pound heavier,' said she, 'and we fattened it expressly for you.'

"'Never mind. I'll have the other, and I'll take it now,' said I.

"'Oh, just as you like,' said she, a little huffed. 'Which is it you want, then?'

"'That white one with the barred tail, right in the middle of the flock.'

"'Oh, very well. Kill it and take it with you.'

"Well, I did what she said, Mr. Holmes, and I carried the bird all the way to Kilburn. I told my pal what I had done, for he was a man that it was easy to tell a thing like that to. He laughed until he choked, and we got a knife and opened the goose. My heart turned to water, for there was no sign of the stone, and I knew that some terrible mistake had occurred. I left the bird, rushed back to my sister's, and hurried into the back yard. There was not a bird to be seen there.

"'Where are they all, Maggie?' I cried.

"'Gone to the dealer's, Jem.'

"'Which dealer's?'

"'Breckinridge, of Covent Garden.'

"'But was there another with a barred tail?' I asked, 'the same as the one I chose?'

"'Yes, Jem; there were two barred-tailed ones, and I could never tell them apart.'

"Well, then, of course I saw it all, and I ran off as hard as my feet would carry me to this man Breckinridge; but he had sold the lot at once, and not one word would he tell me as to where they had gone. You heard him yourselves to-night. Well, he has always answered me like that. My sister thinks that I am going mad. Sometimes I think that I am myself. And now—and now I am myself a branded thief, without ever having touched the wealth for which I sold my character. God help me! God help me!" He burst into convulsive sobbing, with his face buried in his hands.

There was a long silence, broken only by his heavy breathing, and by the measured tapping of Sherlock Holmes's finger-tips upon the edge of the table. Then my friend rose and threw open the door.

"Get out!" said he.

"What, sir! Oh, Heaven bless you!"

"No more words. Get out!"

And no more words were needed. There was a rush, a clatter upon the stairs, the bang of a door, and the crisp rattle of running footfalls from the street.

"After all, Watson," said Holmes, reaching up his hand for his clay pipe, "I am not retained by the police to supply their deficiencies. If Horner were in danger it would be another thing; but this fellow will not appear against him, and the case must collapse. I suppose that I am commuting a felony, but it is just possible that I am saving a soul. This fellow will not go wrong again; he is too terribly frightened. Send him to jail now, and you make him a jail-bird for life. Besides, it is the season of forgiveness. Chance has put in our way a most singular and whimsical problem, and its solution is its own reward. If you will have the goodness to touch the bell, Doctor, we will begin another investigation, in which, also, a bird will be the chief feature."

HANS CHRISTIAN ANDERSEN

The Little Match Girl

It was terribly cold; it snowed and was already almost dark, and evening came on, the last evening of the year. In the cold and gloom a poor little girl, bareheaded and barefoot, was walking through the streets. When she left her own house she certainly had had slippers on, but of what use were they? They were very big slippers, and her mother had used them till then, so big were they. The little maid lost them as she slipped across the road, where two carriages were rattling by terribly fast. One slipper was not to be found again, and a boy had seized the other and run away with it. He thought he could use it very well as a cradle some day when he had children of his own. So now the little girl went with her little naked feet, which were quite red and blue with the cold. In an old apron she carried a number of matches, and a bundle of them in her hand. No one had bought anything off her all day, and no one had given her a farthing.

Shivering with cold and hunger, she crept along, a picture of misery, poor little girl! The snowflakes covered her long fair hair, which fell in pretty curls over her neck; but she did not think of that now. In all the windows lights were shining, and there was a glorious smell of roast goose, for it was New Year's Eve. Yes, she thought of that!

In a corner formed by two houses, one of which projected beyond the other, she sat down, cowering. She had drawn up her little feet, but she was still colder, and she did not dare to go home, for she had sold no matches and did not bring a farthing of money. From her father she would certainly receive a beating; and, besides, it was cold at home, for they had nothing over them but a roof through which the wind whistled, though the largest rents had been stopped with straw and rags.

Her little hands were almost benumbed with the cold. Ah, a match might do her good, if she could only draw one from the bundle and rub it against the wall and warm her hands at it. She drew one out. R-r-atch! How it sputtered and burned! It was a warm bright flame, like a little candle, when she held her hands over it; it was a wonderful little light! It really seemed to the little girl as if she sat before a great polished stove with bright brass feet and a brass cover. How the fire burned! How comfortable it was! But the little flame went out, the stove vanished, and she had only the remains of the burnt match in her hand.

A second was rubbed against the wall. It burned up, and when the light fell upon the wall it became transparent like a thin veil, and she could see through it into the room. On the table a snow-white cloth was spread; upon it stood a shining dinner service; the roast goose smoked gloriously, stuffed with apples and dried plums. And, what was still more splendid to behold, the goose hopped down from the dish and waddled along the floor, with a knife and fork in its breast, to the little girl. Then the match went out and only the thick, damp, cold wall was before her. She lighted another match. Then she was sitting under a beautiful Christmas tree; it was greater and more ornamented than the one she had seen through the glass door at the rich merchant's. Thousands of candles burned upon the green branches, and coloured pictures like those in the print shops looked down upon them. The little girl stretched forth her hand toward them; then the match went out. The Christmas lights mounted higher. She saw them now as stars in the sky; one of them fell down, forming a long line of fire.

"Now someone is dying," thought the little girl, for her old grandmother, the only person who had loved her, and who was now dead, had told her that when a star fell down a soul mounted up to God.

She rubbed another match against the wall; it became bright again, and in the brightness the old grandmother stood clear and shining, mild and lovely.

"Grandmother!" cried the child. "Oh, take me with you! I know you will go when the match is burned out. You will vanish like the warm fire, the warm food, and the great, glorious Christmas tree!"

And she hastily rubbed the whole bundle of matches, for she wished to hold her grandmother fast. And the matches burned with such a glow that it became brighter than in the middle of the day; grandmother had never been so large or so beautiful. She took the little girl in her arms, and both flew in brightness and joy above the earth, very, very high, and up there was neither cold, nor hunger, nor care—they were with God.

But in the corner, leaning against the wall, sat the poor girl with red cheeks and smiling mouth, frozen to death on the last evening of the old year. The New Year's sun rose upon a little corpse! The child sat there, stiff and cold, with the matches, of which one bundle was burned. "She wanted to warm herself," the people said. No one imagined what a beautiful thing she had seen and in what glory she had gone in with her grandmother to the New Year's Day.

Christmas Eve

Saint Francis and Saint Benedight
Blesse this house from wicked wight;
From the night-mare and the goblin,
That is hight good fellow Robin:
Keep it from all evil spirits,
Fairies, weezels, rats, and ferrets:
From curfew time
To the next prime.

It was a brilliant moonlight night, but extremely cold; our chaise whirled rapidly over the frozen ground; the postboy smacked his whip incessantly, and a part of the time his horses were on a gallop. "He knows where he is going," said my companion, laughing, "and is eager to arrive in time for some of the merriment and good cheer of the servants' hall. My father, you must know, is a bigoted devotee of the old school, and prides himself upon keeping up something of old English hospitality. He is a tolerable specimen of what you will rarely meet with nowadays in its purity, the old English country gentleman; for our men of fortune spend so much of their time in town, and fashion is carried so much into the country, that the strong rich peculiarities of ancient rural life are almost polished away. My father, however, from early years, took honest Peacham[*] for his text-book instead of Chesterfield; he determined, in his own mind, that there was no condition more truly honourable and enviable than that of a country gentleman on his paternal lands, and therefore passes the whole of his time on his estate. He is a strenuous advocate for the revival of the old rural games and holiday observances, and is deeply read in the writers, ancient and modern, who have treated on the subject. Indeed, his favourite range of reading is among the authors who flourished at least two centuries since; who, he insists, wrote and thought more like true Englishmen than any of their successors. He even regrets sometimes that he had not been born a few centuries earlier, when England was itself, and had its peculiar manners and customs. As he lives at some distance from the main road, in rather a lonely part of the country, without any rival gentry near him, he has that most enviable of all blessings to an English-man, the opportunity of indulging the bent of his own humour without molestation. Being representative of the oldest family in the neighbourhood, and a great part of the peasantry being his tenants, he is much looked up to, and, in general, is known simply by the appellation of 'The Squire'; a title which has been accorded to the head of the family since time immemorial. I think it best to give you these hints about my

---

[*] Peacham's *Complete Gentleman* 1622.

worthy old father, to prepare you for any eccentricities that might otherwise appear absurd."

We had passed for some time along the wall of a park, and at length the chaise stopped at the gate. It was in a heavy magnificent old style, of iron bars, fancifully wrought at top into flourishes and flowers. The huge square columns that supported the gate were surmounted by the family crest. Close adjoining was the porter's lodge, sheltered under dark fir-trees, and almost buried in shrubbery.

The postboy rang a large porter's bell, which resounded through the still frosty air, and was answered by the distant barking of dogs, with which the mansion-house seemed garrisoned. An old woman immediately appeared at the gate. As the moonlight fell strongly upon her, I had a full view of a little primitive dame, dressed very much in the antique taste, with a neat kerchief and stomacher, and her silver hair peeping from under a cap of snowy whiteness. She came curt-seying forth, with many expressions of simple joy at seeing her young master. Her husband, it seemed, was up at the house keeping Christmas Eve in the servants' hall; they could not do without him, as he was the best hand at a song and story in the household.

My friend proposed that we should alight and walk through the park to the hall, which was at no great distance, while the chaise should follow on. Our road wound through a noble avenue of trees, among the naked branches of which the moon glittered as she rolled through the deep vault of a cloudless sky. The lawn beyond was sheeted with a slight covering of snow, which here and there sparkled as the moonbeams caught a frosty crystal; and at a distance might be seen a thin transparent vapour stealing up from the low grounds and threatening gradually to shroud the landscape.

My companion looked around him with transport. "How often," said he, "have I scampered up this avenue, on returning home on school vacations! How often have I played under these trees when a boy! I feel a degree of filial reverence for them, as we look up to those who have cherished us in childhood. My father was always scrupulous in exacting our holidays, and having us around him on family festivals. He used to direct and superintend our games with the strictness that some parents do the studies of their children. He was very particular that we should play the old English games according to their original form; and consulted old books for precedent and authority for every 'merrie sport'; yet I assure you there never was pedantry so delightful. It was the policy of the good old gentleman to make his children feel that home was the happiest place in the world, and I value this delicious home-feeling as one of the choicest gifts a parent could bestow."

We were interrupted by the clamour of a troop of dogs of all sorts and sizes, "mongrel, puppy, whelp and hound, and curs of low degree," that, disturbed by the ring of the porter's bell, and the rattling of the chaise, came bounding, open-mouthed, across the lawn. "The little dogs and all—Tray, Blanch, and Sweetheart—see, they bark at me!" cried Bracebridge, laughing. At the sound of his voice, the bark was changed into a yelp of delight, and in a moment he was surrounded and almost overpowered by the caresses of the faithful animals.

We had now come in full view of the old family mansion, partly thrown in deep shadow, and partly lit up by the cold moonshine. It was an irregular building, of some magnitude, and seemed to be of the architecture of different periods. One wing was evidently very ancient, with heavy stone-shafted bow windows, jutting out and overrun with ivy, from among the foliage of which the small diamond-shaped panes of glass glittered with the moonbeams. The rest of the house was in the French taste of Charles the Second's time, having been repaired and altered, as my friend told me, by one of his ancestors, who returned with that monarch at the Restoration. The grounds about the house were laid out in the old formal manner of artificial flower-beds, clipped shrubberies, raised terraces, and heavy stone balustrades, ornamented with urns, a leaden statue or two, and a jet of water. The old gentleman, I was told, was extremely careful to preserve this obsolete finery in all its original state. He admired this fashion in gardening: it had an air of magnificence, was courtly and noble, and befitting good old family style. The boasted imitation of nature in modern gardening had sprung up with modern republican notions, but did not suit a monarchical government; it smacked of the levelling system. I could not help smiling at this introduction of politics into gardening, though I expressed some apprehension that I should find the old gentleman rather intolerant in his creed. Frank assured me, however, that it was almost the only instance in which he had ever heard his father meddle with politics; and he believed that he had got this notion from a member of parliament who once passed a few weeks with him. The squire was glad of any argument to defend his clipped yew trees and formal terraces which had been occasionally attacked by modern landscape-gardeners.

As we approached the house, we heard the sound of

music, and now and then a burst of laughter from one end of the building. This, Bracebridge said, must proceed from the servants' hall, where a great deal of revelry was permitted, and even encouraged, by the squire, throughout the twelve days of Christmas, provided everything was done conformably to ancient usage. Here were kept up the old games of hoodman blind, shoe the wild mare, hot cockles, steal the white loaf, bob apple, and snap dragon: the Yule clog and Christmas candle were regularly burnt, and the mistletoe, with its white berries, hung up, to the imminent peril of all the pretty housemaids.[*]

So intent were the servants upon their sports, that we had to ring repeatedly before we could make ourselves heard. On our arrival being announced, the squire came out to receive us, accompanied by his two other sons; one a young officer in the army, home on leave of absence; the other an Oxonian, just from the University. The squire was a fine healthy-looking old gentleman, with silver hair curling lightly round an open florid countenance; in which the physiognomist, with the advantage, like myself, of a previous hint or two, might discover a singular mixture of whim and benevolence.

The family meeting was warm and affectionate; as the evening was far advanced, the squire would not permit us to change our travelling dresses, but ushered us at once to the company, which was assembled in a large old-fashioned hall. It was composed of different branches of a numerous family connection, where there

---

[*] The mistletoe is still hung up in farmhouses and kitchens at Christmas, and the young men have the privilege of kissing the girls under it, plucking each time a berry from the bush. When the berries are all plucked, the privilege ceases.

were the usual proportion of old uncles and aunts, comfortably married dames, superannuated spinsters, blooming country cousins, half-fledged striplings, and bright-eyed boarding-school hoydens. They were variously occupied; some at a round game of cards; others conversing around the fireplace; at one end of the hall was a group of the young folks, some nearly grown up, others of a more tender and budding age, fully engrossed by a merry game; and a profusion of wooden horses, penny trumpets, and tattered dolls, about the floor, showed traces of a troop of little fairy beings, who, having frolicked through a happy day, had been carried off to slumber through a peaceful night.

While the mutual greetings were going on between young Bracebridge and his relatives, I had time to scan the apartment. I have called it a hall, for so it had evidently been in old times, and the squire had evidently endeavoured to restore it to something of its primitive state. Over the heavy projecting fireplace was suspended a picture of a warrior in armour, standing by a white horse, and on the opposite wall hung a helmet, buckler, and lance. At one end an enormous pair of antlers were inserted in the wall, the branches serving as hooks in which to suspend hats, whips, and spurs; and in the corner of the apartment were fowling-pieces, fishing-rods, and other sporting implements. The furniture was of the cumbrous workmanship of former days, though some articles of modern convenience had been added, and the oaken floor had been carpeted; so that the whole presented an odd mixture of parlour and hall.

The grate had been removed from the wide overwhelming fire-place, to make way for a fire of wood, in the midst of which was an enormous log glowing and blazing, and sending forth a vast volume of light and heat; this I understood was the Yule clog, which the squire was particular in having brought in and illumined on a Christmas Eve, according to ancient custom.*

It was really delightful to see the old squire seated in his hereditary elbow chair, by the hospitable fireplace of his ancestors, and looking round him like the sun of a system, beaming warmth and gladness to every heart. Even the very dog that lay stretched at his feet, as he lazily shifted his position and yawned, would look fondly up in his master's face, wag his tail against the floor, and stretch himself again to sleep, confident of kindness and protection. There is an emanation from the heart in genuine hospitality which cannot be described, but is immediately felt, and puts the stranger at once at his ease. I had not been seated many minutes by the comfortable hearth of the worthy old cavalier,

---

* The Yule clog is a great log of wood, sometimes the root of a tree, brought into the house with great ceremony on Christmas Eve, laid in the fire place, and lighted with the brand of last year's clog. While it lasted, there was great drinking, singing; and telling of tales. Sometimes it was accompanied by Christmas candles; but in the cottages the only light was from the ruddy blaze of the great wood fire. The Yule clog was to burn all night; if it went out, it was considered a sign of ill luck.

Herrick mentions it in one of his songs—

> Come, bring with a noise, My merrie, merrie bow,
> The Christmas log to the firing; While my good dame,
> she Bids ye all be free,
> And drink to your heart's desiring.

The Yule clog is still burnt in many farmhouses and kitchens in England, particularly in the north: and there are several superstitions connected with it among the peasantry. If a squinting person come to the house while it is burning, or a person bare-footed, it is considered an ill omen. The brand remaining from the Yule clog is carefully put away to light the next year's Christmas fire.

before I found myself as much at home as if I had been one of the family.

Supper was announced shortly after our arrival. It was served up in a spacious oaken chamber, the panels of which shone with wax, and around which were several family portraits decorated with holly and ivy. Besides the accustomed lights, two great wax tapers, called Christmas candles, wreathed with greens, were placed on a highly polished beaufet among the family plate. The table was abundantly spread with substantial fare; but the squire made his supper of frumenty, a dish made of wheat cakes boiled in milk, with rich spices, being a standing dish in old times for Christmas Eve. I was happy to find my old friend, minced pie, in the retinue of the feast; and finding him to be perfectly orthodox, and that I need not be ashamed of my predilection, I greeted him with all the warmth wherewith we usually greet an old and very genteel acquaintance.

The mirth of the company was greatly promoted by the humours of an eccentric personage whom Mr. Bracebridge always addressed with the quaint appellation of Master Simon. He was a tight brisk little man, with the air of an arrant old bachelor. His nose was shaped like the bill of a parrot; his face slightly pitted with the small-pox, with a dry perpetual bloom on it, like a frost-bitten leaf in autumn. He had an eye of great quickness and vivacity, with a drollery and lurking waggery of expression that was irresistible. He was evidently the wit of the family, dealing very much in sly jokes and innuendoes with the ladies, and making infinite merriment by harping upon old themes; which unfortunately, my ignorance of the family chronicles did not permit me to enjoy. It seemed to be his great delight during supper to keep a young girl next him in a continual agony of stifled laughter, in spite of her awe of the reproving looks of her mother who sat opposite. Indeed, he was the idol of the younger part of the company, who laughed at everything he said or did, and at every turn of his countenance. I could not wonder at it; for he must have been a miracle of accomplishments in their eyes. He could imitate Punch and Judy; make an old woman of his hand, with the assistance of a burnt cork and pocket-handkerchief; and cut an orange into such a ludicrous caricature, that the young folks were ready to die with laughing.

I was let briefly into his history by Frank Bracebridge. He was an old bachelor, of a small independent income, which, by careful management, was sufficient for all his wants. He revolved through the family system like a vagrant comet in its orbit; sometimes visiting one branch, and sometimes another quite remote; as is often the case with gentlemen of extensive connections and small fortunes in England. He had a chirping buoyant disposition, always enjoying the present moment; and his frequent change of scene and company prevented his acquiring those rusty unaccommodating habits with which old bachelors are so uncharitably charged. He was a complete family chronicle, being versed in the genealogy, history, and inter-marriages of the whole house of Bracebridge, which made him a great favourite with the old folks; he was the beau of all the elder ladies and superannuated spinsters, among whom he was habitually considered rather a young fellow, and he was master of the revels among the children; so that there was not a more popular being in the sphere in which he moved than Mr. Simon Bracebridge. Of late years he had resided almost entirely with the squire, to whom he had become a factotum, and whom he particularly delighted by jumping with his humour in respect to old times, and by having a scrap of an old song to suit every occasion. We had presently a specimen of his last-mentioned talent, for no sooner was supper removed, and spiced wines and other beverages peculiar to the season introduced, than Master Simon was called on for a good old Christmas song. He bethought himself for a moment, and then, with a sparkle of the eye, and a voice by no means bad, excepting that it ran occasionally into a falsetto, like the notes of a split reed, he quavered forth a quaint old ditty.

> *Now Christmas is come,*
> *Let us beat up the drum,*
> *And call all our neighbours together,*
> *And when they appear,*
> *Let us make them such cheer,*
> *As will keep out the wind and the weather, &c.*

The supper had disposed every one to gaiety, and an old harper was summoned from the servants' hall, where he had been strumming all the evening, and to all appearance comforting himself with some of the squire's home-brewed. He was a kind of hanger-on, I was told, of the establishment, and, though ostensibly a resident of the village, was oftener to be found in the squire's kitchen than his own home, the old gentleman being fond of the sound of "harpinhall."

The dance, like most dances after supper, was a merry one; some of the older folks joined in it, and the squire himself figured down several couple with a partner, with whom he affirmed he had danced at every Christmas for nearly half a century. Master Simon, who seemed to be a kind of connecting link between the old times and the new, and to be withal a little antiquated in the taste of his accomplishments, evidently piqued himself on his dancing, and was endeavouring to gain credit by the heel and toe, rigadoon, and other graces of the ancient school; but he had unluckily assorted himself with a little romping girl from boarding-school, who by her wild vivacity, kept him continually on the stretch, and defeated all his sober attempts at elegance: such are the ill-assorted matches to which antique gentlemen are unfortunately prone!

The young Oxonian, on the contrary, had led out one of his maiden aunts, on whom the rogue played a thousand little knaveries with impunity; he was full of practical jokes, and his delight was to tease his aunt and cousins; yet, like all madcap youngsters, he was a universal favourite among the women. The most interesting couple in the dance was the young officer and a ward of the squire's, a beautiful blushing girl of seventeen. From several sly glances which I had noticed in the course of the evening, I suspected there was a little kindness growing up between them; and, indeed, the young soldier was just the hero to captivate a romantic girl. He was tall, slender, and handsome, and like most young British officers of late years, had picked up various small accomplishments on the Continent—he could talk French and Italian—draw landscapes, sing very tolerably, dance divinely; but, above all, he had been wounded at Waterloo—what girl of seventeen, well read in poetry and romance, could resist such a mirror of chivalry and perfection!

The moment the dance was over, he caught up a guitar, and lolling against the old marble fireplace, in an attitude which I am half inclined to suspect was studied, began the little French air of the Troubadour.

The squire, however, exclaimed against having anything on Christmas Eve but good old English; upon which the young minstrel, casting up his eye for a moment, as if in an effort of memory, struck into another strain, and, with a charming air of gallantry, gave Herrick's "Night-Piece to Julia."

> Her eyes the glow-worm lend thee,
> The shooting stars attend thee,
> And the elves also, Whose little eyes glow
> Like the sparks of fire befriend thee.
>
> No Will-o'-the-Wisp mislight thee;
> Nor snake nor slow-worm bite thee;
> But on, on the way, Not making a stay,
> Since ghost there is none to affright thee.
>
> Then let not the dark thee cumber;
> What tho' the moon does slumber,
> The stars of the night
> Will lend thee their light,
> Like tapers clear without number;
>
> Then, Julia, let me woo thee,
> Thus, thus to come unto me,
> And when I shall meet
> Thy silvery feet,
> My soul I'll pour into thee.

The song might or might not have been intended in compliment to the fair Julia, for so I found his partner was called; she, however, was certainly unconscious of any such application, for she never looked at the singer, but kept her eyes cast upon the floor. Her face was suffused, it is true, with a beautiful blush, and there was a gentle heaving of the bosom, but all that was doubtless caused by the exercise of the dance; indeed, so great was her indifference, that she amused herself with plucking to pieces a choice bouquet of hot-house flowers, and by the time the song was concluded the nosegay lay in ruins on the floor.

The party now broke up for the night, with the kindhearted old custom of shaking hands. As I passed through the hall, on my way to my chamber, the dying embers of the Yule clog still sent forth a dusky glow, and had it not been the season when "no spirit dares stir abroad," I should have been half tempted to steal from my room at midnight, and peep whether the fairies might not be at their revels about the hearth.

My chamber was in the old part of the mansion, the ponderous furniture of which might have been fabricated in the days of the giants. The room was panelled, with cornices of heavy carved work, in which flowers and grotesque faces were strangely intermingled; and a row of black-looking portraits stared mournfully at me from the walls. The bed was of rich though faded damask, with a lofty tester, and stood in a niche opposite a bow window. I had scarcely got into bed when a strain of music seemed to break forth in the air just below the window. I listened, and found it proceeded from a band, which I concluded to be the waits from some neighbouring village. They went round the house, playing under the windows. I drew aside the curtains to hear them more distinctly. The moonbeams fell through the upper part of the casement, partially lighting up the antiquated apartment. The sounds, as they receded, became more soft and aerial, and seemed to accord with the quiet and moonlight. I listened and listened— they became more and more tender and remote, and, as they gradually died away, my head sunk upon the pillow, and I fell asleep.

ANTHONY TROLLOPE

Christmas at Thompson Hall

CHAPTER I: MRS. BROWN'S SUCCESS

Every one remembers the severity of the Christmas of 187–. I will not designate the year more closely, lest I should enable those who are too curious to investigate the circumstances of this story, and inquire into details which I do not intend to make known. That winter, however, was especially severe, and the cold of the last ten days of December was more felt, I think, in Paris than in any part of England. It may, indeed, be doubted whether there is any town in any country in which thoroughly bad weather is more afflicting than in the French capital. Snow and hail seem to be colder there, and fires certainly are less warm, than in London. And then there is a feeling among visitors to Paris that Paris ought to be gay; that gayety, prettiness, and liveliness are its aims, as money, commerce, and general business are the aims of London, which, with its outside sombre darkness, does often seem to want an excuse for its ugliness. But on this occasion, at this Christmas of

187–, Paris was neither gay, nor pretty, nor lively. You could not walk the streets without being ankle-deep, not in snow, but in snow that had just become slush; and there was falling throughout the day and night of the 23rd of December a succession of damp, half-frozen abominations from the sky which made it almost impossible for men and women to go about their business.

It was at ten o'clock on that evening that an English lady and gentleman arrived at the Grand Hotel on the Boulevard des Italiens. As I have reasons for concealing the names of this married couple, I will call them Mr. and Mrs. Brown. Now, I wish it to be understood that in all the general affairs of life this gentleman and this lady lived happily together, with all the amenities which should bind a husband and a wife. Mrs. Brown was one of a wealthy family, and Mr. Brown, when he married her, had been relieved from the necessity of earning his bread. Nevertheless, she had at once yielded to him when he expressed a desire to spend the winters of their life in the South of France; and he, though he was by disposition somewhat idle, and but little prone to the energetic occupations of life, would generally allow himself, at other periods of the year, to be carried hither and thither by her, whose more robust nature delighted in the excitement of travelling. But on this occasion there had been a little difference between them.

Early in December an intimation had reached Mrs. Brown at Pau that on the coming Christmas there was to be a great gathering of all the Thompsons in the Thompson family hall at Stratford-le-Bow, and that she, who had been a Thompson, was desired to join the party with her husband. On this occasion her only sister was desirous of introducing to the family generally a most excellent young man to whom she had recently become engaged. The Thompsons—the real name, however, is in fact concealed—were a numerous and a thriving people. There were uncles and cousins and brothers who had all done well in the world, and who were all likely to do better still. One had lately been returned to Parliament for the Essex Flats, and was at the time of which I am writing a conspicuous member of the gallant Conservative majority. It was partly in triumph at this success that the great Christmas gathering of the Thompsons was to be held, and an opinion had been expressed by the legislator himself that, should Mrs. Brown, with her husband, fail to join the family on this happy occasion, she and he would be regarded as being but *fainéant* Thompsons.

Since her marriage, which was an affair now nearly eight years old, Mrs. Brown had never passed a Christmas in England. The desirability of doing so had often been mooted by her. Her very soul craved the festivities of holly and mince-pies. There had ever been meetings of the Thompsons at Thompson Hall, though meetings not so significant, not so important to the family, as this one which was now to be collected. More than once had she expressed a wish to see old Christmas again in the old house among the old faces. But her husband had always pleaded a certain weakness about his throat and chest as a reason for remaining among the delights of Pau. Year after year she had yielded, and now this loud summons had come.

It was not without considerable trouble that she had induced Mr. Brown to come as far as Paris. Most unwillingly had he left Pau; and then, twice on his journey—both at Bordeaux and Tours—he had made an attempt to return. From the first moment he had

pleaded his throat, and when at last he had consented
to make the journey, he had stipulated for sleeping at
those two towns and at Paris. Mrs. Brown, who, with
no slightest feeling of fatigue, could have made the
journey from Pau to Stratford without stopping, had
assented to everything, so that they might be at Thompson Hall on Christmas-eve. When Mr. Brown uttered
his unavailing complaints at the first two towns at
which they stayed, she did not, perhaps, quite believe
all that he said of his own condition. We know how
prone the strong are to suspect the weakness of the
weak—as the weak are to be disgusted by the strength
of the strong. There were, perhaps, a few words between
them on the journey, but the result had hitherto been
in favour of the lady. She had succeeded in bringing
Mr. Brown as far as Paris.

Had the occasion been less important, no doubt she
would have yielded. The weather had been bad even
when they left Pau, but as they had made their way
northward it had become worse and still worse. As
they left Tours, Mr. Brown, in a hoarse whisper, had
declared his conviction that the journey would kill him.
Mrs. Brown, however, had unfortunately noticed half
an hour before that he had scolded the waiter on the
score of an overcharged franc or two with a loud and
clear voice. Had she really believed that there was
danger, or even suffering, she would have yielded; but
no woman is satisfied in such a matter to be taken in
by false pretences. She observed that he ate a good
dinner on his way to Paris, and that he took a small
glass of cognac with complete relish, which a man really
suffering from bronchitis surely would not do. So she
persevered, and brought him into Paris, late in the
evening, in the midst of all that slush and snow. Then,

as they sat down to supper, she thought he did speak
hoarsely, and her loving feminine heart began to mis-
give her.

But this now was, at any rate, clear to her—that he
could not be worse off by going on to London than he
would be should he remain in Paris. If a man is to be
ill, he had better be ill in the bosom of his family than
at a hotel. What comfort could he have, what relief, in
that huge barrack? As for the cruelty of the weather,
London could not be worse than Paris, and then she
thought she had heard that sea air is good for a sore
throat. In that bedroom which had been allotted to
them *au quatrième* they could not even get a decent fire.
It would in every way be wrong now to forgo the great
Christmas gathering when nothing could be gained by
staying in Paris.

She had perceived that, as her husband became
really ill, he became also more tractable and less dispu-
tatious. Immediately after that little glass of cognac he
had declared that he would be—if he would go beyond
Paris, and she began to fear that, after all, everything
would have been done in vain. But as they went down
to supper between ten and eleven he was more sub-
dued, and merely remarked that this journey would, he
was sure, be the death of him. It was half past eleven
when they got back to their bedroom, and then he
seemed to speak with good sense, and also with much
real apprehension. "If I can't get something to relieve
me, I know I shall never make my way on," he said. It
was intended that they should leave the hotel at half
past five the next morning, so as to arrive at Stratford,
travelling by the tidal train, at half past seven on
Christmas-eve. The early hour, the long journey, the
infamous weather, the prospect of that horrid gulf

between Boulogne and Folkestone, would have been as nothing to Mrs. Brown, had it not been for that settled look of anguish which had now pervaded her husband's face. "If you don't find something to relieve me, I shall never live through it," he said again, sinking back into the questionable comfort of a Parisian hotel arm-chair.

"But, my dear, what can I do?" she asked, almost in tears, standing over him and caressing him. He was a thin, genteel-looking man, with a fine long soft brown beard, a little bald at the top of the head, but certainly; genteel-looking man. She loved him dearly, and in her softer moods was apt to spoil him with her caresses. "What can I do, my dearie? You know I would do anything if I could. Get into bed, my pet, and be warm, and then to-morrow morning you will be all right." At this moment he was preparing himself for his bed, and she was assisting him. Then she tied a piece of flannel around his throat, and kissed him, and put him in beneath the bedclothes.

"I'll tell you what you can do," he said, very hoarsely. His voice was so bad now that she could hardly hear him. So she crept close to him, and bent over him. She would do anything if he would only say what. Then he told her what was his plan. Down in the salon he had seen a large jar of mustard standing on a sideboard. As he left the room he had observed that this had not been withdrawn with the other appurtenances of the meal. If she could manage to find her way down there, taking with her a handkerchief folded for the purpose, and if she could then appropriate a part of the contents of that jar, and, returning with her prize, apply it to his throat, he thought that he could get some relief, so that he might be able to leave his bed the next morning at five. "But I am afraid it will be very disagreeable for you to go down all alone at this time of night," he croaked out in a piteous whisper.

"Of course I'll go," said she. "I don't mind going in the least. Nobody will bite me"; and she at once began to fold a clean handkerchief. "I won't be two minutes, my darling; and if there is a grain of mustard in the house, I'll have it on your chest almost immediately." She was a woman not easily cowed, and the journey down into the salon was nothing to her. Before she went she tucked the clothes carefully up to his ears, and then she started.

To run along the first corridor till she came to a flight of stairs was easy enough, and easy enough to descend them. Then there was another corridor and another flight, and a third corridor and a third flight, and she began to think that she was wrong. She found herself in a part of the hotel which she had not hitherto visited, and soon discovered by looking through an open door or two that she had found her way among a set of private sitting-rooms which she had not seen before. Then she tried to make her way back, up the same stairs and through the same passages, so that she might start again. She was beginning to think that she had lost herself altogether, and that she would be able to find neither the salon nor her bedroom, when she happily met the night porter. She was dressed in a loose white dressing-gown, with a white net over her loose hair, and with white worsted slippers. I ought, perhaps, to have described her personal appearance sooner. She was a large woman with a commanding bust, thought by some to be handsome, after the manner of Juno. But with strangers there was a certain severity of manner about her—a fortification, as it were, of her virtue against all possible attacks—a declared determination to maintain, at all points, the beautiful character of a British matron, which, much as it had been appreciated at Thompson Hall, had met with some ill-natured criticism among French men and women. At Pau she had been called La Fiere Anglaise. The name had reached her own ears and those of her husband. He had been much annoyed, but she had taken it in good part—had, indeed, been somewhat proud of the title—and had endeavoured to live up to it. With her husband she could, on occasion, be soft, but she was of opinion that with other men a British matron should be stern. She was now greatly in want of assistance; but, nevertheless, when she met the porter she remembered her character. "I have lost my way wandering through these horrid passages," she said in her severest tone. This was in answer to some question from him—some question to which her reply was given very slowly. Then, when he asked where madame wished to go, she paused, again thinking what destination she would announce. No doubt the man could take her back to her bedroom, but if so, the mustard must be renounced, and with the mustard, as she now feared, all hope of reaching Thompson Hall on Christmas-eve. But she, though she was in many respects a brave woman, did not dare to tell the man that she was prowling about the hotel in order that she might make a midnight raid upon the mustard pot. She paused, therefore, for a moment, that she might collect her thoughts, erecting her head as she did so in her best Juno fashion, till the porter was lost in admiration. Thus she gained time to fabricate a tale. She had, she said, dropped her handkerchief under the supper-table; would he show her the way to the salon, in order that she might pick it up? But the porter did more than that, and accompanied her to the room in which she had supped.

Here, of course, there was a prolonged and, it need hardly be said, a vain search. The good-natured man insisted on emptying an enormous receptacle of soiled table napkins, and on turning them over one by one, in order that the lady's property might be found. The lady stood by unhappy, but still patient, and as the man was stooping to his work, her eye was on the mustard pot. There it was, capable of containing enough to blister the throats of a score of sufferers. She edged off a little toward it while the man was busy, trying to persuade herself that he would surely forgive her if she took the mustard and told him her whole story. But the descent from her Juno bearing would have been so great! She must have owned, not only to the quest for mustard, but also to a fib—and she could not do it. The porter was at last of opinion that madame must have made a mistake, and madame acknowledged that she was afraid it was so.

With a longing, lingering eye, with an eye turned back, oh! so sadly to the great jar, she left the room, the porter leading the way. She assured him that she would find it by herself, but he would not leave her till he had put her on to the proper passage. The journey seemed to be longer now even than before; but as she ascended the many stairs she swore to herself that she would not even yet be balked of her object. Should her husband want comfort for his poor throat, and the comfort be there within her reach, and he not have it? She counted every stair as she went up, and marked every turn well. She was sure now that she would know the way, and that she could return to the room without fault. She would go back to the salon. Even though the man should encounter her again, she would go boldly forward and seize the remedy which her poor husband so grievously required.

"Ah, yes," she said, when the porter told her that her room, No. 333, was in the corridor which they had then reached, "I know it all now. I am so much obliged. Do not come a step farther." He was anxious to accompany her up to the very door, but she stood in the passage, and prevailed. He lingered awhile—naturally. Unluckily, she had brought no money with her, and could not give him the two-franc piece which he had earned. Nor could she fetch it from her room, feeling that, were she to return to her husband without the mustard, no second attempt would be possible. The disappointed man turned on his heel at last, and made his way down the stairs and along the passage. It seemed to her to be almost an eternity while she listened to his still audible footsteps. She had gone on, creeping noiselessly up to the very door of her room, and there she stood shading the candle in her hand, till she thought that the man must have wandered away into some farthest corner of that endless building. Then she turned once more and retraced her steps.

There was no difficulty now as to the way. She knew it, every stair. At the head of each flight she stood and listened, but not a sound was to be heard, and then she went on again. Her heart beat high with anxious desire to achieve her object, and at the same time with fear. What might have been explained so easily at first would now be as difficult of explanation. At last she was in the great public vestibule, which she was now visiting for the third time, and of which, at her last visit, she had

taken the bearings accurately. The door was there—
closed, indeed, but it opened easily to the hand. In the
hall and on the stairs and along the passages there had
been gas, but here there was no light beyond that given
by the little taper which she carried. When accompanied by the porter she had not feared the darkness, but
now there was something in the obscurity which made
her dread to walk the length of the room up to the
mustard jar. She paused, and listened, and trembled.
Then she thought of the glories of Thompson Hall, of
the genial warmth of a British Christmas, of that proud
legislator who was her first cousin, and with a rush she
made good the distance, and laid her hand upon the
copious delf. She looked round, but there was no one
there; no sound was heard; not the distant creak of a
shoe, not a rattle from one of those thousand doors. As
she paused with her fair hand upon the top of the jar,
while the other held the white cloth on which the
medicinal compound was to be placed, she looked like
Lady Macbeth as she listened at Duncan's chamber
door.

There was no doubt as to the sufficiency of the contents. The jar was full nearly up to the lips. The mixture
was, no doubt, very different from that good, wholesome English mustard which your cook makes fresh for
you, with a little water, in two minutes. It was impreg-
nated with a sour odour, and was, to English eyes,
unwholesome of colour. But still it was mustard. She
seized the horn spoon, and without further delay
spread an ample sufficiency on the folded square of
the handkerchief. Then she commenced to hurry her
return.

But still there was a difficulty, no thought of which
had occurred to her before. The candle occupied one

hand, so that she had but the other for the sustenance of her treasure. Had she brought a plate or saucer from the salon, it would have been all well. As it was, she was obliged to keep her eye intent on her right hand, and to proceed very slowly on her return journey. She was surprised to find what an aptitude the thing had to slip from her grasp. But still she progressed slowly, and was careful not to miss a turning. At last she was safe at her chamber door. There it was, No. 333.

CHAPTER II: MRS. BROWN'S FAILURE

With her eye still fixed upon her burden, she glanced up at the number of the door—333. She had been determined all through not to forget that. Then she turned the latch and crept in. The chamber also was dark after the gaslight on the stairs, but that was so much the better. She herself had put out the two candles on the dressing-table before she had left her husband. As she was closing the door behind her she paused, and could hear that he was sleeping. She was well aware that she had been long absent—quite long enough for a man to fall into slumber who was given that way. She must have been gone, she thought, fully an hour. There had been no end to that turning over of napkins which she had so well known to be altogether vain. She paused at the centre-table of the room, still looking at the mustard, which she now delicately dried from off her hand. She had had no idea that it would have been so difficult to carry so light and so small an affair. But there it was, and nothing had been lost. She took some small instrument from the washing-stand, and with the handle collected the flowing fragments into the centre. Then the question occurred to her whether, as her husband was sleeping so sweetly, it would be well to disturb him. She listened again, and felt that the slight murmur of a snore with which her ears were regaled was altogether free from any real malady in the throat. Then it occurred to her that, after all, fatigue perhaps had only made him cross. She bethought herself how, during the whole journey, she had failed to believe in his illness. What meals he had eaten! How thoroughly he had been able to enjoy his full complement of cigars! And then that glass of brandy, against which she had raised her voice slightly in feminine opposition. And now he was sleeping there like an infant, with full, round, perfected, almost sonorous workings of the throat. Who does not know that sound, almost of two rusty bits of iron scratching against each other, which comes from a suffering windpipe? There was no semblance of that here. Why disturb him when he was so thoroughly enjoying that rest which, more certainly than anything else, would fit him for the fatigue of the morrow's journey?

I think that, after all her labour, she would have left the pungent cataplasm on the table and have crept gently into bed beside him, had not a thought suddenly struck her of the great injury he had been doing her if he were not really ill. To send her down there, in a strange hotel, wandering among the passages, in the middle of the night, subject to the contumely of any one who might meet her, on a commission which, if it were not sanctified by absolute necessity, would be so thoroughly objectionable! At this moment she hardly did believe that he had ever really been ill. Let him have the cataplasm; if not as a remedy, then as a punishment. It could, at any rate, do him no harm. It was with an idea of avenging rather than of justifying the past labours of the night that she proceeded at once to quick action.

Leaving the candle on the table, so that she might steady her right hand with the left, she hurried stealthily to the bedside. Even though he was behaving badly to her, she would not cause him discomfort by waking him roughly. She would do a wife's duty to him as a British matron should. She would not only put the warm mixture on his neck, but would sit carefully by him for twenty minutes, so that she might relieve him from it when the proper period should have come for removing the counter-irritation from his throat. There would doubtless be some little difficulty in this—in collecting the mustard after it had served her purpose. Had she been at home, surrounded by her own comforts, the application would have been made with some delicate linen bag, through which the pungency of the spice would have penetrated with strength sufficient for the purpose. But the circumstance of the occasion had not admitted this. She had, she felt, done wonders in achieving so much success as this which she had obtained. If there should be anything disagreeable in the operation, he must submit to it. He had asked for mustard for his throat, and mustard he should have.

As these thoughts passed quickly through her mind, leaning over him in the dark, with her eye fixed on the mixture lest it should slip! she gently raised his flowing beard with her left hand, and with her other inverted rapidly, steadily but very softly fixed the handkerchief on his throat. From the bottom of his chin to the spot at which the collar-bones meeting together form the orifice of the chest, it covered the whole noble expanse. There was barely time for a glance, but never had she

been more conscious of the grand proportions of that
manly throat. A sweet feeling of pity came upon her,
causing her to determine to relieve his sufferings in the
shorter space of fifteen minutes. He had been lying on
his back, with his lips apart, and as she held back his
beard, that and her hand nearly covered the features of
his face. But he made no violent effort to free himself
from the encounter. He did not even move an arm or a
leg. He simply emitted a snore louder than any that had
come before. She was aware that it was not his wont to
be so loud—that there was generally something more
delicate and perhaps more querulous in his nocturnal
voice, but then the present circumstances were excep-
tional. She dropped the beard very softly—and there on
the pillow before her lay the face of a stranger. She had
put the mustard plaster on the wrong man.

Not Priam wakened in the dead of night, not Dido
when first she learned that Æneas had fled, not Othello
when he learned that Desdemona had been chaste, not
Medea when she became conscious of her slaughtered
children, could have been more struck with horror than
was this British matron as she stood for a moment
gazing with awe on that stranger's bed. One vain,
half-completed, snatching grasp she made at the handkerchief, and then drew back her hand. If she were to
touch him, would he not wake at once, and find her
standing there in his bedroom? And then how could she
explain it? By what words could she so quickly make
him know the circumstances of that strange occurrence
that he should accept it all before he had said a word
that might offend her? For a moment she stood all but
paralyzed after that faint ineffectual movement of her
arm. Then he stirred his head uneasily on the pillow,
opened wider his lips, and twice in rapid succession

snored louder than before. She started back a couple of paces, and with her body placed between him and the candle, with her face averted, but with her hand still resting on the foot of the bed, she endeavoured to think what duty required of her.

She had injured the man. Though she had done it most unwittingly, there could be no doubt but that she had injured him. If for a moment she could be brave, the injury might in truth be little; but how disastrous might be the consequences if she were now in her cowardice to leave him, who could tell? Applied for fifteen or twenty minutes, a mustard plaster may be the salvation of a throat ill at ease; but if left there throughout the night, upon the neck of a strong man, ailing nothing, only too prone in his strength to slumber soundly, how sad, how painful, for aught she knew how dangerous, might be the effects! And surely it was an error which any man with a heart in his bosom might pardon! Judging from what little she had seen of him, she thought that he must have a heart in his bosom. Was it not her duty to wake him, and then quietly to extricate him from the embarrassment which she had brought upon him?

But in doing this what words should she use? How should she wake him? How should she make him understand her goodness, her beneficence, her sense of duty, before he should have jumped from the bed and rushed to the bell, and have summoned all above, and all below, to the rescue? "Sir, sir, do not move, do not stir, do not scream. I have put a mustard plaster on your throat, thinking that you were my husband. As yet no harm has been done. Let me take it off, and then hold your peace forever." Where is the man of such native constancy and grace of spirit that, at the first moment of waking with a shock, he could hear these words from the mouth of an unknown woman by his bedside, and at once obey them to the letter? Would he not surely jump from his bed, with that horrid compound falling about him—from which there could be no complete relief unless he would keep his present attitude without a motion. The picture which presented itself to her mind as to his probable conduct was so terrible that she found herself unable to incur the risk.

Then an idea presented itself to her mind. We all know how in a moment quick thoughts will course through the subtle brain. She would find that porter and send him to explain it all. There should be no concealment now. She would tell the story and would bid him to find the necessary aid. Alas! as she told herself that she would do so, she knew well that she was only running from the danger which it was her duty to encounter. Once again she put out her hand as though to return along the bed. Then thrice he snorted louder than before, and moved up his knee uneasily beneath the clothes as though the sharpness of the mustard were already working upon his skin. She watched him for a moment longer, and then, with the candle in her hand, she fled.

Poor human nature! Had he been an old man, even a middle-aged man, she would not have left him to his unmerited sufferings. As it was, though she completely recognized her duty, and knew what justice and goodness demanded of her, she could not do it. But there was still left to her that plan of sending the night porter to him. It was not till she was out of the room and had gently closed the door behind her that she began to bethink herself how she had made the mistake. With a glance of her eye she looked up, and then saw the number on the door—353. Remarking to herself, with a Briton's natural criticism on things French, that those horrid foreigners do not know how to make their figures, she scudded rather than ran along the corridor, and then down some stairs and along another passage —so that she might not be found in the neighbourhood should the poor man in his agony rush rapidly from his bed.

In the confusion of her first escape she hardly ventured to look for her own passage—nor did she in the least know how she had lost her way when she came up-stairs with the mustard in her hand. But at the present moment her chief object was the night porter. She went on descending till she came again to that vestibule, and looking up at the clock saw that it was now past one. It was not yet midnight when she left her husband, but she was not at all astonished at the lapse of time. It seemed to her as though she had passed a night among these miseries. And, oh, what a night! But there was yet much to be done. She must find that porter, and then return to her own suffering husband. Ah! what now should she say to him? If he should really be ill, how should she assuage him? And yet how more than ever necessary was it that they should leave that hotel early in the morning—that they should leave Paris by the very earliest and quickest train that would take them as fugitives from their present dangers! The door of the salon was open, but she had no courage to go in search of a second supply. She would have lacked strength to carry it up the stairs. Where, now, oh! where was that man? From the vestibule she made her way into the hall, but everything seemed to be deserted.

Through the glass she could see a light in the court beyond, but she could not bring herself to endeavour even to open the hall doors.

And now she was very cold—chilled to her very bones. All this had been done at Christmas, and during such severity of weather as had never before been experienced by living Parisians. A feeling of great pity for herself gradually came upon her. What wrong had she done, that she should be so grievously punished? Why should she be driven to wander about in this way till her limbs were failing her? And then so absolutely important as it was that her strength should support her in the morning! The man would not die even though he were left there without aid, to rid himself of the cataplasm as best he might. Was it absolutely necessary that she should disgrace herself?

But she could not even procure the means of disgracing herself, if that telling her story to the night porter would have been a disgrace. She did not find him, and at last resolved to make her way back to her own room without further quest. She began to think that she had done all that she could do. No man was ever killed by a mustard plaster on his throat. His discomfort at the worst would not be worse than hers had been—or, too probably, than that of her poor husband. So she went back up the stairs and along the passages, and made her way on this occasion to the door of her room without any difficulty. The way was so well known to her that she could not but wonder that she had failed before. But now her hands had been empty, and her eyes had been at her full command. She looked up, and there was the number, very manifest on this occasion 333. She opened the door most gently, thinking that her husband might be sleeping as soundly as that other man had slept, and she crept into the room.

CHAPTER III: MRS. BROWN ATTEMPTS TO ESCAPE

But her husband was not sleeping. He was not even in bed, as she had left him. She found him sitting there before the fire place, on which one half-burned log still retained a spark of what had once pretended to be a fire. Nothing more wretched than his appearance could be imagined. There was a single lighted candle on the table, on which he was leaning with his two elbows, while his head rested between his hands. He had on a dressing-gown over his nightshirt, but otherwise was not clothed. He shivered audibly, or rather shook himself with the cold, and made the table to chatter, as she entered the room. Then he groaned, and let his head fall from his hands on to the table. It occurred to her at the moment, as she recognized the tone of his querulous voice, and as she saw the form of his neck, that she must have been deaf and blind when she had mistaken that stalwart stranger for her husband. "O my dear," she said, "why are you not in bed?" He answered nothing in words, but only groaned again. "Why did you get up? I left you warm and comfortable."

"Where have you been all night?" he half whispered, half croaked, with an agonizing effort.

"I have been looking for the mustard."

"Have been looking all night, and haven't found it? Where have you been?"

She refused to speak a word to him till she had got him into bed, and then she told her story. But, alas! that which she told was not the true story. As she was persuading him to go back to his rest, and while she arranged the clothes again around him, she with difficulty made up her mind as to what she would do and what she would say. Living or dying, he must be made to start for Thompson Hall at half past five on the next morning. It was no longer a question of the amenities of Christmas, no longer a mere desire to satisfy the family ambition of her own people, no longer an anxiety to see her new brother-in-law. She was conscious that there was in that house one whom she had deeply injured, and from whose vengeance—even from whose aspect—she must fly. How could she endure to see that face which she was so well sure that she would recognize, or to hear the slightest sound of that voice which would be quite familiar to her ears, though it had never spoken a word in her hearing? She must certainly fly on the wings of the earliest train which would carry her toward the old house; but in order that she might do so, she must propitiate her husband.

So she told her story. She had gone forth, as he had bade her, in search of the mustard, and then had suddenly lost her way. Up and down the house she had wandered, perhaps nearly a dozen times. "Had she met no one?" he asked, in that raspy, husky whisper. "Surely there must have been some one about the hotel! Nor was it possible that she could have been roaming about all those hours." "Only one hour, my dear," she said. Then there was a question about the duration of time, in which both of them waxed angry; and as she became angry, her husband waxed stronger, and as he became violent beneath the clothes, the comfortable idea returned to her that he was not perhaps so ill as he would seem to be. She found herself driven to tell him something about the porter, having to account for that lapse of time by explaining how she had driven the poor man to search for the handkerchief which she had never lost.

"Why did you not tell him you wanted the mustard?"

"My dear!"

"Why not? There is nothing to be ashamed of in wanting mustard."

"At one o'clock in the morning! I couldn't do it. To tell you the truth, he wasn't very civil, and I thought that he was—perhaps a little tipsy. Now, my dear, do go to sleep."

"Why didn't you get the mustard?"

"There was none there—nowhere at all about the room. I went down again and searched everywhere. That's what took me so long. They always lock up those kind of things at these French hotels. They are too close-fisted to leave anything out. When you first spoke of it I knew that it would be gone when I got there. Now, my dear, do go to sleep, because we positively must start in the morning."

"That is impossible," said he, jumping up in the bed.

"We must go, my dear. I say that we must go. After all that has passed, I wouldn't not be with Uncle John and my cousin Robert tomorrow evening for more—more—more than I would venture to say."

"Bother!" he exclaimed.

"It's all very well for you to say that, Charles, but you don't know. I say that we must go to-morrow, and we will."

"I do believe you want to kill me, Mary."

"That is very cruel, Charles, and most false, and most unjust. As for making you ill, nothing could be so bad for you as this wretched place, where nobody can get warm either day or night. If anything will cure your throat for you at once, it will be the sea air. And only think how much more comfortable they can make you at Thompson Hall than anywhere in this country. I have so set my heart upon it, Charles, that I will do it. If we are not there to-morrow night, Uncle John won't consider us as belonging to the family."

"I don't believe a word of it."

"Jane told me so in her letter. I wouldn't let you know before because I thought it so unjust. But that has been the reason why I've been so earnest about it all through."

It was a thousand pities that so good a woman should have been driven by the sad stress of circumstances to tell so many fibs. One after another she was compelled to invent them, that there might be a way open to her of escaping the horrors of a prolonged sojourn in that hotel. At length, after much grumbling, he became silent, and she trusted that he was sleeping. He had not as yet said that he would start at the required hour in the morning, but she was perfectly determined in her own mind that he should be made to do so. As he lay there motionless, and as she wandered about the room pretending to pack her things, she more than once almost resolved that she would tell him everything. Surely then he would be ready to make any effort. But there came upon her an idea that he might perhaps fail to see all the circumstances, and that, so failing, he would insist on remaining that he might tender some apology to the injured gentleman. An apology might have been very well had she not left him there in his misery; but what apology would be possible now? She would have to see him and speak to him, and every one in the hotel would know every detail of the story. Every one in France would know that it was she who had gone to the strange man's bed-side and put the mustard plaster on the strange man's throat in the dead of night! She could not tell the story even to her husband, lest even her husband should betray her.

Her own sufferings at the present moment were not light. In her perturbation of mind she had foolishly resolved that she would not herself go to bed. The tragedy of the night had seemed to her too deep for personal comfort. And then, how would it be were she to sleep, and have no one to call her? It was imperative that she should have all her powers ready for thoroughly arousing him. It occurred to her that the servant of the hotel would certainly run her too short of time. She had to work for herself and for him too, and therefore she would not sleep. But she was very cold, and she put on first a shawl over her dressing-gown and then a cloak. She could not consume all the remaining hours of the night in packing one bag and one portmanteau; so that at last she sat down on the narrow red cotton velvet sofa, and, looking at her watch, perceived that as yet it was not much past two o'clock. How was she to get through those other three long, tedious, chilly hours?

Then there came a voice from the bed—"Ain't you coming?"

"I hoped you were asleep, my dear."

"I haven't been asleep at all. You'd better come, if you don't mean to make yourself as ill as I am."

"You are not so very bad, are you, darling?"

"I don't know what you call bad. I never felt my throat so choked in my life before." Still as she listened she thought that she remembered his throat to have been more choked. If the husband of her bosom could play with her feelings and deceive her on such an occasion as this—then—then—then she thought that she would rather not have any husband of her bosom at all. But she did creep into bed, and lay down beside him without saying another word.

Of course she slept, but her sleep was not the sleep of the blest. At every striking of the clock in the quadrangle she would start up in alarm, fearing that she had let the time go by. Though the night was so short, it was very long to her. But he slept like an infant. She could hear from his breathing that he was not quite so well as she could wish him to be, but still he was resting in beautiful tranquillity. Not once did he move when she started up, as she did so frequently. Orders had been given and repeated over and over again that they should be called at five. The man in the office had almost been angry as he assured Mrs. Brown for the fourth time that monsieur and madame would most assuredly be wakened at the appointed time. But still she would trust to no one, and was up and about the room before the clock had struck half past four.

In her heart of hearts she was very tender toward her husband. Now, in order that he might feel a gleam of warmth while he was dressing himself, she collected together the fragments of half-burned wood, and endeavoured to make a little fire. Then she took out from her bag a small pot and a patent lamp and some chocolate, and prepared for him a warm drink, so that he might have it instantly as he was awakened. She would do anything for him in the way of ministering to his comfort—only he must go! Yes, he certainly must go!

And then she wondered how that strange man was bearing himself at the present moment. She would fain have ministered to him too had it been possible; but, ah! it was so impossible! Probably before this he would have been aroused from his troubled slumbers. But then—

how aroused? At what time in the night would the burning heat upon his chest have awakened him to a sense of torture which must have been so altogether incomprehensible to him? Her strong imagination showed to her a clear picture of the scene—clear, though it must have been done in the dark. How he must have tossed and hurled himself under the clothes! how those strong knees must have worked themselves up and down before the potent god of sleep would allow him to return to perfect consciousness! how his fingers, restrained by no reason, would have trampled over his feverish throat, scattering everywhere that unhappy poultice! Then when he should have sat up wide awake, but still in the dark—with her mind's eye she saw it all—feeling that some fire as from the infernal regions had fallen upon him, but whence he would know not, how fiercely wild would be the working of his spirit! Ah, now she knew, now she felt, now she acknowledged, how bound she had been to awaken him at the moment, whatever might have been the personal inconvenience to herself! In such a position what would he do—or rather what had he done? She could follow much of it in her own thoughts: how he would scramble madly from his bed, and, with one hand still on his throat, would snatch hurriedly at the matches with the other. How the light would come, and how then he would rush to the mirror. Ah, what a sight he would behold! She could see it all, to the last wide-spread daub.

But she could not see, she could not tell herself, what in such a position a man would do; at any rate, not what that man would do. Her husband, she thought, would tell his wife, and then the two of them, between them, would put up with it.

There are misfortunes which, if they be published, are simply aggravated by ridicule. But she remembered the features of the stranger as she had seen them at that instant in which she had dropped his beard, and she thought that there was a ferocity in them, a certain tenacity of self-importance, which would not permit their owner to endure such treatment in silence. Would he not storm and rage, and ring the bell, and call all Paris to witness his revenge?

But the storming and the raging had not reached her yet, and now it wanted but a quarter to five. In three-quarters of an hour they would be in that demi-omnibus which they had ordered for themselves, and in half an hour after that they would be flying toward Thompson Hall. Then she allowed herself to think of those coming comforts—of those comforts so sweet, if only they would come! That very day now present to her was the 24th December, and on that very evening she would be sitting in Christmas joy among all her uncles and cousins, holding her new brother-in-law affectionately by the hand. Oh, what a change from Pandemonium to Paradise! from that wretched room, from that miserable house in which there was such ample cause for fear, to all the domestic Christmas bliss of the home of the Thompsons! She resolved that she would not, at any rate, be deterred by any light opposition on the part of her husband. "It wants just a quarter to five," she said, putting her hand steadily upon his shoulder, "and I'll get a cup of chocolate for you, so that you may get up comfortably."

"I've been thinking about it," he said, rubbing his eyes with the back of his hands. "It will be so much better to go over by the mail-train to-night. We should be in time for Christmas just the same."

83

"That will not do at all," she answered, energetically. "Come, Charles, after all the trouble, do not disappoint me."

"It is such a horrid grind."

"Think what I have gone through—what I have done for you! In twelve hours we shall be there, among them all. You won't be so little like a man as not to go on now." He threw himself back upon the bed, and tried to re-adjust the clothes around his neck. "No, Charles, no," she continued; "not if I know it. Take your chocolate and get up. There is not a moment to be lost." With that she laid her hand upon his shoulder, and made him clearly understand that he would not be allowed to take further rest in that bed.

Grumbling, sulky, coughing continually, and declaring that life under such circumstances was not worth having, he did at last get up and dress himself. When once she knew that he was obeying her, she became again tender to him, and certainly took much more than her own share of the trouble of the proceedings. Long before the time was up she was ready, and the porter had been summoned to take the luggage downstairs. When the man came, she was rejoiced to see that it was not he whom she had met among the passages during her nocturnal rambles. He shouldered the box, and told them that they would find coffee and bread and butter in the small *salle à manger* below.

"I told you that it would be so, when you would boil that stuff," said the ungrateful man, who had nevertheless swallowed the hot chocolate when it was given to him.

They followed their luggage down into the hall; but as she went, at every step, the lady looked around her. She dreaded the sight of that porter of the night; she feared lest some potential authority of the hotel should come to her and ask her some horrid question; but of all her fears her greatest fear was that there should arise before her an apparition of that face which she had seen recumbent on its pillow.

As they passed the door of the great salon, Mr. Brown looked in. "Why, there it is still!" said he.

"What?" said she, trembling in every limb.

"The mustard pot."

"They have put it in there since," she exclaimed, energetically, in her despair. "But never mind. The omnibus is here. Come away." And she absolutely took him by the arm.

But at that moment a door behind them opened, and Mrs. Brown heard herself called by her name. And there was the night porter—with a handkerchief in his hand. But the further doings of that morning must be told in a further chapter.

CHAPTER IV: MRS. BROWN DOES ESCAPE

It had been visible to Mrs. Brown from the first moment of her arrival on the ground floor that "something was the matter," if we may be allowed to use such a phrase; and she felt all but convinced that this something had reference to her. She fancied that the people of the hotel were looking at her as she swallowed, or tried to swallow, her coffee. When her husband was paying the bill there was something disagreeable in the eye of the man who was taking the money. Her sufferings were very great, and no one sympathized with her. Her husband was quite at his ease, except that he was complaining of the cold. When she was anxious to get him out into the carriage, he still stood there, leisurely arranging shawl after shawl around his throat. "You can do that quite as well in the omnibus," she had just said to him, very crossly, when there appeared upon the scene through a side door that very night porter whom she dreaded with a soiled pocket-handkerchief in his hand.

Even before the sound of her own name met her ears, Mrs. Brown knew it all. She understood the full horror of her position from that man's hostile face, and from the little article which he held in his hand. If during the watches of the night she had had money in her pocket, if she had made a friend of this greedy fellow by well-timed liberality, all might have been so different! But she reflected that she had allowed him to go unfed after all his trouble, and she knew that he was her enemy. It was the handkerchief that she feared. She thought that she might have brazened out anything but that. No one had seen her enter or leave that strange man's room. No one had seen her dip her hands in that jar. She had, no doubt, been found wandering about the house while the slumberer had been made to suffer so strangely, and there might have been suspicion, and perhaps accusation. But she would have been ready with frequent protestations to deny all charges made against her, and though no one might have believed her, no one could have convicted her. Here, however, was evidence against which she would be unable to stand for a moment. At the first glance she acknowledged the potency of that damning morsel of linen.

During all the horrors of the night she had never given a thought to the handkerchief, and yet she ought to have known that the evidence it would bring against her was palpable and certain. Her name, "M. Brown," was plainly written on the corner. What a fool she had been not to have thought of this! Had she but remembered the plain marking which she, as a careful, well-conducted British matron, had put upon all her clothes, she would at any hazard have recovered the article. Oh that she had waked the man, or bribed the porter, or even told her husband! But now she was, as it were, friendless, without support, without a word that she could say in her own defence, convicted of having committed this assault upon a strange man as he slept in his own bedroom, and then of having left him! The thing must be explained by the truth; but how to explain such truth, how to tell such story in a way to satisfy injured folk, and she with only barely time sufficient to catch the train! Then it occurred to her that they could have no legal right to stop her because the pocket-handkerchief had been found in a strange gentleman's bedroom. "Yes, it is mine," she said, turning to her husband, as the porter, with a loud voice, asked if she were not Madame Brown. "Take it, Charles, and come on." Mr. Brown naturally stood still in astonishment. He did put out his hand, but the porter would not allow the evidence to pass so readily out of his custody.

"What does it all mean?" asked Mr. Brown.

"A gentleman has been—eh—eh—Something has been done to a gentleman in his bedroom," said the clerk.

"Something done to a gentleman!" repeated Mr. Brown.

"Something very bad indeed," said the porter. "Look here"; and he showed the condition of the handkerchief.

"Charles, we shall lose the train," said the affrighted wife.

"What the mischief does it all mean?" demanded the husband.

"Did madame go into the gentleman's room?" asked the clerk. Then there was an awful silence, and all eyes were fixed upon the lady.

"What does it all mean?" demanded the husband. "Did you go into anybody's room?"

"I did," said Mrs. Brown with much dignity, looking round upon her enemies as a stag at bay will look upon the hounds which are attacking him. "Give me the handkerchief." But the night porter quickly put it behind his back. "Charles, we cannot allow ourselves to be delayed. You shall write a letter to the keeper of the hotel explaining it all." Then she essayed to swim out through the front door into the courtyard, in which the vehicle was waiting for them. But three or four men and women interposed themselves, and even her husband did not seem quite ready to continue his journey. "Tonight is Christmas-eve," said Mrs. Brown, "and we shall not be at Thompson Hall. Think of my sister!"

"Why did you go into the man's bedroom, my dear?" whispered Mr. Brown in English.

But the porter heard the whisper, and understood the language—the porter who had not been "tipped." "Ye'es—vy?" asked the porter.

"It was a mistake, Charles; there is not a moment to lose. I can explain it all to you in the carriage." Then the clerk suggested that madame had better postpone her journey a little. The gentleman upstairs had certainly been very badly treated, and had demanded to know why so great an outrage had been perpetrated. The clerk said that he did not wish to send for the police (here Mrs. Brown gasped terribly, and threw herself on her husband's shoulder), but he did not think he could allow the party to go till the gentleman up-stairs had received some satisfaction. It had now become clearly impossible that the journey could be made by the early train. Even Mrs. Brown gave it up herself, and demanded of her husband that she should be taken back to her bedroom.

"But what is to be said to the gentleman?" asked the porter.

Of course it was impossible that Mrs. Brown should be made to tell her story there in the presence of them all. The clerk, when he found he had succeeded in pre-venting her from leaving the house, was satisfied with a promise from Mr. Brown that he would inquire from his wife what were these mysterious circumstances, and would then come down to the office and give some explanation. If it were necessary, he would see the strange gentleman—whom he now ascertained to be a certain Mr. Jones, returning from the east of Europe. He learned also that this Mr. Jones had been most anxious to travel by that very morning train which he and his wife had intended to use; that Mr. Jones had been most particular in giving his orders accordingly; but that at the last moment he had declared himself to be unable even to dress himself, because of the injury which had been done him during the night. When Mr. Brown heard this from the clerk just before he was allowed to take his wife up-stairs, while she was sitting on a sofa in a corner with her face hidden, a look of awful gloom came over his own countenance. What could it be that his wife had done to the man, of so terrible a nature? "You had better come up with me," he said to her, with marital severity; and the poor cowed woman went with him tamely as might have done some patient Grizel. Not a word was spoken till they were in the room and the door was locked. "Now," said he, "what does it all mean?"

It was not till nearly two hours had passed that Mr. Brown came down the stairs very slowly, turning it all over in his mind. He had now gradually heard the absolute and exact truth, and had very gradually learned to believe it. It was first necessary that he should understand that his wife had told him many fibs during the night; but, as she constantly alleged to him when he complained of her conduct in this respect, they had all been told on his behalf. Had she not struggled to get the mustard for his comfort, and when she had secured the prize had she not hurried to put it on—as she had fondly thought—his throat? And though she had fibbed to him afterward, had she not done so in order that he might not be troubled? "You are not angry with me because I was in that man's room?" she asked, looking full into his eyes, but not quite without a sob. He paused a moment, and then declared, with something of a true husband's confidence in his tone, that he was not in the least angry with her on that account. Then she kissed him, and bade him remember that, after all, no one could really injure them. "What harm has been done, Charles? The gentleman won't die because he has had a mustard plaster on his throat. The worst is about Uncle John and dear Jane. They do think so much of Christmas-eve at Thompson Hall!"

Mr. Brown, when he again found himself in the clerk's office, requested that his card might be taken up to Mr. Jones. Mr. Jones had sent down his own card, which was handed to Mr. Brown: "Mr. Barnaby Jones." "And how was it all, sir?" asked the clerk, in a whisper

—a whisper which had at the same time something of authoritative demand and something also of submissive respect. The clerk, of course, was anxious to know the mystery. It is hardly too much to say that every one in that vast hotel was by this time anxious to have the mystery unravelled. But Mr. Brown would tell nothing to any one. "It is merely a matter to be explained between me and Mr. Jones," he said. The card was taken up-stairs, and after a while he was ushered into Mr. Jones's room. It was, of course, that very 353 with which the reader is already acquainted. There was a fire burning, and the remains of Mr. Jones's breakfast were on the table. He was sitting in his dressing-gown and slippers, with his shirt open in the front, and a silk handkerchief very loosely covering his throat. Mr. Brown, as he entered the room, of course looked with considerable anxiety at the gentleman of whose condition he had heard so sad an account; but he could only observe some considerable stiffness of movement and demeanor as Mr. Jones turned his head round to greet him.

"This has been a very disagreeable accident, Mr. Jones," said the husband of the lady.

"Accident! I don't know how it could have been an accident. It has been a most—most—most—a most monstrous—er—er—I must say, interference with a gentleman's privacy and personal comfort."

"Quite so, Mr. Jones, but—on the part of the lady, who is my wife—"

"So I understand. I myself am about to become a married man, and I can understand what your feelings must be. I wish to say as little as possible to harrow them." Here Mr. Brown bowed. "But there's the fact. She did do it."

"She thought it was—me!"

"What!"

"I give you my word as a gentleman, Mr. Jones. When she was putting that mess upon you, she thought it was me! She did indeed." Mr. Jones looked at his new acquaintance and shook his head.

He did not think it possible that any woman would make such a mistake as that.

"I had a very bad sore throat," continued Mr. Brown, "and indeed you may perceive it still"—in saying this he perhaps aggravated a little the sign of his distemper—"and I asked Mrs. Brown to go down and get one—just what she put on you."

"I wish you'd had it," said Mr. Jones, putting his hand up to his neck.

"I wish I had, for your sake as well as mine, and for hers, poor woman. I don't know when she will get over the shock."

"I don't know when I shall. And it has stopped me on my journey. I was to have been to-night, this very night, this Christmas-eve, with the young lady I am engaged to marry. Of course I couldn't travel. The extent of the injury done nobody can imagine at present."

"It has been just as bad to me, sir. We were to have been with our family this Christmas-eve. There were particular reasons—most particular. We were only hindered from going by hearing of your condition."

"Why did she come into my room at all? I can't understand that. A lady always knows her own room at a hotel."

"353—that's yours; 333—that's ours. Don't you see how easy it was? She had lost her way, and she was a little afraid lest the thing should fall down."

"I wish it had with all my heart."

"That's how it was. Now I'm sure, Mr. Jones, you'll take a lady's apology. It was a most unfortunate mistake—most unfortunate; but what more can be said?"

Mr. Jones gave himself up to reflection for a few moments before he replied to this. He supposed that he was bound to believe the story as far as it went. At any rate, he did not know how he could say that he did not believe it. It seemed to him to be almost incredible, especially incredible in regard to that personal mistake, for, except that they both had long beards and brown beards, Mr. Jones thought that there was no point of resemblance between himself and Mr. Brown. But still, even that, he felt, must be accepted. But then why had he been left, deserted, to undergo all those torments? "She found out her mistake at last, I suppose?" he said.

"Oh, yes."

"Why didn't she wake a fellow and take it off again?"

"Ah!"

"She can't have cared very much for a man's comfort, when she went away and left him like that."

"Ah! There was the difficulty, Mr. Jones."

"Difficulty! Who was it that had done it? To come to me in my bedroom in the middle of the night and put that thing on me, and then leave it there and say nothing about it! It seems to me deuced like a practical joke."

"No, Mr. Jones."

"That's the way I look at it," said Mr. Jones, plucking up his courage.

"There isn't a woman in all England or in all France less likely to do such a thing than my wife. She's as steady as a rock, Mr. Jones, and would no more go into another gentleman's bedroom in joke than—Oh dear no! You're going to be a married man yourself."

"Unless all this makes a difference," said Mr. Jones, almost in tears. "I had sworn that I would be with her this Christmas-eve."

"Oh Mr. Jones, I cannot believe that will interfere with your happiness. How could you think that your wife, as is to be, would do such a thing as that in joke?"

"She wouldn't do it at all, joke or any way."

"How can you tell what accident might happen to any one?"

"She'd have wakened the man, then, afterward. I'm sure she would. She would never have left him to suffer in that way. Her heart is too soft. Why didn't she send you to wake me and explain it all? That's what my Jane would have done; and I should have gone and wakened him. But the whole thing is impossible," he said, shaking his head as he remembered that he and his Jane were not in a condition as yet to undergo any such mutual trouble. At last Mr. Jones was brought to acknowledge that nothing more could be done. The lady had sent her apology and told her story, and he must bear the trouble and inconvenience to which she had subjected him. He still, however, had his own opinion about her conduct generally, and could not be brought to give any sign of amity. He simply bowed when Mr. Brown was hoping to induce him to shake hands, and sent no word of pardon to the great offender.

The matter, however, was so far concluded that there was no further question of police interference, nor any doubt but that the lady, with her husband, was to be allowed to leave Paris by the night train. The nature of the accident probably became known to all. Mr. Brown was interrogated by many, and though he professed to declare that he would answer no question, nevertheless he found it better to tell the clerk something of the truth than to allow the matter to be shrouded in mystery. It is to be feared that Mr. Jones, who did not once show himself through the day, but who employed the hours in endeavouring to assuage the injury done him, still lived in the conviction that the lady had played a practical joke on him. But the subject of such a joke never talks about it, and Mr. Jones could not be induced to speak even by the friendly adherence of the night porter. Mrs. Brown also clung to the seclusion of her own bedroom, never once stirring from it till the time came in which she was to be taken down to the omnibus. Up-stairs she ate her meals, and up-stairs she passed her time in packing and unpacking, and in requesting that telegrams might be sent repeatedly to Thompson Hall. In the course of the day two such telegrams were sent, in the latter of which the Thompson family were assured that the Browns would arrive probably in time for breakfast on Christmas-day, certainly in time for church. She asked more than once tenderly after Mr. Jones's welfare, but could obtain no information. "He was very cross, and that's all I know about it," said Mr. Brown. Then she made a remark as to the gentleman's Christian name, which appeared on the card as "Barnaby." "My sister's husband's name will be Burnaby," she said. "And this man's Christian name is Barnaby; that's all the difference," said her husband, with ill-timed jocularity.

We all know how people under a cloud are apt to fail in asserting their personal dignity. On the former day a separate vehicle had been ordered by Mr. Brown to take himself and his wife to the station, but now, after his misfortunes, he contented himself with such provision as the people at the hotel might make for him. At the appointed hour he brought his wife down, thickly veiled. There were many strangers, as she passed through the hall, ready to look at the lady who had done that wonderful thing in the dead of night, but none could see a feature of her face as she stepped across the hall and was hurried into the omnibus. And there were many eyes also on Mr. Jones, who followed her very quickly, for he also, in spite of his sufferings, was leaving Paris on the evening in order that he might be with his English friends on Christmas-day. He, as he went through the crowd, assumed an air of great dignity, to which, perhaps, something was added by his endeavours as he walked to save his poor throat from irritation. He, too, got into the same omnibus, stumbling over the feet of his enemy in the dark. At the station they got their tickets, one close after the other, and then were brought into each other's presence in the waiting-room. I think it must be acknowledged that here Mr. Jones was conscious not only of her presence, but of her consciousness of his presence, and that he assumed an attitude as though he should have said, "Now do you think it possible for me to believe that you mistook me for your husband?" She was perfectly quiet, but sat through that quarter of an hour with her face continually veiled. Mr. Brown made some little overture of conversation to Mr. Jones, but Mr. Jones, though he did mutter some reply, showed plainly enough that he had no desire for further intercourse.

Then came the accustomed stampede, the awful rush, the internecine struggle in which seats had to be found. Seats, I fancy, are regularly found, even by the most tardy, but it always appears that every British father and every British husband is actuated at these stormy moments by a conviction that unless he proves himself a very Hercules he and his daughters and his wife will be left desolate in Paris. Mr. Brown was quite Herculean, carrying two bags and a hatbox in his own hands, besides the cloaks, the coats, the rugs, the sticks, and the umbrellas. But when he had got himself and his wife well seated, with their faces to the engine, with a corner seat for her—there was Mr. Jones immediately opposite to her. Mr. Jones, as soon as he perceived the inconvenience of his position, made a scramble for another place, but he was too late. In that contiguity the journey as far as Calais had to be made. She, poor woman, never once took up her veil. There he sat, without closing an eye, stiff as a ramrod, sometimes showing by little uneasy gestures that the trouble at his neck was still there, but never speaking a word, and hardly moving a limb.

Crossing from Calais to Dover the lady was, of course, separated from her victim. The passage was very bad, and she more than once reminded her husband how well it would have been with them now had they pursued their journey as she had intended—as though they had been detained in Paris by his fault! Mr. Jones, as he laid himself down on his back, gave himself up to wondering whether any man before him had ever been made subject to such absolute injustice. Now and again he put his hand up to his own beard, and began to doubt whether it could have been moved, as it must have been moved, without waking him. What if chloroform had been used? Many such suspicions crossed his mind during the misery of that passage.

They were again together in the same railway carriage from Dover to London. They had now got used to the close neighbourhood, and knew how to endure each the presence of the other. But as yet Mr. Jones had never seen the lady's face. He longed to know what were the features of the woman who had been so blind—if indeed that story were true. Or if it were not true, of what like was the woman who would dare in the middle of the night to play such a trick as that? But still she kept her veil close over her face.

From Cannon Street the Browns took their departure in a cab for the Liverpool Street Station, whence they would be conveyed by the Eastern Counties Railway to Stratford. Now, at any rate, their troubles were over. They would be in ample time not only for Christmas-day church, but for Christmas-day breakfast. "It will be just the same as getting in there last night," said Mr. Brown, as he walked across the platform to place his wife in the carriage for Stratford. She entered it the first, and as she did so, there she saw Mr. Jones seated in the corner! Hitherto she had borne his presence well, but now she could not restrain herself from a little start and a little scream. He bowed his head very slightly, as though acknowledging the compliment, and then down she dropped her veil. When they arrived at Stratford, the journey being over in a quarter of an hour, Jones was out of the carriage even before the Browns.

"There is Uncle John's carriage," said Mrs. Brown, thinking that now, at any rate, she would be able to free herself from the presence of this terrible stranger. No doubt he was a handsome man to look at, but on no face so sternly hostile had she ever before fixed her eyes. She did not, perhaps, reflect that the owner of no other face had ever been so deeply injured by herself.

★

Chapter V: Mrs. Brown At Thompson Hall

"Please, sir, we were to ask for Mr. Jones," said the servant, putting his head into the carriage after both Mr. and Mrs. Brown had seated themselves.

"Mr. Jones!" exclaimed the husband.

"Why ask for Mr. Jones?" demanded the wife. The servant was about to tender some explanation, when Mr. Jones stepped up and said that he was Mr. Jones. "We are going to Thompson Hall," said the lady, with great vigour.

"So am I," said Mr. Jones, with much dignity. It was, however, arranged that he should sit with the coach-man, as there was a rumble behind for the other servant. The luggage was put into a cart, and away all went for Thompson Hall.

"What do you think about it, Mary?" whispered Mr. Brown, after a pause. He was evidently awe-struck by the horror of the occasion.

"I cannot make it out at all. What do you think?"

"I don't know what to think. Jones going to Thompson Hall!"

"He's a very good-looking young man," said Mrs. Brown.

"Well—that's as people think. A stiff, stuck-up fellow, I should say. Up to this moment he has never forgiven you for what you did to him."

"Would you have forgiven his wife, Charles, if she'd done it to you?"

"He hasn't got a wife—yet."

"How do you know?"

"He is coming home now to be married," said Mr. Brown. "He expects to meet the young lady this very

99

Christmas-day. He told me so. That was one of the reasons why he was so angry at being stopped by what you did last night."

"I suppose he knows Uncle John, or he wouldn't be going to the Hall," said Mrs. Brown.

"I can't make it out," said Mr. Brown, shaking his head.

"He looks quite like a gentleman," said Mrs. Brown, "though he has been so stiff. Jones! Barnaby Jones! You're sure it was Barnaby?"

"That was the name on the card."

"Not Burnaby?" asked Mrs. Brown.

"It was Barnaby Jones on the card—just the same as 'Barnaby Rudge'; and as for looking like a gentleman, I'm by no means quite so sure. A gentleman takes an apology when it's offered."

"Perhaps, my dear, that depends on the condition of his throat. If you had had a mustard plaster on all night, you might not have liked it. But here we are at Thompson Hall at last."

Thompson Hall was an old brick mansion, standing within a huge iron gate, with a gravel sweep before it. It had stood there before Stratford was a town, or even a suburb, and had then been known by the name of Bow Place. But it had been in the hands of the present family for the last thirty years, and was now known far and wide as Thompson Hall—a comfortable, roomy, old-fashioned place, perhaps a little dark and dull to look at, but much more substantially built than most of our modern villas. Mrs. Brown jumped with alacrity from the carriage, and with a quick step entered the home of her fore fathers. Her husband followed her more leisurely; but he too felt that he was at home at Thompson Hall. Then Mr. Jones walked in also; but he looked as though he were not at all at home. It was still very early, and no one of the family was as yet down. In these circumstances it was almost necessary that something should be said to Mr. Jones.

"Do you know Mr. Thompson?" asked Mr. Brown.

"I never had the pleasure of seeing him—as yet," answered Mr. Jones, very stiffly.

"Oh—I didn't know. Because you said you were coming here."

"And I have come here. Are you friends of Mr. Thompson?"

"Oh dear yes," said Mrs. Brown. "I was a Thompson myself before I married."

"Oh—indeed!" said Mr. Jones. "How very odd!— very odd indeed."

During this time the luggage was being brought into the house, and two old family servants were offering them assistance. Would the new-comers like to go up to their bedrooms? Then the housekeeper, Mrs. Green, intimated with a wink that Miss Jane would, she was sure, be down quite immediately. The present moment, however, was still very unpleasant. The lady probably had made her guess as to the mystery, but the two gentlemen were still altogether in the dark. Mrs. Brown had no doubt declared her parentage, but Mr. Jones, with such a multitude of strange facts crowding on his mind, had been slow to understand her. Being somewhat suspicious by nature, he was beginning to think whether possibly the mustard had been put by this lady on his throat with some reference to his connection with Thompson Hall. Could it be that she, for some reason of her own, had wished to prevent his coming, and had contrived this untoward stratagem out of her brain? or had she wished to make him ridiculous to the

Thompson family, to whom, as a family, he was at present unknown? It was becoming more and more improbable to him that the whole thing should have been an accident. When, after the first horrid torments of that morning in which he had in his agony invoked the assistance of the night porter, he had begun to reflect on his situation, he had determined that it would be better that nothing further should be said about it. What would life be worth to him if he were to be known wherever he went as the man who had been mustard-plastered in the middle of the night by a strange lady? The worst of a practical joke is that the remembrance of the absurd condition sticks so long to the sufferer. At the hotel that night porter, who had possessed himself of the handkerchief, and had read the name, and had connected that name with the occupant of 333, whom he had found wandering about the house with some strange purpose, had not permitted the thing to sleep. The porter had pressed the matter home against the Browns, and had produced the interview which has been recorded. But during the whole of that day Mr. Jones had been resolving that he would never again either think of the Browns or speak of them. A great injury had been done to him—a most outrageous injustice; but it was a thing which had to be endured. A horrid woman had come across him like a nightmare. All he could do was to endeavour to forget the terrible visitation. Such had been his resolve, in making which he had passed that long day in Paris. And now the Browns had stuck to him from the moment of his leaving his room! He had been forced to travel with them, but had travelled with them as a stranger. He had tried to comfort himself with the reflection that at every fresh stage he would shake them off. In one railway after another the vicinity had been bad—but still they were strangers. Now he found himself in the same house with them, where of course the story would be told. Had not the thing been done on purpose that the story might be told there at Thompson Hall?

Mrs. Brown had acceded to the proposition of the housekeeper, and was about to be taken to her room, when there was heard a sound of footsteps along the passage above and on the stairs, and a young lady came bounding on to the scene. "You have all of you come a quarter of an hour earlier than we thought possible," said the young lady. "I did so mean to be up to receive you!" With that she passed her sister on the stairs—for the young lady was Miss Jane Thompson, sister to our Mrs. Brown—and turned down into the hall. Here Mr. Brown, who had ever been on affectionate terms with his sister-in-law, put himself forward to receive her embraces; but she, apparently not noticing him in her ardour, rushed on and threw herself on to the breast of the other gentleman. "This is my Charles," she said. "Oh, Charles, I thought you never would be here!"

Mr. Charles Burnaby Jones—for such was his name since he had inherited the Jones property in Pembrokeshire—received into his arms the ardent girl of his heart with all that love and devotion to which she was entitled, but could not do so without some external shrinking from her embrace. "Oh, Charles, what is it?" she said.

"Nothing, dearest—only—only—" Then he looked piteously up into Mrs. Brown's face, as though imploring her not to tell the story.

"Perhaps, Jane, you had better introduce us," said Mrs. Brown.

"Introduce you! I thought you had been travelling together, and staying at the same hotel, and all that."

"So we have; but people may be in the same hotel without knowing each other. And we have travelled all the way home with Mr. Jones without in the least knowing who he was."

"How very odd! Do you mean you have never spoken?"

"Not a word," said Mrs. Brown.

"I do so hope you'll love each other," said Jane.

"It sha'n't be my fault if we don't," said Mrs. Brown.

"I'm sure it sha'n't be mine," said Mr. Brown, tendering his hand to the other gentleman. The various feelings of the moment were too much for Mr. Jones, and he could not respond quite as he should have done. But as he was taken up-stairs to his room, he determined that he would make the best of it.

The owner of the house was old Uncle John. He was a bachelor, and with him lived various members of the family. There was the great Thompson of them all, Cousin Robert, who was now member of Parliament for the Essex Flats; and young John, as a certain enterprising Thompson of the age of forty was usually called; and then there was old Aunt Bess; and among other young branches there was Miss Jane Thompson, who was now engaged to marry Mr. Charles Burnaby Jones. As it happened, no other member of the family had as yet seen Mr. Burnaby Jones, and he, being by nature of a retiring disposition, felt himself to be ill at ease when he came into the breakfast parlor among all the Thompsons. He was known to be a gentleman of good family and ample means, and all the Thompsons had approved of the match; but during that first Christmas breakfast he did not seem to accept his condition jovially. His own Jane sat beside him, but then on the other side sat Mrs. Brown. She assumed an immediate intimacy—as women know how to do on such occasions—being determined from the very first to regard her sister's husband as a brother; but he still feared her. She was still to him the woman who had come to him in the dead of night with that horrid mixture—and had then left him.

"It was so odd that both of you should have been detained on the very same day," said Jane.

"Yes, it was odd," said Mrs. Brown, with a smile, looking round upon her neighbour.

"It was abominably bad weather, you know," said Brown.

"But you were both so determined to come," said the old gentleman. "When we got the two telegrams at the same moment, we were sure that there had been some agreement between you."

"Not exactly an agreement," said Mrs. Brown; whereupon Mr. Jones looked as grim as death.

"I'm sure there is something more than we understand yet," said the member of Parliament.

Then they all went to church, as a united family ought to do on Christmas-day, and came home to a fine old English early dinner at three o'clock—a sirloin of beef a foot and half broad, a turkey as big as an ostrich, a plum-pudding bigger than the turkey, and two or three dozen mince-pies. "That's a very large bit of beef," said Mr. Jones, who had not lived much in England latterly.

"It won't look so large," said the old gentleman, "when all our friends down-stairs have had their say to it." "A plum-pudding on Christmas-day can't be too big," he said again, "if the cook will but take time enough over it. I never knew a bit to go to waste yet."

By this time there had been some explanation as to past events between the two sisters. Mrs. Brown had, indeed, told Jane all about it—how ill her husband had been, how she had been forced to go down and look for the mustard, and then what she had done with the mustard.

"I don't think they are a bit alike, you know, Mary, if you mean that," said Jane.

"Well, no; perhaps not quite alike. I only saw his beard, you know. No doubt it was stupid, but I did it."

"Why didn't you take it off again?" asked the sister.

"Oh, Jane, if you'd only think of it! Could you?" Then, of course, all that occurred was explained—how they had been stopped on their journey, how Brown had made the best apology in his power, and how Jones had travelled with them and had never spoken a word. The gentleman had only taken his new name a week since, but of course he had had his new card printed immediately. "I'm sure I should have thought of it, if they hadn't made a mistake of the first name. Charles said it was like Barnaby Rudge."

"Not at all like Barnaby Rudge," said Jane: "Charles Burnaby Jones is a very good name."

"Very good indeed—and I'm sure that after a little bit he won't be at all the worse for the accident."

Before dinner the secret had been told no further, but still there had crept about among the Thompsons, and, indeed, down-stairs also among the retainers, a feeling that there was a secret. The old housekeeper was sure that Miss Mary, as she still called Mrs. Brown, had something to tell, if she could only be induced to tell it, and that this something had reference to

Mr. Jones's personal comfort. The head of the family, who was a sharp old gentleman, felt this also, and the member of Parliament, who had an idea that he especially should never be kept in the dark, was almost angry. Mr. Jones, suffering from some kindred feeling throughout the dinner, remained silent and unhappy. When two or three toasts had been drunk—the Queen's health, the old gentleman's health, the young couple's health, Brown's health, and the general health of all the Thompsons—then tongues were loosened and a question was asked. "I know that there has been something doing in Paris between these young people that we haven't heard as yet," said the uncle. Then Mrs. Brown laughed, and Jane, laughing too, gave Mr. Jones to understand that she, at any rate, knew all about it.

"If there is a mystery, I hope it will be told at once," said the member of Parliament angrily.

"Come, Brown, what is it?" asked another male cousin.

"Well, there was an accident. I'd rather Jones should tell," said he. Jones's brow became blacker than thunder, but he did not say a word. "You mustn't be angry with Mary," Jane whispered into her lover's ear.

"Come, Mary, you never were slow at talking," said the uncle. "I do hate this kind of thing," said the member of Parliament.

"I will tell it all," said Mrs. Brown, very nearly in tears, or else pretending to be very nearly in tears. "I know I was very wrong, and I do beg his pardon; and if he won't say that he forgives me, I never shall be happy again." Then she clasped her hands, and, turning round, looked him piteously in the face.

"Oh, yes; I do forgive you," said Mr. Jones.

"My brother," said she, throwing her arms round

him and kissing him. He recoiled from the embrace, but I think that he attempted to return the kiss. "And now I will tell the whole story," said Mrs. Brown. And she told it, acknowledging her fault with true contrition, and swearing that she would atone for it by life-long sisterly devotion.

"And you mustard-plastered the wrong man!" said the old gentleman, almost rolling off his chair with delight.

"I did," said Mrs. Brown, sobbing; "and I think that no woman ever suffered as I suffered."

"And Jones wouldn't let you leave the hotel?"

"It was the handkerchief stopped us," said Brown.

"If it had turned out to be anybody else," said the member of Parliament, "the results might have been most serious—not to say discreditable."

"That's nonsense, Robert," said Mrs. Brown, who was disposed to resent the use of so severe a word, even from the legislator cousin. "In a strange gentleman's bedroom!" he continued. "It only shows that what I have always said is quite true. You should never go to bed in a strange house without locking your door."

Nevertheless it was a very jovial meeting and before the evening was over Mr. Jones was happy, and had been brought to acknowledge that the mustard plaster would probably not do him any permanent injury.

L. M. MONTGOMERY

A Christmas Inspiration

"Well I really think Santa Claus has been very good to us all," said Jean Lawrence, pulling the pins out of her heavy coil of fair hair and letting it ripple over her shoulders.

"So do I," said Nellie Preston as well as she could with a mouthful of chocolates. "Those blessed home folks of mine seem to have divined by instinct the very things I most wanted."

It was the dusk of Christmas Eve and they were all in Jean Lawrence's room at No. 16 Chestnut Terrace. No. 16 was a boarding-house, and boarding-houses are not proverbially cheerful places in which to spend Christmas, but Jean's room, at least, was a pleasant spot, and all the girls had brought their Christmas presents in to show each other. Christmas came on Sunday that year and the Saturday evening mail at Chestnut Terrace had been an exciting one.

Jean had lighted the pink-globed lamp on her table and the mellow light fell over merry faces as the girls chatted about their gifts. On the table was a big white box heaped with roses that betokened a bit of Christmas extravagance on somebody's part. Jean's brother had sent them to her from Montreal, and all the girls were enjoying them in common.

No. 16 Chestnut Terrace was overrun with girls generally. But just now only five were left; all the others had gone home for Christmas, but these five could not go and were bent on making the best of it.

Belle and Olive Reynolds, who were sitting on the bed – Jean could never keep them off it – were High School girls; they were said to be always laughing, and even the fact that they could not go home for Christmas because a young brother had measles did not dampen their spirits.

Beth Hamilton, who was hovering over the roses, and Nellie Preston, who was eating candy, were art students, and their homes were too far away to visit. As for Jean Lawrence, she was an orphan, and had no home of her own. She worked on the staff of one of the big city newspapers and the other girls were a little in awe of her cleverness, but her nature was a "chummy" one and her room was a favourite rendezvous. Everybody liked frank, open-handed and hearted Jean.

"It was so funny to see the postman when he came this evening," said Olive. "He just bulged with parcels. They were sticking out in every direction."

"We all got our share of them," said Jean with a sigh of content.

"Even the cook got six – I counted."

"Miss Allen didn't get a thing – not even a letter," said Beth quickly. Beth had a trick of seeing things that other girls didn't.

"I forgot Miss Allen. No, I don't believe she did," answered Jean thoughtfully as she twisted up her pretty hair. "How dismal it must be to be so forlorn as that on Christmas Eve of all times. Ugh! I'm glad I have friends."

"I saw Miss Allen watching us as we opened our parcels and letters," Beth went on. "I happened to look up once, and such an expression as was on her face, girls! It was pathetic and sad and envious all at once. It really made me feel bad – for five minutes," she concluded honestly.

"Hasn't Miss Allen any friends at all?" asked Beth.

"No, I don't think she has," answered Jean. "She has lived here for fourteen years, so Mrs. Pickrell says. Think of that, girls! Fourteen years at Chestnut Terrace! Is it any wonder that she is thin and dried-up and snappy?"

"Nobody ever comes to see her and she never goes anywhere," said Beth. "Dear me! She must feel lonely now when everybody else is being remembered by their friends. I can't forget her face tonight; it actually haunts me. Girls, how would you feel if you hadn't anyone belonging to you, and if nobody thought about you at Christmas?"

"Ow!" said Olive, as if the mere idea made her shiver.

A little silence followed. To tell the truth, none of them liked Miss Allen. They knew that she did not like them either, but considered them frivolous and pert, and complained when they made a racket.

"The skeleton at the feast," Jean called her, and certainly the presence of the pale, silent, discontented-looking woman at the No. 16 table did not tend to heighten its festivity.

Presently Jean said with a dramatic flourish, "Girls, I have an inspiration – a Christmas inspiration!"

"What is it?" cried four voices.

"Just this. Let us give Miss Allen a Christmas surprise. She has not received a single present and I'm sure she feels lonely. Just think how we would feel if we were in her place."

"That is true," said Olive thoughtfully. "Do you know, girls, this evening I went to her room with a message from Mrs. Pickrell, and I do believe she had been crying. Her room looked dreadfully bare and cheerless, too. I think she is very poor. What are we to do, Jean?"

"Let us each give her something nice. We can put the things just outside of her door so that she will see them whenever she opens it. I'll give her some of Fred's roses too, and I'll write a Christmassy letter in my very best style to go with them," said Jean, warming up to her ideas as she talked.

The other girls caught her spirit and entered into the plan with enthusiasm.

"Splendid!" cried Beth. "Jean, it is an inspiration, sure enough. Haven't we been horribly selfish – thinking of nothing but our own gifts and fun and pleasure? I really feel ashamed."

"Let us do the thing up the very best way we can," said Nellie, forgetting even her beloved chocolates in her eagerness. "The shops are open yet. Let us go up town and invest."

Five minutes later five capped and jacketed figures were scurrying up the street in the frosty, starlit December dusk. Miss Allen in her cold little room heard their gay voices and sighed. She was crying by herself in the dark. It was Christmas for everybody but her, she thought drearily.

In an hour the girls came back with their purchases.

"Now, let's hold a council of war," said Jean jubilantly. "I hadn't the faintest idea what Miss Allen would like so I just guessed wildly. I got her a lace handkerchief and a big bottle of perfume and a painted photograph frame – and I'll stick my own photo in it for fun. That was really all I could afford. Christmas purchases have left my purse dreadfully lean."

"I got her a glove-box and a pin tray," said Belle, "and Olive got her a calendar and Whittier's poems. And besides we are going to give her half of that big plummy fruit cake Mother sent us from home. I'm sure she hasn't tasted anything so delicious for years, for fruit cakes don't grow on Chestnut Terrace and she never goes anywhere else for a meal."

Beth had bought a pretty cup and saucer and said she meant to give one of her pretty water colours too. Nellie, true to her reputation, had invested in a big box of chocolate creams, a gorgeously striped candy cane, a bag of oranges, and a brilliant lampshade of rose-coloured crepe paper to top off with. "It makes such a lot of show for the money," she explained. "I am bankrupt, like Jean."

"Well, we've got a lot of pretty things," said Jean in a tone of satisfaction. "Now we must do them up nicely. Will you wrap them in tissue paper, girls, and tie them with baby ribbon – here's a box of it – while I write that letter?"

While the others chatted over their parcels Jean wrote her letter, and Jean could write delightful letters. She had a decided talent in that respect, and her correspondents all declared her letters to be things of beauty and joy forever. She put her best into Miss Allen's Christmas letter. Since then she has written many bright and clever things, but I do not believe she ever in her life wrote anything more genuinely original and delightful than that letter. Besides, it breathed the very spirit of Christmas, and all the girls declared that it was splendid. "You must all sign it now," said Jean, "and I'll put it in one of those big envelopes; and, Nellie, won't you write her name on it in fancy letters?"

Which Nellie proceeded to do, and furthermore embellished the envelope by a border of chubby cherubs, dancing hand in hand around it and a sketch of No. 16 Chestnut Terrace in the corner in lieu of a stamp. Not content with this she hunted out a huge sheet of drawing paper and drew upon it an original pen-and-ink design after her own heart. A dudish cat – Miss Allen was fond of the No. 16 cat if she could be said to be fond of anything – was portrayed seated on a rocker arrayed in smoking jacket and cap with a cigar waved airily aloft in one paw while the other held out a placard bearing the legend "Merry Christmas." A second cat in full street costume bowed politely, hat in paw, and waved a banner inscribed with "Happy New Year," while faintly suggested kittens gambolled around the border. The girls laughed until they cried over it and voted it to be the best thing Nellie had yet done in original work.

All this had taken time and it was past eleven o'clock. Miss Allen had cried herself to sleep long ago and everybody else in Chestnut Terrace was abed when five figures cautiously crept down the hall, headed by Jean with a dim lamp. Outside of Miss Allen's door the procession halted and the girls silently arranged their gifts on the floor.

"That's done," whispered Jean in a tone of satisfaction as they tiptoed back. "And now let us go to bed or Mrs. Pickrell, bless her heart, will be down on us for burning so much midnight oil. Oil has gone up, you know, girls."

It was in the early morning that Miss Allen opened her door. But early as it was, another door down the hall was half open too and five rosy faces were peering cautiously out. The girls had been up for an hour for fear they would miss the sight and were all in Nellie's room, which commanded a view of Miss Allen's door.

That lady's face was a study. Amazement, incredulity, wonder, chased each other over it, succeeded by a glow of pleasure. On the floor before her was a snug little pyramid of parcels topped by Jean's letter. On a chair behind it was a bowl of delicious hot-house roses and Nellie's placard.

Miss Allen looked down the hall but saw nothing, for Jean had slammed the door just in time. Half an hour later when they were going down to breakfast Miss Allen came along the hall with outstretched hands to meet them. She had been crying again, but I think her tears were happy ones; and she was smiling now. A cluster of Jean's roses were pinned on her breast.

"Oh, girls, girls," she said, with a little tremble in her voice, "I can never thank you enough. It was so kind and sweet of you. You don't know how much good you have done me."

Breakfast was an unusually cheerful affair at No. 16 that morning. There was no skeleton at the feast and everybody was beaming. Miss Allen laughed and talked like a girl herself.

"Oh, how surprised I was!" she said. "The roses were like a bit of summer, and those cats of Nellie's were so funny and delightful. And your letter too, Jean! I cried and laughed over it. I shall read it every day for a year."

After breakfast everyone went to Christmas service. The girls went uptown to the church they attended. The city was very beautiful in the morning sunshine.

There had been a white frost in the night and the tree-lined avenues and public squares seemed like glimpses of fairyland.

"How lovely the world is," said Jean.

"This is really the very happiest Christmas morning I have ever known," declared Nellie. "I never felt so really Christmassy in my inmost soul before."

"I suppose," said Beth thoughtfully, "that it is because we have discovered for ourselves the old truth that it is more blessed to give than to receive. I've always known it, in a way, but I never realized it before."

"Blessing on Jean's Christmas inspiration," said Nellie. "But, girls, let us try to make it an all-the-year-round inspiration, I say. We can bring a little of our own sunshine into Miss Allen's life as long as we live with her."

"Amen to that!" said Jean heartily.

"Oh, listen, girls – the Christmas chimes!"

And over all the beautiful city was wafted the grand old message of peace on earth and good will to all the world.

G. K. CHESTERTON

The Flying Stars

"The most beautiful crime I ever committed," Flambeau would say in his highly moral old age, "was also, by a singular coincidence, my last. It was committed at Christmas. As an artist I had always attempted to provide crimes suitable to the special season or landscapes in which I found myself, choosing this or that terrace or garden for a catastrophe, as if for a statuary group. Thus squires should be swindled in long rooms panelled with oak; while Jews, on the other hand, should rather find themselves unexpectedly penniless among the lights and screens of the Cafe Riche. Thus, in England, if I wished to relieve a dean of his riches (which is not so easy as you might suppose), I wished to frame him, if I make myself clear, in the green lawns and grey towers of some cathedral town. Similarly, in France, when I had got money out of a rich and wicked peasant (which is almost impossible), it gratified me to get his indignant head relieved against a grey line of clipped poplars, and those solemn plains of Gaul over which broods the mighty spirit of Millet.

"Well, my last crime was a Christmas crime, a cheery, cosy, English middle-class crime; a crime of Charles Dickens. I did it in a good old middle-class house near Putney, a house with a crescent of carriage drive, a house with a stable by the side of it, a house with the name on the two outer gates, a house with a monkey tree. Enough, you know the species. I really think my imitation of Dickens's style was dexterous and literary. It seems almost a pity I repented the same evening."

Flambeau would then proceed to tell the story from the inside; and even from the inside it was odd. Seen from the outside it was perfectly incomprehensible, and it is from the outside that the stranger must study it. From this standpoint the drama may be said to have begun when the front doors of the house with the stable opened on the garden with the monkey tree, and a young girl came out with bread to feed the birds on the afternoon of Boxing Day. She had a pretty face, with brave brown eyes; but her figure was beyond conjecture, for she was so wrapped up in brown furs that it was hard to say which was hair and which was fur. But for the attractive face she might have been a small toddling bear.

The winter afternoon was reddening towards evening, and already a ruby light was rolled over the bloomless beds, filling them, as it were, with the ghosts of the dead roses. On one side of the house stood the stable, on the other an alley or cloister of laurels led to the larger garden behind. The young lady, having scattered bread for the birds (for the fourth or fifth time that day, because the dog ate it), passed unobtrusively down the lane of laurels and into a glimmering plantation of evergreens behind. Here she gave an exclamation of wonder, real or ritual, and looking up at the high garden wall above her, beheld it fantastically bestridden by a somewhat fantastic figure.

"Oh, don't jump, Mr. Crook," she called out in some alarm; "it's much too high."

The individual riding the party wall like an aerial horse was a tall, angular young man, with dark hair sticking up like a hair brush, intelligent and even distinguished lineaments, but a sallow and almost alien complexion. This showed the more plainly because he wore an aggressive red tie, the only part of his costume of which he seemed to take any care. Perhaps it was a symbol. He took no notice of the girl's alarmed adjuration, but leapt like a grasshopper to the ground beside her, where he might very well have broken his legs.

"I think I was meant to be a burglar," he said placidly, "and I have no doubt I should have been if I hadn't happened to be born in that nice house next door. I can't see any harm in it, anyhow."

"How can you say such things?" she remonstrated.

"Well," said the young man, "if you're born on the wrong side of the wall, I can't see that it's wrong to climb over it."

"I never know what you will say or do next," she said.

"I don't often know myself," replied Mr. Crook; "but then I am on the right side of the wall now."

"And which is the right side of the wall?" asked the young lady, smiling.

"Whichever side you are on," said the young man named Crook.

As they went together through the laurels towards the front garden a motor horn sounded thrice, coming nearer and nearer, and a car of splendid speed, great elegance, and a pale green colour swept up to the front doors like a bird and stood throbbing.

"Hullo, hullo!" said the young man with the red tie, "here's somebody born on the right side, anyhow. I didn't know, Miss Adams, that your Santa Claus was so modern as this."

"Oh, that's my godfather, Sir Leopold Fischer. He always comes on Boxing Day."

Then, after an innocent pause, which unconsciously betrayed some lack of enthusiasm, Ruby Adams added:

"He is very kind."

John Crook, journalist, had heard of that eminent City magnate; and it was not his fault if the City magnate had not heard of him; for in certain articles in *The Clarion* or *The New Age* Sir Leopold had been dealt with austerely. But he said nothing and grimly watched the unloading of the motor-car, which was rather a long process. A large, neat chauffeur in green got out from the front, and a small, neat manservant in grey got out from the back, and between them they deposited Sir Leopold on the door-step and began to unpack him, like some very carefully protected parcel. Rugs enough to stock a bazaar, furs of all the beasts of the forest, and scarves of all the colours of the rainbow were unwrapped one by one, till they revealed something resembling the human form; the form of a friendly, but foreign-looking old gentleman, with a grey goat-like beard and a beaming smile, who rubbed his big fur gloves together.

Long before this revelation was complete the two big doors of the porch had opened in the middle, and Colonel Adams (father of the furry young lady) had come out himself to invite his eminent guest inside. He was a tall, sunburnt, and very silent man, who wore a red smoking-cap like a fez, making him look like one of the English Sirdars or Pashas in Egypt. With him was his brother-in-law, lately come from Canada, a big and rather boisterous young gentleman-farmer, with a yellow beard, by name James Blount. With him also was the more insignificant figure of the priest from the neighbouring Roman Church; for the colonel's late wife had been a Catholic, and the children, as is common in such cases, had been trained to follow her. Everything seemed undistinguished about the priest, even down to his name, which was Brown; yet the colonel had always found something companionable about him, and frequently asked him to such family gatherings.

In the large entrance hall of the house there was ample room even for Sir Leopold and the removal of his wraps. Porch and vestibule, indeed, were unduly large in proportion to the house, and formed, as it were, a big room with the front door at one end, and the bottom of the staircase at the other. In front of the large hall fire, over which hung the colonel's sword, the process was completed and the company, including the saturnine Crook, presented to Sir Leopold Fischer. That venerable financier, however, still seemed struggling with portions of his well-lined attire, and at length produced from a very interior tail-coat pocket, a black oval case which he radiantly explained to be his Christmas present for his god-daughter. With an unaffected vain-glory that had something disarming about it he held out the case before them all; it flew open at a touch and half-blinded them. It was just as if a crystal fountain had spurted in their eyes. In a nest of orange velvet lay like three eggs, three white and vivid diamonds that seemed to set the very air on fire all round them. Fischer stood beaming benevolently and drinking deep of the astonishment and ecstasy of the girl, the grim admiration and gruff thanks of the colonel, the wonder of the whole group.

"I'll put 'em back now, my dear," said Fischer, returning the case to the tails of his coat. "I had to be careful of 'em coming down. They're the three great African diamonds called 'The Flying Stars,' because they've been stolen so often. All the big criminals are on the track; but even the rough men about in the streets and hotels could hardly have kept their hands off them. I might have lost them on the road here. It was quite possible."

"Quite natural, I should say," growled the man in the red tie. "I shouldn't blame 'em if they had taken 'em. When they ask for bread, and you don't even give them a stone, I think they might take the stone for themselves."

"I won't have you talking like that," cried the girl, who was in a curious glow. "You've only talked like that since you became a horrid what's-his-name. You know what I mean. What do you call a man who wants to embrace the chimney-sweep?"

"A saint," said Father Brown.

"I think," said Sir Leopold, with a supercilious smile, "that Ruby means a Socialist."

"A radical does not mean a man who lives on radishes," remarked Crook, with some impatience; "and a Conservative does not mean a man who preserves jam. Neither, I assure you, does a Socialist mean a man who desires a social evening with the chimney-sweep. A Socialist means a man who wants all the chimneys swept and all the chimney-sweeps paid for it."

"But who won't allow you," put in the priest in a low voice, "to own your own soot."

Crook looked at him with an eye of interest and even respect. "Does one want to own soot?" he asked.

"One might," answered Brown, with speculation in his eye. "I've heard that gardeners use it. And I once made six children happy at Christmas when the conjuror didn't come, entirely with soot—applied externally."

"Oh, splendid," cried Ruby. "Oh, I wish you'd do it to this company." The boisterous Canadian, Mr. Blount, was lifting his loud voice in applause, and the astonished financier his (in some considerable deprecation), when a knock sounded at the double front doors. The priest opened them and they showed again the front garden of evergreens, monkey-tree and all, now gathering gloom against a gorgeous violet sunset. The scene thus framed was so coloured and quaint, like a back scene in a play, that they forgot a moment the insignificant figure standing in the door. He was dusty-looking and in a frayed coat, evidently a common messenger. "Any of you gentlemen Mr. Blount?" he asked, and held forward a letter doubtfully. Mr. Blount started, and stopped in his shout of assent. Ripping up the envelope with evident astonishment he read it; his face clouded a little, and then cleared, and he turned to his brother-in-law and host.

"I'm sick at being such a nuisance, colonel," he said, with the cheery colonial conventions; "but would it upset you if an old acquaintance called on me here tonight on business? In point of fact it's Florian, that famous French acrobat and comic actor; I knew him years ago out West (he was a French-Canadian by birth), and he seems to have business for me, though I hardly guess what."

"Of course, of course," replied the colonel carelessly.

"My dear chap, any friend of yours. No doubt he will prove an acquisition."

"He'll black his face, if that's what you mean," cried Blount, laughing. "I don't doubt he'd black everyone else's eyes. I don't care; I'm not refined. I like the jolly old pantomime where a man sits on his top hat."

"Not on mine, please," said Sir Leopold Fischer, with dignity.

"Well, well," observed Crook, airily, "don't let's quarrel. There are lower jokes than sitting on a top hat."

Dislike of the red-tied youth, born of his predatory opinions and evident intimacy with the pretty godchild, led Fischer to say, in his most sarcastic, magisterial manner: "No doubt you have found something much lower than sitting on a top hat. What is it, pray?"

"Letting a top hat sit on you, for instance," said the Socialist.

"Now, now, now," cried the Canadian farmer with his barbarian benevolence, "don't let's spoil a jolly evening. What I say is let's do something for the company tonight. Not blacking faces or sitting on hats, if you don't like those—but something of the sort. Why couldn't we have a proper old English pantomime—clown, columbine, and so on. I saw one when I left England at twelve years old, and it's blazed in my brain like a bonfire ever since. I came back to the old country only last year, and I find the thing's extinct. Nothing but a lot of snivelling fairy plays. I want a hot poker and a policeman made into sausages, and they give me princesses moralising by moonlight, Blue Birds, or something. Blue Beard's more in my line, and him I liked best when he turned into the pantaloon."

"I'm all for making a policeman into sausages," said

John Crook. "It's a better definition of Socialism than some recently given. But surely the get-up would be too big a business."

"Not a scrap," cried Blount, quite carried away. "A harlequinade's the quickest thing we can do, for two reasons. First, one can gag to any degree; and, second, all the objects are household things—tables and trowel-horses and washing baskets, and things like that."

"That's true," admitted Crook, nodding eagerly and walking about. "But I'm afraid I can't have my police-man's uniform? Haven't killed a policeman lately."

Blount frowned thoughtfully a space, and then smote his thigh. "Yes, we can!" he cried. "I've got Florian's address here, and he knows every *costumier* in London. I'll 'phone him to bring a police dress when he comes." And he went bounding away to the telephone.

"Oh, it's glorious, godfather," cried Ruby, almost dancing. "I'll be columbine and you shall be panta-loon."

The millionaire held himself stiff with a sort of hea-then solemnity. "I think, my dear," he said, "you must get someone else for pantaloon."

"I will be pantaloon, if you like," said Colonel Adams, taking his cigar out of his mouth, and speaking for the first and last time.

"You ought to have a statue," cried the Canadian, as he came back, radiant, from the telephone. "There, we are all fitted. Mr. Crook shall be clown; he's a journal-ist and knows all the oldest jokes. I can be harlequin, that only wants long legs and jumping about. My friend Florian 'phones he's bringing the police costume; he's changing on the way. We can act it in this very hall, the audience sitting on those broad stairs opposite, one row above another. These front doors can be the back scene,

125

either open or shut. Shut, you see an English interior. Open, a moonlit garden. It all goes by magic." And snatching a chance piece of billiard chalk from his pocket, he ran it across the hall floor, half-way between the front door and the staircase, to mark the line of the footlights.

How even such a banquet of bosh was got ready in the time remained a riddle. But they went at it with that mixture of recklessness and industry that lives when youth is in a house; and youth was in that house that night, though not all may have isolated the two faces and hearts from which it flamed. As always happens, the invention grew wilder and wilder through the very tameness of the bourgeois conventions from which it had to create. The columbine looked charming in an outstanding skirt that strangely resembled the large lamp-shade in the drawing-room. The clown and pantaloon made themselves white with flour from the cook, and red with rouge from some other domestic, who remained (like all true Christian benefactors) anonymous. The harlequin, already clad in silver paper out of cigar boxes, was, with difficulty, prevented from smashing the old Victorian lustre chandeliers, that he might cover himself with resplendent crystals. In fact he would certainly have done so, had not Ruby unearthed some old pantomime paste jewels she had worn at a fancy dress party as the Queen of Diamonds. Indeed, her uncle, James Blount, was getting almost out of hand in his excitement; he was like a schoolboy. He put a paper donkey's head unexpectedly on Father Brown, who bore it patiently, and even found some private manner of moving his ears. He even essayed to put the paper donkey's tail to the coat-tails of Sir Leopold Fischer. This, however, was frowned down. "Uncle is too absurd," cried Ruby to Crook, round whose shoulders she had seriously placed a string of sausages. "Why is he so wild?"

"He is harlequin to your columbine," said Crook. "I am only the clown who makes the old jokes."

"I wish you were the harlequin," she said, and left the string of sausages swinging.

Father Brown, though he knew every detail done behind the scenes, and had even evoked applause by his transformation of a pillow into a pantomime baby, went round to the front and sat among the audience with all the solemn expectation of a child at his first matinee. The spectators were few, relations, one or two local friends, and the servants; Sir Leopold sat in the front seat, his full and still fur-collared figure largely obscuring the view of the little cleric behind him; but it has never been settled by artistic authorities whether the cleric lost much. The pantomime was utterly chaotic, yet not contemptible; there ran through it a rage of improvisation which came chiefly from Crook the clown. Commonly he was a clever man, and he was inspired tonight with a wild omniscience, a folly wiser than the world, that which comes to a young man who has seen for an instant a particular expression on a particular face. He was supposed to be the clown, but he was really almost everything else, the author (so far as there was an author), the prompter, the scene-painter, the scene-shifter, and, above all, the orchestra. At abrupt intervals in the outrageous performance he would hurl himself in full costume at the piano and bang out some popular music equally absurd and appropriate.

The climax of this, as of all else, was the moment when the two front doors at the back of the scene flew open, showing the lovely moonlit garden, but showing more prominently the famous professional guest; the great Florian, dressed up as a policeman. The clown at the piano played the constabulary chorus in the "Pirates of Penzance," but it was drowned in the deafening applause, for every gesture of the great comic actor was an admirable though restrained version of the carriage and manner of the police. The harlequin leapt upon him and hit him over the helmet; the pianist playing "Where did you get that hat?" he faced about in admirably simulated astonishment, and then the leaping harlequin hit him again (the pianist suggesting a few bars of "Then we had another one"). Then the harlequin rushed right into the arms of the policeman and fell on top of him, amid a roar of applause. Then it was that the strange actor gave that celebrated imitation of a dead man, of which the fame still lingers round Putney. It was almost impossible to believe that a living person could appear so limp.

The athletic harlequin swung him about like a sack or twisted or tossed him like an Indian club; all the time to the most maddeningly ludicrous tunes from the piano. When the harlequin heaved the comic constable heavily off the floor the clown played "I arise from dreams of thee." When he shuffled him across his back, "With my bundle on my shoulder," and when the harlequin finally let fall the policeman with a most convincing thud, the lunatic at the instrument struck into a jingling measure with some words which are still believed to have been, "I sent a letter to my love and on the way I dropped it."

At about this limit of mental anarchy Father Brown's view was obscured altogether; for the City magnate in front of him rose to his full height and thrust his hands savagely into all his pockets. Then he sat down nervously, still fumbling, and then stood up again. For an instant it seemed seriously likely that he would stride across the footlights; then he turned a glare at the clown playing the piano; and then he burst in silence out of the room.

The priest had only watched for a few more minutes the absurd but not inelegant dance of the amateur harlequin over his splendidly unconscious foe. With real though rude art, the harlequin danced slowly backwards out of the door into the garden, which was full of moonlight and stillness. The vamped dress of silver paper and paste, which had been too glaring in the footlights, looked more and more magical and silvery as it danced away under a brilliant moon. The audience was closing in with a cataract of applause, when Brown felt his arm abruptly touched, and he was asked in a whisper to come into the colonel's study.

He followed his summoner with increasing doubt, which was not dispelled by a solemn comicality in the scene of the study. There sat Colonel Adams, still unaffectedly dressed as a pantaloon, with the knobbed whalebone nodding above his brow, but with his poor old eyes sad enough to have sobered a Saturnalia. Sir Leopold Fischer was leaning against the mantelpiece and heaving with all the importance of panic.

"This is a very painful matter, Father Brown," said Adams. "The truth is, those diamonds we all saw this afternoon seem to have vanished from my friend's tail-coat pocket. And as you—"

"As I," supplemented Father Brown, with a broad grin, "was sitting just behind him—"

"Nothing of the sort shall be suggested," said Colonel Adams, with a firm look at Fischer, which rather implied that some such thing *had* been suggested. "I only ask you to give me the assistance that any gentleman might give."

"Which is turning out his pockets," said Father Brown, and proceeded to do so, displaying seven and sixpence, a return ticket, a small silver crucifix, a small breviary, and a stick of chocolate.

The colonel looked at him long, and then said, "Do you know, I should like to see the inside of your head more than the inside of your pockets. My daughter is one of your people, I know; well, she has lately—" and he stopped.

"She has lately," cried out old Fischer, "opened her father's house to a cut-throat Socialist, who says openly he would steal anything from a richer man. This is the end of it. Here is the richer man—and none the richer."

"If you want the inside of my head you can have it," said Brown rather wearily. "What it's worth you can say afterwards. But the first thing I find in that disused pocket is this: that men who mean to steal diamonds don't talk Socialism. They are more likely," he added demurely, "to denounce it."

Both the others shifted sharply and the priest went on:

"You see, we know these people, more or less. That Socialist would no more steal a diamond than a Pyramid. We ought to look at once to the one man we don't know. The fellow acting the policeman—Florian. Where is he exactly at this minute, I wonder."

The pantaloon sprang erect and strode out of the room. An interlude ensued, during which the millionaire stared at the priest, and the priest at his breviary; then the pantaloon returned and said, with *staccato* gravity, "The policeman is still lying on the stage. The curtain has gone up and down six times; he is still lying there."

Father Brown dropped his book and stood staring with a look of blank mental ruin. Very slowly a light began to creep in his grey eyes, and then he made the scarcely obvious answer.

"Please forgive me, colonel, but when did your wife die?"

"Wife!" replied the staring soldier, "she died this year two months. Her brother James arrived just a week too late to see her."

The little priest bounded like a rabbit shot. "Come on!" he cried in quite unusual excitement. "Come on! We've got to go and look at that policeman!"

They rushed on to the now curtained stage, breaking rudely past the columbine and clown (who seemed whispering quite contentedly), and Father Brown bent over the prostrate comic policeman.

"Chloroform," he said as he rose; "I only guessed it just now."

There was a startled stillness, and then the colonel said slowly, "Please say seriously what all this means."

Father Brown suddenly shouted with laughter, then stopped, and only struggled with it for instants during the rest of his speech. "Gentlemen," he gasped, "there's not much time to talk. I must run after the criminal. But this great French actor who played the police-man—this clever corpse the harlequin waltzed with and dandled and threw about—he was—" His voice again failed him, and he turned his back to run.

"He was?" called Fischer inquiringly.

"A real policeman," said Father Brown, and ran away into the dark. There were hollows and bowers at the extreme end of that leafy garden, in which the laurels and other immortal shrubs showed against sapphire sky and silver moon, even in that mid-winter, warm colours as of the south. The green gaiety of the waving laurels, the rich purple indigo of the night, the moon like a monstrous crystal, make an almost irresponsible romantic picture; and among the top branches of the garden trees a strange figure is climbing, who looks not so much romantic as impossible. He sparkles from head to heel, as if clad in ten million moons; the real moon catches him at every movement and sets a new inch of him on fire. But he swings, flashing and successful, from the short tree in this garden to the tall, rambling tree in the other, and only stops there because a shade has slid under the smaller tree and has unmistakably called up to him.

"Well, Flambeau," says the voice, "you really look like a Flying Star; but that always means a Falling Star at last."

The silver, sparkling figure above seems to lean forward in the laurels and, confident of escape, listens to the little figure below.

"You never did anything better, Flambeau. It was clever to come from Canada (with a Paris ticket, I suppose) just a week after Mrs. Adams died, when no one was in a mood to ask questions. It was cleverer to have marked down the Flying Stars and the very day of Fischer's coming. But there's no cleverness, but mere genius, in what followed. Stealing the stones, I suppose, was nothing to you. You could have done it by sleight of hand in a hundred other ways besides that pretence of putting a paper donkey's tail to Fisher's coat. But in the rest you eclipsed yourself."

The silvery figure among the green leaves seems to linger as if hypnotised, though his escape is easy behind him; he is staring at the man below. "Oh, yes," says the man below, "I know all about it. I know you not only forced the pantomime, but put it to a double use. You were going to steal the stones quietly; news came by an accomplice that you were already suspected, and a capable police officer was coming to rout you up that very night. A common thief would have been thankful for the warning and fled; but you are a poet. You already had the clever notion of hiding the jewels in a blaze of false stage jewellery. Now, you saw that if the dress were a harlequin's the appearance of a policeman would be quite in keeping. The worthy officer started from Putney police station to find you, and walked into the queerest trap ever set in this world. When the front door opened he walked straight on to the stage of a Christmas pantomime, where he could be kicked, clubbed, stunned and drugged by the dancing harlequin, amid roars of laughter from all the most respectable people in Putney. Oh, you will never do anything better. And now, by the way, you might give me back those diamonds."

The green branch on which the glittering figure swung, rustled as if in astonishment; but the voice went on:

"I want you to give them back, Flambeau, and I want you to give up this life. There is still youth and honour and humour in you; don't fancy they will last in that trade. Men may keep a sort of level of good, but no man has ever been able to keep on one level of evil. That road goes down and down. The kind man drinks and turns cruel; the frank man kills and lies about it. Many a man I've known started like you to be an honest outlaw, a merry robber of the rich, and ended stamped into slime. Maurice Blum started out as an anarchist of principle, a father of the poor; he ended a greasy spy and tale-bearer that both sides used and despised. Harry Burke started his free money movement sincerely enough; now he's sponging on a half-starved sister for endless brandies and sodas. Lord Amber went into wild society in a sort of chivalry; now he's paying blackmail to the lowest vultures in London. Captain Barillon was the great gentleman-apache before your time; he died in a madhouse, screaming with fear of the "narks" and receivers that had betrayed him and hunted him down. I know the woods look very free behind you, Flambeau; I know that in a flash you could melt into them like a monkey. But some day you will be an old grey monkey, Flambeau. You will sit up in your free forest cold at heart and close to death, and the tree-tops will be very bare."

Everything continued still, as if the small man below held the other in the tree in some long invisible leash; and he went on:

"Your downward steps have begun. You used to boast of doing nothing mean, but you are doing something mean tonight. You are leaving suspicion on an honest boy with a good deal against him already; you are separating him from the woman he loves and who loves him. But you will do meaner things than that before you die."

Three flashing diamonds fell from the tree to the turf. The small man stooped to pick them up, and when he looked up again the green cage of the tree was emptied of its silver bird.

The restoration of the gems (accidentally picked up by Father Brown, of all people) ended the evening in uproarious triumph; and Sir Leopold, in his height of good humour, even told the priest that though he himself had broader views, he could respect those whose creed required them to be cloistered and ignorant of this world.

CHARLES DICKENS

A Christmas Dinner

Christmas time! That man must be a misanthrope indeed, in whose breast something like a jovial feeling is not roused—in whose mind some pleasant associations are not awakened—by the recurrence of Christmas. There are people who will tell you that Christmas is not to them what it used to be; that each succeeding Christmas has found some cherished hope, or happy prospect, of the year before, dimmed or passed away; that the present only serves to remind them of reduced circumstances and straitened incomes—of the feasts they once bestowed on hollow friends, and of the cold looks that meet them now, in adversity and misfortune. Never heed such dismal reminiscences. There are few men who have lived long enough in the world, who cannot call up such thoughts any day in the year. Then do not select the merriest of the three hundred and sixty-five for your doleful recollections, but draw your chair nearer the blazing fire—fill the glass and send round the song—and if your room be smaller than it was a dozen years ago, or if your glass be filled with reeking punch, instead of sparkling wine, put a good face on the matter, and empty it off-hand, and fill another, and troll off the old ditty you used to sing, and thank God it's no worse. Look on the merry faces of your children (if you have any) as they sit round the fire. One little seat may be empty; one slight form that gladdened the father's heart, and roused the mother's pride to look upon, may not be there. Dwell not upon the past; think not that one short year ago, the fair child now resolving into dust, sat before you, with the bloom of health upon its cheek, and the gaiety of infancy in its joyous eye. Reflect upon your present blessings—of which every man has many—not on your past misfortunes, of which all men have some. Fill your glass again, with a merry face and contented heart. Our life on it, but your Christmas shall be merry, and your new year a happy one!

Who can be insensible to the outpourings of good feeling, and the honest interchange of affectionate attachment, which abound at this season of the year? A Christmas family-party! We know nothing in nature more delightful! There seems a magic in the very name of Christmas. Petty jealousies and discords are forgotten; social feelings are awakened, in bosoms to which they have long been strangers; father and son, or brother and sister, who have met and passed with averted gaze, or a look of cold recognition, for months before, proffer and return the cordial embrace, and bury their past animosities in their present happiness. Kindly hearts that have yearned towards each other, but have been withheld by false notions of pride and self-dignity, are again reunited, and all is kindness and benevolence! Would that Christmas lasted the whole year through (as it ought), and that the prejudices and passions which deform our better nature, were never called into action among those to whom they should ever be strangers!

The Christmas family-party that we mean, is not a mere assemblage of relations, got up at a week or two's notice, originating this year, having no family precedent in the last, and not likely to be repeated in the next. No. It is an annual gathering of all the accessible members of the family, young or old, rich or poor; and all the children look forward to it for two months beforehand, in a fever of anticipation. Formerly, it was held at grandpapa's; but grandpapa getting old, and grandmamma getting old too, and rather infirm, they have given up house-keeping, and domesticated themselves with uncle George; so, the party always takes place at uncle George's house, but grandmamma sends in most of the good things, and grandpapa always *will* toddle down, all the way to Newgate-market, to buy the turkey, which he engages a porter to bring home behind him in triumph, always insisting on the man's being rewarded with a glass of spirits, over and above his hire, to drink "a merry Christmas and a happy new year" to aunt George. As to grandmamma, she is very secret and mysterious for two or three days beforehand, but not sufficiently so, to prevent rumours getting afloat that she has purchased a beautiful new cap with pink ribbons for each of the servants, together with sundry books, and pen-knives and pencil-cases, for the younger branches; to say nothing of divers secret additions to the order originally given by aunt George at the pastry-cook's, such as another dozen of mince pies for the dinner, and a large plum-cake for the children.

On Christmas-eve, grandmamma is always in excellent spirits, and after employing all the children, during the day, in stoning the plums, and all that, insists, regularly every year, on uncle George coming down into the kitchen, taking off his coat, and stirring the pudding for half an hour or so, which uncle George good-humouredly does, to the vociferous delight of the children and servants. The evening concludes with a glorious game of blind-man's-buff, in an early stage of which grandpapa takes great care to be caught, in order that he may have an opportunity of displaying his dexterity.

On the following morning, the old couple, with as many of the children as the pew will hold, go to church in great state: leaving aunt George at home dusting decanters and filling casters, and uncle George carrying bottles into the dining-parlour, and calling for cork-screws, and getting into everybody's way.

When the church-party return to lunch, grandpapa produces a small sprig of mistletoe from his pocket, and tempts the boys to kiss their little cousins under it—a proceeding which affords both the boys and the old gentleman unlimited satisfaction, but which rather outrages grandmamma's ideas of decorum, until grandpapa says, that when he was just thirteen years and three months old, *he* kissed grandmamma under a mistletoe too, on which the children clap their hands, and laugh very heartily, as do aunt George and uncle George; and grandmamma looks pleased, and says, with a benevolent smile, that grandpapa was an impudent young dog, on which the children laugh very heartily again, and grandpapa more heartily than any of them.

But all these diversions are nothing to the subsequent excitement when grandmamma in a high cap, and silk gown; and grandpapa with a beautifully plaited shirt-frill, and white neckerchief; seat themselves on one side of the drawing-room fire, with uncle George's children and little cousins innumerable, seated in the front, waiting the arrival of the expected visitors. Suddenly a hackney-coach is heard to stop, and uncle George, who has been looking out of the window, exclaims "Here's Jane!" on which the children rush to the door, and helter-skelter down-stairs; and uncle Robert and aunt Jane, and the dear little baby, and the nurse, and the whole party, are ushered up-stairs amidst tumultuous shouts of "Oh, my!" from the children, and frequently repeated warnings not to hurt baby from the nurse. And grandpapa takes the child, and grandmamma kisses her daughter, and the confusion of this first entry has scarcely subsided, when some other aunts and uncles with more cousins arrive, and the grown-up cousins flirt with each other, and so do the little cousins too, for that matter, and nothing is to be heard but a confused din of talking, laughing, and merriment.

A hesitating double knock at the street-door, heard during a momentary pause in the conversation, excites a general inquiry of "Who's that?" and two or three children, who have been standing at the window, announce in a low voice, that it's "poor aunt Margaret." Upon which, aunt George leaves the room to welcome the new-comer; and grandmamma draws herself up, rather stiff and stately; for Margaret married a poor man without her consent, and poverty not being a sufficiently weighty punishment for her offence, has been discarded by her friends, and debarred the society of her dearest relatives. But Christmas has come round, and the unkind feelings that have struggled against better dispositions during the year, have melted away before its genial influence, like half-formed ice beneath the morning sun. It is not difficult in a moment of angry feeling for a parent to denounce a disobedient child; but, to banish her at a period of general good-will and hilarity, from the hearth, round which she has sat on so many anniversaries of the same day, expanding by slow degrees from infancy to girlhood, and then bursting, almost imperceptibly, into a woman, is widely different. The air of conscious rectitude, and cold forgiveness, which the old lady has assumed, sits ill upon her; and when the poor girl is led in by her sister, pale in looks and broken in hope—not from poverty, for that she could bear, but from the consciousness of undeserved neglect, and unmerited unkindness—it is easy to see how much of it is assumed. A momentary pause succeeds; the girl breaks suddenly from her sister and throws herself, sobbing, on her mother's neck. The father steps hastily forward, and takes her husband's hand. Friends crowd round to offer their hearty congratulations, and happiness and harmony again prevail.

As to the dinner, it's perfectly delightful—nothing goes wrong, and everybody is in the very best of spirits, and disposed to please and be pleased. Grandpapa relates a circumstantial account of the purchase of the turkey, with a slight digression relative to the purchase of previous turkeys, on former Christmas-days, which grandmamma corroborates in the minutest particular. Uncle George tells stories, and carves poultry, and takes wine, and jokes with the children at the side-table, and winks at the cousins that are making love, or being made love to, and exhilarates everybody with his good humour and hospitality; and when, at last, a stout servant staggers in with a gigantic pudding, with a sprig of holly in the top, there is such a laughing, and shouting, and clapping of little chubby hands, and kicking up of fat dumpy legs, as can only be equalled by the applause with which the astonishing feat of pouring lighted brandy into mince-pies, is received by the younger visitors. Then the dessert!—and the wine!—and the fun! Such beautiful speeches, and *such* songs, from aunt Margaret's husband, who turns out to be such a nice man, and *so* attentive to grandmamma! Even grandpapa not only sings his annual song with unprecedented vigour, but on being honoured with an unanimous encore, according to annual custom, actually comes out with a new one which nobody but grandmamma ever heard before; and a young scapegrace of a cousin, who has been in some disgrace with the old people, for certain heinous sins of omission and commission—neglecting to call, and persisting in drinking Burton Ale—astonishes everybody into convulsions of laughter by volunteering the most extraordinary comic songs that ever were heard. And thus the evening passes, in a strain of rational good-will and cheerfulness, doing more to awaken the sympathies of every member of the party in behalf of his neighbour, and to perpetuate their good feeling during the ensuing year, than half the homilies that have ever been written, by half the Divines that have ever lived.

The Fir-tree

Out in the woods stood a nice little Fir-tree. The place he had was a very good one; the sun shone on him; as to fresh air, there was enough of that, and round him grew many large-sized comrades, pines as well as firs. But the little Fir wanted so very much to be a grown-up tree.

He did not think of the warm sun and of the fresh air; he did not care for the little cottage children that ran about and prattled when they were in the woods looking for wild strawberries. The children often came with a whole pitcher full of berries, or a long row of them threaded on a straw, and sat down near the young Tree and said, "Oh, how pretty he is! What a nice little Fir!" But this was what the Tree could not bear to hear.

At the end of a year he had shot up a good deal, and after another year he was another long bit taller; for with fir-trees one can always tell by the shoots how many years old they are.

"Oh, were I but such a high tree as the others are!"

sighed he. "Then I should be able to spread out my branches and with the tops look into the wide world! Then would the birds build nests among my branches; and when there was a breeze I could bend with as much stateliness as the others!"

Neither the sunbeams, nor the birds, nor the red clouds which morning and evening sailed above him gave the little Tree any pleasure.

In winter, when the snow lay glittering on the ground, a hare would often come leaping along and jump right over the little Tree. Oh, that made him so angry! But two winters were past, and in the third the Tree was so large that the hare was obliged to go round it. "To grow and grow, to get older and be tall," thought the Tree, "that, after all, is the most delightful thing in the world!"

In autumn the woodcutters always came and felled some of the largest trees. This happened every year; and the young Fir-tree, that had now grown to a very comely size, trembled at the sight; for the magnificent great trees fell to the earth with noise and cracking, the branches were lopped off, and the trees looked long and bare; they were hardly to be recognized; and then they were laid in carts, and the horses dragged them out of the wood.

Where did they go to? What became of them?

In spring, when the Swallows and the Storks came, the Tree asked them, "Don't you know where they have been taken? Have you not met them anywhere?"

The Swallows did not know anything about it; but the Stork looked musing, nodded his head, and said, "Yes, I think I know. I met many ships as I was flying hither from Egypt; on the ships were magnificent masts, and I venture to assert that it was they that smelt so of fir. I may congratulate you, for they lifted themselves on high most majestically!"

"Oh, were I but old enough to fly across the sea! But how does the sea look in reality? What is it like?"

"That would take a long time to explain," said the Stork; and with these words off he went.

"Rejoice in thy growth!" said the Sunbeams; "rejoice in thy vigorous growth and in the fresh life that moveth within thee!"

And the Wind kissed the Tree, and the Dew wept tears over him; but the Fir understood it not.

When Christmas came, quite young trees were cut down, trees which often were not even as large or of the same age as this Fir-tree who could never rest but always wanted to be off. These young trees, and they were always the finest-looking, retained their branches; they were laid on carts, and the horses drew them out of the wood.

"Where are they going to?" asked the Fir. "They are not taller than I; there was one indeed that was considerably shorter—and why do they retain all their branches? Whither are they taken?"

"We know! We know!" chirped the Sparrows. "We have peeped in at the windows in the town below! We know whither they are taken! The greatest splendour and the greatest magnificence one can imagine await them. We peeped through the windows and saw them planted in the middle of the warm room, and ornamented with the most splendid things—with gilded apples, with gingerbread, with toys and many hundred lights!"

"And then?" asked the Fir-tree, trembling in every bough. "And then? What happens then?"

"We did not see anything more; it was incomparably beautiful."

"I would fain know if I am destined for so glorious a career," cried the Tree, rejoicing. "That is still better than to cross the sea! What a longing do I suffer! Were Christmas but come! I am now tall, and my branches spread like the others that were carried off last year! Oh, were I but already on the cart! Were I in the warm room with all the splendour and magnificence! Yes; then something better, something still grander, will surely follow, or wherefore should they thus ornament me? Something better, something still grander, *must* follow—but what? Oh, how I long, how I suffer! I do not know myself what is the matter with me!"

"Rejoice in our presence!" said the Air and the Sunlight; "rejoice in thy own fresh youth!"

But the Tree did not rejoice at all; he grew and grew, and was green both winter and summer. People that saw him said, "What a fine tree!" and toward Christmas he was one of the first that was cut down. The ax struck deep into the very pith; the tree fell to the earth with a sigh; he felt a pang—it was like a swoon; he could not think of happiness, for he was sorrowful at being separated from his home, from the place where he had sprung up. He well knew that he should never see his dear old comrades, the little bushes and flowers around him, any more, perhaps not even the birds! The departure was not at all agreeable.

The Tree only came to himself when he was unloaded in a courtyard with the other trees, and heard a man say, "That one is splendid; we don't want the others." Then two servants came in rich livery and carried the Fir-tree into a large and splendid drawing room. Portraits were hanging on the walls, and near the white porcelain stove stood two large Chinese vases with lions on the covers. There, too, were large easy chairs, silken sofas, large tables full of picture books and full of toys worth hundreds and hundreds of crowns—at least the children said so. And the Fir-tree was stuck upright in a cask that was filled with sand; but no one could see that it was a cask, for green cloth was hung all around it, and it stood on a large, gaily coloured carpet. Oh, how the tree quivered! What was to happen? The servants as well as the young ladies decorated it. On one branch there hung little nets cut out of coloured paper, and each net was filled with sugarplums; and among the other boughs gilded apples and walnuts were suspended, looking as though they had grown there, and little blue and white tapers were placed among the leaves. Dolls that looked for all the world like men—the Tree had never beheld such before—were seen among the foliage, and at the very top a large star of gold tinsel was fixed. It was really splendid—beyond description splendid.

"This evening!" said they all; "how it will shine this evening!"

"Oh," thought the Tree, "if the evening were but come! If the tapers were but lighted! And then I wonder what will happen! Perhaps the other trees from the forest will come to look at me! Perhaps the sparrows will beat against the windowpanes! I wonder if I shall take root here and winter and summer stand covered with ornaments!"

He knew very much about the matter! But he was so impatient that for sheer longing he got a pain in his back, and this with trees is the same thing as a headache with us.

The candles were now lighted. What brightness!

What splendour! The Tree trembled so in every bough that one of the tapers set fire to the foliage. It blazed up splendidly.

"Help! help!" cried the young ladies, and they quickly put out the fire.

Now the Tree did not even dare tremble. What a state he was in! He was so uneasy lest he should lose something of his splendor that he was quite bewildered amid the glare and brightness, when suddenly both folding doors opened and a troop of children rushed in as if they would upset the Tree. The older persons followed quietly; the little ones stood quite still. But it was only for a moment; then they shouted so that the whole place re-echoed with their rejoicing; they danced round the Tree, and one present after the other was pulled off.

"What are they about?" thought the Tree. "What is to happen now?" And the lights burned down to the very branches, and as they burned down they were put out one after the other, and then the children had permission to plunder the Tree. So they fell upon it with such violence that all its branches cracked; if it had not been fixed firmly in the cask it would certainly have tumbled down.

The children danced about with their beautiful playthings; no one looked at the Tree except the old nurse, who peeped between the branches; but it was only to see if there was a fig or an apple left that had been forgotten.

"A story! A story!" cried the children, drawing a little fat man toward the Tree. He seated himself under it and said, "Now we are in the shade, and the Tree can listen too. But I shall tell only one story. Now which will you have: that about Ivedy-Avedy, or about Klumpy-

Dumpy who tumbled downstairs, and yet after all came to the throne and married the princess?"

"Ivedy-Avedy," cried some; "Klumpy-Dumpy," cried the others. There was such a bawling and screaming. The Fir-tree alone was silent, and he thought to himself, "Am I not to bawl with the rest—am I to do nothing whatever?" for he was one of the company and had done what he had to do.

And the man told about Klumpy-Dumpy that tumbled down, who notwithstanding came to the throne and at last married the princess. And the children clapped their hands and cried out, "Oh, go on! Do go on!" They wanted to hear about Ivedy-Avedy, too, but the little man only told them about Klumpy-Dumpy. The Fir-tree stood quite still and absorbed in thought; the birds in the wood had never related the like of this. "Klumpy-Dumpy fell downstairs, and yet he married the princess! Yes, yes! That's the way of the world!" thought the Fir-tree, and believed it all, because the man who told the story was so good-looking. "Well, well! Who knows, perhaps I may fall downstairs, too, and get a princess as wife!" And he looked forward with joy to the morrow, when he hoped to be decked out again with lights, playthings, fruits, and tinsel.

"I won't tremble tomorrow!" thought the Fir-tree. "I will enjoy to the full all my splendour! Tomorrow I shall hear again the story of Klumpy-Dumpy, and perhaps that of Ivedy-Avedy, too." And the whole night the Tree stood still and in deep thought.

In the morning the servant and the housemaid came in.

"Now, then, the splendour will begin again," thought the Fir. But they dragged him out of the room, and up

149

the stairs into the loft; and here in a dark corner, where no daylight could enter, they left him. "What's the meaning of this?" thought the Tree. "What am I to do here? What shall I hear now, I wonder?" And he leaned against the wall, lost in reverie. Time enough had he, too, for his reflections, for days and nights passed on, and nobody came up; and when at last somebody did come it was only to put some great trunks in a corner out of the way. There stood the Tree, quite hidden; it seemed as if he had been entirely forgotten.

"'Tis now winter out-of-doors!" thought the Tree. "The earth is hard and covered with snow; men cannot plant me now, and therefore I have been put up here under shelter till the springtime comes! How thoughtful that is! How kind man is, after all! If it only were not so dark here and so terribly lonely! Not even a hare. And out in the woods it was so pleasant when the snow was on the ground, and the hare leaped by; yes, even when he jumped over me; but I did not like it then. It is really terribly lonely here!"

"Squeak! Squeak!" said a little Mouse, at the same moment peeping out of his hole. And then another little one came.

They snuffed about the Fir-tree and rustled among the branches.

"It is dreadfully cold," said the Mouse. "But for that it would be delightful here, old Fir, wouldn't it?"

"I am by no means old," said the Fir-tree. "There's many a one considerably older than I am."

"Where do you come from," asked the Mice, "and what can you do?" They were so extremely curious. "Tell us about the most beautiful spot on the earth. Have you never been there? Were you never in the larder where cheeses lie on the shelves and hams hang from above, where one dances about on tallow candles; that place where one enters lean and comes out again fat and portly?"

"I know no such place," said the Tree. "But I know the wood, where the sun shines, and where the little birds sing." And then he told all about his youth; and the little Mice had never heard the like before; and they listened and said, "Well, to be sure! How much you have seen! How happy you must have been!"

"I!" said the Fir-tree, thinking over what he had himself related. "Yes, in reality those were happy times." And then he told about Christmas Eve, when he was decked out with cakes and candles.

"Oh," said the little Mice, "how fortunate you have been, old Fir-tree!"

"I am by no means old," said he. "I came from the wood this winter; I am in my prime, and am only rather short for my age."

"What delightful stories you know!" said the Mice; and the next night they came with four other little Mice, who were to hear what the Tree recounted; and the more he related the more plainly he remembered all himself; and it appeared as if those times had really been happy times. "But they may still come—they may still come. Klumpy-Dumpy fell downstairs, and yet he got a princess!" And he thought at the moment of a nice little Birch-tree growing out in the wood; to the Fir that would be a real charming princess.

"Who is Klumpy-Dumpy?" asked the Mice. So then the Fir-tree told the whole fairy tale, for he could remember every single word of it; and the little Mice jumped for joy up to the very top of the Tree. Next night two more Mice came, and on Sunday two Rats, even; but they said the stories were not interesting, which vexed the little Mice; and they, too, now began to think them not so very amusing, either.

"Do you know only one story?" asked the Rats.

"Only that one," answered the Tree. "I heard it on my happiest evening; but I did not then know how happy I was."

"It is a very stupid story! Don't you know one about bacon and tallow candles? Can't you tell any larder stories?"

"No," said the Tree.

"Then good-by," said the Rats; and they went home.

At last the little Mice stayed away also; and the Tree sighed. "After all, it was very pleasant when the sleek little Mice sat round me and listened to what I told them. Now that, too, is over. But I will take good care to enjoy myself when I am brought out again."

But when was that to be? Why, one morning there came a quantity of people and set to work in the loft. The trunks were moved, the tree was pulled out and thrown—rather hard, it is true—down on the floor, but a man drew him toward the stairs, where the daylight shone.

"Now a merry life will begin again," thought the Tree. He felt the fresh air, the first sunbeam—and now he was out in the courtyard.

All passed so quickly, there was so much going on around him, that the Tree quite forgot to look to himself. The court adjoined a garden, and all was in flower; the roses hung so fresh and odorous over the balustrade, the lindens were in blossom, the Swallows flew by and said, "Quirre-vit! My husband is come!" but it was not the Fir-tree that they meant.

"Now, then, I shall really enjoy life," said he, exultingly, and spread out his branches; but, alas! they were all withered and yellow. It was in a corner that he lay, among weeds and nettles. The golden star of tinsel was still on the top of the Tree, and glittered in the sunshine.

In the courtyard some of the merry children were playing who had danced at Christmas round the Fir-tree and were so glad at the sight of him. One of the youngest ran and tore off the golden star.

"Only look what is still on the ugly old Christmas tree!" said he, trampling on the branches so that they all cracked beneath his feet.

And the Tree beheld all the beauty of the flowers and the freshness in the garden; he beheld himself and wished he had remained in his dark corner in the loft; he thought of his first youth in the wood, of the merry Christmas Eve, and of the little Mice who had listened with so much pleasure to the story of Klumpy-Dumpy.

"'Tis over! 'Tis past!" said the poor Tree. "Had I but rejoiced when I had reason to do so! But now 'tis past, 'tis past!"

And the gardener's boy chopped the Tree into small pieces; there was a whole heap lying there. The wood flamed up splendidly under the large brewing cauldron, and it sighed so deeply! Each sigh was like a shot.

The boys played about in the court, and the youngest wore the gold star on his breast which the Tree had had on the happiest evening of his life. However, that was over now—the Tree gone, the story at an end. All, all was over; every tale must end at last.

O. Henry

The Gift of the Magi

One dollar and eighty-seven cents. That was all. And sixty cents of it was in pennies. Pennies saved one and two at a time by bulldozing the grocer and the vegetable man and the butcher until one's cheeks burned with the silent imputation of parsimony that such close dealing implied. Three times Della counted it. One dollar and eighty-seven cents. And the next day would be Christmas.

There was clearly nothing to do but flop down on the shabby little couch and howl. So Della did it. Which instigates the moral reflection that life is made up of sobs, sniffles, and smiles, with sniffles predominating.

While the mistress of the home is gradually subsiding from the first stage to the second, take a look at the home. A furnished flat at $8 per week. It did not exactly beggar description, but it certainly had that word on the lookout for the mendicancy squad.

In the vestibule below was a letter-box into which no letter would go, and an electric button from which no mortal finger could coax a ring. Also appertaining there

unto was a card bearing the name "Mr. James Dillingham Young."

The "Dillingham" had been flung to the breeze
during a former period of prosperity when its possessor
was being paid $30 per week. Now, when the income
was shrunk to $20, the letters of "Dillingham" looked
blurred, as though they were thinking seriously of con-
tracting to a modest and unassuming D. But whenever
Mr. James Dillingham Young came home and reached
his flat above he was called "Jim" and greatly hugged
by Mrs. James Dillingham Young, already introduced to
you as Della. Which is all very good.

Della finished her cry and attended to her cheeks
with the powder rag. She stood by the window and
looked out dully at a grey cat walking a grey fence in a
grey backyard. To-morrow would be Christmas Day,
and she had only $1.87 with which to buy Jim a present.
She had been saving every penny she could for months,
with this result. Twenty dollars a week doesn't go far.
Expenses had been greater than she had calculated.
They always are. Only $1.87 to buy a present for Jim.
Her Jim. Many a happy hour she had spent planning
for something nice for him. Something fine and rare
and sterling—something just a little bit near to being
worthy of the honour of being owned by Jim.

There was a pier-glass between the windows of the
room. Perhaps you have seen a pier-glass in an $8 flat.
A very thin and very agile person may, by observing his
reflection in a rapid sequence of longitudinal stops,
obtain a fairly accurate conception of his looks. Della,
being slender, had mastered the art.

Suddenly she whirled from the window and stood
before the glass. Her eyes were shining brilliantly,
but her face had lost its colour within twenty seconds.

Rapidly she pulled down her hair and let it fall to its full length.

Now, there were two possessions of the James Dillingham Youngs in which they both took a mighty pride. One was Jim's gold watch that had been his father's and grandfather's. The other was Della's hair. Had the Queen of Sheba lived in the flat across the airshaft, Della would have let her hair hang out the window some day to dry just to depreciate Her Majesty's jewels and gifts. Had King Solomon been the janitor, with all his treasures piled up in the basement, Jim would have pulled out his watch every time he passed, just to see him pluck at his beard from envy.

So now Della's beautiful hair fell about her, rippling and shining like a cascade of brown waters. It reached below her knee and made itself almost garment for her. And then she did it up again nervously and quickly. Once she faltered for a minute and stood still while a tear or two splashed on the worn red carpet.

On went her old brown jacket; on went her old brown hat. With a whirl of skirts and with the brilliant sparkle still in her eyes, she fluttered out the door and down the stairs to the street.

Where she stopped the sign read: "Mme. Sofronie. Hair Goods of All Kinds." One flight up Della ran, and collected herself, panting. Madame, large, too white, chilly, hardly looked the "Sofronie."

"Will you buy my hair?" asked Della.

"I buy hair," said Madame. "Take yer hat off and let's have a sight at the looks of it."

Down rippled the brown cascade.

"Twenty dollars," said Madame, lifting the mass with a practised hand.

"Give it to me quick," said Della.

Oh, and the next two hours tripped by on rosy wings. Forget the hashed metaphor. She was ransacking the stores for Jim's present.

She found it at last. It surely had been made for Jim and no one else. There was no other like it in any of the stores, and she had turned all of them inside out. It was a platinum fob chain simple and chaste in design, properly proclaiming its value by substance alone and not by meretricious ornamentation—as all good things should do. It was even worthy of The Watch. As soon as she saw it she knew that it must be Jim's. It was like him. Quietness and value—the description applied to both. Twenty-one dollars they took from her for it, and she hurried home with the 87 cents. With that chain on his watch Jim might be properly anxious about the time in any company. Grand as the watch was, he sometimes looked at it on the sly on account of the old leather strap that he used in place of a chain.

When Della reached home her intoxication gave way a little to prudence and reason. She got out her curling irons and lighted the gas and went to work repairing the ravages made by generosity added to love. Which is always a tremendous task, dear friends—a mammoth task.

Within forty minutes her head was covered with tiny, close-lying curls that made her look wonderfully like a truant schoolboy. She looked at her reflection in the mirror long, carefully, and critically.

"If Jim doesn't kill me," she said to herself, "before he takes a second look at me, he'll say I look like a Coney Island chorus girl. But what could I do—oh! what could I do with a dollar and eighty-seven cents?"

At 7 o'clock the coffee was made and the frying-pan

was on the back of the stove hot and ready to cook the chops.

Jim was never late. Della doubled the fob chain in her hand and sat on the corner of the table near the door that he always entered. Then she heard his step on the stair away down on the first flight, and she turned white for just a moment. She had a habit of saying little silent prayers about the simplest everyday things, and now she whispered: "Please God, make him think I am still pretty."

The door opened and Jim stepped in and closed it. He looked thin and very serious. Poor fellow, he was only twenty-two—and to be burdened with a family! He needed a new overcoat and he was without gloves.

Jim stopped inside the door, as immovable as a setter at the scent of quail. His eyes were fixed upon Della, and there was an expression in them that she could not read, and it terrified her. It was not anger, nor surprise, nor disapproval, nor horror, nor any of the sentiments that she had been prepared for. He simply stared at her fixedly with that peculiar expression on his face.

Della wriggled off the table and went for him.

"Jim, darling," she cried, "don't look at me that way. I had my hair cut off and sold it because I couldn't have lived through Christmas without giving you a present. It'll grow out again—you won't mind, will you? I just had to do it. My hair grows awfully fast. Say 'Merry Christmas!' Jim, and let's be happy. You don't know what a nice—what a beautiful, nice gift I've got for you."

"You've cut off your hair?" asked Jim, laboriously, as if he had not arrived at that patent fact yet even after the hardest mental labour.

"Cut it off and sold it," said Della. "Don't you like

me just as well, anyhow? I'm me without my hair, ain't I?"

Jim looked about the room curiously.

"You say your hair is gone?" he said, with an air almost of idiocy.

"You needn't look for it," said Della. "It's sold, I tell you—sold and gone, too. It's Christmas Eve, boy. Be good to me, for it went for you. Maybe the hairs of my head were numbered," she went on with a sudden serious sweetness, "but nobody could ever count my love for you. Shall I put the chops on, Jim?"

Out of his trance Jim seemed quickly to wake. He enfolded his Della. For ten seconds let us regard with discreet scrutiny some inconsequential object in the other direction. Eight dollars a week or a million a year—what is the difference? A mathematician or a wit would give you the wrong answer. The magi brought valuable gifts, but that was not among them. This dark assertion will be illuminated later on.

Jim drew a package from his overcoat pocket and threw it upon the table.

"Don't make any mistake, Dell," he said, "about me. I don't think there's anything in the way of a haircut or a shave or a shampoo that could make me like my girl any less. But if you'll unwrap that package you may see why you had me going a while at first."

White fingers and nimble tore at the string and paper. And then an ecstatic scream of joy; and then, alas! a quick feminine change to hysterical tears and wails, necessitating the immediate employment of all the comforting powers of the lord of the flat.

For there lay The Combs—the set of combs, side and back, that Della had worshipped for long in a Broadway window. Beautiful combs, pure tortoise shell, with jeweled rims—just the shade to wear in the beautiful vanished hair. They were expensive combs, she knew, and her heart had simply craved and yearned over them without the least hope of possession. And now, they were hers, but the tresses that should have adorned the coveted adornments were gone.

But she hugged them to her bosom, and at length she was able to look up with dim eyes and a smile and say: "My hair grows so fast, Jim!"

And then Della leaped up like a little singed cat and cried, "Oh, oh!"

Jim had not yet seen his beautiful present. She held it out to him eagerly upon her open palm. The dull precious metal seemed to flash with a reflection of her bright and ardent spirit.

"Isn't it a dandy, Jim? I hunted all over town to find it. You'll have to look at the time a hundred times a day now. Give me your watch. I want to see how it looks on it."

Instead of obeying, Jim tumbled down on the couch and put his hands under the back of his head and smiled.

"Dell," said he, "let's put our Christmas presents away and keep 'em a while. They're too nice to use just at present. I sold the watch to get the money to buy your combs. And now suppose you put the chops on."

The magi, as you know, were wise men—wonderfully wise men—who brought gifts to the Babe in the manger. They invented the art of giving Christmas presents. Being wise, their gifts were no doubt wise ones, possibly bearing the privilege of exchange in case of duplication. And here I have lamely related to you the uneventful chronicle of two foolish children in a flat who most unwisely sacrificed for each other the greatest treasures of their house. But in a last word to the wise of these days let it be said that of all who give gifts these two were the wisest. Of all who give and receive gifts, such as they are wisest. Everywhere they are wisest. They are the magi.

A Kidnapped Santa Claus

Santa Claus lives in the Laughing Valley, where stands the big rambling castle in which his toys are manufactured. His workmen, selected from the ryls, knooks, pixies and fairies, live with him, and every one is as busy as can be from one year's end to another.

It is called the Laughing Valley because everything there is happy and gay. The brook chuckles to itself as it leaps rollicking between its green banks; the wind whistles merrily in the trees; the sunbeams dance lightly over the soft grass, and the violets and wild-flowers look smilingly up from their green nests. To laugh one needs to be happy; to be happy one needs to be content. And throughout the Laughing Valley of Santa Claus contentment reigns supreme.

On one side is the mighty Forest of Burzee. At the other side stands the huge mountain that contains the Caves of the Daemons. And between them the Valley lies smiling and peaceful.

One would think that our good old Santa Claus, who devotes his days to making children happy, would have no enemies on all the earth; and, as a matter of fact, for a long period of time he encountered nothing but love wherever he might go.

But the Daemons who live in the mountain caves grew to hate Santa Claus very much, and all for the simple reason that he made children happy.

The Caves of the Daemons are five in number. A broad pathway leads up to the first cave, which is a finely arched cavern at the foot of the mountain, the entrance being beautifully carved and decorated. In it resides the Daemon of Selfishness. Back of this is another cavern inhabited by the Daemon of Envy. The cave of the Daemon of Hatred is next in order, and through this, one passes to the home of the Daemon of Malice—situated in a dark and fearful cave in the very heart of the mountain. I do not know what lies beyond this. Some say there are terrible pitfalls leading to death and destruction, and this may very well be true. However, from each one of the four caves mentioned there is a small, narrow tunnel leading to the fifth cave—a cozy little room occupied by the Daemon of Repentance. And as the rocky floors of these passages are well worn by the track of passing feet, I judge that many wanderers in the Caves of the Daemons have escaped through the tunnels to the abode of the Daemon of Repentance, who is said to be a pleasant sort of fellow who gladly opens for one a little door admitting you into fresh air and sunshine again.

Well, these Daemons of the Caves, thinking they had great cause to dislike old Santa Claus, held a meeting one day to discuss the matter.

"I'm really getting lonesome," said the Daemon of Selfishness. "For Santa Claus distributes so many pretty Christmas gifts to all the children that they

163

become happy and generous, through his example, and keep away from my cave."

"I'm having the same trouble," rejoined the Daemon of Envy. "The little ones seem quite content with Santa Claus, and there are few, indeed, that I can coax to become envious."

"And that makes it bad for me!" declared the Daemon of Hatred. "For if no children pass through the caves of Selfishness and Envy, none can get to *my* cavern."

"Or to mine," added the Daemon of Malice.

"For my part," said the Daemon of Repentance, "it is easily seen that if children do not visit your caves they have no need to visit mine; so I am quite as neglected as you are."

"And all because of this person they call Santa Claus!" exclaimed the Daemon of Envy. "He is simply ruining our business, and something must be done at once."

To this they readily agreed; but what to do was another and more difficult matter to settle. They knew that Santa Claus worked all through the year at his castle in the Laughing Valley, preparing the gifts he was to distribute on Christmas Eve; and at first they resolved to try to tempt him into their caves, that they might lead him on to the terrible pitfalls that ended in destruction.

So the very next day, while Santa Claus was busily at work, surrounded by his little band of assistants, the Daemon of Selfishness came to him and said, "These toys are wonderfully bright and pretty. Why do you not keep them for yourself? It's a pity to give them to those noisy boys and fretful girls, who break and destroy them so quickly."

"Nonsense!" cried the old graybeard, his bright eyes twinkling merrily as he turned toward the tempting Daemon; "the boys and girls are never so noisy and fretful after receiving my presents, and if I can make them happy for one day in the year I am quite content." So the Daemon went back to the others, who awaited him in their caves, and said, "I have failed, for Santa Claus is not at all selfish."

The following day the Daemon of Envy visited Santa Claus. Said he, "The toy-shops are full of playthings quite as pretty as these you are making. What a shame it is that they should interfere with your business! They make toys by machinery much quicker than you can make them by hand; and they sell them for money, while you get nothing at all for your work."

But Santa Claus refused to be envious of the toy-shops.

"I can supply the little ones but once a year—on Christmas Eve," he answered; "for the children are many, and I am but one. And as my work is one of love and kindness I would be ashamed to receive money for my little gifts. But throughout all the year the children must be amused in some way, and so the toy-shops are able to bring much happiness to my little friends. I like the toy-shops, and am glad to see them prosper."

In spite of this second rebuff, the Daemon of Hatred thought he would try to influence Santa Claus. So the next day he entered the busy workshop and said, "Good morning, Santa! I have bad news for you."

"Then run away, like a good fellow," answered Santa Claus. "Bad news is something that should be kept secret and never told."

"You cannot escape this, however," declared the Daemon; "for in the world are a good many who do not believe in Santa Claus, and these you are bound to hate bitterly, since they have so wronged you."

"Stuff and rubbish!" cried Santa.

"And there are others who resent your making children happy and who sneer at you and call you a foolish old rattlepate! You are quite right to hate such base slanderers, and you ought to be revenged upon them for their evil words."

"But I *don't* hate 'em!" exclaimed Santa Claus, positively. "Such people do me no real harm, but merely render themselves and their children unhappy. Poor things! I'd much rather help them any day than injure them."

Indeed, the Daemons could not tempt old Santa Claus in any way. On the contrary, he was shrewd enough to see that their object in visiting him was to make mischief and trouble. So the Daemons abandoned honeyed words and determined to use force.

It is well known that no harm can come to Santa Claus while he is in the Laughing Valley, for the fairies, and ryls, and knooks all protect him. But on Christmas Eve he drives his reindeer out into the big world, carrying a sleigh-load of toys and pretty gifts to the children; and this was the time and the occasion when his enemies had the best chance to injure him. So the Daemons laid their plans and awaited the arrival of Christmas Eve.

The moon shone big and white in the sky, and the snow lay crisp and sparkling on the ground as Santa Claus cracked his whip and sped away out of the Valley into the great world beyond. The roomy sleigh was packed full with huge sacks of toys, and as the reindeer dashed onward our jolly old Santa laughed and whistled and sang for very joy. For in all his merry life this was the one day in the year when he was happiest—the day he lovingly bestowed the treasures of his workshop upon the little children.

It would be a busy night for him, he well knew. As he whistled and shouted and cracked his whip again, he reviewed in mind all the towns and cities and farm-houses where he was expected, and figured that he had just enough presents to go around and make every child happy. The reindeer knew exactly what was expected of them, and dashed along so swiftly that their feet scarcely seemed to touch the snow-covered ground.

Suddenly a strange thing happened: a rope shot through the moonlight and a big noose that was in the end of it settled over the arms and body of Santa Claus and drew tight. Before he could resist or even cry out he was jerked from the seat of the sleigh and tumbled head foremost into a snowbank, while the reindeer rushed onward with the load of toys and carried it quickly out of sight and sound.

Such a surprising experience confused old Santa for a moment, and when he had collected his senses he found that the wicked Daemons had pulled him from the snowdrift and bound him tightly with many coils of the stout rope. And then they carried the kidnapped Santa Claus away to their mountain, where they thrust the prisoner into a secret cave and chained him to the rocky wall so that he could not escape.

"Ha, ha!" laughed the Daemons, rubbing their hands together with cruel glee. "What will the children do now? How they will cry and scold and storm when they find there are no toys in their stockings and no gifts on their Christmas trees! And what a lot of punishment they will receive from their parents, and how they will flock to our caves of Selfishness, and Envy, and Hatred, and Malice! We have done a mighty clever thing, we Daemons of the Caves!"

Now it so chanced that on this Christmas Eve the good Santa Claus had taken with him in his sleigh Nuter the Ryl, Peter the Knook, Kilter the Pixie, and a small fairy named Wisk—his four favorite assistants. These little people he had often found very useful in helping him to distribute his gifts to the children, and when their master was so suddenly dragged from the sleigh they were all snugly tucked underneath the seat, where the sharp wind could not reach them.

The tiny immortals knew nothing of the capture of Santa Claus until some time after he had disappeared. But finally they missed his cheery voice, and as their master always sang or whistled on his journeys, the silence warned them that something was wrong.

Little Wisk stuck out his head from underneath the seat and found Santa Claus gone and no one to direct the flight of the reindeer.

"Whoa!" he called out, and the deer obediently slackened speed and came to a halt.

Peter and Nuter and Kilter all jumped upon the seat and looked back over the track made by the sleigh. But Santa Claus had been left miles and miles behind.

"What shall we do?" asked Wisk, anxiously, all the mirth and mischief banished from his wee face by this great calamity.

"We must go back at once and find our master," said Nuter the Ryl, who thought and spoke with much deliberation.

"No, no!" exclaimed Peter the Knook, who, cross and crabbed though he was, might always be depended upon in an emergency. "If we delay, or go back, there will not be time to get the toys to the children before morning; and that would grieve Santa Claus more than anything else."

"It is certain that some wicked creatures have captured him," added Kilter, thoughtfully; "and their object must be to make the children unhappy. So our first duty is to get the toys distributed as carefully as if Santa Claus were himself present. Afterward we can search for our master and easily secure his freedom."

This seemed such good and sensible advice that the others at once resolved to adopt it. So Peter the Knook called to the reindeer, and the faithful animals again sprang forward and dashed over hill and valley, through forest and plain, until they came to the houses wherein children lay sleeping and dreaming of the pretty gifts they would find on Christmas morning.

The little immortals had set themselves a difficult task; for although they had assisted Santa Claus on many of his journeys, their master had always directed and guided them and told them exactly what he wished them to do. But now they had to distribute the toys according to their own judgment, and they did not understand children as well as did old Santa. So it is no wonder they made some laughable errors.

Mamie Brown, who wanted a doll, got a drum instead; and a drum is of no use to a girl who loves dolls. And Charlie Smith, who delights to romp and play out of doors, and who wanted some new rubber boots to keep his feet dry, received a sewing-box filled with colored worsteds and threads and needles, which made him so provoked that he thoughtlessly called our dear Santa Claus a fraud.

Had there been many such mistakes the Daemons

would have accomplished their evil purpose and made the children unhappy. But the little friends of the absent Santa Claus labored faithfully and intelligently to carry out their master's ideas, and they made fewer errors than might be expected under such unusual circumstances.

And, although they worked as swiftly as possible, day had begun to break before the toys and other presents were all distributed; so for the first time in many years the reindeer trotted into the Laughing Valley, on their return, in broad daylight, with the brilliant sun peeping over the edge of the forest to prove they were far behind their accustomed hour.

Having put the deer in the stable, the little folk began to wonder how they might rescue their master; and they realized they must discover, first of all, what had happened to him and where he was.

So Wisk the Fairy transported himself to the bower of the Fairy Queen, which was located deep in the heart of the Forest of Burzee; and once there, it did not take him long to find out all about the naughty Daemons and how they had kidnapped the good Santa Claus to prevent his making children happy. The Fairy Queen also promised her assistance, and then, fortified by this powerful support, Wisk flew back to where Nuter and Peter and Kilter awaited him, and the four counselled together and laid plans to rescue their master from his enemies.

It is possible that Santa Claus was not as merry as usual during the night that succeeded his capture. For although he had faith in the judgment of his little friends he could not avoid a certain amount of worry, and an anxious look would creep at times into his kind old eyes as he thought of the disappointment that might await his dear little children. And the Daemons, who guarded him by turns, one after another, did not neglect to taunt him with contemptuous words in his helpless condition.

When Christmas Day dawned the Daemon of Malice was guarding the prisoner, and his tongue was sharper than that of any of the others.

"The children are waking up, Santa!" he cried; "they are waking up to find their stockings empty! Ho, ho! How they will quarrel, and wail, and stamp their feet in anger! Our caves will be full to-day, old Santa! Our caves are sure to be full!"

But to this, as to other like taunts, Santa Claus answered nothing. He was much grieved by his capture, it is true; but his courage did not forsake him. And, finding that the prisoner would not reply to his jeers, the Daemon of Malice presently went away, and sent the Daemon of Repentance to take his place.

This last personage was not so disagreeable as the others. He had gentle and refined features, and his voice was soft and pleasant in tone.

"My brother Daemons do not trust me overmuch," said he, as he entered the cavern; "but it is morning, now, and the mischief is done. You cannot visit the children again for another year."

"That is true," answered Santa Claus, almost cheerfully; "Christmas Eve is past, and for the first time in centuries I have not visited my children."

"The little ones will be greatly disappointed," murmured the Daemon of Repentance, almost regretfully, "but that cannot be helped now. Their grief is likely to make the children selfish and envious and hateful, and if they come to the Caves of the Daemons to-day I shall get a chance to lead some of them to my Cave of Repentance."

"Do you never repent, yourself?" asked Santa Claus, curiously. "Oh, yes, indeed," answered the Daemon. "I am even now repenting that I assisted in your capture. Of course it is too late to remedy the evil that has been done; but repentance, you know, can come only after an evil thought or deed, for in the beginning there is nothing to repent of."

"So I understand," said Santa Claus. "Those who avoid evil need never visit your cave."

"As a rule, that is true," replied the Daemon; "yet you, who have done no evil, are about to visit my cave at once; for to prove that I sincerely regret my share in your capture I am going to permit you to escape."

This speech greatly surprised the prisoner, until he reflected that it was just what might be expected of the Daemon of Repentance. The fellow at once busied himself untying the knots that bound Santa Claus and unlocking the chains that fastened him to the wall. Then he led the way through a long tunnel until they both emerged in the Cave of Repentance.

"I hope you will forgive me," said the Daemon, pleadingly. "I am not really a bad person, you know; and I believe I accomplish a great deal of good in the world."

With this he opened a back door that let in a flood of sunshine, and Santa Claus sniffed the fresh air gratefully.

"I bear no malice," said he to the Daemon, in a gentle voice; "and I am sure the world would be a dreary place without you. So, good morning, and a Merry Christmas to you!"

With these words he stepped out to greet the bright

morning, and a moment later he was trudging along, whistling softly to himself, on his way to his home in the Laughing Valley.

Marching over the snow toward the mountain was a vast army, made up of the most curious creatures imaginable. There were numberless knooks from the forest, as rough and crooked in appearance as the gnarled branches of the trees they ministered to. And there were dainty ryls from the fields, each one bearing the emblem of the flower or plant it guarded. Behind these were many ranks of pixies, gnomes and nymphs, and in the rear a thousand beautiful fairies floating along in gorgeous array.

This wonderful army was led by Wisk, Peter, Nuter and Kilter, who had assembled it to rescue Santa Claus from captivity and to punish the Daemons who had dared to take him away from his beloved children.

And, although they looked so bright and peaceful, the little immortals were armed with powers that would be very terrible to those who had incurred their anger. Woe to the Daemons of the Caves if this mighty army of vengeance ever met them!

But lo! coming to meet his loyal friends appeared the imposing form of Santa Claus, his white beard floating in the breeze and his bright eyes sparkling with pleasure at this proof of the love and veneration he had inspired in the hearts of the most powerful creatures in existence.

And while they clustered around him and danced with glee at his safe return, he gave them earnest thanks for their support. But Wisk, and Nuter, and Peter, and Kilter, he embraced affectionately. "It is useless to pursue the Daemons," said Santa Claus to the army. "They have their place in the world, and can never be destroyed. But that is a great pity, nevertheless," he continued, musingly.

So the fairies, and knooks, and pixies, and ryls all escorted the good man to his castle, and there left him to talk over the events of the night with his little assistants.

Wisk had already rendered himself invisible and flown through the big world to see how the children were getting along on this bright Christmas morning; and by the time he returned, Peter had finished telling Santa Claus of how they had distributed the toys.

"We really did very well," cried the Fairy, in a pleased voice; "for I found little unhappiness among the children this morning. Still, you must not get captured again, my dear master, for we might not be so fortunate another time in carrying out your ideas."

He then related the mistakes that had been made, and which he had not discovered until his tour of inspection. And Santa Claus at once sent him with rubber boots for Charlie Smith, and a doll for Mamie Brown; so that even those two disappointed ones became happy.

As for the wicked Daemons of the Caves, they were filled with anger and chagrin when they found that their clever capture of Santa Claus had come to naught. Indeed, no one on that Christmas Day appeared to be at all selfish, or envious, or hateful. And, realizing that while the children's saint had so many powerful friends it was folly to oppose him, the Daemons never again attempted to interfere with his journeys on Christmas Eve.

J. M. BARRIE

The Ghost of Christmas Eve

A few years ago, as some may remember, a startling
ghost paper appeared in the monthly organ of the Society for Haunting Houses. The writer guaranteed the
truth of his statement, and even gave the name of the
Yorkshire manor-house in which the affair took place.
The article and the discussion to which it gave rise
agitated me a good deal, and I consulted Pettigrew
about the advisability of clearing up the mystery. The
writer wrote that he "distinctly saw his arm pass
through the apparition and come out at the other side,"
and indeed I still remember his saying so next morning.
He had a scared face, but I had presence of mind to
continue eating my rolls and marmalade as if my briar
had nothing to do with the miraculous affair.

Seeing that he made a "paper" of it, I suppose he is
justified in touching up the incidental details. He says,
for instance, that were told the story of the ghost which
is said to haunt the house, just before going to bed. As
far as I remember, it was only mentioned at luncheon,
and then sceptically. Instead of there being snow falling

outside and an eerie wind wailing through the skeleton trees, the night was still and muggy. Lastly, I did not know, until the journal reached my hands, that he was put into the room known as The Haunted Chamber, nor that in that room the fire is noted for casting weird shadows upon the walls. This, however, may be so. The legend of the manor-house ghost he tells precisely as it is known to me. The tragedy dates back to the time of Charles I., and is led up to by a pathetic love-story, which I need not give. Suffice it that for seven days and nights the old steward had been anxiously awaiting the return of his young master and mistress from their honeymoon. On Christmas Eve, after he had gone to bed, there was a great clanging of the door-bell. Flinging on a dressing-gown, he hastened down-stairs. According to the story, a number of servants watched him, and saw by the light of his candle that his face was an ashy white. He took off the chains of the door, unbolted it, and pulled it open. What he saw no human being knows; but it must have been something awful, for without a cry the old steward fell dead in the hall. Perhaps the strangest part of the story is this: that the shadow of a burly man, holding a pistol in his hand, entered by the open door, stepped over the steward's body, and, gliding up the stairs, disappeared, no one could say where. Such is the legend. I shall not tell the many ingenious explanations of it that have been offered. Every Christmas Eve, however, the silent scene is said to be gone through again; and tradition declares that no person lives for twelve months at whom the ghostly intruder points his pistol.

On Christmas Day the gentleman who tells the tale in the scientific journal created some sensation at the breakfast-table by solemnly asserting that he had seen the ghost. Most of the men present scouted his story, which may be condensed into a few words. He had retired to his bedroom at a fairly early hour, and as he opened the door his candle-light was blown out. He tried to get a light from the fire, but it was too low, and eventually he went to bed in the semi-darkness. He was wakened—he did not know at what hour—by the clanging of a bell. He sat up in bed, and the ghost-story came in a rush to his mind. His fire was dead, and the room was consequently dark; yet by and by he knew, though he heard no sound, that his door had opened. He cried out, "Who is that?" but got no answer. By an effort he jumped up and went to the door, which was ajar. His bedroom was on the first floor, and looking up the stairs he could see nothing. He felt a cold sensation at his heart, however, when he looked the other way. Going slowly and without a sound down the stairs, was an old man in a dressing-gown. He carried a candle. From the top of the stairs only part of the hall is visible, but as the apparition disappeared the watcher had the courage to go down a few steps after him. At first nothing was to be seen, for the candle-light had vanished. A dim light, however, entered by the long narrow windows which flank the hall-door, and after a moment the onlooker could see that the hall was empty. He was marvelling at this sudden disappearance of the steward, when, to his horror, he saw a body fall upon the hall floor within a few feet of the door. The watcher cannot say whether he cried out, nor how long he stood there trembling. He came to himself with a start as he realized that something was coming up the stairs. Fear prevented his taking flight, and in a moment the thing was at his side. Then he saw indistinctly that it was not the figure he had seen descend. He saw a younger man in a heavy overcoat, but with no hat on his head. He wore on his face a look of extravagant triumph. The guest boldly put out his hand towards the figure. To his amazement his arm went through it. The ghost paused for a moment and looked behind it. It was then the watcher realized that it carried a pistol in its right hand. He was by this time in a highly strung condition, and he stood trembling lest the pistol should be pointed at him. The apparition, however, rapidly glided up the stairs and was soon lost to sight. Such are the main facts of the story; none of which I contradicted at the time.

I cannot say absolutely that I can clear up this mystery; but my suspicions are confirmed by a good deal of circumstantial evidence. This will not be understood unless I explain my strange infirmity. Wherever I went I used to be troubled with a presentiment that I had left my pipe behind. Often even at the dinner-table, I paused in the middle of a sentence as if stricken with sudden pain. Then my hand went down to my pocket. Sometimes, even after I felt my pipe, I had a conviction that it was stopped, and only by a desperate effort did I keep myself from producing it and blowing down it. I distinctly remember once dreaming three nights in succession that I was on the Scotch express without it. More than once, I know, I have wandered in my sleep, looking for it in all sorts of places, and after I went to bed I generally jumped out, just to make sure of it. My strong belief, then, is that I was the ghost seen by the writer of the paper. I fancy that I rose in my sleep, lighted a candle and wandered down to the hall to feel if my pipe was safe in my coat, which was hanging there. The light had gone out when I was in the hall. Probably the body seen to fall on the hall floor was some other coat which I had flung there to get more easily at my own. I cannot account for the bell; but perhaps the gentleman in the Haunted Chamber dreamt that part of the affair. I had put on the overcoat before reascending; indeed, I may say that next morning I was surprised to find it on a chair in my bedroom, also to notice that there were several long streaks of candle-grease on my dressing-gown. I conclude that the pistol, which gave my face such a look of triumph, was my briar, which I found in the morning beneath my pillow. The strangest thing of all, perhaps, is that when I awoke there was a smell of tobacco-smoke in the bedroom.

LOUISA MAY ALCOTT

A Country Christmas

"A handful of good life is worth a bushel of learning."

"Dear Emily,—I have a brilliant idea, and at once hasten to share it with you. Three weeks ago I came up here to the wilds of Vermont to visit my old aunt, also to get a little quiet and distance in which to survey certain new prospects which have opened before me, and to decide whether I will marry a millionnaire and become a queen of society, or remain 'the charming Miss Vaughan' and wait till the conquering hero comes.

"Aunt Plumy begs me to stay over Christmas, and I have consented, as I always dread the formal dinner with which my guardian celebrates the day.

"My brilliant idea is this. I'm going to make it a real old-fashioned frolic, and won't you come and help me? You will enjoy it immensely I am sure, for Aunt is a character, Cousin Saul worth seeing, and Ruth a far prettier girl than any of the city rose-buds coming out this season. Bring Leonard Randal along with you to take notes for his new books; then it will be fresher and truer than the last, clever as it was.

"The air is delicious up here, society amusing, this old farmhouse full of treasures, and your bosom friend pining to embrace you. Just telegraph yes or no, and we will expect you on Tuesday.

"Ever yours,

"SOPHIE VAUGHAN."

"They will both come, for they are as tired of city life and as fond of change as I am," said the writer of the above, as she folded her letter and went to get it posted without delay.

Aunt Plumy was in the great kitchen making pies; a jolly old soul, with a face as ruddy as a winter apple, a cheery voice, and the kindest heart that ever beat under a gingham gown. Pretty Ruth was chopping the mince, and singing so gaily as she worked that the four-and-twenty immortal blackbirds could not have put more music into a pie than she did. Saul was piling wood into the big oven, and Sophie paused a moment on the threshold to look at him, for she always enjoyed the sight of this smart cousin, whom she likened to a Norse viking, with his fair hair and beard, keen blue eyes, and six feet of manly height, with shoulders that looked broad and strong enough to bear any burden.

His back was toward her, but he saw her first, and turned his flushed face to meet her, with the sudden lighting up it always showed when she approached.

"I've done it, Aunt; and now I want Saul to post the letter, so we can get a speedy answer."

"Just as soon as I can hitch up, cousin," and Saul pitched in his last log, looking ready to put a girdle round the earth in less than forty minutes.

"Well, dear, I ain't the least mite of objection, as long as it pleases you. I guess we can stan' it if your city folks can. I presume to say things will look kind of sing'lar to 'em but I s'pose that's what they come for. Idle folks do dreadful queer things to amuse 'em;" and Aunt Plumy leaned on the rolling-pin to smile and nod with a shrewd twinkle of her eye, as if she enjoyed the prospect as much as Sophie did.

"I shall be afraid of 'em, but I'll try not to make you ashamed of me," said Ruth, who loved her charming cousin even more than she admired her.

"No fear of that, dear. They will be the awkward ones, and you must set them at ease by just being your simple selves, and treating them as if they were every-day people. Nell is very nice and jolly when she drops her city ways, as she must here. She will enter into the spirit of the fun at once, and I know you'll all like her. Mr. Randal is rather the worse for too much praise and petting, as successful people are apt to be, so a little plain talk and rough work will do him good. He is a true gentleman in spite of his airs and elegance, and he will take it all in good part, if you treat him like a man and not a lion."

"I'll see to him," said Saul, who had listened with great interest to the latter part of Sophie's speech, evidently suspecting a lover, and enjoying the idea of supplying him with a liberal amount of "plain talk and rough work."

"I'll keep 'em busy if that's what they need, for there will be a sight to do, and we can't get help easy up here. Our darters don't hire out much. Work to home till they marry, and don't go gaddin' 'round gettin' their heads full of foolish notions, and forgettin' all the useful things their mothers taught 'em."

Aunt Plumy glanced at Ruth as she spoke, and a sudden color in the girl's cheeks proved that the words hit certain ambitious fancies of this pretty daughter of the house of Basset.

"They shall do their parts and not be a trouble, I'll see to that, for you certainly are the dearest aunt in the world to let me take possession of you and yours in this way," cried Sophie, embracing the old lady with warmth.

Saul wished the embrace could be returned by proxy, as his mother's hands were too floury to do more than hover affectionately round the delicate face that looked so fresh and young beside her wrinkled one. As it could not be done, he fled temptation and "hitched up" without delay.

The three women laid their heads together in his absence, and Sophie's plan grew apace, for Ruth longed to see a real novelist and a fine lady, and Aunt Plumy, having plans of her own to further, said "Yes, dear," to every suggestion.

Great was the arranging and adorning that went on that day in the old farmhouse, for Sophie wanted her friends to enjoy this taste of country pleasures, and knew just what additions would be indispensable to their comfort; what simple ornaments would be in keeping with the rustic stage on which she meant to play the part of prima donna.

Next day a telegram arrived accepting the invitation, for both the lady and the lion. They would arrive that afternoon, as little preparation was needed for this impromptu journey, the novelty of which was its chief charm to these *blase* people.

Saul wanted to get out the double sleigh and span, for he prided himself on his horses, and a fall of snow came most opportunely to beautify the landscape and add a new pleasure to Christmas festivities.

But Sophie declared that the old yellow sleigh, with Punch, the farm-horse, must be used, as she wished everything to be in keeping; and Saul obeyed, thinking he had never seen anything prettier than his cousin when she appeared in his mother's old-fashioned camlet cloak and blue silk pumpkin hood. He looked remarkably well himself in his fur coat, with hair and beard brushed till they shone like spun gold, a fresh color in his cheek, and the sparkle of amusement in his eyes, while excitement gave his usually grave face the animation it needed to be handsome.

Away they jogged in the creaking old sleigh, leaving Ruth to make herself pretty, with a fluttering heart, and Aunt Plumy to dish up a late dinner fit to tempt the most fastidious appetite.

"She has not come for us, and there is not even a stage to take us up. There must be some mistake," said Emily Herrick, as she looked about the shabby little station where they were set down.

"That is the never-to-be-forgotten face of our fair friend, but the bonnet of her grandmother, if my eyes do not deceive me," answered Randal, turning to survey the couple approaching in the rear.

"Sophie Vaughan, what do you mean by making such a guy of yourself?" exclaimed Emily, as she kissed the smiling face in the hood and stared at the quaint cloak.

"I'm dressed for my part, and I intend to keep it up. This is our host, my cousin, Saul Basset. Come to the sleigh at once, he will see to your luggage," said Sophie, painfully conscious of the antiquity of her array as her eyes rested on Emily's pretty hat and mantle, and the masculine elegance of Randal's wraps.

They were hardly tucked in when Saul appeared with a valise in one hand and a large trunk on his shoulder, swinging both on to a wood-sled that stood near by as easily as if they had been hand-bags.

"That is your hero, is it? Well, he looks it, calm and comely, taciturn and tall," said Emily, in a tone of approbation.

"He should have been named Samson or Goliath; though I believe it was the small man who slung things about and turned out the hero in the end," added Randal, surveying the performance with interest and a touch of envy, for much pen work had made his own hands as delicate as a woman's.

"Saul doesn't live in a glass house, so stones won't hurt him. Remember sarcasm is forbidden and sincerity the order of the day. You are country folks now, and it will do you good to try their simple, honest ways for a few days."

Sophie had no time to say more, for Saul came up and drove off with the brief remark that the baggage would "be along right away."

Being hungry, cold and tired, the guests were rather silent during the short drive, but Aunt Plumy's hospitable welcome, and the savory fumes of the dinner awaiting them, thawed the ice and won their hearts at once.

"Isn't it nice? Aren't you glad you came?" asked Sophie, as she led her friends into the parlor, which she had redeemed from its primness by putting bright chintz curtains to the windows, hemlock boughs over the old portraits, a china bowl of flowers on the table, and a splendid fire on the wide hearth.

"It is perfectly jolly, and this is the way I begin to enjoy myself," answered Emily, sitting down upon the home-made rug, whose red flannel roses bloomed in a blue list basket.

"If I may add a little smoke to your glorious fire, it will be quite perfect. Won't Samson join me?" asked Randal, waiting for permission, cigar-case in hand.

"He has no small vices, but you may indulge yours," answered Sophie, from the depths of a grandmotherly chair.

Emily glanced up at her friend as if she caught a new tone in her voice, then turned to the fire again with a wise little nod, as if confiding some secret to the reflection of herself in the bright brass and iron.

"His Delilah does not take this form. I wait with interest to discover if he has one. What a daisy the sister is. Does she ever speak?" asked Randal, trying to lounge on the haircloth sofa, where he was slipping uncomfortably about.

"Oh yes, and sings like a bird. You shall hear her when she gets over her shyness. But no trifling, mind you, for it is a jealously guarded daisy and not to be picked by any idle hand," said Sophie warningly, as she recalled Ruth's blushes and Randal's compliments at dinner.

"I should expect to be annihilated by the big brother if I attempted any but the 'sincerest' admiration and respect. Have no fears on that score, but tell us what is to follow this superb dinner. An apple bee, spinning match, husking party, or primitive pastime of some sort, I have no doubt."

"As you are new to our ways I am going to let you rest this evening. We will sit about the fire and tell stories. Aunt is a master hand at that, and Saul has reminiscences of the war that are well worth hearing if we can only get him to tell them."

"Ah, he was there, was he?"

"Yes, all through it, and is Major Basset, though he likes his plain name best. He fought splendidly and had several wounds, though only a mere boy when he earned his scars and bars. I'm very proud of him for that," and Sophie looked so as she glanced at the photograph of a stripling in uniform set in the place of honor on the high mantel-piece.

"We must stir him up and hear these martial memories. I want some new incidents, and shall book all I can get, if I may."

Here Randal was interrupted by Saul himself, who came in with an armful of wood for the fire. "Anything more I can do for you, cousin?" he asked, surveying the scene with a rather wistful look.

"Only come and sit with us and talk over war times with Mr. Randal."

"When I've foddered the cattle and done my chores I'd be pleased to. What regiment were you in?" asked Saul, looking down from his lofty height upon the slender gentleman, who answered briefly,—

"In none. I was abroad at the time."

"Sick?"

"No, busy with a novel."

"Took four years to write it?"

"I was obliged to travel and study before I could finish it. These things take more time to work up than outsiders would believe."

"Seems to me our war was a finer story than any you could find in Europe, and the best way to study it would be to fight it out. If you want heroes and heroines you'd have found plenty of 'em there."

"I have no doubt of it, and shall be glad to atone for

my seeming neglect of them by hearing about your own exploits, Major."

Randal hoped to turn the conversation gracefully, but Saul was not to be caught, and left the room, saying, with a gleam of fun in his eye,—

"I can't stop now; heroes can wait, pigs can't."

The girls laughed at this sudden descent from the sublime to the ridiculous, and Randal joined them, feeling his condescension had not been unobserved.

As if drawn by the merry sound Aunt Plumy appeared, and being established in the rockingchair fell to talking as easily as if she had known her guests for years.

"Laugh away, young folks, that's better for digestion than any of the messes people use. Are you troubled with dyspepsy, dear? You didn't seem to take your vittles very hearty, so I mistrusted you was delicate," she said, looking at Emily, whose pale cheeks and weary eyes told the story of late hours and a gay life.

"I haven't eaten so much for years, I assure you, Mrs. Basset; but it was impossible to taste all your good things. I am not dyspeptic, thank you, but a little seedy and tired, for I've been working rather hard lately."

"Be you a teacher? or have you a 'perfessun,' as they call a trade nowadays?" asked the old lady in a tone of kindly interest, which prevented a laugh at the idea of Emily's being anything but a beauty and a belle. The others kept their countenances with difficulty, and she answered demurely,—

"I have no trade as yet, but I dare say I should be happier if I had."

"Not a doubt on't, my dear."

"What would you recommend, ma'am?"

"I should say dressmakin' was rather in your line, ain't it? Your clothes is dreadful tasty, and do you credit if you made 'em yourself," and Aunt Plumy surveyed with feminine interest the simple elegance of the travelling dress which was the masterpiece of a French modiste.

"No, ma'am, I don't make my own things, I'm too lazy. It takes so much time and trouble to select them that I have only strength left to wear them."

"Housekeepin' used to be the favorite perfessun in my day. It ain't fashionable now, but it needs a sight of trainin' to be perfect in all that's required, and I've an idee it would be sight healthier and usefuller than the paintin' and music and fancy work young women do nowadays."

"But every one wants some beauty in their lives, and each one has a different sphere to fill, if one can only find it."

"'Pears to me there's no call for so much art when nater is full of beauty for them that can see and love it. As for 'spears' and so on, I've a notion if each of us did up our own little chores smart and thorough we needn't go wanderin' round to set the world to rights. That's the Lord's job, and I presume to say He can do it without any advice of ourn."

Something in the homely but true words seemed to rebuke the three listeners for wasted lives, and for a moment there was no sound but the crackle of the fire, the brisk click of the old lady's knitting needles, and Ruth's voice singing overhead as she made ready to join the party below.

"To judge by that sweet sound you have done one of your 'chores' very beautifully, Mrs. Basset, and in spite of the follies of our day, succeeded in keeping one girl healthy, happy and unspoiled," said Emily, looking up into the peaceful old face with her own lovely one full of respect and envy.

"I do hope so, for she's my ewe lamb, the last of four dear little girls; all the rest are in the burying ground 'side of father. I don't expect to keep her long, and don't ought to regret when I lose her, for Saul is the best of sons; but daughters is more to mothers somehow, and I always yearn over girls that is left without a broodin' wing to keep 'em safe and warm in this world of tribulation."

Aunt Plumy laid her hand on Sophie's head as she spoke, with such a motherly look that both girls drew nearer, and Randal resolved to put her in a book without delay.

Presently Saul returned with little Ruth hanging on his arm and shyly nestling near him as he took the three-cornered leathern chair in the chimney nook, while she sat on a stool close by. "Now the circle is complete and the picture perfect. Don't light the lamps yet, please, but talk away and let me make a mental study of you. I seldom find so charming a scene to paint," said Randal, beginning to enjoy himself immensely, with a true artist's taste for novelty and effect.

"Tell us about your book, for we have been reading it as it comes out in the magazine, and are much exercised about how it's going to end," began Saul, gallantly throwing himself into the breach for a momentary embarrassment fell upon the women at the idea of sitting for their portraits before they were ready.

"Do you really read my poor serial up here, and do me the honor to like it?" asked the novelist both flattered and amused, for his work was of the aesthetic sort, microscopic studies of character, and careful pictures of modern life.

"Sakes alive, why shouldn't we?" cried Aunt Plumy. "We have some eddication, though we ain't very genteel. We've got a town libry, kep up by the women mostly, with fairs and tea parties and so on. We have all the magazines reg'lar and Saul reads out the pieces while Ruth sews and I knit, my eyes bein' poor. Our winter is long and evenins would be kinder lonesome if we didn't have novils and newspapers to cheer 'em up."

"I am very glad I can help to beguile them for you. Now tell me what you honestly think of my work? Criticism is always valuable, and I should really like yours, Mrs. Basset," said Randal, wondering what the good woman would make of the delicate analysis and worldly wisdom on which he prided himself.

Short work, as Aunt Plumy soon showed him, for she rather enjoyed freeing her mind at all times and decidedly resented the insinuation that country folk could not appreciate light literature as well as city people.

"I ain't no great of a jedge about anything but nat'ralness of books, and it really does seem as if some of your men and women was dreadful uncomfortable creaters. 'Pears to me it ain't wise to be always pickin' ourselves to pieces and pryin' into things that ought to come gradual by way of experience and the visitations of Providence. Flowers won't blow worth a cent ef you pull 'em open. Better wait and see what they can do alone. I do relish the smart sayins, the odd ways of furrin parts, and the sarcastic slaps at folkses weak spots. But massy knows, we can't live on spice-cake and Charlotte Ruche, and I do feel as if books was more sustainin' ef they was full of every-day people and things, like good bread and butter. Them that goes to the heart and ain't soon forgotten is the kind I hanker for. Mis Terry's books now, and Mis Stowe's, and Dickens's Christmas pieces,—them is real sweet and cheerin', to my mind."

As the blunt old lady paused it was evident she had produced a sensation, for Saul smiled at the fire, Ruth looked dismayed at this assault upon one of her idols, and the young ladies were both astonished and amused at the keenness of the new critic who dared express what they had often felt. Randal, however, was quite composed and laughed good-naturedly, though secretly feeling as if a pail of cold water had been poured over him.

"Many thanks, madam; you have discovered my weak point with surprising accuracy. But you see I cannot help 'picking folks to pieces,' as you have expressed it; that is my gift, and it has its attractions, as the sale of my books will testify. People like the 'spice-bread,' and as that is the only sort my oven will bake, I must keep on in order to make my living."

"So rumsellers say, but it ain't a good trade to foller, and I'd chop wood 'fore I'd earn my livin' harmin' my feller man. 'Pears to me I'd let my oven cool a spell, and hunt up some homely, happy folks to write about; folks that don't borrer trouble and go lookin' for holes in their neighbors' coats, but take their lives brave and cheerful; and rememberin' we are all human, have pity on the weak, and try to be as full of mercy, patience and lovin' kindness as Him who made us. That sort of a book would do a heap of good; be real warmin' and strengthenin', and make them that read it love the man that wrote it, and remember him when he was dead and gone."

"I wish I could!" and Randal meant what he said, for

he was as tired of his own style as a watch-maker might be of the magnifying glass through which he strains his eyes all day. He knew that the heart was left out of his work, and that both mind and soul were growing morbid with dwelling on the faulty, absurd and meta-physical phases of life and character. He often threw down his pen and vowed he would write no more; but he loved ease and the books brought money readily; he was accustomed to the stimulant of praise and missed it as the toper misses his wine, so that which had once been a pleasure to himself and others was fast becom-ing a burden and a disappointment.

The brief pause which followed his involuntary betrayal of discontent was broken by Ruth, who ex-claimed, with a girlish enthusiasm that overpowered girlish bashfulness,—

"*I* think all the novels are splendid! I hope you will write hundreds more, and I shall live to read 'em."

"Bravo, my gentle champion! I promise that I will write one more at least, and have a heroine in it whom your mother will both admire and love," answered Randal, surprised to find how grateful he was for the girl's approval, and how rapidly his trained fancy began to paint the background on which he hoped to copy this fresh, human daisy.

Abashed by her involuntary outburst, Ruth tried to efface herself behind Saul's broad shoulder, and he brought the conversation back to its starting-point by saying in a tone of the most sincere interest,—

"Speaking of the serial, I am very anxious to know how your hero comes out. He is a fine fellow, and I can't decide whether he is going to spoil his life marry-ing that silly woman, or do something grand and generous, and not be made a fool of."

"Upon my soul, I don't know myself. It is very hard to find new finales. Can't you suggest something, Major? then I shall not be obliged to leave my story without an end, as people complain I am rather fond of doing."

"Well, no, I don't think I've anything to offer. Seems to me it isn't the sensational exploits that show the hero best, but some great sacrifice quietly made by a common sort of man who is noble without knowing it. I saw a good many such during the war, and often wish I could write them down, for it is surprising how much courage, goodness and real piety is stowed away in common folks ready to show when the right time comes."

"Tell us one of them, and I'll bless you for a hint. No one knows the anguish of an author's spirit when he can't ring down the curtain on an effective tableau," said Randal, with a glance at his friends to ask their aid in eliciting an anecdote or reminiscence.

"Tell about the splendid fellow who held the bridge, like Horatius, till help came up. That was a thrilling story, I assure you," answered Sophie, with an inviting smile.

But Saul would not be his own hero, and said briefly:

"Any man can be brave when the battle-fever is on him, and it only takes a little physical courage to dash ahead." He paused a moment, with his eyes on the snowy landscape without, where twilight was deepening; then, as if constrained by the memory that winter scene evoked, he slowly continued,—

"One of the bravest things I ever knew was done by a poor fellow who has been a hero to me ever since, though I only met him that night. It was after one of the big battles of that last winter, and I was knocked

194

over with a broken leg and two or three bullets here and there. Night was coming on, snow falling, and a sharp wind blew over the field where a lot of us lay, dead and alive, waiting for the ambulance to come and pick us up. There was skirmishing going on not far off, and our prospects were rather poor between frost and fire. I was calculating how I'd manage, when I found too poor chaps close by who were worse off, so I braced up and did what I could for them. One had an arm blown away, and kept up a dreadful groaning. The other was shot bad, and bleeding to death for want of help, but never complained. He was nearest, and I liked his pluck, for he spoke cheerful and made me ashamed to growl. Such times make dreadful brutes of men if they haven't something to hold on to, and all three of us were most wild with pain and cold and hunger, for we'd fought all day fasting, when we heard a rumble in the road below, and saw lanterns bobbing round. That meant life to us, and we all tried to holler; two of us were pretty faint but I managed a good yell, and they heard it.

"'Room for one more. Hard luck, old boys, but we are full and must save the worst wounded first. Take a drink, and hold on till we come back,' says one of them with the stretcher.

"'Here's the one to go,' I says, pointin' out my man, for I saw by the light that he was hard hit.

"'No, that one. He's got more chances than I, or this one; he's young and got a mother; I'll wait,' said the good feller, touchin' my arm, for he'd heard me mutterin' to myself about this dear old lady. We always want mother when we are down, you know."

Saul's eyes turned to the beloved face with a glance of tenderest affection, and Aunt Plumy answered with a dismal groan at the recollection of his need that night, and her absence.

"Well, to be short, the groaning chap was taken, and my man left. I was mad, but there was no time for talk, and the selfish one went off and left that poor feller to run his one chance. I had my rifle, and guessed I could hobble up to use it if need be; so we settled back to wait without much hope of help, everything being in a muddle. And wait we did till morning, for that ambulance did not come back till next day, when most of us were past needing it.

"I'll never forget that night. I dream it all over again as plain as if it was real. Snow, cold, darkness, hunger, thirst, pain, and all round us cries and cursing growing less and less, till at last only the wind went moaning over that meadow. It was awful! so lonesome, helpless, and seemingly God-forsaken. Hour after hour we lay there side by side under one coat, waiting to be saved or die, for the wind grew strong and we grew weak."

Saul drew a long breath, and held his hands to the fire as if he felt again the sharp suffering of that night.

"And the man?" asked Emily, softly, as if reluctant to break the silence.

"He was a man! In times like that men talk like brothers and show what they are. Lying there, slowly freezing, Joe Cummings told me about his wife and babies, his old folks waiting for him, all depending on him, yet all ready to give him up when he was needed. A plain man, but honest and true, and loving as a woman; I soon saw that as he went on talking, half to me and half to himself, for sometimes he wandered a little toward the end. I've read books, heard sermons, and seen good folks, but nothing ever came so close or did me so much good as seeing this man die. He had one chance and gave it cheerfully. He longed for those he loved, and let 'em go with a good-by they couldn't hear. He suffered all the pains we most shrink from without a murmur, and kept my heart warm while his own was growing cold. It's no use trying to tell that part of it; but I heard prayers that night that meant something, and I saw how faith could hold a soul up when everything was gone but God."

Saul stopped there with a sudden huskiness in his deep voice, and when he went on it was in the tone of one who speaks of a dear friend.

"Joe grew still by and by, and I thought he was asleep, for I felt his breath when I tucked him up; and his hand held on to mine. The cold sort of numbed me, and I dropped off, too weak and stupid to think or feel. I never should have waked up if it hadn't been for Joe. When I came to, it was morning, and I thought I was dead, for all I could see was that great field of white mounds, like graves, and a splendid sky above. Then I looked for Joe, remembering; but he had put my coat back over me, and lay stiff and still under the snow that covered him like a shroud, all except his face. A bit of my cape had blown over it, and when I took it off and the sun shone on his dead face, I declare to you it was so full of heavenly peace I felt as if that common man had been glorified by God's light, and rewarded by God's 'Well done.' That's all."

No one spoke for a moment, while the women wiped their eyes, and Saul dropped his as if to hide something softer than tears.

"It was very noble, very touching. And you? how did you get off at last?" asked Randal, with real admiration and respect in his usually languid face.

"Crawled off," answered Saul, relapsing into his former brevity of speech.

"Why not before, and save yourself all that misery?"

"Couldn't leave Joe."

"Ah, I see; there were two heroes that night."

"Dozens, I've no doubt. Those were times that made heroes of men, and women, too."

"Tell us more;" begged Emily, looking up with an expression none of her admirers ever brought to her face by their softest compliments or wiliest gossip.

"I've done my part. It's Mr. Randal's turn now," and Saul drew himself out of the ruddy circle of firelight, as if ashamed of the prominent part he was playing.

Sophie and her friend had often heard Randal talk, for he was an accomplished *raconteur*, but that night he exerted himself, and was unusually brilliant and entertaining, as if upon his mettle. The Bassets were charmed. They sat late and were very merry, for Aunt Plumy got up a little supper for them, and her cider was as exhilarating as champagne. When they parted for the night and Sophie kissed her aunt, Emily did the same, saying heartily,—

"It seems as if I'd known you all my life, and this is certainly the most enchanting old place that ever was."

"Glad you like it, dear. But it ain't all fun, as you'll find out to-morrow when you go to work, for Sophie says you must," answered Mrs. Basset, as her guests trooped away, rashly promising to like everything.

They found it difficult to keep their word when they were called at half past six next morning. Their rooms were warm, however, and they managed to scramble down in time for breakfast, guided by the fragrance of coffee and Aunt Plumy's shrill voice singing the good old hymn—

*"Lord, in the morning Thou shalt hear
My voice ascending high."*

An open fire blazed on the hearth, for the cooking was done in the lean-to, and the spacious, sunny kitchen was kept in all its old-fashioned perfection, with the wooden settle in a warm nook, the tall clock behind the door, copper and pewter utensils shining on the dresser, old china in the corner closet and a little spinning wheel rescued from the garret by Sophie to adorn the deep window, full of scarlet geraniums, Christmas roses, and white chrysanthemums.

The young lady, in a checked apron and mobcap, greeted her friends with a dish of buckwheats in one hand, and a pair of cheeks that proved she had been learning to fry these delectable cakes.

"You do 'keep it up' in earnest, upon my word; and very becoming it is, dear. But won't you ruin your complexion and roughen your hands if you do so much of this new fancy-work?" asked Emily, much amazed at this novel freak.

"I like it, and really believe I've found my proper sphere at last. Domestic life seems so pleasant to me that I feel as if I'd better keep it up for the rest of my life," answered Sophie, making a pretty picture of herself as she cut great slices of brown bread, with the early sunshine touching her happy face.

"The charming Miss Vaughan in the role of a farmer's wife. I find it difficult to imagine, and shrink from the thought of the wide-spread dismay such a fate will produce among her adorers," added Randal, as he basked in the glow of the hospitable fire.

"She might do worse; but come to breakfast and do honor to my handiwork," said Sophie, thinking of her worn-out millionnaire, and rather nettled by the satiric smile on Randal's lips.

"What an appetite early rising gives one. I feel equal to almost anything, so let me help wash cups," said Emily, with unusual energy, when the hearty meal was over and Sophie began to pick up the dishes as if it was her usual work.

Ruth went to the window to water the flowers, and Randal followed to make himself agreeable, remembering her defence of him last night. He was used to admiration from feminine eyes, and flattery from soft lips, but found something new and charming in the innocent delight which showed itself at his approach in blushes more eloquent than words, and shy glances from eyes full of hero-worship.

"I hope you are going to spare me a posy for tomorrow night, since I can be fine in no other way to do honor to the dance Miss Sophie proposes for us," he said, leaning in the bay window to look down on the little girl, with the devoted air he usually wore for pretty women.

"Anything you like! I should be so glad to have you wear my flowers. There will be enough for all, and I've nothing else to give to people who have made me as happy as cousin Sophie and you," answered Ruth, half drowning her great calla as she spoke with grateful warmth.

"You must make her happy by accepting the invitation to go home with her which I heard given last night. A peep at the world would do you good, and be a pleasant change, I think."

"Oh, very pleasant! but would it do me good?" and Ruth looked up with sudden seriousness in her blue eyes, as a child questions an elder, eager, yet wistful.

"Why not?" asked Randal, wondering at the hesitation.

"I might grow discontented with things here if I saw splendid houses and fine people. I am very happy now, and it would break my heart to lose that happiness, or ever learn to be ashamed of home."

"But don't you long for more pleasure, new scenes and other friends than these?" asked the man, touched by the little creature's loyalty to the things she knew and loved.

"Very often, but mother says when I'm ready they will come, so I wait and try not to be impatient." But Ruth's eyes looked out over the green leaves as if the longing was very strong within her to see more of the unknown world lying beyond the mountains that hemmed her in.

"It is natural for birds to hop out of the nest, so I shall expect to see you over there before long, and ask you how you enjoy your first flight," said Randal, in a paternal tone that had a curious effect on Ruth.

To his surprise, she laughed, then blushed like one of her own roses, and answered with a demure dignity that was very pretty to see.

"I intend to hop soon, but it won't be a very long flight or very far from mother. She can't spare me, and nobody in the world can fill her place to me."

"Bless the child, does she think I'm going to make love to her," thought Randal, much amused, but quite mistaken. Wiser women had thought so when he assumed the caressing air with which he beguiled them into the little revelations of character he liked to use, as the south wind makes flowers open their hearts to give up their odor, then leaves them to carry it elsewhere, the more welcome for the stolen sweetness.

"Perhaps you are right. The maternal wing is a safe shelter for confiding little souls like you, Miss Ruth. You will be as comfortable here as your flowers in this sunny window," he said, carelessly pinching geranium leaves, and ruffling the roses till the pink petals of the largest fluttered to the floor.

As if she instinctively felt and resented something in the man which his act symbolized, the girl answered quietly, as she went on with her work, "Yes, if the frost does not touch me, or careless people spoil me too soon."

Before Randal could reply Aunt Plumy approached like a maternal hen who sees her chicken in danger.

"Saul is goin' to haul wood after he's done his chores, mebbe you'd like to go along? The view is good, the roads well broke, and the day uncommon fine."

"Thanks; it will be delightful, I dare say," politely responded the lion, with a secret shudder at the idea of a rural promenade at 8 A. M. in the winter.

"Come on, then; we'll feed the stock, and then I'll show you how to yoke oxen," said Saul, with a twinkle in his eye as he led the way, when his new aide had muffled himself up as if for a polar voyage.

"Now, that's too bad of Saul! He did it on purpose, just to please you, Sophie," cried Ruth presently, and the girls ran to the window to behold Randal bravely following his host with a pail of pigs' food in each hand, and an expression of resigned disgust upon his aristocratic face.

"To what base uses may we come," quoted Emily, as they all nodded and smiled upon the victim as he looked back from the barn-yard, where he was clamorously welcomed by his new charges.

"It is rather a shock at first, but it will do him good,

and Saul won't be too hard upon him, I'm sure," said Sophie, going back to her work, while Ruth turned her best buds to the sun that they might be ready for a peace-offering tomorrow.

There was a merry clatter in the big kitchen for an hour; then Aunt Plumy and her daughter shut themselves up in the pantry to perform some culinary rites, and the young ladies went to inspect certain antique costumes laid forth in Sophie's room.

"You see, Em, I thought it would be appropriate to the house and season to have an old-fashioned dance. Aunt has quantities of ancient finery stowed away, for great-grandfather Basset was a fine old gentleman and his family lived in state. Take your choice of the crimson, blue or silver-gray damask. Ruth is to wear the worked muslin and quilted white satin skirt, with that coquettish hat."

"Being dark, I'll take the red and trim it up with this fine lace. You must wear the blue and primrose, with the distracting high-heeled shoes. Have you any suits for the men?" asked Emily, throwing herself at once into the all-absorbing matter of costume.

"A claret velvet coat and vest, silk stockings, cocked hat and snuff-box for Randal. Nothing large enough for Saul, so he must wear his uniform. Won't Aunt Plumy be superb in this plum-colored satin and immense cap?"

A delightful morning was spent in adapting the faded finery of the past to the blooming beauty of the present, and time and tongues flew till the toot of a horn called them down to dinner.

The girls were amazed to see Randal come whistling up the road with his trousers tucked into his boots, blue mittens on his hands, and an unusual amount of energy in his whole figure, as he drove the oxen, while Saul laughed at his vain attempts to guide the bewildered beasts.

"It's immense! The view from the hill is well worth seeing, for the snow glorifies the landscape and reminds one of Switzerland. I'm going to make a sketch of it this afternoon; better come and enjoy the delicious freshness, young ladies."

Randal was eating with such an appetite that he did not see the glances the girls exchanged as they promised to go.

"Bring home some more winter-green, I want things to be real nice, and we haven't enough for the kitchen," said Ruth, dimpling with girlish delight as she imagined herself dancing under the green garlands in her grandmother's wedding gown.

It was very lovely on the hill, for far as the eye could reach lay the wintry landscape sparkling with the brief beauty of sunshine on virgin snow. Pines sighed overhead, hardy birds flitted to and fro, and in all the trodden spots rose the little spires of evergreen ready for its Christmas duty. Deeper in the wood sounded the measured ring of axes, the crash of falling trees, while the red shirts of the men added color to the scene, and a fresh wind brought the aromatic breath of newly cloven hemlock and pine.

"How beautiful it is! I never knew before what winter woods were like. Did you, Sophie?" asked Emily, sitting on a stump to enjoy the novel pleasure at her ease.

"I've found out lately; Saul lets me come as often as I like, and this fine air seems to make a new creature of me," answered Sophie, looking about her with sparkling eyes, as if this was a kingdom where she reigned supreme.

"Something is making a new creature of you, that is very evident. I haven't yet discovered whether it is the air or some magic herb among that green stuff you are gathering so diligently;" and Emily laughed to see the color deepen beautifully in her friend's half-averted face.

"Scarlet is the only wear just now, I find. If we are lost like babes in the woods there are plenty of red-breasts to cover us with leaves," and Randal joined Emily's laugh, with a glance at Saul, who had just pulled his coat off.

"You wanted to see this tree go down, so stand from under and I'll show you how it's done," said the farmer, taking up his axe, not unwilling to gratify his guests and display his manly accomplishments at the same time.

It was a fine sight, the stalwart man swinging his axe with magnificent strength and skill, each blow sending a thrill through the stately tree, till its heart was reached and it tottered to its fall. Never pausing for breath Saul shook his yellow mane out of his eyes, and hewed away, while the drops stood on his forehead and his arm ached, as bent on distinguishing himself as if he had been a knight tilting against his rival for his lady's favor.

"I don't know which to admire most, the man or his muscle. One doesn't often see such vigor, size and comeliness in these degenerate days," said Randal, mentally booking the fine figure in the red shirt.

"I think we have discovered a rough diamond. I only wonder if Sophie is going to try and polish it," answered Emily, glancing at her friend, who stood a little apart, watching the rise and fall of the axe as intently as if her fate depended on it.

Down rushed the tree at last, and, leaving them to

examine a crow's nest in its branches, Saul went off to his men, as if he found the praises of his prowess rather too much for him.

Randal fell to sketching, the girls to their garland-making, and for a little while the sunny woodland nook was full of lively chat and pleasant laughter, for the air exhilarated them all like wine. Suddenly a man came running from the wood, pale and anxious, saying, as he hastened by for help, "Blasted tree fell on him! Bleed to death before the doctor comes!"

"Who? who?" cried the startled trio.

But the man ran on, with some breathless reply, in which only a name was audible—"Basset."

"The deuce it is!" and Randal dropped his pencil, while the girls sprang up in dismay. Then, with one impulse, they hastened to the distant group, half visible behind the fallen trees and corded wood.

Sophie was there first, and forcing her way through the little crowd of men, saw a redshirted figure on the ground, crushed and bleeding, and threw herself down beside it with a cry that pierced the hearts of those who heard it.

In the act she saw it was not Saul, and covered her bewildered face as if to hide its joy. A strong arm lifted her, and the familiar voice said cheeringly,—

"I'm all right, dear. Poor Bruce is hurt, but we've sent for help. Better go right home and forget all about it."

"Yes, I will, if I can do nothing;" and Sophie meekly returned to her friends who stood outside the circle over which Saul's head towered, assuring them of his safety.

Hoping they had not seen her agitation, she led

Emily away, leaving Randal to give what aid he could
and bring them news of the poor wood-chopper's state.

Aunt Plumy produced the "camphire" the moment
she saw Sophie's pale face, and made her lie down,
while the brave old lady trudged briskly off with ban-
dages and brandy to the scene of action. On her return
she brought comfortable news of the man, so the little
flurry blew over and was forgotten by all but Sophie,
who remained pale and quiet all the evening, tying
evergreen as if her life depended on it.

"A good night's sleep will set her up. She ain't used
to such things, dear child, and needs cosseting'," said
Aunt Plumy, purring over her until she was in her bed,
with a hot stone at her feet and a bowl of herb tea to
quiet her nerves.

An hour later when Emily went up, she peeped in to
see if Sophie was sleeping nicely, and was surprised
to find the invalid wrapped in a dressing-gown writing
busily.

"Last will and testament, or sudden inspiration,
dear? How are you? faint or feverish, delirious or in the
dumps! Saul looks so anxious, and Mrs. Basset hushes
us all up so, I came to bed, leaving Randal to entertain
Ruth."

As she spoke Emily saw the papers disappear in a
portfolio, and Sophie rose with a yawn.

"I was writing letters, but I'm sleepy now. Quite over
my foolish fright, thank you. Go and get your beauty
sleep that you may dazzle the natives to-morrow."

"So glad, good night;" and Emily went away, saying
to herself, "Something is going on, and I must find out
what it is before I leave. Sophie can't blind me."

But Sophie did all the next day, being delightfully

gay at the dinner, and devoting herself to the young minister who was invited to meet the distinguished novelist, and evidently being afraid of him, gladly basked in the smiles of his charming neighbor. A dashing sleigh-ride occupied the afternoon, and then great was the fun and excitement over the costumes.

Aunt Plumy laughed till the tears rolled down her cheeks as the girls compressed her into the plum-colored gown with its short waist, leg-of-mutton sleeves, and narrow skirt. But a worked scarf hid all deficiencies, and the towering cap struck awe into the soul of the most frivolous observer.

"Keep an eye on me; girls, for I shall certainly split somewheres or lose my head-piece off when I'm trottin' round. What would my blessed mother say if she could see me rigged out in her best things?" and with a smile and a sigh the old lady departed to look after "the boys," and see that the supper was all right.

Three prettier damsels never tripped down the wide staircase than the brilliant brunette in crimson brocade, the pensive blonde in blue, or the rosy little bride in old muslin and white satin.

A gallant court gentleman met them in the hall with a superb bow, and escorted them to the parlor, where Grandma Basset's ghost was discovered dancing with a modern major in full uniform.

Mutual admiration and many compliments followed, till other ancient ladies and gentlemen arrived in all manner of queer costumes, and the old house seemed to wake from its humdrum quietude to sudden music and merriment, as if a past generation had returned to keep its Christmas there.

The village fiddler soon struck up the good old tunes,

and then the strangers saw dancing that filled them with mingled mirth and envy; it was so droll, yet so hearty. The young men, unusually awkward in their grand-fathers' kneebreeches, flapping vests, and swallow-tail coats, footed it bravely with the buxom girls who were the prettier for their quaintness, and danced with such vigor that their high combs stood awry, their furbelows waved wildly, and their cheeks were as red as their breast-knots, or hose.

It was impossible to stand still, and one after the other the city folk yielded to the spell, Randal leading off with Ruth, Sophie swept away by Saul, and Emily being taken possession of by a young giant of eighteen, who spun her around with a boyish impetuosity that took her breath away. Even Aunt Plumy was discovered jigging it alone in the pantry, as if the music was too much for her, and the plates and glasses jingled gaily on the shelves in time to Money Musk and Fishers' Hornpipe.

A pause came at last, however, and fans fluttered, heated brows were wiped, jokes were made, lovers exchanged confidences, and every nook and corner held a man and maid carrying on the sweet game which is never out of fashion. There was a glitter of gold lace in the back entry, and a train of blue and primrose shone in the dim light. There was a richer crimson than that of the geraniums in the deep window, and a dainty shoe tapped the bare floor impatiently as the brilliant black eyes looked everywhere for the court gentleman, while their owner listened to the gruff prattle of an enamored boy. But in the upper hall walked a little white ghost as if waiting for some shadowy companion, and when a dark form appeared ran to take its arm, saying, in a tone of soft satisfaction,—

"I was so afraid you wouldn't come!"

"Why did you leave me, Ruth?" answered a manly voice in a tone of surprise, though the small hand slipping from the velvet coat-sleeve was replaced as if it was pleasant to feel it there.

A pause, and then the other voice answered demurely,—

"Because I was afraid my head would be turned by the fine things you were saying."

"It is impossible to help saying what one feels to such an artless little creature as you are. It does me good to admire anything so fresh and sweet, and won't harm you."

"It might if—"

"If what, my daisy?"

"I believed it," and a laugh seemed to finish the broken sentence better than the words.

"You may, Ruth, for I do sincerely admire the most genuine girl I have seen for a long time. And walking here with you in your bridal white I was just asking myself if I should not be a happier man with a home of my own and a little wife hanging on my arm than drifting about the world as I do now with only myself to care for."

"I know you would!" and Ruth spoke so earnestly that Randal was both touched and startled, fearing he had ventured too far in a mood of unwonted sentiment, born of the romance of the hour and the sweet frankness of his companion.

"Then you don't think it would be rash for some sweet woman to take me in hand and make me happy, since fame is a failure?"

"Oh, no; it would be easy work if she loved you. I know some one—if I only dared to tell her name."

"Upon my soul, this is cool," and Randal looked down, wondering if the audacious lady on his arm could be shy Ruth.

If he had seen the malicious merriment in her eyes he would have been more humiliated still, but they were modestly averted, and the face under the little hat was full of a soft agitation rather dangerous even to a man of the world.

"She is a captivating little creature, but it is too soon for anything but a mild flirtation. I must delay further innocent revelations or I shall do something rash."

While making this excellent resolution Randal had been pressing the hand upon his arm and gently pacing down the dimly lighted hall with the sound of music in his ears, Ruth's sweetest roses in his button-hole, and a loving little girl beside him, as he thought.

"You shall tell me by and by when we are in town. I am sure you will come, and meanwhile don't forget me."

"I am going in the spring, but I shall not be with Sophie," answered Ruth, in a whisper.

"With whom then? I shall long to see you."

"With my husband. I am to be married in May."

"The deuce you are!" escaped Randal, as he stopped short to stare at his companion, sure she was not in earnest.

But she was, for as he looked the sound of steps coming up the back stairs made her whole face flush and brighten with the unmistakable glow of happy love, and she completed Randal's astonishment by running into the arms of the young minister, saying with an irrepressible laugh, "Oh, John, why didn't you come before?"

The court gentleman was all right in a moment, and

the coolest of the three as he offered his congratulations and gracefully retired leaving the lovers to enjoy the tryst he had delayed. But as he went down stairs his brows were knit, and he slapped the broad railing smartly with his cocked hat as if some irritation must find vent in a more energetic way than merely saying, "Confound the little baggage!" under his breath.

Such an amazing supper came from Aunt Plumy's big pantry that the city guests could not eat for laughing at the queer dishes circulating through the rooms, and copiously partaken of by the hearty young folks.

Doughnuts and cheese, pie and pickles, cider and tea, baked beans and custards, cake and cold turkey, bread and butter, plum pudding and French bonbons, Sophie's contribution.

"May I offer you the native delicacies, and share your plate? Both are very good, but the china has run short, and after such vigorous exercise as you have had you must need refreshment. I'm sure I do!" said Randal, bowing before Emily with a great blue platter laden with two doughnuts, two wedges of pumpkin pie and two spoons.

The smile with which she welcomed him, the alacrity with which she made room beside her and seemed to enjoy the supper he brought, was so soothing to his ruffled spirit that he soon began to feel that there is no friend like an old friend, that it would not be difficult to name a sweet woman who would take him in hand and would make him happy if he cared to ask her, and he began to think he would by and by, it was so pleasant to sit in that green corner with waves of crimson brocade flowing over his feet, and a fine face softening beautifully under his eyes.

The supper was not romantic, but the situation was,

and Emily found that pie ambrosial food eaten with the man she loved, whose eyes talked more eloquently than the tongue just then busy with a doughnut. Ruth kept away, but glanced at them as she served her company, and her own happy experience helped her to see that all was going well in that quarter. Saul and Sophie emerged from the back entry with shining countenances, but carefully avoided each other for the rest of the evening. No one observed this but Aunt Plumy from the recesses of her pantry and she folded her hands as if well content as she murmured fervently over a pan full of crullers, "Bless the dears! Now I can die happy."

Every one thought Sophie's old-fashioned dress immensely becoming, and several of his former men said to Saul with blunt admiration, "Major, you look to-night as you used to after we'd gained a big battle."

"I feel as if I had," answered the splendid Major, with eyes much brighter than his buttons, and a heart under them infinitely prouder than when he was promoted on the field of honor, for his Waterloo was won.

There was more dancing, followed by games, in which Aunt Plumy shone pre-eminent, for the supper was off her mind and she could enjoy herself. There were shouts of merriment as the blithe old lady twirled the platter, hunted the squirrel, and went to Jerusalem like a girl of sixteen; her cap in a ruinous condition, and every seam of the purple dress straining like sails in a gale. It was great fun, but at midnight it came to an end, and the young folks, still bubbling over with innocent jollity, went jingling away along the snowy hills, unanimously pronouncing Mrs. Basset's party the best of the season.

"Never had such a good time in my life!" exclaimed Sophie, as the family stood together in the kitchen where the candles among the wreaths were going out, and the floor was strewn with wrecks of past joy.

"I'm proper glad, dear. Now you all go to bed and lay as late as you like to-morrow. I'm so kinder worked up I couldn't sleep, so Saul and me will put things to rights without a mite of noise to disturb you;" and Aunt Plumy sent them off with a smile that was a benediction Sophie thought.

"The dear old soul speaks as if midnight was an unheard-of hour for Christians to be up. What would she say if she knew how we seldom go to bed till dawn in the ball season? I'm so wide awake I've half a mind to pack a little. Randal must go at two, he says, and we shall want his escort," said Emily, as the girls laid away their brocades in the press in Sophie's room. "I'm not going. Aunt can't spare me, and there is nothing to go for yet," answered Sophie, beginning to take the white chrysanthemums out of her pretty hair.

"My dear child, you will die of ennui up here. Very nice for a week or so, but frightful for a winter. We are going to be very gay, and cannot get on without you," cried Emily dismayed at the suggestion.

"You will have to, for I'm not coming. I am very happy here, and so tired of the frivolous life I lead in town, that I have decided to try a better one," and Sophie's mirror reflected a face full of the sweetest content.

"Have you lost your mind? experienced religion? or any other dreadful thing? You always were odd, but this last freak is the strangest of all. What will your guardian say, and the world?" added Emily in the awe-stricken tone of one who stood in fear of the omnipotent Mrs. Grundy.

"Guardy will be glad to be rid of me, and I don't care that for the world," cried Sophie, snapping her fingers with a joyful sort of recklessness which completed Emily's bewilderment.

"But Mr. Hammond? Are you going to throw away millions, lose your chance of making the best match in the city, and driving the girls of our set out of their wits with envy?"

Sophie laughed at her friend's despairing cry, and turning round said quietly,—

"I wrote to Mr. Hammond last night, and this evening received my reward for being an honest girl. Saul and I are to be married in the spring when Ruth is."

Emily fell prone upon the bed as if the announcement was too much for her, but was up again in an instant to declare with prophetic solemnity,—

"I knew something was going on, but hoped to get you away before you were lost. Sophie, you will repent. Be warned, and forget this sad delusion."

"Too late for that. The pang I suffered yesterday when I thought Saul was dead showed me how well I loved him. To-night he asked me to stay, and no power in the world can part us. Oh! Emily, it is all so sweet, so beautiful, that *everything* is possible, and I know I shall be happy in this dear old home, full of love and peace and honest hearts. I only hope you may find as true and tender a man to live for as my Saul."

Sophie's face was more eloquent than her fervent words, and Emily beautifully illustrated the inconsistency of her sex by suddenly embracing her friend, with the incoherent exclamation, "I think I have, dear! Your brave Saul is worth a dozen old Hammonds, and I do believe you are right."

It is unnecessary to tell how, as if drawn by the irresistible magic of sympathy, Ruth and her mother crept in one by one to join the midnight conference and add their smiles and tears, tender hopes and proud delight to the joys of that memorable hour. Nor how Saul, unable to sleep, mounted guard below, and meeting Randal prowling down to soothe his nerves with a surreptitious cigar found it impossible to help confiding to his attentive ear the happiness that would break bounds and overflow in unusual eloquence.

Peace fell upon the old house at last, and all slept as if some magic herb had touched their eyelids, bringing blissful dreams and a glad awakening.

"Can't we persuade you to come with us, Miss Sophie?" asked Randal next day, as they made their adieux.

"I'm under orders now, and dare not disobey my superior officer," answered Sophie, handing her Major his driving gloves, with a look which plainly showed that she had joined the great army of devoted women who enlist for life and ask no pay but love.

"I shall depend on being invited to your wedding, then, and yours, too, Miss Ruth," added Randal, shaking hands with "the little baggage," as if he had quite forgiven her mockery and forgotten his own brief lapse into sentiment.

Before she could reply Aunt Plumy said, in a tone of calm conviction, that made them all laugh, and some of them look conscious,—

"Spring is a good time for weddin's, and I shouldn't wonder if there was quite a number."

"Nor I," and Saul and Sophie smiled at one another as they saw how carefully Randal arranged Emily's wraps.

Then with kisses, thanks and all the good wishes that happy hearts could imagine, the guests drove away, to remember long and gratefully that pleasant country Christmas.

E. NESBIT

The Conscience-Pudding

It was Christmas, nearly a year after Mother died. I
cannot write about Mother – but I will just say one
thing. If she had only been away for a little while, and
not for always, we shouldn't have been so keen on
having a Christmas. I didn't understand this then,
but I am much older now, and I think it was just
because everything was so different and horrid we felt
we *must* do something and perhaps we were not particular enough *what*. Things make you much more
unhappy when you loaf about than when you are doing
events.

Father had to go away just about Christmas. He had
heard that his wicked partner, who ran away with his
money, was in France, and he thought he could catch
him, but really he was in Spain, where catching criminals is never practised. We did not know this till
afterwards.

Before Father went away he took Dora and Oswald
into his study, and said –

'I'm awfully sorry I've got to go away, but it is very

serious business, and I must go. You'll be good while I'm away, kiddies, won't you?'

We promised faithfully. Then he said –

'There are reasons – you wouldn't understand if I tried to tell you – but you can't have much of a Christmas this year. But I've told Matilda to make you a good plain pudding. Perhaps next Christmas will be brighter.'

(It was; for the next Christmas saw us the affluent nephews and nieces of an Indian uncle – but that is quite another story, as good old Kipling says.)

When Father had been seen off at Lewisham Station with his bags, and a plaid rug in a strap, we came home again, and it was horrid. There were papers and things littered all over his room where he had packed. We tidied the room up – it was the only thing we could do for him. It was Dicky who accidentally broke his shaving-glass, and H.O. made a paper boat out of a letter we found out afterwards Father particularly wanted to keep. This took us some time, and when we went into the nursery the fire was black out, and we could not get it alight again, even with the whole *Daily Chronicle*. Matilda, who was our general then, was out, as well as the fire, so we went and sat in the kitchen. There is always a good fire in kitchens. The kitchen hearthrug was not nice to sit on, so we spread newspapers on it.

It was sitting in the kitchen, I think, that brought to our minds my father's parting words – about the pudding, I mean.

Oswald said, 'Father said we couldn't have much of a Christmas for secret reasons, and he said he had told Matilda to make us a plain pudding.'

The plain pudding instantly cast its shadow over the deepening gloom of our young minds.

'I wonder *how* plain she'll make it?' Dicky said. 'As plain as plain, you may depend,' said Oswald. 'A here-am-I-where-are-you pudding – that's her sort.'

The others groaned, and we gathered closer round the fire till the newspapers rustled madly.

'I believe I could make a pudding that *wasn't* plain, if I tried,' Alice said. 'Why shouldn't we?'

'No chink,' said Oswald, with brief sadness. 'How much would it cost?' Nöel asked, and added that Dora had twopence and H.O. had a French halfpenny.

Dora got the cookery-book out of the dresser drawer, where it lay doubled up among clothes-pegs, dirty dusters, scallop shells, string, penny novelettes, and the dining-room corkscrew. The general we had then – it seemed as if she did all the cooking on the cookery-book instead of on the baking-board, there were traces of so many bygone meals upon its pages.

'It doesn't say Christmas pudding at all,' said Dora.

'Try plum,' the resourceful Oswald instantly counselled.

Dora turned the greasy pages anxiously.

'"Plum-pudding, 518.

'"A rich, with flour, 517.

'"Christmas, 517.

'"Cold brandy sauce for, 241."

'We shouldn't care about that, so it's no use looking.

'"Good without eggs, 518.

'"Plain, 518."

'We don't want *that* anyhow. "Christmas, 517" – that's the one.'

It took her a long time to find the page. Oswald got a shovel of coals and made up the fire. It blazed up like the devouring elephant the *Daily Telegraph* always calls it. Then Dora read –

"'Christmas plum-pudding. Time six hours.'"

'To eat it in?' said H.O.

'No, silly! to make it.'

'Forge ahead, Dora,' Dicky replied.

Dora went on –

"'2072. One pound and a half of raisins; half a pound of currants; three-quarters of a pound of bread-crumbs; half a pound of flour; three-quarters of a pound of beef suet; nine eggs; one wine glassful of brandy; half a pound of citron and orange peel; half a nutmeg; and a little ground ginger." I wonder *how* little ground ginger.'

'A teacupful would be enough, I think,' Alice said; 'we must not be extravagant.'

'We haven't got anything yet to be extravagant *with*,' said Oswald, who had toothache that day. 'What would you do with the things if you'd got them?'

'You'd "chop the suet as fine as possible" – I wonder how fine that is?' replied Dora and the book together – '"and mix it with the bread-crumbs and flour; add the currants washed and dried.'"

'Not starched, then,' said Alice.

"'The citron and orange peel cut into thin slices" – I wonder what they call thin? Matilda's thin bread-and-butter is quite different from what I mean by it – "and the raisins stoned and divided." How many heaps would you divide them into?'

'Seven, I suppose,' said Alice, 'one for each person and one for the pot – I mean pudding.'

"'Mix it all well together with the grated nutmeg and ginger. Then stir in nine eggs well beaten, and the brandy" – we'll leave that out, I think – "and again mix it thoroughly together that every ingredient may be moistened; put it into a buttered mould, tie over tightly,

221

and boil for six hours. Serve it ornamented with holly and brandy poured over it."'

'I should think holly and brandy poured over it would be simply beastly,' said Dicky.

'I expect the book knows. I daresay holly and water would do as well though. "This pudding may be made a month before" – it's no use reading about that though, because we've only got four days to Christmas.'

'It's no use reading about any of it,' said Oswald, with thoughtful repeatedness, 'because we haven't got the things, and we haven't got the coin to get them.'

'We might get the tin somehow,' said Dicky.

'There must be lots of kind people who would subscribe to a Christmas pudding for poor children who hadn't any,' Nöel said.

'Well, I'm going skating at Penn's,' said Oswald. 'It's no use thinking about puddings. We must put up with it plain.'

So he went, and Dicky went with him.

When they returned to their home in the evening the fire had been lighted again in the nursery, and the others were just having tea. We toasted our bread-and-butter on the bare side, and it gets a little warm among the butter. This is called French toast. 'I like English better, but it is more expensive,' Alice said –

'Matilda is in a frightful rage about your putting those coals on the kitchen fire, Oswald. She says we shan't have enough to last over Christmas as it is. And Father gave her a talking to before he went about them – asked her if she ate them, she says – but I don't believe he did. Anyway, she's locked the coal-cellar door, and she's got the key in her pocket. I don't see how we can boil the pudding.'

'What pudding?' said Oswald dreamily. He was thinking of a chap he had seen at Penn's who had cut the date 1899 on the ice with four strokes.

'*The* pudding,' Alice said. 'Oh, we've had such a time, Oswald! First Dora and I went to the shops to find out exactly what the pudding would cost – it's only two and elevenpence halfpenny, counting in the holly.'

'It's no good,' Oswald repeated; he is very patient and will say the same thing any number of times. 'It's no good. You know we've got no tin.'

'Ah,' said Alice, 'but Nöel and I went out, and we called at some of the houses in Granville Park and Dartmouth Hill – and we got a lot of sixpences and shillings, besides pennies, and one old gentleman gave us half-a-crown. He was so nice. Quite bald, with a knitted red and blue waistcoat. We've got eight-and-sevenpence.'

Oswald did not feel quite sure Father would like us to go asking for shillings and sixpences, or even half-crowns from strangers, but he did not say so. The money had been asked for and got, and it couldn't be helped – and perhaps he wanted the pudding – I am not able to remember exactly why he did not speak up and say, 'This is wrong', but anyway he didn't.

Alice and Dora went out and bought the things next morning. They bought double quantities, so that it came to five shillings and eleven pence, and was enough to make a noble pudding. There was a lot of holly left over for decorations. We used very little for the sauce. The money that was left we spent very anxiously in other things to eat, such as dates and figs and toffee. We did not tell Matilda about it. She was a red-haired girl, and apt to turn shirty at the least thing.

Concealed under our jackets and overcoats, we

carried the parcels up to the nursery, and hid them in the treasure-chest we had there. It was the bureau drawer. It was locked up afterwards because the treacle got all over the green baize and the little drawers inside it while we were waiting to begin to make the pudding. It was the grocer told us we ought to put treacle in the pudding, mind also about not so much ginger as a teacupful.

When Matilda had begun to pretend to scrub the floor (she pretended this three times a week so as to have an excuse not to let us in the kitchen, but I know she used to read novelettes most of the time, because Alice and I had a squint through the window more than once), we barricaded the nursery door and set to work. We were very careful to be quite clean. We washed our hands as well as the currants. I have sometimes thought we did not get all the soap off the currants. The pudding smelt like a washing-day when the time came to cut it open. And we washed a corner of the table to chop the suet on. Chopping suet looks easy till you try.

Father's machine he weighs letters with did to weigh out the things. We did this very carefully, in case the grocer had not done so. Everything was right except the raisins. H.O. had carried them home. He was very young then, and there was a hole in the corner of the paper bag and his mouth was sticky.

Lots of people have been hanged to a gibbet in chains on evidence no worse than that, and we told H.O. so till he cried. This was good for him. It was not unkindness to H.O., but part of our duty.

Chopping suet as fine as possible is much harder than any one would think, as I said before. So is crumbling bread – especially if your loaf is new, like ours was. When we had done them the bread-crumbs and the suet were both very large and lumpy, and of a dingy grey colour, something like pale slate pencil.

They looked a better colour when we had mixed them with the flour. The girls had washed the currants with Brown Windsor soap and the sponge. Some of the currants got inside the sponge and kept coming out in the bath for days afterwards. I see now that this was not quite nice. We cut the candied peel as thin as we wish people would cut our bread-and-butter. We tried to take the stones out of the raisins, but they were too sticky, so we just divided them up in seven lots. Then we mixed the other things in the wash-hand basin from the spare bedroom that was always spare. We each put in our own lot of raisins and turned it all into a pudding-basin, and tied it up in one of Alice's pinafores, which was the nearest thing to a proper pudding-cloth we could find – at any rate clean. What was left sticking to the wash-hand basin did not taste so bad.

'It's a little bit soapy,' Alice said, 'but perhaps that will boil out; like stains in table-cloths.'

It was a difficult question how to boil the pudding. Matilda proved furious when asked to let us, just because some one had happened to knock her hat off the scullery door and Pincher had got it and done for it. However, part of the embassy nicked a saucepan while the others were being told what Matilda thought about the hat, and we got hot water out of the bathroom and made it boil over our nursery fire. We put the pudding in – it was now getting on towards the hour of tea – and let it boil. With some exceptions – owing to the fire going down, and Matilda not hurrying up with coals – it boiled for an hour and a quarter. Then Matilda came suddenly in and said, 'I'm not going to have you messing about in here with my saucepans';

and she tried to take it off the fire. You will see that we couldn't stand this; it was not likely. I do not remember who it was that told her to mind her own business, and I think I have forgotten who caught hold of her first to make her chuck it. I am sure no needless violence was used. Anyway, while the struggle progressed, Alice and Dora took the saucepan away and put it in the boot-cupboard under the stairs and put the key in their pocket.

This sharp encounter made every one very hot and cross. We got over it before Matilda did, but we brought her round before bedtime. Quarrels should always be made up before bedtime. It says so in the Bible. If this simple rule was followed there would not be so many wars and martyrs and law suits and inquisitions and bloody deaths at the stake.

All the house was still. The gas was out all over the house except on the first landing, when several darkly shrouded figures might have been observed creeping downstairs to the kitchen.

On the way, with superior precaution, we got out our saucepan. The kitchen fire was red, but low; the coal-cellar was locked, and there was nothing in the scuttle but a little coal-dust and the piece of brown paper that is put in to keep the coals from tumbling out through the bottom where the hole is. We put the saucepan on the fire and plied it with fuel – two *Chronicles*, a *Telegraph*, and two *Family Herald* novelettes were burned in vain. I am almost sure the pudding did not boil at all that night.

'Never mind,' Alice said. 'We can each nick a piece of coal every time we go into the kitchen tomorrow.'

This daring scheme was faithfully performed, and by night we had nearly half a waste-paper basket of coal, coke, and cinders. And in the depth of night once more we might have been observed, this time with our collier-like waste-paper basket in our guarded hands.

There was more fire left in the grate that night, and we fed it with the fuel we had collected. This time the fire blazed up, and the pudding boiled like mad. This was the time it boiled two hours – at least I think it was about that, but we dropped asleep on the kitchen tables and dresser. You dare not be lowly in the night in the kitchen, because of the beetles. We were aroused by a horrible smell. It was the pudding cloth burning. All the water had secretly boiled itself away. We filled it up at once with cold, and the saucepan cracked. So we cleaned it and put it back on the shelf and took another and went to bed. You see what a lot of trouble we had over the pudding. Every evening till Christmas, which had now become only the day after tomorrow, we sneaked down in the inky midnight and boiled that pudding for as long as it would.

On Christmas morning we chopped the holly for the sauce, but we put hot water (instead of brandy) and moist sugar. Some of them said it was not so bad. Oswald was not one of these.

Then came the moment when the plain pudding Father had ordered smoked upon the board. Matilda brought it in and went away at once. She had a cousin out of Woolwich Arsenal to see her that day, I remember. Those far-off days are quite distinct in memory's recollection still.

Then we got out our own pudding from its hiding-place and gave it one last hurried boil – only seven minutes, because of the general impatience which Oswald and Dora could not cope with.

We had found means to secrete a dish, and we now

tried to dish the pudding up, but it stuck to the basin, and had to be dislodged with the chisel. The pudding was horribly pale. We poured the holly sauce over it, and Dora took up the knife and was just cutting it when a few simple words from H.O. turned us from happy and triumphing cookery artists to persons in despair.

He said: 'How pleased all those kind ladies and gentlemen would be if they knew *we* were the poor children they gave the shillings and sixpences and things for!'

We all said, *'What?'* It was no moment for politeness.

'I say,' H.O. said, 'they'd be glad if they knew it was us was enjoying the pudding, and not dirty little, really poor children.'

'You should say "you were", not "you was",' said Dora, but it was as in a dream and only from habit.

'Do you mean to say' – Oswald spoke firmly, yet not angrily – 'that you and Alice went and begged for money for poor children, and then *kept* it?'

'We didn't keep it,' said H.O., 'we spent it.'

'We've kept the *things,* you little duffer!' said Dicky, looking at the pudding sitting alone and uncared for on its dish. 'You begged for money for poor children, and then *kept* it. It's stealing, that's what it is. I don't say so much about you – you're only a silly kid – but Alice knew better. Why did you do it?'

He turned to Alice, but she was now too deep in tears to get a word out.

H.O. looked a bit frightened, but he answered the question. We have taught him this. He said –

'I thought they'd give us more if I said poor children than if I said just us.'

'That's cheating,' said Dicky – 'downright beastly, mean, low cheating.'

'I'm not,' said H.O.; 'and you're another.' Then he began to cry too. I do not know how the others felt, but I understand from Oswald that he felt that now the honour of the house of Bastable had been stamped on in the dust, and it didn't matter what happened. He looked at the beastly holly that had been left over from the sauce and was stuck up over the pictures. It now appeared hollow and disgusting, though it had got quite a lot of berries, and some of it was the varied kind – green and white. The figs and dates and toffee were set out in the doll's dinner service. The very sight of it all made Oswald blush sickly. He owns he would have liked to cuff H.O., and, if he did for a moment wish to shake Alice, the author, for one, can make allowances.

Now Alice choked and spluttered, and wiped her eyes fiercely, and said, 'It's no use ragging H.O. It's my fault. I'm older than he is.'

H.O. said, 'It couldn't be Alice's fault. I don't see as it was wrong.'

'That, not as,' murmured Dora, putting her arm round the sinner who had brought this degrading blight upon our family tree, but such is girls' undetermined and affectionate silliness. 'Tell sister all about it, H.O. dear. Why couldn't it be Alice's fault?'

H.O. cuddled up to Dora and said snufflingly in his nose –

'Because she hadn't got nothing to do with it. I collected it all. She never went into one of the houses. She didn't want to.'

'And then took all the credit of getting the money,' said Dicky savagely.

Oswald said, 'Not much *credit*,' in scornful tones.

'Oh, you are *beastly*, the whole lot of you, except Dora!' Alice said, stamping her foot in rage and despair.

'I tore my frock on a nail going out, and I didn't want to go back, and I got H.O. to go to the houses alone, and I waited for him, outside. And I asked him not to say anything because I didn't want Dora to know about the frock – it's my best. And *I* don't know what he said inside. He never told me. But I'll bet anything he didn't *mean* to cheat.'

'You *said* lots of kind people would be ready to give money to get pudding for poor children. So I asked them to.'

Oswald, with his strong right hand, waved a wave of passing things over.

'We'll talk about that another time,' he said; 'just now we've got weightier things to deal with.'

He pointed to the pudding, which had grown cold during the conversation to which I have alluded. H.O. stopped crying, but Alice went on with it. Oswald now said –

'We're a base and outcast family. Until that pudding's out of the house we shan't be able to look any one in the face. We must see that that pudding goes to poor children – not grisling, grumpy, whiney-piney, pretending poor children – but real poor ones, just as poor as they can stick.'

'And the figs too – and the dates,' said Nöel, with regretting tones.

'Every fig,' said Dicky sternly. 'Oswald is quite right.'

This honourable resolution made us feel a bit better. We hastily put on our best things, and washed ourselves a bit, and hurried out to find some really poor people to give the pudding to. We cut it in slices ready, and put it in a basket with the figs and dates and toffee. We would not let H.O. come with us at first because he wanted to. And Alice would not come because of him.

So at last we had to let him. The excitement of tearing into your best things heals the hurt that wounded honour feels, as the poetry writer said – or at any rate it makes the hurt feel better.

We went out into the streets. They were pretty quiet – nearly everybody was eating its Christmas dessert. But presently we met a woman in an apron. Oswald said very politely –

'Please, are you a poor person?' And she told us to get along with us.

The next we met was a shabby man with a hole in his left boot.

Again Oswald said, 'Please, are you a poor person, and have you any poor little children?'

The man told us not to come any of our games with him, or we should laugh on the wrong side of our faces. We went on sadly. We had no heart to stop and explain to him that we had no games to come.

The next was a young man near the Obelisk. Dora tried this time.

She said, 'Oh, if you please we've got some Christmas pudding in this basket, and if you're a poor person you can have some.'

'Poor as Job,' said the young man in a hoarse voice, and he had to come up out of a red comforter to say it.

We gave him a slice of the pudding, and he bit into it without thanks or delay. The next minute he had thrown the pudding slap in Dora's face, and was clutching Dicky by the collar.

'Blime if I don't chuck ye in the river, the whole bloomin' lot of you!' he exclaimed.

The girls screamed, the boys shouted, and though Oswald threw himself on the insulter of his sister with all his manly vigour, yet but for a friend of Oswald's, who is in the police, passing at that instant, the author shudders to think what might have happened, for he was a strong young man, and Oswald is not yet come to his full strength, and the Quaggy runs all too near.

Our policeman led our assailant aside, and we waited anxiously, as he told us to. After long uncertain moments the young man in the comforter loafed off grumbling, and our policeman turned to us.

'Said you give him a dollop o'pudding, and it tasted of soap and hair-oil.'

I suppose the hair-oil must have been the Brown Windsoriness of the soap coming out. We were sorry, but it was still our duty to get rid of the pudding. The Quaggy was handy, it is true, but when you have collected money to feed poor children and spent it on pudding it is not right to throw that pudding in the river. People do not subscribe shillings and sixpences and half-crowns to feed a hungry flood with Christmas pudding.

Yet we shrank from asking any more people whether they were poor persons, or about their families, and still more from offering the pudding to chance people who might bite into it and taste the soap before we had time to getaway.

It was Alice, the most paralysed with disgrace of all of us, who thought of the best idea.

She said, 'Let's take it to the workhouse. At any rate they're all poor there, and they mayn't go out without leave, so they can't run after us to do anything to us after the pudding. No one would give them leave to go out to pursue people who had brought them pudding, and wreck vengeance on them, and at any rate we shall get rid of the – conscience-pudding – it's a sort of conscience-money, you know – only it isn't money but pudding.'

The workhouse is a good way, but we stuck to it, though very cold, and hungrier than we thought possible when we started, for we had been so agitated we had not even stayed to eat the plain pudding our good father had so kindly and thoughtfully ordered for our Christmas dinner.

The big bell at the workhouse made a man open the door to us, when we rang it. Oswald said (and he spoke because he is next eldest to Dora, and she had had jolly well enough of saying anything about pudding) – he said –

'Please we've brought some pudding for the poor people.'

He looked us up and down, and he looked at our basket, then he said: 'You'd better see the Matron.'

We waited in a hall, feeling more and more uncomfy, and less and less like Christmas. We were very cold indeed, especially our hands and our noses. And we felt less and less able to face the Matron if she was horrid, and one of us at least wished we had chosen the Quaggy for the pudding's long home, and made it up to the robbed poor in some other way afterwards.

Just as Alice was saying earnestly in the burning cold ear of Oswald, 'Let's put down the basket and make a bolt for it. Oh, Oswald, *let's!*' a lady came along the passage. She was very upright, and she had eyes that went through you like blue gimlets. I should not like to be obliged to thwart that lady if she had any design, and mine was opposite. I am glad this is not likely to occur.

She said, 'What's all this about a pudding?'

H.O. said at once, before we could stop him, 'They

say I've stolen the pudding, so we've brought it here for the poor people.'

'No, we didn't!' 'That wasn't why!'

'The money was given!' 'It was meant for the poor!' 'Shut up, H.O.!' said the rest of us all at once.

Then there was an awful silence. The lady gimleted us again one by one with her blue eyes.

Then she said: 'Come into my room. You all look frozen.'

She took us into a very jolly room with velvet curtains and a big fire, and the gas lighted, because now it was almost dark, even out of doors. She gave us chairs, and Oswald felt as if his was a dock, he felt so criminal, and the lady looked so Judgular.

Then she took the arm-chair by the fire herself, and said, 'Who's the eldest?'

'I am,' said Dora, looking more like a frightened white rabbit than I've ever seen her.

'Then tell me all about it.'

Dora looked at Alice and began to cry. That slab of pudding in the face had totally unnerved the gentle girl. Alice's eyes were red, and her face was puffy with crying; but she spoke up for Dora and said –

'Oh, please let Oswald tell. Dora can't. She's tired with the long walk. And a young man threw a piece of it in her face, and –'

The lady nodded and Oswald began. He told the story from the very beginning, as he has always been taught to, though he hated to lay bare the family honour's wound before a stranger, however judgelike and gimlet-eyed.

He told all – not concealing the pudding throwing, nor what the young man said about soap.

'So,' he ended, 'we want to give the conscience-pudding to you. It's like conscience-money – you know what that is, don't you? But if you really think it is soapy and not just the young man's horridness, perhaps you'd better not let them eat it. But the figs and things are all right.'

When he had had one the lady said, for most of us were crying more or less –

'Come, cheer up! It's Christmas-time, and he's very little – your brother, I mean. And I think the rest of you seem pretty well able to take care of the honour of the family. I'll take the conscience-pudding off your minds. Where are you going now?'

'Home, I suppose,' Oswald said. And he thought how nasty and dark and dull it would be: The fire out most likely and Father away.

'And your father's not at home, you say,' the blue-gimlet lady went on. 'What do you say to having tea with me, and then seeing the entertainment we have got up for our old people?'

Then the lady smiled and the blue gimlets looked quite merry.

The room was so warm and comfortable and the invitation was the last thing we expected. It was jolly of her, I do think.

No one thought quite at first of saying how pleased we should be to accept her kind invitation. Instead we all just said 'Oh!' but in a tone which must have told her we meant 'Yes, please', very deeply.

Oswald (this has more than once happened) was the first to restore his manners. He made a proper bow like he has been taught, and said –

'Thank you very much. We should like it very much. It is very much nicer than going home. Thank you very much.'

I need not tell the reader that Oswald could have made up a much better speech if he had had more time to make it up in, or if he had not been so filled with mixed flusteredness and furification by the shameful events of the day.

We washed our faces and hands and had a first rate muffin and crumpet tea, with slices of cold meats, and many nice jams and cakes. A lot of other people were there, most of them people who were giving the entertainment to the aged poor.

After tea it was the entertainment. Songs and conjuring and a play called 'Box and Cox', very amusing, and a lot of throwing things about in it – bacon and chops and things – and nigger minstrels. We clapped till our hands were sore.

When it was over we said goodbye. In between the songs and things Oswald had had time to make up a speech of thanks to the lady.

He said –

'We all thank you heartily for your goodness. The entertainment was beautiful. We shall never forget your kindness and hospitableness.'

The lady laughed, and said she had been very pleased to have us. A fat gentleman said –

'And your teas? I hope you enjoyed those – eh?'

Oswald had not had time to make up an answer to that, so he answered straight from the heart, and said –

'Ra – *ther!*'

And every one laughed and slapped us boys on the back and kissed the girls, and the gentleman who played the bones in the nigger minstrels saw us home. We ate the cold pudding that night, and H.O. dreamed that something came to eat him, like it advises you to in the advertisements on the hoardings. The grown-ups said it was the pudding, but I don't think it could have been that, because, as I have said more than once, it was so very plain.

Some of H.O.'s brothers and sisters thought it was a judgement on him for pretending about who the poor children were he was collecting the money for. Oswald does not believe such a little boy as H.O. would have a real judgement made just for him and nobody else, whatever he did.

But it certainly is odd. H.O. was the only one who had bad dreams, and he was also the only one who got any of the things we bought with that ill-gotten money, because, you remember, he picked a hole in the raisin-paper as he was bringing the parcel home. The rest of us had nothing, unless you count the scrapings of the pudding-basin, and those don't really count at all.

THOMAS HARDY

The Thieves Who Couldn't Help Sneezing

Many years ago, when oak-trees now past their prime were about as large as elderly gentlemen's walking-sticks, there lived in Wessex a yeoman's son, whose name was Hubert. He was about fourteen years of age, and was as remarkable for his candour and lightness of heart as for his physical courage, of which, indeed, he was a little vain.

One cold Christmas Eve his father, having no other help at hand, sent him on an important errand to a small town several miles from home. He travelled on horseback, and was detained by the business till a late hour in the evening. At last, however, it was completed; he returned to the inn, the horse was saddled, and he started on his way. His journey homeward lay through the Vale of Blackmore, a fertile but somewhat lonely district, with heavy clay roads and crooked lanes. In those days, too, a great part of it was thickly wooded.

It must have been about nine o'clock when, riding along amid the over-hanging trees upon his stout-legged cob, Jerry, and singing a Christmas carol, to be in harmony with the season, Hubert fancied that he heard a noise among the boughs. This recalled to his mind that the spot he was traversing bore an evil name. Men had been waylaid there. He looked at Jerry, and wished he had been of any other colour than light gray; for on this account the docile animal's form was visible even here in the dense shade. "What do I care?" he said aloud, after a few minutes of reflection. "Jerry's legs are too nimble to allow any highwayman to corrie near me."

"Ha! ha! indeed," was said in a deep voice; and the next moment a man darted from the thicket on his right hand, another man from the thicket on his left hand, and another from a tree-trunk a few yards ahead. Hubert's bridle was seized, he was pulled from his horse, and although he struck out with all his might, as a brave boy would naturally do, he was overpowered. His arms were tied behind him, his legs bound tightly together, and he was thrown into the ditch. The robbers, whose faces he could now dimly perceive to be artificially blackened, at once departed, leading off the horse.

As soon as Hubert had a little recovered himself, he found that by great exertion he was able to extricate his legs from the cord; but, in spite of every endeavour, his arms remained bound as fast as before. All, therefore, that he could do was to rise to his feet and proceed on his way with his arms behind him, and trust to chance for getting them unfastened. He knew that it would be impossible to reach home on foot that night, and in such a condition; but he walked on. Owing to the confusion which this attack caused in his brain, he lost his way, and would have been inclined to lie down and rest till morning among the dead leaves had he not known the danger of sleeping without wrappers in a frost so severe. So he wandered further onwards, his arms wrung and numbed by the cord which pinioned him, and his heart aching for the loss of poor Jerry, who never had been known to kick, or bite, or show a single vicious habit. He was not a little glad when he discerned through the trees a distant light. Towards this he made his way, and presently found himself in front of a large mansion with flanking wings, gables, and towers, the battlements and chimneys showing their shapes against the stars.

All was silent; but the door stood wide open, it being from this door that the light shone which had attracted him. On entering he found himself in a vast apartment arranged as a dining-hall, and brilliantly illuminated. The walls were covered with a great deal of dark wainscoting, formed into moulded panels, carvings, closet-doors, and the usual fittings of a house of that kind. But what drew his attention most was the large table in the midst of the hall, upon which was spread a sumptuous supper, as yet untouched. Chairs were placed around, and it appeared as if something had occurred to interrupt the meal just at the time when all were ready to begin.

Even had Hubert been so inclined, he could not have eaten in his helpless state, unless by dipping his mouth into the dishes, like a pig or cow. He wished first to obtain assistance; and was about to penetrate further into the house for that purpose when he heard hasty footsteps in the porch and the words, "Be quick!" uttered in the deep voice which had reached him when he was dragged from the horse. There was only just time for him to dart under the table before three men entered the dining-hall. Peeping from beneath the hanging edges of the tablecloth, he perceived that their faces, too, were blackened, which at once removed any remaining doubts he may have felt that these were the same thieves.

"Now, then," said the first—the man with the deep voice—"let us hide ourselves. They will all be back again in a minute. That was a good trick to get them out of the house—eh?"

"Yes. You well imitated the cries of a man in distress," said the second.

"Excellently," said the third.

"But they will soon find out that it was a false alarm. Come, where shall we hide? It must be some place we can stay in for two or three hours, till all are in bed and asleep. Ah! I have it. Come this way! I have learnt that the further closet is not opened once in a twelve-month; it will serve our purpose exactly."

The speaker advanced into a corridor which led from the hall. Creeping a little farther forward, Hubert could discern that the closet stood at the end, facing the dining-hall. The thieves entered it, and closed the door. Hardly breathing, Hubert glided forward, to learn a little more of the intention, if possible; and, coming close, he could hear the robbers whispering about the different rooms where the jewels, plate, and other valuables of the house were kept, which they plainly meant to steal.

They had not been long in hiding when a gay chattering of ladies and gentlemen was audible on the terrace without. Hubert felt that it would not do to be caught prowling about the house, unless he wished to be taken for a robber himself; and he slipped softly back to the hall, out the door, and stood in a dark corner of the porch, where he could see everything without being himself seen. In a moment or two a whole troop of personages came gliding past him into the house. There were an elderly gentleman and lady, eight or nine young ladies, as many young men, besides half-a-dozen men-servants and maids. The mansion had apparently been quite emptied of its occupants.

"Now, children and young people, we will resume our meal," said the old gentleman. "What the noise could have been I cannot understand. I never felt so certain in my life that there was a person being murdered outside my door."

Then the ladies began saying how frightened they had been, and how they had expected an adventure, and how it had ended in nothing at all.

"Wait a while," said Hubert to himself. "You'll have adventure enough by-and-by, ladies."

It appeared that the young men and women were married sons and daughters of the old couple, who had come that day to spend Christmas with their parents.

The door was then closed, Hubert being left outside in the porch. He thought this a proper moment for asking their assistance; and, since he was unable to knock with his hands, began boldly to kick the door.

"Hullo! What disturbance are you making here?" said a footman who opened it; and, seizing Hubert by the shoulder, he pulled him into the dining-hall. "Here's a strange boy I have found making a noise in the porch, Sir Simon."

Everybody turned.

"Bring him forward," said Sir Simon, the old gentleman before mentioned. "What were you doing there, my boy?"

"Why, his arms are tied!" said one of the ladies.

"Poor fellow!" said another.

Hubert at once began to explain that he had been waylaid on his journey home, robbed of his horse, and mercilessly left in this condition by the thieves.

"Only to think of it!" exclaimed Sir Simon.

"That's a likely story," said one of the gentlemen-guests, incredulously. "Doubtful, hey?" asked Sir Simon.

"Perhaps he's a robber himself," suggested a lady.

"There is a curiously wild, wicked look about him, certainly, now that I examine him closely," said the old mother.

Hubert blushed with shame; and, instead of continuing his story, and relating that robbers were concealed in the house, he doggedly held his tongue, and half resolved to let them find out their danger for themselves.

"Well, untie him," said Sir Simon. "Come, since it is Christmas Eve, we'll treat him well. Here, my lad; sit down in that empty seat at the bottom of the table, and make as good a meal as you can. When you have had your fill we will listen to more particulars of your story."

The feast then proceeded; and Hubert, now at liberty, was not at all sorry to join in. The more they ate and drank the merrier did the company become; the wine flowed freely, the logs flared up the chimney, the ladies laughed at the gentlemen's stories; in short, all went as noisily and as happily as a Christmas gathering in old times possibly could do.

Hubert, in spite of his hurt feelings at their doubts of his honesty, could not help being warmed both in mind and in body by the good cheer, the scene, and the example of hilarity set by his neighbours. At last he laughed as heartily at their stories and repartees as the old Baronet, Sir Simon, himself. When the meal was almost over one of the sons, who had drunk a little too much wine, after the manner of men in that century, said to Hubert, "Well, my boy, how are you? Can you take a pinch of snuff?" He held out one of the snuff-boxes which were then becoming common among young and old throughout the country.

"Thank you," said Hubert, accepting a pinch.

"Tell the ladies who you are, what you are made of, and what you can do," the young man continued, slapping Hubert upon the shoulder.

"Certainly," said our hero, drawing himself up, and thinking it best to put a bold face on the matter. "I am a traveling magician."

"Indeed!"

"What shall we hear next?"

"Can you call up spirits from the vasty deep, young wizard?"

"I can conjure up a tempest in a cupboard," Hubert replied.

"Ha-ha!" said the old Baronet, pleasantly rubbing his hands. "We must see this performance. Girls, don't go away: here's something to be seen."

"Not dangerous, I hope?" said the old lady.

Hubert rose from the table. "Hand me your snuff-box, please," he said to the young man who had made free with him. "And now," he continued, "without the least noise, follow me. If any of you speak it will break the spell."

They promised obedience. He entered the corridor, and, taking off his shoes, went on tiptoe to the closet door, the guests advancing in a silent group at a little distance behind him. Hubert next placed a stool in front of the door, and, by standing upon it, was tall enough to reach to the top. He then, just as noiselessly, poured all the snuff from the box along the upper edge of the door, and, with a few short puffs of breath, blew the snuff through the chink into the interior of the closet. He held up his finger to the assembly, that they might be silent.

"Dear me, what's that?" said the old lady, after a minute or two had elapsed.

A suppressed sneeze had come from inside the closet. Hubert held up his finger again.

"How very singular," whispered Sir Simon. "This is most interesting."

Hubert took advantage of the moment to gently slide the bolt of the closet door into its place. "More snuff," he said, calmly.

"More snuff," said Sir Simon. Two or three gentlemen passed their boxes, and the contents were blown in at the top of the closet. Another sneeze, not quite so well suppressed as the first, was heard: then another, which seemed to say that it would not be suppressed under any circumstances whatever. At length there arose a perfect storm of sneezes.

"Excellent, excellent for one so young!" said Sir Simon. "I am much interested in this trick of throwing the voice—called, I believe, ventriloquism."

"More snuff," said Hubert.

"More snuff," said Sir Simon. Sir Simon's man brought a large jar of the best scented Scotch.

Hubert once more charged the upper chink of the closet, and blew the snuff into the interior, as before. Again he charged, and again, emptying the whole contents of the jar. The tumult of sneezes became really extraordinary to listen to—there was no cessation. It was like wind, rain, and sea battling in a hurricane.

"I believe there are men inside, and that it is no trick at all!" exclaimed Sir Simon, the truth flashing on him.

"There are," said Hubert. "They are come to rob the house; and they are the same who stole my horse."

The sneezes changed to spasmodic groans. One of the thieves, hearing Hubert's voice, cried, "Oh! mercy! mercy! let us out of this!"

"Where's my horse?" said Hubert.

"Tied to the tree in the hollow behind Short's Gibbet. Mercy! mercy! let us out, or we shall die of suffocation!"

All the Christmas guests now perceived that this was no longer sport, but serious earnest. Guns and cudgels were procured; all the men-servants were called in, and arranged in position outside the closet. At a signal Hubert withdrew the bolt, and stood on the defensive. But the three robbers, far from attacking them, were found crouching in the corner, gasping for breath. They made no resistance; and, being pinioned, were placed in an outhouse till the morning.

Hubert now gave the remainder of his story to the assembled company, and was profusely thanked for the services he had rendered. Sir Simon pressed him to stay over the night, and accept the use of the best bedroom the house afforded, which had been occupied by Queen Elizabeth and King Charles successively when on their visits to this part of the country. But Hubert declined, being anxious to find his horse Jerry, and to test the truth of the robbers' statements concerning him.

Several of the guests accompanied Hubert to the spot behind the gibbet, alluded to by the thieves as where Jerry was hidden. When they reached the knoll and looked over, behold! there the horse stood, uninjured, and quite unconcerned. At sight of Hubert he neighed joyfully; and nothing could exceed Hubert's gladness at finding him. He mounted, wished his friends "Good-night!" and cantered off in the direction they pointed out, reaching home safely about four o'clock in the morning.

WILLIAM DEAN HOWELLS

Christmas Every Day

The little girl came into her papa's study, as she always did Saturday morning before breakfast, and asked for a story. He tried to beg off that morning, for he was very busy, but she would not let him. So he began:

"Well, once there was a little pig—" She put her hand over his mouth and stopped him at the word.

She said she had heard little pig-stories till she was perfectly sick of them.

"Well, what kind of story *shall* I tell, then?"

"About Christmas. It's getting to be the season. It's past Thanksgiving already."

"It seems to me," her papa argued, "that I've told as often about Christmas as I have about little pigs."

"No difference! Christmas is more interesting."

"Well!" Her papa roused himself from his writing by a great effort. "Well, then, I'll tell you about the little girl that wanted it Christmas every day in the year. How would you like that?"

"First-rate!" said the little girl; and she nestled into comfortable shape in his lap, ready for listening.

"Very well, then, this little pig—Oh, what are you pounding me for?"

"Because you said little pig instead of little girl."

"I should like to know what's the difference between a little pig and a little girl that wanted it Christmas every day!"

"Papa," said the little girl, warningly, "if you don't go on, I'll *give* it to you!" And at this her papa darted off like lightning, and began to tell the story as fast as he could.

Well, once there was a little girl who liked Christmas so much that she wanted it to be Christmas every day in the year; and as soon as Thanksgiving was over she began to send postal-cards to the old Christmas Fairy to ask if she mightn't have it. But the old Fairy never answered any of the postals; and after a while the little girl found out that the Fairy was pretty particular, and wouldn't notice anything but letters—not even correspondence cards in envelopes; but real letters on sheets of paper, and sealed outside with a mono-gram—or your initial, anyway. So, then, she began to send her letters; and in about three weeks—or just the day before Christmas, it was—she got a letter from the Fairy, saying she might have it Christmas every day for a year, and then they would see about having it longer.

The little girl was a good deal excited already, preparing for the old-fashioned, once-a-year Christmas that was coming the next day, and perhaps the Fairy's promise didn't make such an impression on her as it would have made at some other time. She just resolved to keep it to herself, and surprise every-body with it as it kept coming true; and then it slipped out of her mind altogether.

She had a splendid Christmas. She went to bed early, so as to let Santa Claus have a chance at the stockings, and in the morning she was up the first of anybody and went and felt them, and found hers all lumpy with packages of candy, and oranges and grapes, and pocket-books and rubber balls, and all kinds of small presents, and her big brother's with nothing but the tongs in them, and her young lady sister's with a new silk umbrella, and her papa's and mamma's with potatoes and pieces of coal wrapped up in tissue-paper, just as they always had every Christmas. Then she waited around till the rest of the family were up, and she was the first to burst into the library, when the doors were opened, and look at the large presents laid out on the library-table— books, and portfolios, and boxes of stationery, and breastpins, and dolls, and little stoves, and dozens of handkerchiefs, and inkstands, and skates, and snow-shovels, and photograph-frames, and little easels, and boxes of water-colors, and Turkish paste, and nougat, and candied cherries, and dolls' houses, and waterproofs—and the big Christmas-tree, lighted and standing in a waste-basket in the middle.

She had a splendid Christmas all day. She ate so much candy that she did not want any breakfast; and the whole forenoon the presents kept pouring in that the expressman had not had time to deliver the night before; and she went round giving the presents she had got for other people, and came home and ate turkey and cranberry for dinner, and plum-pudding and nuts and raisins and oranges and more candy, and then went out and coasted, and came in with a stomach-ache, crying; and her papa said he would see if his house was turned into that sort of fool's paradise another year; and they had a light supper, and pretty early everybody went to bed cross.

Here the little girl pounded her papa in the back, again. "Well, what now? Did I say pigs?"

"You made them *act* like pigs."

"Well, didn't they?"

"No matter; you oughtn't to put it into a story."

"Very well, then, I'll take it all out."

Her father went on:

The little girl slept very heavily, and she slept very late, but she was wakened at last by the other children dancing round her bed with their stockings full of presents in their hands.

"What is it?" said the little girl, and she rubbed her eyes and tried to rise up in bed.

"Christmas! Christmas! Christmas!" they all shouted, and waved their stockings.

"Nonsense! It was Christmas yesterday."

Her brothers and sisters just laughed. "We don't know about that. It's Christmas to-day, anyway. You come into the library and see."

Then all at once it flashed on the little girl that the Fairy was keeping her promise, and her year of Christmases was beginning. She was dreadfully sleepy, but she sprang up like a lark—a lark that had overeaten itself and gone to bed cross—and darted into the library. There it was again! Books, and port-folios, and boxes of stationery, and breastpins—

"You needn't go over it all, papa; I guess I can remember just what was there," said the little girl.

Well, and there was the Christmas-tree blazing away, and the family picking out their presents, but looking pretty sleepy, and her father perfectly puzzled, and her mother ready to cry. "I'm sure I don't see how I'm to dispose of all these things," said her mother, and her father said it seemed to him they had had something just like it the day before, but he supposed he must have dreamed it. This struck the little girl as the best kind of a joke; and so she ate so much candy she didn't want any breakfast, and went round carrying presents, and had turkey and cranberry for dinner, and then went out and coasted, and came in with a—

"Papa!"

"Well, what now?"

"What did you promise, you forgetful thing?"

"Oh! oh yes!"

Well, the next day, it was just the same thing over again, but everybody getting crosser; and at the end of a week's time so many people had lost their tempers that you could pick up lost tempers anywhere; they perfectly strewed the ground. Even when people tried to recover their tempers they usually got somebody else's, and it made the most dreadful mix.

The little girl began to get frightened, keeping the secret all to herself; she wanted to tell her mother, but she didn't dare to; and she was ashamed to ask the Fairy to take back her gift, it seemed ungrateful and ill-bred, and she thought she would try to stand it, but she hardly knew how she could, for a whole year. So it went on and on, and it was Christmas on St. Valentine's Day and Washington's Birthday, just the same as any day, and it didn't skip even the First of April, though everything was counterfeit that day, and that was some *little* relief.

After a while coal and potatoes began to be awfully scarce, so many had been wrapped up in tissue-paper to fool papas and mammas with. Turkeys got to be about a thousand dollars a piece—

"Papa!"

"Well, what?"

"You're beginning to fib."

"Well, *two* thousand, then."

And they got to passing off almost anything for turkeys—half-grown humming-birds, and even roes out of the *Arabian Nights*—the real turkeys were so scarce. And cranberries—well, they asked a diamond apiece for cranberries. All the woods and orchards were cut down for Christmas-trees, and where the woods and orchards used to be it looked just like a stubble-field, with the stumps. After a while they had to make Christmas-trees out of rags, and stuff them with bran, like old-fashioned dolls; but there were plenty of rags, because people got so poor, buying presents for one another, that they couldn't get any new clothes, and they just wore their old ones to tatters. They got so poor that everybody had to go to the poor-house, except the confectioners, and the fancy-store keepers, and the picture-book sellers, and the expressmen; and *they* all got so rich and proud that they would hardly wait upon a person when he came to buy. It was perfectly shameful!

Well, after it had gone on about three or four months, the little girl, whenever she came into the room in the morning and saw those great ugly, lumpy stockings dangling at the fireplace, and the disgusting presents around everywhere, used to just sit down and burst out crying. In six months she was perfectly exhausted; she couldn't even cry any more; she just lay on the lounge and rolled her eyes and panted. About the beginning of October she took to sitting down on dolls wherever she found them—French dolls, or any kind—she hated the sight of them so; and by Thanksgiving she was crazy, and just slammed her presents across the room.

By that time people didn't carry presents around nicely any more. They flung them over the fence, or through the window, or anything; and, instead of running their tongues out and taking great pains to write "For dear Papa," or "Mamma," or "Brother," or "Sister," or "Susie," or "Sammie," or "Billie," or "Bobbie," or "Jimmie," or "Jennie," or whoever it was, and troubling to get the spelling right, and then sign-ing their names, and "Xmas, 18—," they used to write in the gift-books, "Take it, you horrid old thing!" and then go and bang it against the front door. Nearly everybody had built barns to hold their presents, but pretty soon the barns over-flowed, and then they used to let them lie out in the rain, or anywhere. Some-times the police used to come and tell them to shovel their presents off the sidewalk, or they would arrest them.

"I thought you said everybody had gone to the poor-house," interrupted the little girl.

"They did go, at first," said her papa; "but after a while the poor-houses got so full that they had to send the people back to their own houses. They tried to cry, when they got back, but they couldn't make the least sound."

"Why couldn't they?"

"Because they had lost their voices, saying 'Merry Christmas' so much. Did I tell you how it was on the Fourth of July?"

"No; how was it?" And the little girl nestled closer, in expectation of something uncommon.

Well, the night before, the boys stayed up to celebrate, as they always do, and fell asleep before twelve o'clock, as usual, expecting to be wakened by the bells and cannon. But it was nearly eight o'clock before the first boy in the United States woke up, and then he found out what the trouble was. As soon as he could get his clothes on he ran out of the house and smashed a big cannon-torpedo down on the pavement; but it didn't make any more noise than a damp wad of paper; and after he tried about twenty or thirty more, he began to pick them up and look at them. Every single torpedo was a big raisin! Then he just streaked it upstairs, and examined his firecrackers and toy pistol and two-dollar collection of fireworks, and found that they were nothing but sugar and candy painted up to look like fireworks! Before ten o'clock every boy in the United States found out that his Fourth of July things had turned into Christmas things; and then they just sat down and cried—they were so mad. There are about twenty million boys in the United States, and so you can imagine what a noise they made. Some men got together before night, with a little powder that hadn't turned into purple sugar yet, and they said they would fire off one cannon, anyway. But the cannon burst into a thousand pieces, for it was nothing but rock-candy, and some of the men nearly got killed. The Fourth of July orations all turned into Christmas carols, and when anybody tried to read the Declaration, instead of saying, "When in the course of human events it becomes necessary," he was sure to sing, "God rest you, merry gentlemen." It was perfectly awful.

The little girl drew a deep sigh of satisfaction.

"And how was it at Thanksgiving?"

Her papa hesitated. "Well, I'm almost afraid to tell you. I'm afraid you'll think it's wicked."

"Well, tell, anyway," said the little girl.

Well, before it came Thanksgiving it had leaked out who had caused all these Christmases. The little girl had suffered so much that she had talked about it in her sleep; and after that hardly anybody would play with her. People just perfectly despised her, because if it had not been for her greediness it wouldn't have happened; and now, when it came Thanksgiving, and she wanted them to go to church, and have squash-pie and turkey, and show their gratitude, they said that all the turkeys had been eaten up for her old Christmas dinners, and if she would stop the Christmases, they would see about the gratitude. Wasn't it dreadful? And the very next day the little girl began to send letters to the Christmas Fairy, and then telegrams, to stop it. But it didn't do any good; and then she got to calling at the Fairy's house, but the girl that came to the door always said, "Not at home," or "Engaged," or "At dinner," or something like that; and so it went on till it came to the old once-a-year

Christmas Eve. The little girl fell asleep, and when she woke up in the morning—

"She found it was all nothing but a dream," suggested the little girl.

"No, indeed!" said her papa. "It was all every bit true!"

"Well, what *did* she find out, then?"

"Why, that it wasn't Christmas at last, and wasn't ever going to be, any more. Now it's time for breakfast."

The little girl held her papa fast around the neck. "You sha'n't go if you're going to leave it *so!*"

"How do you want it left?"

"Christmas once a year."

"All right," said her papa; and he went on again.

Well, there was the greatest rejoicing all over the country, and it extended clear up into Canada. The people met together everywhere, and kissed and cried for joy. The city carts went around and gathered up all the candy and raisins and nuts, and dumped them into the river; and it made the fish perfectly sick; and the whole United States, as far out as Alaska, was one blaze of bonfires, where the children were burning up their gift-books and presents of all kinds. They had the greatest *time!*

The little girl went to thank the old Fairy because she had stopped its being Christmas, and she said she hoped she would keep her promise and see that Christmas never, never came again. Then the Fairy frowned, and asked her if she was sure she knew what she meant; and the little girl asked her, Why not? and the old Fairy said that now she was behaving just as greedily as ever, and she'd better look out. This made the little girl think it all over carefully again—, and she said she would be willing to have it Christmas about once in a thousand years; and then she said a hundred, and then she said ten, and at last she got down to one. Then the Fairy said that was the good old way that had pleased people ever since Christmas began, and she was agreed. Then the little girl said, "What're your shoes made of?" And the Fairy said, "Leather." And the little girl said, "Bargain's done forever," and skipped off, and hippity-hopped the whole way home, she was so glad.

"How will that do?" asked the papa.

"First-rate!" said the little girl; but she hated to have the story stop, and was rather sober.

However, her mamma put her head in at the door, and asked her papa, "Are you never coming to breakfast? What have you been telling that child?"

"Oh, just a moral tale."

The little girl caught him around the neck again.

"*We* know! Don't you tell *what*, papa! Don't you tell *what!*"

CHARLES DICKENS

A Christmas Tree

I have been looking on, this evening, at a merry company of children assembled round that pretty German toy, a Christmas Tree. The tree was planted in the middle of a great round table, and towered high above their heads. It was brilliantly lighted by a multitude of little tapers; and everywhere sparkled and glittered with bright objects. There were rosy-cheeked dolls, hiding behind the green leaves; and there were real watches (with movable hands, at least, and an endless capacity of being wound up) dangling from innumerable twigs; there were French-polished tables, chairs, bedsteads, wardrobes, eight-day clocks, and various other articles of domestic furniture (wonderfully made, in tin, at Wolverhampton), perched among the boughs, as if in preparation for some fairy housekeeping; there were jolly, broad-faced little men, much more agreeable in appearance than many real men—and no wonder, for their heads took off, and showed them to be full of sugarplums; there were fiddles and drums; there were tambourines, books, work-boxes, paint-boxes, sweetmeat-boxes, peep-show boxes, and all kinds of boxes; there were trinkets for the elder girls, far brighter than any grown-up gold and jewels; there were baskets and pincushions in all devices; there were guns, swords, and banners; there were witches standing in enchanted rings of pasteboard, to tell fortunes; there were teetotums, humming-tops, needle-cases, pen-wipers, smelling-bottles, conversation-cards, bouquet-holders; real fruit, made artificially dazzling with gold leaf; imitation apples, pears, and walnuts, crammed with surprises; in short, as a pretty child, before me, delight-edly whispered to another pretty child, her bosom friend, "There was everything, and more." This motley collection of odd objects, clustering on the tree like magic fruit, and flashing back the bright looks directed towards it from every side—some of the diamond-eyes admiring it were hardly on a level with the table, and a few were languishing in timid wonder on the bosoms of pretty mothers, aunts, and nurses—made a lively real-isation of the fancies of childhood; and set me thinking how all the trees that grow and all the things that come into existence on the earth, have their wild adornments at that well-remembered time.

Being now at home again, and alone, the only person in the house awake, my thoughts are drawn back, by a fascination which I do not care to resist, to my own childhood. I begin to consider, what do we all remem-ber best upon the branches of the Christmas Tree of our own young Christmas days, by which we climbed to real life.

Straight, in the middle of the room, cramped in the freedom of its growth by no encircling walls or soon-reached ceiling, a shadowy tree arises; and, looking up into the dreamy brightness of its top—for I observe in this tree the singular property that it appears to grow downward towards the earth—I look into my youngest Christmas recollections!

All toys at first, I find. Up yonder, among the green holly and red berries, is the Tumbler with his hands in his pockets, who wouldn't lie down, but whenever he was put upon the floor, persisted in rolling his fat body about, until he rolled himself still, and brought those lobster eyes of his to bear upon me—when I affected to laugh very much, but in my heart of hearts was extremely doubtful of him. Close beside him is that infernal snuff-box, out of which there sprang a demoniacal Counsellor in a black gown, with an obnoxious head of hair, and a red cloth mouth, wide open, who was not to be endured on any terms, but could not be put away either; for he used suddenly, in a highly magnified state, to fly out of Mammoth Snuff-boxes in dreams, when least expected. Nor is the frog with cobbler's wax on his tail, far off; for there was no knowing where he wouldn't jump; and when he flew over the candle, and came upon one's hand with that spotted back—red on a green ground—he was horrible. The cardboard lady in a blue-silk skirt, who was stood up against the candlestick to dance, and whom I see on the same branch, was milder, and was beautiful; but I can't say as much for the larger cardboard man, who used to be hung against the wall and pulled by a string; there was a sinister expression in that nose of his; and when he got his legs round his neck (which he very often did), he was ghastly, and not a creature to be alone with.

When did that dreadful Mask first look at me? Who put it on, and why was I so frightened that the sight of it is an era in my life? It is not a hideous visage in itself;

it is even meant to be droll, why then were its stolid features so intolerable? Surely not because it hid the wearer's face. An apron would have done as much; and though I should have preferred even the apron away, it would not have been absolutely insupportable, like the mask. Was it the immovability of the mask? The doll's face was immovable, but I was not afraid of *her*. Perhaps that fixed and set change coming over a real face, infused into my quickened heart some remote suggestion and dread of the universal change that is to come on every face, and make it still? Nothing reconciled me to it. No drummers, from whom proceeded a melancholy chirping on the turning of a handle; no regiment of soldiers, with a mute band, taken out of a box, and fitted, one by one, upon a stiff and lazy little set of lazytongs; no old woman, made of wires and a brown-paper composition, cutting up a pie for two small children; could give me a permanent comfort, for a long time. Nor was it any satisfaction to be shown the Mask, and see that it was made of paper, or to have it locked up and be assured that no one wore it. The mere recollection of that fixed face, the mere knowledge of its existence anywhere, was sufficient to awake me in the night all perspiration and horror, with, "O, I know it's coming! O, the mask!"

I never wondered what the dear old donkey with the panniers—there he is! was made of, then! His hide was real to the touch, I recollect. And the great black horse with the round red spots all over him—the horse that I could even get upon—I never wondered what had brought him to that strange condition, or thought that such a horse was not commonly seen at Newmarket. The four horses of no colour, next to him, that went into the waggon of cheeses, and could be taken out and stabled under the piano, appear to have bits of fur-tippet for their tails, and other bits for their manes, and to stand on pegs instead of legs, but it was not so when they were brought home for a Christmas present. They were all right, then; neither was their harness unceremoniously nailed into their chests, as appears to be the case now. The tinkling works of the music-cart, I *did* find out, to be made of quill tooth-picks and wire; and I always thought that little tumbler in his shirt sleeves, perpetually swarming up one side of a wooden frame, and coming down, head foremost, on the other, rather a weak-minded person—though good-natured; but the Jacob's Ladder, next him, made of little squares of red wood, that went flapping and clattering over one another, each developing a different picture, and the whole enlivened by small bells, was a mighty marvel and a great delight.

Ah! The Doll's house!—of which I was not proprietor, but where I visited. I don't admire the Houses of Parliament half so much as that stone-fronted mansion with real glass windows, and door-steps, and a real balcony—greener than I ever see now, except at watering places; and even they afford but a poor imitation. And though it *did* open all at once, the entire house-front (which was a blow, I admit, as cancelling the fiction of a staircase), it was but to shut it up again, and I could believe. Even open, there were three distinct rooms in it: a sitting-room and bed-room, elegantly furnished, and best of all, a kitchen, with uncommonly soft fire-irons, a plentiful assortment of diminutive utensils—oh, the warmingpan!—and a tin man—cook in profile, who was always going to fry two fish. What Barmecide justice have I done to the noble feasts wherein the set of wooden platters figured, each with its own peculiar delicacy, as a ham or turkey, glued tight on to it, and garnished with something green, which I recollect as moss! Could all the Temperance Societies of these later days, united, give me such a tea-drinking as I have had through the means of yonder little set of blue crockery, which really would hold liquid (it ran out of the small wooden cask, I recollect, and tasted of matches), and which made tea, nectar. And if the two legs of the ineffectual little sugar-tongs did tumble over one another, and want purpose, like Punch's hands, what does it matter? And if I did once shriek out, as a poisoned child, and strike the fashionable company with consternation, by reason of having drunk a little teaspoon, inadvertently dissolved in too hot tea, I was never the worse for it, except by a powder!

Upon the next branches of the tree, lower down, hard by the green roller and miniature gardening-tools, how thick the books begin to hang. Thin books, in themselves, at first, but many of them, and with deliciously smooth covers of bright red or green. What fat black letters to begin with! "A was an archer, and shot at a frog." Of course he was. He was an apple-pie also, and there he is! He was a good many things in his time, was A, and so were most of his friends, except X, who had so little versatility, that I never knew him to get beyond Xerxes or Xantippe—like Y, who was always confined to a Yacht or a Yew Tree; and Z condemned for ever to be a Zebra or a Zany. But, now, the very tree itself changes, and becomes a bean-stalk—the marvellous bean-stalk up which Jack climbed to the Giant's house! And now, those dreadfully interesting, double-headed giants, with their clubs over their shoulders, begin to stride along the boughs in a perfect throng, dragging knights and ladies home for dinner by the hair of their heads. And Jack—how noble, with his sword of sharpness, and his shoes of swiftness! Again those old meditations come upon me as I gaze up at him; and I debate within myself whether there was more than one Jack (which I am loath to believe possible), or only one genuine original admirable Jack, who achieved all the recorded exploits.

Good for Christmas-time is the ruddy colour of the cloak, in which—the tree making a forest of itself for her to trip through, with her basket—Little Red Riding-Hood comes to me one Christmas-eve to give me information of the cruelty and treachery of that dissembling Wolf who ate her grandmother, without making any impression on his appetite, and then ate her, after making that ferocious joke about his teeth. She was my first love. I felt that if I could have married Little Red Riding-Hood, I should have known perfect bliss. But, it was not to be; and there was nothing for it but to look out the Wolf in the Noah's Ark there, and put him late in the procession on the table, as a monster who was to be degraded. O, the wonderful Noah's Ark! It was not found seaworthy when put in a washing-tub, and the animals were crammed in at the roof, and needed to have their legs well shaken down before they could be got in, even there—and then, ten to one but they began to tumble out at the door, which was but imperfectly fastened with a wire latch—but what was *that*—against it! Consider the noble fly, a size or two smaller than the elephant: the lady-bird, the butterfly— all triumphs of art! Consider the goose, whose feet were so small, and whose balance was so indifferent, that he usually tumbled forward, and knocked down all the animal creation. Consider Noah and his family, like idiotic tobacco-stoppers; and how the leopard stuck to warm little fingers; and how the tails of the larger animals used gradually to resolve themselves into frayed bits of string!

Hush! Again a forest, and somebody up in a tree—not Robin Hood, not Valentine, not the Yellow Dwarf (I have passed him and all Mother Bunch's wonders, without mention), but an Eastern King with a glittering scimitar and turban. By Allah! two Eastern Kings, for I see another, looking over his shoulder! Down upon the grass, at the tree's foot, lies the full length of a coal-black Giant, stretched asleep, with his head in a lady's lap; and near them is a glass box, fastened with four locks of shining steel, in which he keeps the lady prisoner when he is awake. I see the four keys at his girdle now. The lady makes signs to the two kings in the tree, who softly descend. It is the setting—in of the bright Arabian Nights.

Oh, now all common things become uncommon and enchanted to me. All lamps are wonderful; all rings are talismans. Common flower-pots are full of treasure, with a little earth scattered on the top; trees are for Ali Baba to hide in; beef-steaks are to throw down into the Valley of Diamonds, that the precious stones may stick to them, and be carried by the eagles to their nests, whence the traders, with loud cries, will scare them. Tarts are made, according to the recipe of the Vizier's son of Bussorah, who turned pastrycook after he was set down in his drawers at the gate of Damascus; cobblers are all Mustaphas, and in the habit of sewing up people cut into four pieces, to whom they are taken blind-fold.

Any iron ring let into stone is the entrance to a cave which only waits for the magician, and the little fire, and the necromancy, that will make the earth shake. All the dates imported come from the same tree as that unlucky date, with whose shell the merchant knocked out the eye of the genie's invisible son. All olives are of the stock of that fresh fruit, concerning which the Commander of the Faithful overheard the boy conduct the fictitious trial of the fraudulent olive merchant; all apples are akin to the apple purchased (with two others) from the Sultan's gardener for three sequins, and which the tall black slave stole from the child. All dogs are associated with the dog, really a transformed man, who jumped upon the baker's counter, and put his paw on the piece of bad money. All rice recalls the rice which the awful lady, who was a ghoule, could only peck by grains, because of her nightly feasts in the burial-place. My very rocking-horse,—there he is, with his nostrils turned completely inside-out, indicative of Blood!—should have a peg in his neck, by virtue thereof to fly away with me, as the wooden horse did with the Prince of Persia, in the sight of all his father's Court.

Yes, on every object that I recognise among those upper branches of my Christmas Tree, I see this fairy light! When I wake in bed, at daybreak, on the cold, dark, winter mornings, the white snow dimly beheld, outside, through the frost on the window-pane, I hear Dinarzade. "Sister, sister, if you are yet awake, I pray you finish the history of the Young King of the Black Islands." Scheherazade replies, "If my lord the Sultan will suffer me to live another day, sister, I will not only finish that, but tell you a more wonderful story yet." Then, the gracious Sultan goes out, giving no orders for the execution, and we all three breathe again.

At this height of my tree I begin to see, cowering among the leaves—it may be born of turkey, or of pudding, or mince pie, or of these many fancies, jumbled with Robinson Crusoe on his desert island, Philip Quarll among the monkeys, Sandford and Merton with Mr. Barlow, Mother Bunch, and the Mask—or it may be the result of indigestion, assisted by imagination and over-doctoring—a prodigious nightmare. It is so exceedingly indistinct, that I don't know why it's frightful—but I know it is. I can only make out that it is an immense array of shapeless things, which appear to be planted on a vast exaggeration of the lazy-tongs that used to bear the toy soldiers, and to be slowly coming close to my eyes, and receding to an immeasurable distance. When it comes closest, it is worse. In connection with it I descry remembrances of winter nights incredibly long; of being sent early to bed, as a punishment for some small offence, and waking in two hours, with a sensation of having been asleep two nights; of the laden hopelessness of morning ever dawning; and the oppression of a weight of remorse.

And now, I see a wonderful row of little lights rise smoothly out of the ground, before a vast green curtain. Now, a bell rings—a magic bell, which still sounds in my ears unlike all other bells—and music plays, amidst a buzz of voices, and a fragrant smell of orange-peel and oil. Anon, the magic bell commands the music to cease, and the great green curtain rolls itself up majestically, and The Play begins! The devoted dog of Montargis avenges the death of his master, foully murdered in the Forest of Bondy; and a humorous Peasant with a red nose and a very little hat, whom I take from this hour forth to my bosom as a friend (I think he was a Waiter or an Hostler at a village Inn, but many years have passed since he and I have met), remarks that the sassigassity of that dog is indeed surprising; and ever-more this jocular conceit will live in my remembrance fresh and unfading, overtopping all possible jokes, unto the end of time. Or now, I learn with bitter tears how poor Jane Shore, dressed all in white, and with her brown hair hanging down, went starving through the streets; or how George Barnwell killed the worthiest uncle that ever man had, and was afterwards so sorry for it that he ought to have been let off. Comes swift to comfort me, the Pantomime—stupendous Phenomenon!—when clowns are shot from loaded mortars into the great chandelier, bright constellation that it is; when Harlequins, covered all over with scales of pure gold, twist and sparkle, like amazing fish; when Pantaloon (whom I deem it no irreverence to compare in my own mind to my grandfather) puts red-hot pokers in his pocket, and cries "Here's somebody coming!" or taxes the Clown with petty larceny, by saying, "Now, I sawed you do it!" when Everything is capable, with the greatest ease, of being changed into Anything; and "Nothing is, but thinking makes it so." Now, too, I perceive my first experience of the dreary sensation—often to return in after-life—of being unable, next day, to get back to the dull, settled world; of wanting to live for ever in the bright atmosphere I have quitted; of doting on the little Fairy, with the wand like a celestial Barber's Pole, and pining for a Fairy immortality along with her. Ah, she comes back, in many shapes, as my eye wanders down the branches of my Christmas Tree, and goes as often, and has never yet stayed by me!

Out of this delight springs the toy-theatre,—there it is, with its familiar proscenium, and ladies in feathers, in the boxes!—and all its attendant occupation with paste and glue, and gum, and water colours, in the getting-up of The Miller and his Men, and Elizabeth, or the Exile of Siberia. In spite of a few besetting accidents and failures (particularly an unreasonable disposition in the respectable Kelmar, and some others, to become faint in the legs, and double up, at exciting points of the drama), a teeming world of fancies so suggestive and all-embracing, that, far below it on my Christmas Tree, I see dark, dirty, real Theatres in the day-time, adorned with these associations as with the freshest garlands of the rarest flowers, and charming me yet.

But hark! The Waits are playing, and they break my childish sleep! What images do I associate with the Christmas music as I see them set forth on the Christmas Tree? Known before all the others, keeping far apart from all the others, they gather round my little bed. An angel, speaking to a group of shepherds in a field; some travellers, with eyes uplifted, following a star; a baby in a manger; a child in a spacious temple, talking with grave men; a solemn figure, with a mild and beautiful face, raising a dead girl by the hand; again, near a city gate, calling back the son of a widow, on his bier, to life; a crowd of people looking through the opened roof of a chamber where he sits, and letting down a sick person on a bed, with ropes; the same, in a tempest, walking on the water to a ship; again, on a sea-shore, teaching a great multitude; again, with a child upon his knee, and other children round; again, restoring sight to the blind, speech to the dumb, hearing to the deaf, health to the sick, strength to the lame, knowledge to the ignorant; again, dying upon a Cross, watched by armed soldiers, a thick darkness coming on, the earth beginning to shake, and only one voice heard, "Forgive them, for they know not what they do."

Still, on the lower and maturer branches of the Tree,

Christmas associations cluster thick. School-books shut up; Ovid and Virgil silenced; the Rule of Three, with its cool impertinent inquiries, long disposed of; Terence and Plautus acted no more, in an arena of huddled desks and forms, all chipped, and notched, and inked; cricket-bats, stumps, and balls, left higher up, with the smell of trodden grass and the softened noise of shouts in the evening air; the tree is still fresh, still gay. If I no more come home at Christmas-time, there will be boys and girls (thank Heaven!) while the World lasts; and they do! Yonder they dance and play upon the branches of my Tree, God bless them, merrily, and my heart dances and plays too!

And I do come home at Christmas. We all do, or we all should. We all come home, or ought to come home, for a short holiday—the longer, the better—from the great boarding school, where we are for ever working at our arithmetical slates, to take, and give a rest. As to going a visiting, where can we not go, if we will; where have we not been, when we would; starting our fancy from our Christmas Tree!

Away into the winter prospect. There are many such upon the tree! On, by low-lying, misty grounds, through fens and fogs, up long hills, winding dark as caverns between thick plantations, almost shutting out the sparkling stars; so, out on broad heights, until we stop at last, with sudden silence, at an avenue. The gate-bell has a deep, half-awful sound in the frosty air; the gate swings open on its hinges; and, as we drive up to a great house, the glancing lights grow larger in the windows, and the opposing rows of trees seem to fall solemnly back on either side, to give us place. At inter-vals, all day, a frightened hare has shot across this whitened turf; or the distant clatter of a herd of deer trampling the hard frost, has, for the minute, crushed the silence too. Their watchful eyes beneath the fern may be shining now, if we could see them, like the icy dewdrops on the leaves; but they are still, and all is still. And so, the lights growing larger, and the trees falling back before us, and closing up again behind us, as if to forbid retreat, we come to the house.

There is probably a smell of roasted chestnuts and other good comfortable things all the time, for we are telling Winter Stories—Ghost Stories, or more shame for us—round the Christmas fire; and we have never stirred, except to draw a little nearer to it. But, no matter for that. We came to the house, and it is an old house, full of great chimneys where wood is burnt on ancient dogs upon the hearth, and grim portraits (some of them with grim legends, too) lower distrustfully from the oaken panels of the walls. We are a middle-aged nobleman, and we make a generous supper with our host and hostess and their guests—it being Christmas-time, and the old house full of company—and then we go to bed. Our room is a very old room. It is hung with tapestry. We don't like the portrait of a cavalier in green, over the fireplace. There are great black beams in the ceiling, and there is a great black bedstead, supported at the foot by two great black figures, who seem to have come off a couple of tombs in the old baronial church in the park, for our particular accommodation. But, we are not a superstitious nobleman, and we don't mind. Well! we dismiss our servant, lock the door, and sit before the fire in our dressing-gown, musing about a great many things. At length we go to bed. Well! we can't sleep. We toss and tumble, and can't sleep. The embers on the hearth burn fitfully and make the room look ghostly. We can't help peeping out over the counterpane, at the two black figures and the cavalier—that wicked-looking cavalier—in green. In the flickering light they seem to advance and retire: which, though we are not by any means a superstitious nobleman, is not agreeable. Well! we get nervous—more and more nervous. We say "This is very foolish, but we can't stand this; we'll pretend to be ill, and knock up somebody." Well! we are just going to do it, when the locked door opens, and there comes in a young woman, deadly pale, and with long fair hair, who glides to the fire, and sits down in the chair we have left there, wringing her hands. Then, we notice that her clothes are wet. Our tongue cleaves to the roof of our mouth, and we can't speak; but, we observe her accurately. Her clothes are wet; her long hair is dabbled with moist mud; she is dressed in the fashion of two hundred years ago; and she has at her girdle a bunch of rusty keys. Well! there she sits, and we can't even faint, we are in such a state about it. Presently she gets up, and tries all the locks in the room with the rusty keys, which won't fit one of them; then, she fixes her eyes on the portrait of the cavalier in green, and says, in a low, terrible voice, "The stags know it!" After that, she wrings her hands again, passes the bedside, and goes out at the door. We hurry on our dressing-gown, seize our pistols (we always travel with pistols), and are following, when we find the door locked. We turn the key, look out into the dark gallery; no one there. We wander away, and try to find our servant. Can't be done. We pace the gallery till daybreak; then return to our deserted room, fall asleep, and are awakened by our servant (nothing ever haunts him) and the shining sun. Well! we make a wretched breakfast, and all the company say we look queer. After breakfast, we go over the house with our host, and then we take him to the portrait of the cavalier in green, and then it all comes out. He was false to a young house-keeper once attached to that family, and famous for her beauty, who drowned herself in a pond, and whose body was discovered, after a long time, because the stags refused to drink of the water. Since which, it has been whispered that she traverses the house at midnight (but goes especially to that room where the cavalier in green was wont to sleep), trying the old locks with the rusty keys. Well! we tell our host of what we have seen, and a shade comes over his features, and he begs it may be hushed up; and so it is. But, it's all true; and we said so, before we died (we are dead now) to many responsible people.

There is no end to the old houses, with resounding galleries, and dismal state—bedchambers, and haunted wings shut up for many years, through which we may ramble, with an agreeable creeping up our back, and encounter any number of ghosts, but (it is worthy of remark perhaps) reducible to a very few general types and classes; for, ghosts have little originality, and "walk" in a beaten track. Thus, it comes to pass, that a certain room in a certain old hall, where a certain bad lord, baronet, knight, or gentleman, shot himself, has certain planks in the floor from which the blood *will not* be taken out. You may scrape and scrape, as the present owner has done, or plane and plane, as his father did, or scrub and scrub, as his grandfather did, or burn and burn with strong acids, as his great-grandfather did, but, there the blood will still be—no redder and no paler—no more and no less—always just the same. Thus, in such another house there is a haunted door, that never will keep open; or another door that never will keep shut, or a haunted sound of a spinning-wheel, or a hammer, or a footstep, or a cry, or a sigh, or a horse's tramp, or the rattling of a chain. Or else, there is a turret-clock, which, at the midnight hour, strikes thirteen when the head of the family is going to die; or a shadowy, immovable black carriage which at such a time is always seen by somebody, waiting near the great gates in the stable-yard. Or thus, it came to pass how Lady Mary went to pay a visit at a large wild house in the Scottish Highlands, and, being fatigued with her long journey, retired to bed early, and innocently said, next morning, at the breakfast-table, "How odd, to have so late a party last night, in this remote place, and not to tell me of it, before I went to bed!" Then, every one asked Lady Mary what she meant? Then, Lady Mary replied, "Why, all night long, the carriages were driving round and round the terrace, underneath my window!" Then, the owner of the house turned pale, and so did his Lady, and Charles Macdoodle of Macdoodle signed to Lady Mary to say no more, and every one was silent. After breakfast, Charles Macdoodle told Lady Mary that it was a tradition in the family that those rumbling carriages on the terrace betokened death. And so it proved, for, two months afterwards, the Lady of the mansion died. And Lady Mary, who was a Maid of Honour at Court, often told this story to the old Queen Charlotte; by this token that the old King always said, "Eh, eh? What, what? Ghosts, ghosts? No such thing, no such thing!" And never left off saying so, until he went to bed.

Or, a friend of somebody's whom most of us know, when he was a young man at college, had a particular friend, with whom he made the compact that, if it were possible for the Spirit to return to this earth after its separation from the body, he of the twain who first died, should reappear to the other. In course of time, this compact was forgotten by our friend; the two young men having progressed in life, and taken diverging paths that were wide asunder. But, one night, many years afterwards, our friend being in the North of England, and staying for the night in an inn, on the Yorkshire Moors, happened to look out of bed; and there, in the moonlight, leaning on a bureau near the window, steadfastly regarding him, saw his old college friend! The appearance being solemnly addressed, replied, in a kind of whisper, but very audibly, "Do not come near me. I am dead. I am here to redeem my promise. I come from another world, but may not disclose its secrets!" Then, the whole form becoming paler, melted, as it were, into the moonlight, and faded away.

Or, there was the daughter of the first occupier of the picturesque Elizabethan house, so famous in our neighbourhood. You have heard about her? No! Why, *She* went out one summer evening at twilight, when she was a beautiful girl, just seventeen years of age, to gather flowers in the garden; and presently came running, terrified, into the hall to her father, saying, "Oh, dear father, I have met myself!" He took her in his arms, and told her it was fancy, but she said, "Oh no! I met myself in the broad walk, and I was pale and gathering withered flowers, and I turned my head, and held them up!" And, that night, she died; and a picture of her story was begun, though never finished, and they say it is somewhere in the house to this day, with its face to the wall.

Or, the uncle of my brother's wife was riding home on horseback, one mellow evening at sunset, when, in a green lane close to his own house, he saw a man standing before him, in the very centre of a narrow way.

"Why does that man in the cloak stand there!" he thought. "Does he want me to ride over him?" But the figure never moved. He felt a strange sensation at seeing it so still, but slackened his trot and rode forward. When he was so close to it, as almost to touch it with his stirrup; his horse shied, and the figure glided up the bank, in a curious, unearthly manner—backward, and without seeming to use its feet—and was gone. The uncle of my brother's wife, exclaiming, "Good Heaven! It's my cousin Harry, from Bombay!" put spurs to his horse, which was suddenly in a profuse sweat, and, wondering at such strange behaviour, dashed round to the front of his house. There, he saw the same figure, just passing in at the long French window of the drawing-room, opening on the ground. He threw his bridle to a servant, and hastened in after it. His sister was sitting there, alone. "Alice, where's my cousin Harry?"

"Your cousin Harry, John?"

"Yes. From Bombay. I met him in the lane just now, and saw him enter here, this instant." Not a creature had been seen by any one; and in that hour and minute, as it afterwards appeared, this cousin died in India.

Or, it was a certain sensible old maiden lady, who died at ninety-nine, and retained her faculties to the last, who really did see the Orphan Boy; a story which has often been incorrectly told, but, of which the real truth is this—because it is, in fact, a story belonging to our family—and she was a connexion of our family. When she was about forty years of age, and still an uncommonly fine woman (her lover died young, which was the reason why she never married, though she had many offers), she went to stay at a place in Kent, which her brother, an Indian-Merchant, had newly bought.

There was a story that this place had once been held in trust by the guardian of a young boy; who was himself the next heir, and who killed the young boy by harsh and cruel treatment. She knew nothing of that. It has been said that there was a Cage in her bedroom in which the guardian used to put the boy. There was no such thing. There was only a closet. She went to bed, made no alarm whatever in the night, and in the morning said composedly to her maid when she came in, "Who is the pretty forlorn-looking child who has been peeping out of that closet all night?" The maid replied by giving a loud scream, and instantly decamping. She was surprised; but she was a woman of remarkable strength of mind, and she dressed herself and went downstairs, and closeted herself with her brother. "Now, Walter," she said, "I have been disturbed all night by a pretty, forlorn-looking boy, who has been constantly peeping out of that closet in my room, which I can't open. This is some trick."

"I am afraid not, Charlotte," said he, "for it is the legend of the house. It is the Orphan Boy. What did he do?"

"He opened the door softly," said she, "and peeped out. Sometimes, he came a step or two into the room. Then, I called to him, to encourage him, and he shrunk, and shuddered, and crept in again, and shut the door."

"The closet has no communication, Charlotte," said her brother, "with any other part of the house, and it's nailed up." This was undeniably true, and it took two carpenters a whole forenoon to get it open, for examination. Then, she was satisfied that she had seen the Orphan Boy. But, the wild and terrible part of the story is, that he was also seen by three of her brother's sons, in succession, who all died young. On the occasion of each child being taken ill, he came home in a heat, twelve hours before, and said, Oh, Mamma, he had been playing under a particular oak-tree, in a certain meadow, with a strange boy—a pretty, forlorn-looking boy, who was very timid, and made signs! From fatal experience, the parents came to know that this was the Orphan Boy, and that the course of that child whom he chose for his little playmate was surely run.

Legion is the name of the German castles, where we sit up alone to wait for the Spectre—where we are shown into a room, made comparatively cheerful for our reception—where we glance round at the shadows, thrown on the blank walls by the crackling fire—where we feel very lonely when the village innkeeper and his pretty daughter have retired, after laying down a fresh store of wood upon the hearth, and setting forth on the small table such supper-cheer as a cold roast capon, bread, grapes, and a flask of old Rhine wine—where the reverberating doors close on their retreat, one after another, like so many peals of sullen thunder—and where, about the small hours of the night, we come into the knowledge of divers supernatural mysteries. Legion is the name of the haunted German students, in whose society we draw yet nearer to the fire, while the school-boy in the corner opens his eyes wide and round, and flies off the footstool he has chosen for his seat, when the door accidentally blows open. Vast is the crop of such fruit, shining on our Christmas Tree; in blossom, almost at the very top; ripening all down the boughs!

Among the later toys and fancies hanging there—as idle often and less pure—be the images once associated with the sweet old Waits, the softened music in the night, ever unalterable! Encircled by the social thoughts of Christmas-time, still let the benignant figure of my childhood stand unchanged! In every cheerful image and suggestion that the season brings, may the bright star that rested above the poor roof, be the star of all the Christian World! A moment's pause, O vanishing tree, of which the lower boughs are dark to me as yet, and let me look once more! I know there are blank spaces on thy branches, where eyes that I have loved have shone and smiled; from which they are departed. But, far above, I see the raiser of the dead girl, and the Widow's Son; and God is good! If Age be hiding for me in the unseen portion of thy downward growth, O, may I, with a grey head, turn a child's heart to that figure yet, and a child's trustfulness and confidence!

Now, the tree is decorated with bright merriment, and song, and dance, and cheerfulness. And they are welcome. Innocent and welcome be they ever held; beneath the branches of the Christmas Tree, which cast no gloomy shadow! But, as it sinks into the ground, I hear a whisper going through the leaves. "This, in commemoration of the law of love and kindness, mercy and compassion. This, in remembrance of Me!"

Bertie's Christmas Eve

It was Christmas Eve, and the family circle of Luke Steffink, Esq., was aglow with the amiability and random mirth which the occasion demanded. A long and lavish dinner had been partaken of, waits had been round and sung carols, the house-party had regaled itself with more caroling on its own account, and there had been romping which, even in a pulpit reference, could not have been condemned as ragging. In the midst of the general glow, however, there was one black unkindled cinder.

Bertie Steffink, nephew of the aforementioned Luke, had early in life adopted the profession of ne'er-do-weel; his father had been something of the kind before him. At the age of eighteen Bertie had commenced that round of visits to our Colonial possessions, so seemly and desirable in the case of a Prince of the Blood, so suggestive of insincerity in a young man of the middle-class. He had gone to grow tea in Ceylon and fruit in British Columbia, and to help sheep to grow wool in Australia. At the age of twenty he had just returned from some similar errand in Canada, from which it may be gathered that the trial he gave to these various experiments was of the summary drum-head nature. Luke Steffink, who fulfilled the troubled role of guardian and deputy-parent to Bertie, deplored the persistent manifestation of the homing instinct on his nephew's part, and his solemn thanks earlier in the day for the blessing of reporting a united family had no reference to Bertie's return.

Arrangements had been promptly made for packing the youth off to a distant corner of Rhodesia, whence return would be a difficult matter; the journey to this uninviting destination was imminent, in fact a more careful and willing traveller would have already begun to think about his packing. Hence Bertie was in no mood to share in the festive spirit which displayed itself around him, and resentment smouldered within him at the eager, self-absorbed discussion of social plans for the coming months which he heard on all sides. Beyond depressing his uncle and the family circle generally by singing "Say au revoir, and not good-bye," he had taken no part in the evening's conviviality.

Eleven o'clock had struck some half-hour ago, and the elder Steffinks began to throw out suggestions leading up to that process which they called retiring for the night.

"Come, Teddie, it's time you were in your little bed, you know," said Luke Steffink to his thirteen-year-old son.

"That's where we all ought to be," said Mrs. Steffink.

"There wouldn't be room," said Bertie.

The remark was considered to border on the scandalous; everybody ate raisins and almonds with the nervous industry of sheep feeding during threatening weather.

"In Russia," said Horace Bordenby, who was staying in the house as a Christmas guest, "I've read that the peasants believe that if you go into a cow-house or stable at midnight on Christmas Eve you will hear the animals talk. They're supposed to have the gift of speech at that one moment of the year."

"Oh, *do* let's *all* go down to the cow-house and listen to what they've got to say?" exclaimed Beryl, to whom anything was thrilling and amusing if you did it in a troop.

Mrs. Steffink made a laughing protest, but gave a virtual consent by saying, "We must all wrap up well, then." The idea seemed a scatterbrained one to her, and almost heathenish, but it afforded an opportunity for "throwing the young people together," and as such she welcomed it. Mr. Horace Bordenby was a young man with quite substantial prospects, and he had danced with Beryl at a local subscription ball a sufficient number of times to warrant the authorized inquiry on the part of the neighbours whether "there was anything in it." Though Mrs. Steffink would not have put it in so many words, she shared the idea of the Russian peasantry that on this night the beast might speak.

The cow-house stood at the junction of the garden with a small paddock, an isolated survival, in a suburban neighbourhood, of what had once been a small farm. Luke Steffink was complacently proud of his cow-house and his two cows; he felt that they gave him a stamp of solidity which no number of Wyandottes or Orpingtons could impart. They even seemed to link him in a sort of inconsequent way with those patriarchs who derived importance from their floating capital of flocks and herds, he-asses and she-asses. It had been an anxious and momentous occasion when he had had to decide definitely between "the Byre" and "the Ranch" for the naming of his villa residence. A December midnight was hardly the moment he would have chosen for showing his farm-building to visitors, but since it was a fine night, and the young people were anxious for an excuse for a mild frolic, Luke consented to chaperon the expedition. The servants had long since gone to bed, so the house was left in charge of Bertie, who scornfully declined to stir out on the pretext of listening to bovine conversation.

"We must go quietly," said Luke, as he headed the procession of giggling young folk, brought up in the rear by the shawled and hooded figure of Mrs. Steffink; "I've always laid stress on keeping this a quiet and orderly neighbourhood."

It was a few minutes to midnight when the party reached the cow-house and made its way in by the light of Luke's stable lantern. For a moment every one stood in silence, almost with a feeling of being in church.

"Daisy—the one lying down—is by a shorthorn bull out of a Guernsey cow," announced Luke in a hushed voice, which was in keeping with the fore-going impression.

"Is she?" said Bordenby, rather as if he had expected her to be by Rembrandt.

"Myrtle is—"

Myrtle's family history was cut short by a little scream from the women of the party.

The cow-house door had closed noiselessly behind them and the key had turned gratingly in the lock; then they heard Bertie's voice pleasantly wishing them good night and his footsteps retreating along the garden path.

Luke Steffink strode to the window; it was a small square opening of the old-fashioned sort, with iron bars let into the stonework.

"Unlock the door this instant," he shouted, with as much air of menacing authority as a hen might assume when screaming through the bars of a coop at a marauding hawk. In reply to his summons the hall-door closed with a defiant bang.

A neighbouring clock struck the hour of midnight. If the cows had received the gift of human speech at that moment they would not have been able to make themselves heard. Seven or eight other voices were engaged in describing Bertie's present conduct and his general character at a high pressure of excitement and indignation.

In the course of half an hour or so everything that it was permissible to say about Bertie had been said some dozens of times, and other topics began to come to the front—the extreme mustiness of the cow-house, the possibility of it catching fire, and the probability of it being a Rowton House for the vagrant rats of the neighbourhood. And still no sign of deliverance came to the unwilling vigil-keepers.

Towards one o'clock the sound of rather boisterous and undisciplined carol-singing approached rapidly, and came to a sudden anchorage, apparently just outside the garden-gate. A motor-load of youthful "bloods," in a high state of conviviality, had made a temporary halt for repairs; the stoppage, however did not extend to the vocal efforts of the party, and the watchers in the cow-shed were treated to a highly un-authorized rendering of "Good King Wenceslas" in which the adjective "good" appeared to be very carelessly applied.

The noise had the effect of bringing Bertie out into the garden, but he utterly ignored the pale, angry faces peering out at the cow-house window, and concentrated his attention on the revellers outside the gate.

"Wassail, you chaps!" he shouted.

"Wassail, old sport!" they shouted back; "we'd jolly well drink y'r health, only we've nothing to drink it in."

"Come and wassail inside," said Bertie hospitably; "I'm all alone, and there's heaps of 'wet.'"

They were total strangers, but his touch of kindness made them instantly his kin. In another moment the unauthorized version of King Wenceslas, which, like many other scandals, grew worse on repetition, went echoing up the garden path; two of the revellers gave an impromptu performance on the way by executing the staircase waltz up the terraces of what Luke Steffink, hitherto with some justification, called his rock-garden. The rock part of it was still there when the waltz had been accorded its third encore. Luke, more than ever like a cooped hen behind the cow-house bars, was in a position to realize the feelings of concert-goers unable to countermand the call for an encore which they neither desire nor deserve.

The hall door closed with a bang on Bertie's guests and the sounds of merriment became faint and muffled to the weary watchers at the other end of the garden. Presently two ominous pops, in quick succession, made themselves distinctly heard.

"They've got at the champagne!" exclaimed Mrs. Steffink.

"Perhaps it's the sparkling Moselle," said Luke hopefully.

Three or four more pops were heard.

"The champagne *and* the sparkling Moselle," said Mrs. Steffink.

Luke uncorked an expletive which, like brandy in a temperance household, was only used on rare emergencies. Mr. Horace Bordenby had been making use of similar expressions under his breath for a considerable time past. The experiment of "throwing the young people together" had been prolonged beyond a point when it was likely to produce any romantic result.

Some forty minutes later the hall door opened and disgorged a crowd that had thrown off any restraint of shyness that might have influenced its earlier actions. Its vocal efforts in the direction of carol-singing were now supplemented by instrumental music; a Christmas-tree that had been prepared for the children of the gardener and other household retainers had yielded a rich spoil of tin trumpets, rattles, and drums. The life-story of King Wenceslas had been dropped, Luke was thankful to notice, but it was intensely irritating for the chilled prisoners in the cow-house to be told that it was a hot time in the old town to-night, together with some accurate but entirely superfluous information as to the imminence of Christmas morning. Judging by the protests which began to be shouted from the upper windows of neighbouring houses, the sentiments prevailing in the cow-house were heartily echoed in other quarters. The revellers found their car, and, what was more remarkable managed to drive off in it, with a parting fanfare of tin trumpets. The lively beat of a drum disclosed the fact that the master of the revels remained on the scene.

"Bertie!" came in an angry, imploring chorus of shouts and screams from the cow-house window.

"Hullo," cried the owner of the name, turning his rather errant steps in the direction of the summons; "are you people still there? Must have heard everything cows got to say by this time. If you haven't, no use waiting. After all, it's a Russian legend, and Russian Chrismush Eve not due for 'nother fortnight. Better come out."

After one or two ineffectual attempts he managed to pitch the key of the cow-house door in through the window. Then, lifting his voice in the strains of "I'm afraid to go home in the dark," with a lusty drum accompaniment, he led the way back to the house. The hurried procession of the released that followed in his steps came in for a good deal of the adverse comment that his exuberant display had evoked.

It was the happiest Christmas Eve he had ever spent. To quote his own words, he had a rotten Christmas.

Christmas; Or, The Good Fairy

"Oh, *dear!* Christmas is coming in a fort-night, and I have got to think up presents for everybody!" said young Ellen Stuart, as she leaned languidly back in her chair. "Dear me, it's so tedious! Everybody has got everything that can be thought of."

"Oh, no," said her confidential adviser, Miss Lester, in a soothing tone. "You have means of buying everything you can fancy; and when every shop and store is glittering with all manner of splendors, you cannot surely be at a loss."

"Well, now, just listen. To begin with, there's mamma. What can I get for her? I have thought of ever so many things. She has three card cases, four gold thimbles, two or three gold chains, two writing desks of different patterns; and then as to rings, brooches, boxes, and all other things, I should think she might be sick of the sight of them. I am sure I am," said she, languidly gazing on her white and jeweled fingers.

This view of the case seemed rather puzzling to the

adviser, and there was silence for a few minutes, when Ellen, yawning, resumed:

"And then there's cousins Jane and Mary; I suppose they will be coming down on me with a whole load of presents; and Mrs. B. will send me something—she did last year; and then there's cousins William and Tom—I must get them something; and I would like to do it well enough, if I only knew what to get."

"Well," said Eleanor's aunt, who had been sitting quietly rattling her knitting needles during this speech, "it's a pity that you had not such a subject to practice on as I was when I was a girl. Presents did not fly about in those days as they do now. I remember, when I was ten years old, my father gave me a most marvelously ugly sugar dog for a Christmas gift, and I was perfectly delighted with it, the very idea of a present was so new to us."

"Dear aunt, how delighted I should be if I had any such fresh, unsophisticated body to get presents for! But to get and get for people that have more than they know what to do with now; to add pictures, books, and gilding when the centre tables are loaded with them now, and rings and jewels when they are a perfect drug! I wish myself that I were not sick, and sated, and tired with having everything in the world given me."

"Well, Eleanor," said her aunt, "if you really do want unsophisticated subjects to practice on, I can put you in the way of it. I can show you more than one family to whom you might seem to be a very good fairy, and where such gifts as you could give with all ease would seem like a magic dream."

"Why, that would really be worth while, aunt."

"Look over in that back alley," said her aunt. "You see those buildings?"

"That miserable row of shanties? Yes."

"Well, I have several acquaintances there who have never been tired of Christmas gifts or gifts of any other kind. I assure you, you could make quite a sensation over there."

"Well, who is there? Let us know."

"Do you remember Owen, that used to make your shoes?"

"Yes, I remember something about him."

"Well, he has fallen into a consumption, and cannot work any more; and he, and his wife, and three little children live in one of the rooms."

"How do they get along?"

"His wife takes in sewing sometimes, and sometimes goes out washing. Poor Owen! I was over there yesterday; he looks thin and wasted, and his wife was saying that he was parched with constant fever, and had very little appetite. She had, with great self-denial, and by restricting herself almost of necessary food, got him two or three oranges; and the poor fellow seemed so eager after them."

"Poor fellow!" said Eleanor, involuntarily.

"Now," said her aunt, "suppose Owen's wife should get up on Christmas morning and find at the door a couple of dozen of oranges, and some of those nice white grapes, such as you had at your party last week; don't you think it would make a sensation?"

"Why, yes, I think very likely it might; but who else, aunt? You spoke of a great many."

"Well, on the lower floor there is a neat little room, that is always kept perfectly trim and tidy; it belongs to a young couple who have nothing beyond the husband's day wages to live on. They are, nevertheless, as cheerful and chipper as a couple of wrens; and she is up and down half a dozen times a day, to help poor Mrs. Owen. She has a baby of her own about five months old, and of course does all the cooking, washing, and ironing for herself and husband; and yet, when Mrs. Owen goes out to wash, she takes her baby, and keeps it whole days for her."

"I'm sure she deserves that the good fairies should smile on her," said Eleanor; "one baby exhausts my stock of virtues very rapidly."

"But you ought to see her baby," said Aunt E.; "so plump, so rosy, and good-natured, and always clean as a lily. This baby is a sort of household shrine; nothing is too sacred or too good for it; and I believe the little thrifty woman feels only one temptation to be extravagant, and that is to get some ornaments to adorn this little divinity."

"Why, did she ever tell you so?"

"No; but one day, when I was coming down stairs, the door of their room was partly open, and I saw a peddler there with open box. John, the husband, was standing with a little purple cap on his hand, which he was regarding with mystified, admiring air, as if he didn't quite comprehend it, and trim little Mary gazing at it with longing eyes.

"'I think we might get it,' said John.

"'Oh, no,' said she, regretfully; 'yet I wish we could, it's so pretty!'"

"Say no more, aunt. I see the good fairy must pop a cap into the window on Christmas morning. Indeed, it shall be done. How they will wonder where it came from, and talk about it for months to come!"

"Well, then," continued her aunt, "in the next street to ours there is a miserable building, that looks as if it were just going to topple over; and away up in the third story, in a little room just under the eaves, live two poor, lonely old women. They are both nearly on to ninety. I was in there day before yesterday. One of them is constantly confined to her bed with rheumatism; the other, weak and feeble, with failing sight and trembling hands, totters about, her only helper; and they are entirely dependent on charity."

"Can't they do anything? Can't they knit?" said Eleanor.

"You are young and strong, Eleanor, and have quick eyes and nimble fingers; how long would it take you to knit a pair of stockings?"

"I?" said Eleanor. "What an idea! I never tried, but I think I could get a pair done in a week, perhaps."

"And if somebody gave you twenty-five cents for them, and out of this you had to get food, and pay room rent, and buy coal for your fire, and oil for your lamp—"

"Stop, aunt, for pity's sake!"

"Well, I will stop; but they can't: they must pay so much every month for that miserable shell they live in, or be turned into the street. The meal and flour that some kind person sends goes off for them just as it does for others, and they must get more or starve; and coal is now scarce and high priced."

"O aunt, I'm quite convinced, I'm sure; don't run me down and annihilate me with all these terrible realities. What shall I do to play good fairy to these old women?"

"If you will give me full power, Eleanor, I will put up a basket to be sent to them that will give them something to remember all winter."

"Oh, certainly I will. Let me see if I can't think of something myself."

293

"Well, Eleanor, suppose, then, some fifty or sixty years hence, if you were old, and your father, and mother, and aunts, and uncles, now so thick around you, lay cold and silent in so many graves—you have somehow got away off to a strange city, where you were never known—you live in a miserable garret, where snow blows at night through the cracks, and the fire is very apt to go out in the old cracked stove—you sit crouching over the dying embers the evening before Christmas—nobody to speak to you, nobody to care for you, except another poor old soul who lies moaning in the bed. Now, what would you like to have sent you?"

"O aunt, what a dismal picture!"

"And yet, Ella, all poor, forsaken old women are made of young girls, who expected it in their youth as little as you do, perhaps."

"Say no more, aunt. I'll buy—let me see—a comfortable warm shawl for each of these poor women; and I'll send them—let me see—oh, some tea—nothing goes down with old women like tea; and I'll make John wheel some coal over to them; and, aunt, it would not be a very bad thought to send them a new stove. I remember, the other day, when mamma was pricing stoves, I saw some such nice ones for two or three dollars."

"For a new hand, Ella, you work up the idea very well," said her aunt.

"But how much ought I to give, for any one case, to these women, say?"

"How much did you give last year for any single Christmas present?"

"Why, six or seven dollars for some; those elegant souvenirs were seven dollars; that ring I gave Mrs. B. was twenty."

"And do you suppose Mrs. B. was any happier for it?"

"No, really, I don't think she cared much about it; but I had to give her something, because she had sent me something the year before, and I did not want to send a paltry present to one in her circumstances."

"Then, Ella, give the same to any poor, distressed, suffering creature who really needs it, and see in how many forms of good such a sum will appear. That one hard, cold, glittering ring, that now cheers nobody, and means nothing, that you give because you must, and she takes because she must, might, if broken up into smaller sums, send real warm and heartfelt gladness through many a cold and cheerless dwelling, through many an aching heart."

"You are getting to be an orator, aunt; but don't you approve of Christmas presents, among friends and equals?"

"Yes, indeed," said her aunt, fondly stroking her head. "I have had some Christmas presents that did me a world of good—a little book mark, for instance, that a certain niece of mine worked for me, with wonderful secrecy, three years ago, when she was not a young lady with a purse full of money—that book mark was a true Christmas present; and my young couple across the way are plotting a profound surprise to each other on Christmas morning. John has contrived, by an hour of extra work every night, to lay by enough to get Mary a new calico dress; and she, poor soul, has bargained away the only thing in the jewelry line she ever possessed, to be laid out on a new hat for him.

"I know, too, a washerwoman who has a poor lame boy—a patient, gentle little fellow—who has lain quietly for weeks and months in his little crib, and his mother is going to give him a splendid Christmas present."

"What is it, pray?"

"A whole orange! Don't laugh. She will pay ten whole cents for it; for it shall be none of your common oranges, but a picked one of the very best going! She has put by the money, a cent at a time, for a whole month; and nobody knows which will be happiest in it, Willie or his mother. These are such Christmas presents as I like to think of—gifts coming from love, and tending to produce love; these are the appropriate gifts of the day."

"But don't you think that it's right for those who *have* money to give expensive presents, supposing always, as you say, they are given from real affection?"

"Sometimes, undoubtedly. The Saviour did not condemn her who broke an alabaster box of ointment—very precious—simply as a proof of love, even although the suggestion was made, 'This might have been sold for three hundred pence, and given to the poor.' I have thought he would regard with sympathy the fond efforts which human love sometimes makes to express itself by gifts, the rarest and most costly. How I rejoiced with all my heart, when Charles Elton gave his poor mother that splendid Chinese shawl and gold watch! because I knew they came from the very fulness of his heart to a mother that he could not do too much for—a mother that has done and suffered everything for him. In some such cases, when resources are ample, a costly gift seems to have a graceful appropriateness; but I cannot approve of it if it exhausts all the means of doing for the poor; it is better, then, to give a simple offering, and to do something for those who really need it."

Eleanor looked thoughtful; her aunt laid down her knitting, and said, in a tone of gentle seriousness, "Whose birth does Christmas commemorate, Ella?"

"Our Saviour's, certainly, aunt."

"Yes," said her aunt. "And when and how was he born? In a stable! laid in a manger; thus born, that in all ages he might be known as the brother and friend of the poor. And surely, it seems but appropriate to commemorate his birthday by an especial remembrance of the lowly, the poor, the outcast, and distressed; and if Christ should come back to our city on a Christmas day, where should we think it most appropriate to his character to find him? Would he be carrying splendid gifts to splendid dwellings, or would he be gliding about in the cheerless haunts of the desolate, the poor, the forsaken, and the sorrowful?"

And here the conversation ended.

"What sort of Christmas presents is Ella buying?" said Cousin Tom, as the servant handed in a portentous-looking package, which had been just rung in at the door.

"Let's open it," said saucy Will. "Upon my word, two great gray blanket shawls! These must be for you and me, Tom! And what's this? A great bolt of cotton flannel and gray yarn stockings!"

The door bell rang again, and the servant brought in another bulky parcel, and deposited it on the marble-topped centre table.

"What's here?" said Will, cutting the cord. "Whew! a perfect nest of packages! Oolong tea! oranges! grapes! white sugar! Bless me, Ella must be going to house-keeping!"

"Or going crazy!" said Tom; "and on my word," said

he, looking out of the window, "there's a drayman ringing at our door, with a stove, with a teakettle set in the top of it!"

"Ella's cook stove, of course," said Will; and just at this moment the young lady entered, with her purse hanging gracefully over her hand.

"Now, boys, you are too bad!" she exclaimed, as each of the mischievous youngsters was gravely marching up and down, attired in a gray shawl.

"Didn't you get them for us? We thought you did," said both. "Ella, I want some of that cotton flannel, to make me a pair of pantaloons," said Tom.

"I say, Ella," said Will, "when are you going to housekeeping? Your cooking stove is standing down in the street; 'pon my word, John is loading some coal on the dray with it."

"Ella, isn't that going to be sent to my office?" said Tom; "do you know I do so languish for a new stove with a teakettle in the top, to heat a fellow's shaving-water!"

Just then, another ring at the door, and the grinning servant handed in a small brown paper parcel for Miss Ella. Tom made a dive at it, and tearing off the brown paper, discovered a jaunty little purple velvet cap, with silver tassels.

"My smoking cap, as I live!" said he; "only I shall have to wear it on my thumb, instead of my head—too small entirely," said he, shaking his head gravely.

"Come, you saucy boys," said Aunt E., entering briskly. "What are you teasing Ella for?"

"Why, do see this lot of things, aunt! What in the world is Ella going to do with them?"

"Oh, I know!"

"You know! Then I can guess, aunt, it is some of your

charitable works. You are going to make a juvenile Lady Bountiful of El, eh?"

Ella, who had colored to the roots of her hair at the *expose* of her very unfashionable Christmas preparations, now took heart, and bestowed a very gentle and salutary little cuff on the saucy head that still wore the purple cap, and then hastened to gather up her various purchases.

"Laugh away," said she, gayly; "and a good many others will laugh, too, over these things. I got them to make people laugh—people that are not in the habit of laughing!"

"Well, well, I see into it," said Will; "and I tell you I think right well of the idea, too. There are worlds of money wasted, at this time of the year, in getting things that nobody wants, and nobody cares for after they are got; and I am glad, for my part, that you are going to get up a variety in this line; in fact, I should like to give you one of these stray leaves to help on," said he, dropping a ten dollar note into her paper. "I like to encourage girls to think of something besides breastpins and sugar candy."

But our story spins on too long. If anybody wants to see the results of Ella's first attempts at *good fairyism*, they can call at the doors of two or three old buildings on Christmas morning, and they shall hear all about it.

NATHANIEL HAWTHORNE

The Snow-Image

One afternoon of a cold winter's day, when the sun shone forth with chilly brightness, after a long storm, two children asked leave of their mother to run out and play in the new-fallen snow. The elder child was a little girl, whom, because she was of a tender and modest disposition, and was thought to be very beautiful, her parents, and other people who were familiar with her, used to call Violet. But her brother was known by the style and title of Peony, on account of the ruddiness of his broad and round little phiz, which made everybody think of sunshine and great scarlet flowers. The father of these two children, a certain Mr. Lindsey, it is important to say, was an excellent but exceedingly matter-of-fact sort of man, a dealer in hardware, and was sturdily accustomed to take what is called the common-sense view of all matters that came under his consideration. With a heart about as tender as other people's, he had a head as hard and impenetrable, and therefore, perhaps, as empty, as one of the iron pots which it was a part of his business to sell. The mother's character, on the other hand, had a strain of poetry in it, a trait of unworldly beauty,—a delicate and dewy flower, as it were, that had survived out of her imaginative youth, and still kept itself alive amid the dusty realities of matrimony and mother-hood.

So, Violet and Peony, as I began with saying, besought their mother to let them run out and play in the new snow; for, though it had looked so dreary and dismal, drifting downward out of the gray sky, it had a very cheerful aspect, now that the sun was shining on it. The children dwelt in a city, and had no wider play-place than a little garden before the house, divided by a white fence from the street, and with a pear-tree and two or three plum-trees overshadowing it, and some rose-bushes just in front of the parlor windows. The trees and shrubs, however, were now leafless, and their twigs were enveloped in the light snow, which thus made a kind of wintry foliage, with here and there a pendent icicle for the fruit.

"Yes, Violet,—yes, my little Peony," said their kind mother; "you may go out and play in the new snow."

Accordingly, the good lady bundled up her darlings in woollen jackets and wadded sacks, and put comforters round their necks, and a pair of striped gaiters on each little pair of legs, and worsted mittens on their hands, and gave them a kiss apiece, by way of a spell to keep away Jack Frost. Forth sallied the two children, with a hop-skip-and-jump, that carried them at once into the very heart of a huge snow-drift, whence Violet emerged like a snow-bunting, while little Peony floundered out with his round face in full bloom. Then what a merry time had they! To look at them frolicking in the wintry garden, you would have thought that the dark and pitiless storm had been sent for no other purpose but to provide a new plaything for Violet and Peony; and that they themselves had been created, as the snowbirds were, to take delight only in the tempest, and in the white mantle which it spread over the earth.

At last when they had frosted one another all over with handfuls of snow, Violet, after laughing heartily at little Peony's figure, was struck with a new idea.

"You look exactly like a snow-image, Peony," said she, "if your cheeks were not so red. And that puts me in mind! Let us make an image out of snow,—an image of a little girl,—and it shall be our sister, and shall run about and play with us all winter long. Won't it be nice?"

"O, yes!" cried Peony, as plainly as he could speak, for was but a little boy. "That will be nice! And mamma shall see it!"

"Yes," answered Violet; "mamma shall see the new little girl. But she must not make her come into the warm parlor; for, you know, our little snow-sister will not love the warmth."

And forthwith the children began this great business of making a snow-image that should run about; while their mother, who was sitting at the window and over-heard some of their talk, could not help smiling at the gravity with which they set about it. They really seemed to imagine that there would be no difficulty whatever in creating a live little girl out of the snow. And, to say the truth, if miracles are ever to be wrought, it will be by putting our hands to the work in precisely such a simple and undoubting frame of mind as that in which Violet and Peony now undertook to perform one, without so much as knowing that it was a miracle. So thought the mother; and thought, likewise, that the new snow, just fallen from heaven, would be excellent material to make new beings of, if it were not so very cold. She gazed at the children a moment longer, delighting to watch their little figures,—the girl, tall for her age, graceful and agile and so delicately colored that she looked like a cheerful thought, more than a physical reality,—while Peony expanded in breadth rather than height, and rolled along on his short and sturdy legs, as substantial as an elephant, though not quite so big. Then the mother resumed her work. What it was I forget; but she was either trimming a silken bonnet for Violet or darning a pair of stockings for little Peony's short legs. Again, however, and again, and yet other agains, she could not help turning her head to the window to see how the children got on with their snow-image.

Indeed, it was an exceedingly pleasant sight, those bright little souls at their tasks! Moreover, it was really wonderful to observe how knowingly and skilfully they managed the matter. Violet assumed the chief direction and told Peony what to do, while, with her own delicate fingers, she shaped out all the nicer parts of the snow-figure. It seemed, in fact, not so much to be made by the children, as to grow up under their hands while they were playing and prattling about it. Their mother was quite surprised at this? and the longer she looked the more and more surprised she grew.

"What remarkable children mine are!" thought she smiling with a mother's pride; and smiling at herself, too, for being so proud of them. "What other children could have made anything so like a little girl's figure out of snow, at the first trial? Well;—but now I must finish Peony's new frock, for his grandfather is coming to-morrow, and I want the little fellow to look handsome."

So she took up the frock, and was soon as busily at

work again with her needle as the two children with their snow-image. But still, as the needle travelled hither and thither through the seams of the dress the mother made her toil light and happy by listening to the airy voices of Violet and Peony. They kept talking to one another all the time, their tongues being quite as active as their feet and hands. Except at intervals she could not distinctly hear what was said, but had merely a sweet impression that they were in a most loving mood, and were enjoying themselves highly, and that the business of making the snow-image went prosperously on. Now and then, however, when Violet and Peony happened to raise their voices, the words were as audible as if they had been spoken in the very parlor, where the mother sat. O, how delightfully those words echoed in her heart, even though they meant nothing so very wise or wonderful, after all!

But you must know a mother listens with her heart, much more than with her ears; and thus she is often delighted with the thrills of celestial music, when other people can hear nothing of the kind.

"Peony, Peony!" cried Violet to her brother, who had gone to another part of the garden, "bring me some of that fresh snow, Peony, from the very furthest corner, where we have not been trampling. I want it to shape our little snow-sister's bosom with. You know that part must be quite pure, just as it came out of the sky!"

"Here it is, Violet!" answered Peony, in his bluff tone,—but a very sweet tone, too,—as he came floundering through the half-trodden drifts. "Here is the snow for her little bosom. O, Violet, how beau-ti-ful she begins to look!"

"Yes," said Violet, thoughtfully and quietly; "our snow-sister does look very lovely. I did not quite know,

Peony, that we could make such a sweet little girl as this."

The mother, as she listened, thought how fit and delightful an incident it would be, if fairies, or, still better, if angel-children were to come from paradise, and play invisibly with her own darlings, and help them to make their snow-image, giving it the features of celestial babyhood! Violet and Peony would not be aware of their immortal playmates,—only they would see that the image grew very beautiful while they worked at it, and would think that they themselves had done it all.

"My little girl and boy deserve such playmates, if mortal children ever did!" said the mother to herself; and then she smiled again at her own motherly pride.

Nevertheless, the idea seized upon her imagination; and, ever and anon, she took a glimpse out of the window, half dreaming that she might see the golden-haired children of paradise sporting with her own golden-haired Violet and bright-cheeked Peony.

Now, for a few moments, there was a busy and earnest, but indistinct hum of the two children's voices, as Violet and Peony wrought together with one happy consent. Violet still seemed to be the guiding spirit while Peony acted rather as a laborer, and brought her the snow from far and near. And yet the little urchin evidently had a proper understanding of the matter, too! "Peony, Peony!" cried Violet; for her brother was again at the other side of the garden. "Bring me those light wreaths of snow that have rested on the lower branches of the pear-tree. You can clamber on the snow-drift, Peony, and reach them easily. I must have them to make some ringlets for our snow-sister's head!"

"Here they are, Violet!" answered the little boy. "Take

care you do not break them. Well done! Well done! How pretty!"

"Does she not look sweetly?" said Violet, with a very satisfied tone; "and now we must have some little shining bits of ice, to make the brightness of her eyes. She is not finished yet. Mamma will see how very beautiful she is; but papa will say, 'Tush! nonsense!—come in out of the cold!'"

"Let us call mamma to look out," said Peony; and then he shouted lustily, "Mamma! mamma!! mamma!!! Look out, and see what a nice 'ittle girl we are making!"

The mother put down her work, for an instant, and looked out of the window. But it so happened that the sun—for this was one of the shortest days of the whole year—had sunken so nearly to the edge of the world, that his setting shine came obliquely into the lady's eyes. So she was dazzled, you must understand, and could not very distinctly observe what was in the garden. Still, however, through all that bright, blinding dazzle of the sun and the new snow, she beheld a small white figure in the garden, that seemed to have a wonderful deal of human likeness about it. And she saw Violet and Peony,—indeed, she looked more at them than at the image,—she saw the two children still at work; Peony bringing fresh snow, and Violet applying it to the figure as scientifically as a sculptor adds clay to his model. Indistinctly as she discerned the snow-child, the mother thought to herself that never before was there a snow-figure so cunningly made, nor ever such a dear little girl and boy to make it.

"They do everything better than other children," said she, very complacently. "No wonder they make better snow-images!"

She sat down again to her work, and made as much

haste with it as possible; because twilight would soon come, and Peony's frock was not yet finished, and grandfather was expected, by railroad, pretty early in the morning. Faster and faster, therefore, went her flying fingers. The children, likewise, kept busily at work in the garden, and still the mother listened, whenever she could catch a word. She was amused to observe how their little imaginations had got mixed up with what they were doing, and were carried away by it. They seemed positively to think that the snow-child would run about and play with them.

"What a nice playmate she will be for us, all winter long!" said Violet. "I hope papa will not be afraid of her giving us a cold! Shan't you love her dearly, Peony?"

"O, yes!" cried Peony. "And I will hug her, and she shall sit down close by me, and drink some of my warm milk!"

"O, no, Peony!" answered Violet, with grave wisdom. "That will not do at all. Warm milk will not be wholesome for our little snow-sister. Little snow-people, like her, eat nothing but icicles. No, no, Peony; we must not give her anything warm to drink!"

There was a minute or two of silence; for Peony, whose short legs were never weary, had gone on a pilgrimage again to the other side of the garden. All of a sudden, Violet cried out, loudly and joyfully.

"Look here, Peony! Come quickly! A light has been shining on her cheek out of that rose-colored cloud! and the color does not go away! Is not that beautiful?"

"Yes; it is beau-ti-ful," answered Peony, pronouncing the three syllables with deliberate accuracy. "O, Violet, only look at her hair! It is all like gold!"

"O, certainly," said Violet, with tranquillity, as if it were very much a matter of course. "That color, you know, comes from the golden clouds, that we see up there in the sky. She is almost finished now. But her lips must be made very red,—redder than her cheeks. Perhaps, Peony, it will make them red, if we both kiss them."

Accordingly, the mother heard two smart little smacks, as if both her children were kissing the snow-image on its frozen mouth. But, as this did not seem to make the lips quite red enough, Violet next proposed that the snow-child should be invited to kiss Peony's scarlet cheek.

"Come, 'ittle snow-sister, kiss me;" cried Peony. "There, she has kissed you," added Violet, "and now her lips are very red. And she blushed a little, too!"

"O what a cold kiss!" cried Peony.

Just then, there came a breeze of the pure west wind, sweeping through the garden and rattling the parlor windows. It sounded so wintry cold, that the mother was about to tap on the window-pane with her thimbled finger, to summon the two children in, when they both cried out to her with one voice. The tone was not a tone of surprise, although they were evidently a good deal excited; it appeared rather as if they were very much rejoiced at some event that had now happened, but which they had been looking for, and had reckoned upon all along.

"Mamma! mamma! We have finished our little snow-sister, and she is running about the garden with us!"

"What imaginative little beings my children are!" thought the mother, putting the last few stitches into Peony's frock. "And it is strange, too, that they make me almost as much a child as they themselves are! I can hardly help believing, now, that the snow-image has really come to life!"

"Dear mamma!" cried Violet, "pray look out, and see what a sweet playmate we have!"

The mother, being thus entreated, could no longer delay to look forth from the window. The sun was now gone out of the sky, leaving, however, a rich inheritance of his brightness among those purple and golden clouds which make the sunsets of winter so magnificent. But there was not the slightest gleam or dazzle, either on the window or on the snow; so that the good lady could look all over the garden, and see everything and every-body in it. And what do you think she saw there? Violet and Peony, of course, her own two darling children. Ah, but whom or what did she besides? Why, if you will believe me, there was a small figure of a girl, dressed all in white, with rose-tinged cheeks and ringlets of golden hue, playing about the garden with the two children! A stranger though she was, the child seemed to be on as familiar terms with Violet and Peony, and they with her, as if all the three had been playmates during the whole of their little lives. The mother thought to herself that it must certainly be the daughter of one of the neigh-bors, and that, seeing Violet and Peony in the garden, the child had run across the street to play with them. So this kind lady went to the door, intending to invite the little runaway into her comfortable parlor; for now that the sunshine was withdrawn, the atmosphere out of doors, was already growing very cold.

But, after opening the house-door, she stood an instant on the threshold, hesitating whether she ought to ask the child to come in, or whether she should even speak to her. Indeed, she almost doubted whether it were a real child, after all, or only a light wreath of the new-fallen snow, blown hither and thither about the garden by the intensely cold west wind. There was certainly something very singular in the aspect of the little stranger. Among all the children of the neighborhood, the lady could remember no such face, with its pure white, and delicate rose-color, and the golden ringlets tossing about the forehead and cheeks. And as for her dress, which was entirely of white, and fluttering in the breeze, it was such as no reasonable woman would put upon a little girl, when sending her out to play, in the depth of winter. It made this kind and careful mother shiver only to look at those small feet, with nothing in the world on them, except a very thin pair of white slippers. Nevertheless, airily as she was clad, the child seemed to feel not the slightest inconvenience from the cold, but danced so lightly over the snow that the tips of her toes left hardly a print in its surface; while Violet could but just keep pace with her, and Peony's short legs compelled him to lag behind.

Once in the course of their play, the strange child placed herself between Violet and Peony, and taking a hand of each, skipped merrily forward, and they along with her. Almost immediately, however, Peony pulled away his little fist, and began to rub it as if the fingers were tingling with cold; while Violet also released herself, though with less abruptness, gravely remarking that it was better not to take hold of hands. The white-robed damsel said not a word, but danced about, just as merrily as before. If Violet and Peony did not choose to play with her, she could make just as good a playmate of the brisk and cold west wind, which kept blowing her all about the garden, and took such liberties with her, that they seemed to have been friends for a long time. All this while, the mother stood on the threshold, wondering how a little girl could look so much like a flying snow-drift, or how a snow-drift could look so very like a little girl.

She called Violet, and whispered to her.

"Violet, my darling, what is this child's name?" asked she. "Does she live near us?"

"Why, dearest mamma," answered Violet, laughing to think that her mother did not comprehend so very plain an affair, "this is our little snow-sister, whom we have just been making!"

"Yes, dear mamma," cried Peony, running to his mother, and looking up simply into her face. "This is our snow-image! Is it not a nice 'ittle child?"

At this instant a flock of snow-birds came flitting through the air. As was very natural, they avoided Violet and Peony. But—and this looked strange,—they flew at once to the white-robed child, fluttered eagerly about her head, alighted on her shoulders, and seemed to claim her as an old acquaintance. She, on her part, was evidently as glad to see these little birds, old Winter's grandchildren, as they were to see her, and welcomed them by holding out both her hands. Hereupon, they each and all tried to alight on her two palms and ten small fingers and thumbs, crowding one another off, with an immense fluttering of their tiny wings. One dear little bird nestled tenderly in her bosom; another put its bill to her lips. They were as joyous, all the while, and seemed as much in their element, as you may have seen them when sporting with a snow storm.

Violet and Peony stood laughing at this pretty sight; for they enjoyed the merry time which their new play-mate was having with these small-winged visitants, almost as much as if they themselves took part in it.

"Violet," said her mother, greatly perplexed, "tell me the truth, without any jest. Who is this little girl?"

"My darling mamma," answered Violet, looking seriously into her mother's face, and apparently surprised that she should need any further explanation, "I have told you truly who she is. It is our little snow-image, which Peony and I have been making. Peony will tell you so, as well as I."

"Yes, mamma," asseverated Peony, with much gravity in his crimson little phiz; "this is 'ittle snow-child. Is not she a nice one? But, mamma, her hand, is, oh, so very cold!"

While mamma still hesitated what to think and what to do, the street-gate was thrown open, and the father of Violet and Peony appeared, wrapped in a pilot-cloth sack, with a fur cap drawn down over his ears, and the thickest of gloves upon his hands. Mr. Lindsey was a middle-aged man, with a weary and yet a happy look in his wind-flushed and frost-pinched face, as if he had been busy all the day long, and was glad to get back to his quiet home. His eyes brightened at the sight of his wife and children, although he could not help uttering a word or two of surprise, at finding the whole family in the open air, on so bleak a day, and after sunset too. He soon perceived the little white stranger, sporting to and fro in the garden, like a dancing snow-wreath, and the flock of snow-birds fluttering about her head.

"Pray, what little girl may that be?" inquired this very sensible man. "Surely her mother must be crazy, to let her go out in such bitter weather as it has been today, with only that flimsy white gown, and those thin slippers!"

"My dear husband," said his wife, "I know no more about the little thing than you do. Some neighbor's child, I suppose. Our Violet and Peony," she added, laughing at herself for repeating so absurd a story, "insist that she is nothing but a snow-image, which they have been busy about in the garden, almost all the afternoon."

As she said this, the mother glanced her eyes toward the spot where the children's snow-image had been made. What was her surprise, on perceiving that there was not the slightest trace of so much labor!—no image at all!—no piled-up heap of snow!—nothing whatever, save the prints of little footsteps around a vacant space!

"This is very strange!" said she.

"What is strange, dear mother?" asked Violet. "Dear father, do not you see how it is? This is our snow-image, which Peony and I have made, because we wanted another playmate. Did not we, Peony?"

"Yes, papa," said crimson Peony. "This be our 'ittle snow-sister. Is she not beau-ti-ful? But she gave me such a cold kiss!"

"Poh, nonsense, children!" cried their good, honest father, who, as we have already intimated, had an exceedingly common-sensible way of looking at matters. "Do not tell me of making live figures out of snow. Come, wife; this little stranger must not stay out in the bleak air a moment longer. We will bring her into the parlor; and you shall give her a supper of warm bread and milk, and make her as comfortable as you can. Meanwhile, I will inquire among the neighbors; or, if necessary, send the city-crier about the streets, to give notice of a lost child."

So saying, this honest and very kind-hearted man was going toward the little white damsel, with the best intentions in the world. But Violet and Peony, each seizing their father by the hand, earnestly besought him not to make her come in.

"Dear father," cried Violet, putting herself before

him, "it is true what I have been telling you! This is our little snow-girl, and she cannot live any longer than while she breathes the cold west wind. Do not make her come into the hot room!"

"Yes, father," shouted Peony, stamping his little foot, so mightily was he in earnest, "this be nothing but our 'ittle snow-child! She will not love the hot fire!"

"Nonsense, children, nonsense, nonsense!" cried the father, half vexed, half laughing at what he considered their foolish obstinacy. "Run into the house, this moment! It is too late to play any longer, now. I must take care of this little girl immediately, or she will catch her death-a-cold!"

"Husband! dear husband!" said his wife, in a low voice,—for she had been looking narrowly at the snow-child, and was more perplexed than ever,—"there is something very singular in all this. You will think me foolish,—but—but—may it not be that some invisible angel has been attracted by the simplicity and good faith with which our children set about their under-taking? May he not have spent an hour of his immortality in playing with those dear little souls? and so the result is what we call a miracle. No, no! Do not laugh at me; I see what a foolish thought it is!"

"My dear wife," replied the husband, laughing heart-ily, "you are as much a child as Violet and Peony."

And in one sense so she was, for all through life she had kept her heart full of childlike simplicity and faith, which was as pure and clear as crystal; and, looking at all matters through this transparent medium, she sometimes saw truths so profound, that other people laughed at them as nonsense and absurdity.

But now kind Mr. Lindsey had entered the garden, breaking away from his two children, who still sent their shrill voices after him, beseeching him to let the snow-child stay and enjoy herself in the cold west wind. As he approached, the snow-birds took to flight. The little white damsel, also, fled backward, shaking her head, as if to say, "Pray, do not touch me!" and roguishly, as it appeared, leading him through the deepest of the snow. Once, the good man stumbled, and floundered down upon his face, so that, gathering himself up again, with the snow sticking to his rough pilot-cloth sack, he looked as white and wintry as a snow-image of the largest size. Some of the neighbors, meanwhile, seeing him from their windows, wondered what could possess poor Mr. Lindsey to be running about his garden in pursuit of a snow-drift, which the west wind was driving hither and thither! At length, after a vast deal of trouble, he chased the little stranger into a corner, where she could not possibly escape him. His wife had been looking on, and, it being nearly twilight, was wonder-struck to observe how the snow-child gleamed and sparkled, and how she seemed to shed a glow all round about her; and when driven into the corner, she positively glistened like a star! It was a frosty kind of brightness, too, like that of an icicle in the moonlight. The wife thought it strange that good Mr. Lindsey should see nothing remarkable in the snow-child's appearance.

"Come, you odd little thing!" cried the honest man, seizing her by the hand, "I have caught you at last, and will make you comfortable in spite of yourself. We will put a nice warm pair of worsted stockings on your frozen little feet, and you shall have a good thick shawl to wrap yourself in. Your poor white nose, I am afraid, is actually frost-bitten. But we will make it all right. Come along in."

And so, with a most benevolent smile on his

sagacious visage, all purple as it was with the cold, this very well meaning gentleman took the snow-child by the hand and led her towards the house. She followed him, droopingly and reluctant; for all the glow and sparkle was gone out of her figure; and whereas just before she had resembled a bright, frosty, star-gemmed evening, with a crimson gleam on the cold horizon, she now looked as dull and languid as a thaw. As kind Mr. Lindsey led her up the steps of the door, Violet and Peony looked into his face,—their eyes full of tears, which froze before they could run down their cheeks,—and again entreated him not to bring their snow-image into the house.

"Not bring her in!" exclaimed the kind-hearted man. "Why, you are crazy, my little Violet!—quite crazy, my small Peony! She is so cold, already, that her hand has almost frozen mine, in spite of my thick gloves. Would you have her freeze to death?"

His wife, as he came up the steps, had been taking another long, earnest, almost awe-stricken gaze at the little white stranger. She hardly knew whether it was a dream or no; but she could not help fancying that she saw the delicate print of Violet's fingers on the child's neck. It looked just as if, while Violet was shaping out the image, she had given it a gentle pat with her hand, and had neglected to smooth the impression quite away.

"After all, husband," said the mother, recurring to her idea that the angels would be as much delighted to play with Violet and Peony as she herself was, "after all she does look strangely like a snow-image! I do believe she is made of snow!"

A puff of the west wind blew against the snow-child, and again she sparkled like a star.

"Snow!" repeated good Mr. Lindsey, drawing the reluctant guest over his hospitable threshold. "No wonder she looks like snow. She is half frozen, poor little thing! But a good fire will put everything to rights."

Without further talk, and always with the same best intentions, this highly benevolent and common-sensible individual led the little white damsel—drooping, drooping, drooping, more and more—out of the frosty air, and into his comfortable parlor. A Heidenberg stove, filled to the brim with intensely burning anthracite, was sending a bright gleam through the isinglass of its iron door, and causing the vase of water on its top to fume and bubble with excitement. A warm, sultry smell was diffused throughout the room. A thermometer on the wall furthest from the stove stood at eighty degrees. The parlor was hung with red curtains, and covered with a red carpet, and looked just as warm as it felt. The difference betwixt the atmosphere here and the cold wintry twilight out of doors, was like stepping at once from Nova Zembla to the hottest part of India, or from the North Pole into an oven. O, this was a fine place for the little white stranger!

The common-sensible man placed the snow-child on the hearthrug, right in front of the hissing and fuming stove.

"Now she will be comfortable!" cried Mr. Lindsey, rubbing his hands and looking about him with the pleasantest smile you ever saw. "Make yourself at home, my child."

Sad, sad and drooping, looked the little white maiden, as she stood on the hearth-rug, with the hot blast of the stove striking through her like a pestilence. Once, she threw a glance wistfully toward the windows, and caught a glimpse through its red curtains, of the snow-covered roofs, and the stars glimmering frostily, and all the delicious intensity of the cold night. The bleak wind rattled the window-panes, as if it were summoning her to come forth. But there stood the snow-child, drooping, before the hot stove!

But the common-sensible man saw nothing amiss. "Come, wife," said he, "let her have a pair of thick stockings and a woollen shawl or blanket directly; and tell Dora to give her some warm supper as soon as the milk boils. You, Violet and Peony, amuse your little friend. She is out of spirits, you see, at finding herself in a strange place. For my part I will go around among the neighbors, and find out where she belongs."

The mother, meanwhile, had gone in search of the shawl and stockings; for her own view of the matter, however subtle and delicate, had given way, as it always did, to the stubborn materialism of her husband. Without heeding the remonstrances of his two children, who still kept murmuring that their little snow-sister did not love the warmth, good Mr. Lindsey took his departure, shutting the parlor door carefully behind him. Turning up the collar of his sack over his ears, he emerged from the house, and had barely reached the street-gate, when he was recalled by the screams of Violet and Peony, and the rapping of a thimbled finger against the parlor window.

"Husband! husband!" cried his wife, showing her horror-stricken face through the window-panes. "There is no need of going for the child's parents!"

"We told you so, father!" screamed Violet and Peony, as he reentered the parlor. "You would bring her in; and now our poor—dear—beau-ti-ful little snow-sister is thawed!"

And their own sweet little faces were already dissolved in tears; so that their father, seeing what strange things occasionally happen in this every-day world, felt not a little anxious lest his children might be going to thaw too! In the utmost perplexity, he demanded an explanation of his wife. She could only reply, that, being summoned to the parlor by the cries of Violet and Peony, she found no trace of the little white maiden, unless it were the remains of a heap of snow, which, while she was gazing at it, melted quite away upon the hearth-rug.

"And there you see all that is left of it!" added she, pointing to a pool of water, in front of the stove.

"Yes, father," said Violet, looking reproachfully at him, through her tears, "there is all that is left of our dear little snow-sister!"

"Naughty father!" cried Peony, stamping his foot, and—I shudder to say—shaking his little fist at the common-sensible man. "We told you how it would be! What for did you bring her in?"

And the Heidenberg stove, through the isinglass of its door, seemed to glare at good Mr. Lindsey, like a red-eyed demon, triumphing in the mischief which it had done!

This, you will observe, was one of those rare cases, which yet will occasionally happen, where common-sense finds itself at fault. The remarkable story of the snow-image, though to that sagacious class of people to whom good Mr. Lindsey belongs it may seem but a childish affair, is, nevertheless, capable of being moralized in various methods,—greatly for their edification. One of its lessons, for instance, might be, that it behooves men, and especially men of benevolence, to consider well what they are about, and, before acting on their philanthropic purposes, to be quite sure that they comprehend the nature and all the relations of the business in hand. What has been established as an element of good to one being may prove absolute mischief to another, even as the warmth of the parlor was proper enough for children of flesh and blood like Violet and Peony,—though by no means very wholesome, even for them,—but involved nothing short of annihilation to the unfortunate snow-image.

But, after all, there is no teaching anything to wise men of good Mr. Lindsey's stamp. They know everything——oh, to be sure!—everything that has been, and everything that is, and everything that by any future possibility can be. And, should some phenomenon of nature or providence transcend their system, they will not recognize it, even if it come to pass under their very noses.

"Wife," said Mr. Lindsey, after a fit of silence, "see what a quantity of snow the children have brought in on their feet! It has made quite a puddle here before the stove. Pray tell Dora to bring some towels and sop it up!"

FYODOR DOSTOEVSKY [trans. Garnett]

A Christmas Tree And a Wedding

The other day I saw a wedding . . . but no, I had better tell you about the Christmas tree. The wedding was nice, I liked it very much; but the other incident was better. I don't know how it was that, looking at that wedding, I thought of that Christmas tree. This was what happened. Just five years ago, on New Year's Eve, I was invited to a children's party. The giver of the party was a well-known and business-like personage, with connections, with a large circle of acquaintances, and a good many schemes on hand, so that it may be supposed that this party was an excuse for getting the parents together and discussing various interesting matters in an innocent, casual way. I was an outsider; I had no interesting matter to contribute, and so I spent the evening rather independently. There was another gentleman present who was, I fancied, of no special rank or family, and who, like me, had simply turned up at this family festivity. He was the first to catch my eye. He was a tall, lanky man, very grave and very correctly dressed. But one could see that he was in no mood for merrymaking and family festivity; whenever he with-drew into a corner he left off smiling and knitted his bushy black brows. He had not a single acquaintance in the party except his host. One could see that he was fearfully bored, but that he was valiantly keeping up the part of a man perfectly happy and enjoying himself. I learned afterwards that this was a gentleman from the provinces, who had a critical and perplexing piece of business in Petersburg, who had brought a letter of introduction to our host, for whom our host was, by no means *con amore,* using his interest, and whom he had invited, out of civility, to his children's party. He did not play cards, cigars were not offered him, every one avoided entering into conversation with him most likely recognising the bird from its feathers; and so the gentleman was forced to sit the whole evening stroking his whiskers simply to have something to do with his hands. His whiskers were certainly very fine. But he stroked them so zealously that, looking at him, one might have supposed that the whiskers were created first and the gentleman only attached to them in order to stroke them.

In addition to this individual who assisted in this way at our host's family festivity (he had five fat, well-fed boys), I was attracted, too, by another gentleman. But he was quite of a different sort. He was a personage. He was called Yulian Mastakovitch. From the first glance one could see that he was an honoured guest, and stood in the same relation to our host as our host stood in relation to the gentleman who was stroking his whis-kers. Our host and hostess said no end of polite things to him, waited on him hand and foot, pressed him to drink, flattered him, brought their visitors up to be introduced to him, but did not take him to be introduced to any one else. I noticed that tears glistened in our host's eyes when he remarked about the party that he had rarely spent an evening so agreeably. I felt as it were frightened in the presence of such a personage, and so, after admiring the children, I went away into a little parlour, which was quite empty, and sat down in an arbour of flowers which filled up almost half the room.

The children were all incredibly sweet, and resolutely refused to model themselves on the "grown-ups," regardless of all the admonitions of their governesses and mammas. They stripped the Christmas tree to the last sweetmeat in the twinkling of an eye, and had succeeded in breaking half the playthings before they knew what was destined for which. Particularly charming was a black-eyed, curly headed boy, who kept trying to shoot me with his wooden gun. But my attention was still more attracted by his sister, a girl of eleven, quiet, dreamy, pale, with big, prominent, dreamy eyes, exquisite as a little Cupid. The children hurt her feelings in some way, and so she came away from them to the same empty parlour in which I was sitting, and played with her doll in the corner. The visitors respectfully pointed out her father, a wealthy contractor, and some one whispered that three hundred thousand roubles were already set aside for her dowry. I turned round to glance at the group who were interested in such a circumstance, and my eye fell on Yulian Mastakovitch, who, with his hands behind his back and his head on one side, was listening with the greatest attention to these gentlemen's idle gossip. Afterwards I could not help admiring the discrimination of the host and hostess in the distribution of the children's presents. The little girl, who had already a portion of three hundred

thousand roubles, received the costliest doll. Then followed presents diminishing in value in accordance with
the rank of the parents of these hippy children; finally,
the child of lowest degree, a thin, freckled, red-haired
little boy of ten, got nothing but a book of stories about
the marvels of nature and tears of devotion, etc., without pictures or even woodcuts. He was the son of a poor
widow, the governess of the children of the house, an
oppressed and scared little boy. He was dressed in a
short jacket of inferior napkin. After receiving his book
he walked round the other toys for a long time; he
longed to play with the other children, but did not dare;
it was evident that he already felt and understood his
position. I love watching children. Their first independent approaches to life are extremely interesting. I
noticed that the red-haired boy was so fascinated by the
costly toys of the other children, especially by a theatre
in which he certainly longed to take some part, that he
made up his mind to sacrifice his dignity. He smiled
and began playing with the other children, he gave
away his apple to a fat-faced little boy who had a mass
of goodies tied up in a pocket-handkerchief already,
and even brought himself to carry another boy on his
back, simply not to be turned away from the theatre,
but an insolent youth gave him a heavy thump a minute
later. The child did not dare to cry. Then the governess,
his mother, made her appearance, and told him not to
interfere with the other children's playing. The boy
went away to the same room in which was the little girl.
She let him join her, and the two set to work very
eagerly dressing the expensive doll.

I had been sitting more than half an hour in the ivy
arbour, listening to the little prattle of the red-haired
boy and the beauty with the dowry of three hundred

thousand, who was nursing her doll, when Yulian Mastakovitch suddenly walked into the room. He had taken advantage of the general commotion following a quarrel among the children to step out of the drawing-room. I had noticed him a moment before talking very cordially to the future heiress's papa, whose acquaintance he had just made, of the superiority of one branch of the service over another. Now he stood in hesitation and seemed to be reckoning something on his fingers.

"Three hundred . . . three hundred," he was whispering. "Eleven . . . twelve . . . thirteen," and so on. "Sixteen—five years! Supposing it is at four per cent—five times twelve is sixty; yes, to that sixty . . . well, in five years we may assume it will be four hundred. Yes! . . . But he won't stick to four per cent, the rascal. He can get eight or ten. Well, five hundred, let us say, five hundred at least . . . that's certain; well, say a little more for frills. H'm! . . ."

His hesitation was at an end, he blew his nose and was on the point of going out of the room when he suddenly glanced at the little girl and stopped short. He did not see me behind the pots of greenery. It seemed to me that he was greatly excited. Either his calculations had affected his imagination or something else, for he rubbed his hands and could hardly stand still. This excitement reached its utmost limit when he stopped and bent another resolute glance at the future heiress. He was about to move forward, but first looked round, then moving on tiptoe, as though he felt guilty, he advanced towards the children. He approached with a little smile, bent down and kissed her on the head. The child, not expecting this attack, uttered a cry of alarm.

"What are you doing here, sweet child?" he asked in a whisper, looking round and patting the girl's cheek.

"We are playing."

"Ah! With him?" Yulian Mastakovitch looked askance at the boy. "You had better go into the drawing-room, my dear," he said to him.

The boy looked at him open-eyed and did not utter a word. Yulian Mastakovitch looked round him again, and again bent down to the little girl.

"And what is this you've got—a dolly, dear child?" he asked.

"Yes, a dolly," answered the child, frowning and a little shy.

"A dolly . . . and do you know, dear child, what your dolly is made of?"

"I don't know . . ." the child answered in a whisper, hanging her head.

"It's made of rags, darling. You had better go into the drawing room to your playmates, boy," said Yulian Mastakovitch, looking sternly at the boy. The boy and girl frowned and clutched at each other. They did not want to be separated.

"And do you know why they gave you that doll?" asked Yulian Mastakovitch, dropping his voice to a softer and softer tone.

"I don't know."

"Because you have been a sweet and well-behaved child all the week."

At this point Yulian Mastakovitch, more excited than ever, speaking in most dulcet tones, asked at last, in a hardly audible voice choked with emotion and impatience—

"And will you love me, dear little girl, when I come and see your papa and mamma?"

Saying this, Yulian Mastakovitch tried once more to kiss "the dear little girl," but the red-haired boy, seeing that the little girl was on the point of tears, clutched her hand and began whimpering from sympathy for her. Yulian Mastakovitch was angry in earnest.

"Go away, go away from here, go away!" he said to the boy. "Go into the drawing-room! Go in there to your playmates!"

"No, he needn't, he needn't! You go away," said the little girl. "Leave him alone, leave him alone," she said, almost crying. Some one made a sound at the door. Yulian Mastakovitch instantly raised his majestic person and took alarm. But the red-haired boy was even more alarmed than Yulian Mastakovitch; he abandoned the little girl and, slinking along by the wall, stole out of the parlour into the dining-room. To avoid arousing suspicion, Yulian Mastakovitch, too, went into the dining-room. He was as red as a lobster, and, glancing into the looking-glass, seemed to be ashamed at himself. He was perhaps vexed with himself for his impetuosity and hastiness. Possibly, he was at first so much impressed by his calculations, so inspired and fascinated by them, that in spite of his seriousness and dignity he made up his mind to behave like a boy, and directly approach the object of his attentions, even though she could not be really the object of his attentions for another five years at least. I followed the estimable gentleman into the dining-room and there beheld a strange spectacle. Yulian Mastakovitch, flushed with vexation and anger, was frightening the red-haired boy, who, retreating from him, did not know where to run in his terror.

"Go away; what are you doing here? Go away, you scamp; are you after the fruit here, eh? Get along, you naughty boy! Get along, you sniveller, to your playmates!"

The panic-stricken boy in his desperation tried creeping under the table. Then his persecutor, in a fury, took out his large batiste handkerchief and began flicking it under the table at the child, who kept perfectly quiet. It must be observed that Yulian Mastakovitch was a little inclined to be fat. He was a sleek, red-faced, solidly built man, paunchy, with thick legs; what is called a fine figure of a man, round as a nut. He was perspiring, breathless, and fearfully flushed. At last he was almost rigid, so great was his indignation and perhaps—who knows?—his jealousy. I burst into loud laughter. Yulian Mastakovitch turned round and, in spite of all his consequence, was overcome with confusion. At that moment from the opposite door our host came in. The boy crept out from under the table and wiped his elbows and his knees. Yulian Mastakovitch hastened to put to his nose the handkerchief which he was holding in his hand by one end.

Our host looked at the three of us in some perplexity; but as a man who knew something of life, and looked at it from a serious point of view, he at once availed himself of the chance of catching his visitor by himself.

"Here, this is the boy," he said, pointing to the red-haired boy, "for whom I had the honour to solicit your influence."

"Ah!" said Yulian Mastakovitch, who had hardly quite recovered himself.

"The son of my children's governess," said our host, in a tone of a petitioner, "a poor woman, the widow of an honest civil servant; and therefore . . . and therefore, Yulian Mastakovitch, if it were possible . . ."

"Oh, no, no!" Yulian Mastakovitch made haste to answer; "no, excuse me, Filip Alexyevitch, it's quite impossible. I've made inquiries; there's no vacancy, and if there were, there are twenty applicants who have far more claim than he . . . I am very sorry, very sorry . . ."

"What a pity," said our host. "He is a quiet, well-behaved boy."

"A great rascal, as I notice," answered Yulian Mastakovitch, with a nervous twist of his lip. "Get along, boy; why are you standing there? Go to your playmates," he said, addressing the child.

At that point he could not contain himself, and glanced at me out of one eye. I, too, could not contain myself, and laughed straight in his face. Yulian Mastakovitch turned away at once, and in a voice calculated to reach my ear, asked who was that strange young man? They whispered together and walked out of the room. I saw Yulian Mastakovitch afterwards shaking his head incredulously as our host talked to him.

After laughing to my heart's content I returned to the drawing room. There the great man, surrounded by fathers and mothers of families, including the host and hostess, was saying something very warmly to a lady to whom he had just been introduced. The lady was holding by the hand the little girl with whom Yulian Mastakovitch had had the scene in the parlour a little while before. Now he was launching into praises and raptures over the beauty, the talents, the grace and the charming manners of the charming child. He was unmistakably making up to the mamma. The mother listened to him almost with tears of delight. The father's lips were smiling. Our host was delighted at the general satisfaction. All the guests, in fact, were sympathetically gratified; even the children's games were checked that they might not hinder the conversation: the whole atmosphere was saturated with reverence. I heard afterwards the mamma of the interesting child, deeply touched, beg Yulian Mastakovitch, in carefully chosen phrases, to do her the special honour of bestowing upon them the precious gift of his acquaintance, and heard with what unaffected delight Yulian Mastakovitch accepted the invitation, and how afterwards the guests, dispersing in different directions, moving away with the greatest propriety, poured out to one another the most touchingly flattering comments upon the contractor, his wife, his little girl, and, above all, upon Yulian Mastakovitch.

"Is that gentleman married?" I asked, almost aloud, of one of my acquaintances, who was standing nearest to Yulian Mastakovitch. Yulian Mastakovitch flung a searching and vindictive glance at me.

"No!" answered my acquaintance, chagrined to the bottom of his heart by the awkwardness of which I had intentionally been guilty . . . I passed lately by a certain church; I was struck by the crowd of people in carriages. I heard people talking of the wedding. It was a cloudy day, it was beginning to sleet. I made my way through the crowd at the door and saw the bridegroom. He was a sleek, well-fed, round, paunchy man, very gorgeously dressed up. He was running fussily about, giving orders. At last the news passed through the crowd that the bride was coming. I squeezed my way through the crowd and saw a marvellous beauty, who could scarcely have reached her first season. But the beauty was pale and melancholy. She looked preoccupied; I even fancied that her eyes were red with recent weeping. The classic severity of every feature of her face gave a certain dignity and seriousness to her beauty. But through that sternness and dignity, through that melancholy, could be seen the look of childish innocence; something indescribably naive, fluid, youthful, which seemed mutely begging for mercy.

People were saying that she was only just sixteen. Glancing attentively at the bridegroom, I suddenly recognised him as Yulian Mastakovitch, whom I had not seen for five years. I looked at her. My God! I began to squeeze my way as quickly as I could out of the church. I heard people saying in the crowd that the bride was an heiress, that she had a dowry of five hundred thousand . . . and a trousseau worth ever so much.

"It was a good stroke of business, though!" I thought as I made my way into the street.

L. M. MONTGOMERY

Christmas at Red Butte

"Of course Santa Claus will come," said Jimmy Martin confidently. Jimmy was ten, and at ten it is easy to be confident. "Why, he's *got* to come because it is Christmas Eve, and he always *has* come. You know that, twins."

Yes, the twins knew it and, cheered by Jimmy's superior wisdom, their doubts passed away. There had been one terrible moment when Theodora had sighed and told them they mustn't be too much disappointed if Santa Claus did not come this year because the crops had been poor, and he mightn't have had enough presents to go around. "That doesn't make any difference to Santa Claus," scoffed Jimmy. "You know as well as I do, Theodora Prentice, that Santa Claus is rich whether the crops fail or not. They failed three years ago, before Father died, but Santa Claus came all the same. Prob'bly you don't remember it, twins, 'cause you were too little, but I do. Of course he'll come, so don't you worry a mite. And he'll bring my skates and your dolls. He knows we're expecting them, Theodora, 'cause we wrote him a letter last week, and threw it up the chimney. And there'll be candy and nuts, of course, and Mother's gone to town to buy a turkey. I tell you we're going to have a ripping Christmas."

"Well, don't use such slangy words about it, Jimmy-boy," sighed Theodora. She couldn't bear to dampen their hopes any further, and perhaps Aunt Elizabeth might manage it if the colt sold well. But Theodora had her painful doubts, and she sighed again as she looked out of the window far down the trail that wound across the prairie, red-lighted by the declining sun of the short wintry afternoon.

"Do people always sigh like that when they get to be sixteen?" asked Jimmy curiously. "You didn't sigh like that when you were only fifteen, Theodora. I wish you wouldn't. It makes me feel funny – and it's not a nice kind of funniness either."

"It's a bad habit I've got into lately," said Theodora, trying to laugh. "Old folks are dull sometimes, you know, Jimmy-boy."

"Sixteen *is* awful old, isn't it?" said Jimmy reflectively. "I'll tell you what *I'm* going to do when I'm sixteen, Theodora. I'm going to pay off the mortgage, and buy mother a silk dress, and a piano for the twins. Won't that be elegant? I'll be able to do that 'cause I'm a man. Of course if I was only a girl I couldn't."

"I hope you'll be a good kind brave man and a real help to your mother," said Theodora softly, sitting down before the cosy fire and lifting the fat little twins into her lap.

"Oh, I'll be good to her, never you fear," assured Jimmy, squatting comfortably down on the little fur rug before the stove – the skin of the coyote his father had killed four years ago. "I believe in being good to your mother when you've only got the one. Now tell us a story, Theodora – a real jolly story, you know, with lots of fighting in it. Only please don't kill anybody. I like to hear about fighting, but I like to have all the people come out alive." Theodora laughed, and began a story about the Riel Rebellion of '85 – a story which had the double merit of being true and exciting at the same time. It was quite dark when she finished, and the twins were nodding, but Jimmy's eyes were wide open and sparkling.

"That was great," he said, drawing a long breath. "Tell us another."

"No, it's bedtime for you all," said Theodora firmly. "One story at a time is my rule, you know."

"But I want to sit up till Mother comes home," objected Jimmy.

"You can't. She may be very late, for she would have to wait to see Mr. Porter. Besides, you don't know what time Santa Claus might come – if he comes at all. If he were to drive along and see you children up instead of being sound asleep in bed, he might go right on and never call at all."

This argument was too much for Jimmy.

"All right, we'll go. But we have to hang up our stockings first. Twins, get yours."

The twins toddled off in great excitement, and brought back their Sunday stockings, which Jimmy proceeded to hang along the edge of the mantel shelf. This done, they all trooped obediently off to bed. Theodora gave another sigh, and seated herself at the window, where she could watch the moonlit prairie for Mrs. Martin's homecoming and knit at the same time.

I am afraid that you will think from all the sighing Theodora was doing that she was a very melancholy and despondent young lady. You couldn't think anything more unlike the real Theodora. She was the jolliest, bravest girl of sixteen in all Saskatchewan, as her shining brown eyes and rosy, dimpled cheeks would have told you; and her sighs were not on her own account, but simply for fear the children were going to be disappointed. She knew that they would be almost heartbroken if Santa Claus did not come, and that this would hurt the patient hardworking little mother more than all else.

Five years before this, Theodora had come to live with Uncle George and Aunt Elizabeth in the little log house at Red Butte. Her own mother had just died, and Theodora had only her big brother Donald left, and Donald had Klondike fever. The Martins were poor, but they had gladly made room for their little niece, and Theodora had lived there ever since, her aunt's right-hand girl and the beloved playmate of the children. They had been very happy until Uncle George's death two years before this Christmas Eve; but since then there had been hard times in the little log house, and though Mrs. Martin and Theodora did their best, it was a woefully hard task to make both ends meet, especially this year when their crops had been poor. Theodora and her aunt had made every sacrifice possible for the children's sake, and at least Jimmy and the twins had not felt the pinch very severely yet.

At seven Mrs. Martin's bells jingled at the door and Theodora flew out. "Go right in and get warm, Auntie," she said briskly. "I'll take Ned away and unharness him."

"It's a bitterly cold night," said Mrs. Martin wearily. There was a note of discouragement in her voice that struck dismay to Theodora's heart.

"I'm afraid it means no Christmas for the children tomorrow," she thought sadly, as she led Ned away to the stable. When she returned to the kitchen Mrs. Martin was sitting by the fire, her face in her chilled hands, sobbing convulsively.

"Auntie – oh, Auntie, don't!" exclaimed Theodora impulsively. It was such a rare thing to see her plucky, resolute little aunt in tears. "You're cold and tired – I'll have a nice cup of tea for you in a trice."

"No, it isn't that," said Mrs. Martin brokenly. "It was seeing those stockings hanging there. Theodora, I couldn't get a thing for the children – not a single thing. Mr. Porter would only give forty dollars for the colt, and when all the bills were paid there was barely enough left for such necessaries as we must have. I suppose I ought to feel thankful I could get those. But the thought of the children's disappointment tomorrow is more than I can bear. It would have been better to have told them long ago, but I kept building on getting more for the colt. Well, it's weak and foolish to give way like this. We'd better both take a cup of tea and go to bed. It will save fuel."

When Theodora went up to her little room her face was very thoughtful. She took a small box from her table and carried it to the window. In it was a very pretty little gold locket hung on a narrow blue ribbon. Theodora held it tenderly in her fingers, and looked out over the moonlit prairie with a very sober face. Could she give up her dear locket – the locket Donald had given her just before he started for the Klondike? She had never thought she could do such a thing. It was almost the only thing she had to remind her of Donald – handsome, merry, impulsive, warmhearted Donald, who had gone away four years ago with a smile on his bonny face and splendid hope in his heart.

"Here's a locket for you, Gift o' God," he had said gaily – he had such a dear loving habit of calling her by the beautiful meaning of her name. A lump came into Theodora's throat as she remembered it. "I couldn't afford a chain too, but when I come back I'll bring you a rope of Klondike nuggets for it."

Then he had gone away. For two years letters had come from him regularly. Then he wrote that he had joined a prospecting party to a remote wilderness. After that was silence, deepening into anguish of suspense that finally ended in hopelessness. A rumour came that Donald Prentice was dead. None had returned from the expedition he had joined. Theodora had long ago given up all hope of ever seeing Donald again. Hence her locket was doubly dear to her.

But Aunt Elizabeth had always been so good and loving and kind to her. Could she not make the sacrifice for her sake? Yes, she could and would. Theodora flung up her head with a gesture that meant decision. She took out of the locket the bits of hair – her mother's and Donald's – which it contained (perhaps a tear or two fell as she did so) and then hastily donned her warmest cap and wraps. It was only three miles to Spencer; she could easily walk it in an hour and, as it was Christmas Eve, the shops would be open late. She must walk, for Ned could not be taken out again, and the mare's foot was sore. Besides, Aunt Elizabeth must not know until it was done.

As stealthily as if she were bound on some nefarious errand, Theodora slipped downstairs and out of the house. The next minute she was hurrying along the trail in the moonlight. The great dazzling prairie was around her, the mystery and splendour of the northern night all about her. It was very calm and cold, but Theodora walked so briskly that she kept warm. The trail from Red Butte to Spencer was a lonely one. Mr. Lurgan's house, halfway to town, was the only dwelling on it.

When Theodora reached Spencer she made her way at once to the only jewellery store the little town contained. Mr. Benson, its owner, had been a friend of her uncle's, and Theodora felt sure that he would buy her locket. Nevertheless her heart beat quickly, and her breath came and went uncomfortably fast as she went in. Suppose he wouldn't buy it. Then there would be no Christmas for the children at Red Butte.

"Good evening, Miss Theodora," said Mr. Benson briskly. "What can I do for you?"

"I'm afraid I'm not a very welcome sort of customer, Mr. Benson," said Theodora, with an uncertain smile. "I want to sell, not buy. Could you – will you buy this locket?"

Mr. Benson pursed up his lips, took up the locket, and examined it. "Well, I don't often buy second-hand stuff," he said, after some reflection, "but I don't mind obliging you, Miss Theodora. I'll give you four dollars for this trinket."

Theodora knew the locket had cost a great deal more than that, but four dollars would get what she wanted, and she dared not ask for more. In a few minutes the locket was in Mr. Benson's possession, and Theodora, with four crisp new bills in her purse, was hurrying to the toy store. Half an hour later she was on her way back to Red Butte, with as many parcels as she could carry – Jimmy's skates, two lovely dolls for the twins, packages of nuts and candy, and a nice plump turkey.

Theodora beguiled her lonely tramp by picturing the children's joy in the morning.

About a quarter of a mile past Mr. Lurgan's house the trail curved suddenly about a bluff of poplars. As Theodora rounded the turn she halted in amazement. Almost at her feet the body of a man was lying across the road. He was clad in a big fur coat, and had a fur cap pulled well down over his forehead and ears. Almost all of him that could be seen was a full bushy beard. Theodora had no idea who he was, or where he had come from. But she realized that he was unconscious, and that he would speedily freeze to death if help were not brought. The footprints of a horse galloping across the prairie suggested a fall and a runaway, but Theodora did not waste time in speculation. She ran back at full speed to Mr. Lurgan's, and roused the house-hold. In a few minutes Mr. Lurgan and his son had hitched a horse to a wood-sleigh, and hurried down the trail to the unfortunate man.

Theodora, knowing that her assistance was not needed, and that she ought to get home as quickly as possible, went on her way as soon as she had seen the stranger in safe keeping. When she reached the little log house she crept in, cautiously put the children's gifts in their stockings, placed the turkey on the table where Aunt Elizabeth would see it the first thing in the morning, and then slipped off to bed, a very weary but very happy girl.

The joy that reigned in the little log house the next day more than repaid Theodora for her sacrifice.

"Whoopee, didn't I tell you that Santa Claus would come all right!" shouted the delighted Jimmy. "Oh, what splendid skates!"

The twins hugged their dolls in silent rapture, but Aunt Elizabeth's face was the best of all.

Then the dinner had to be prepared, and everybody had a hand in that. Just as Theodora, after a grave peep into the oven, had announced that the turkey was done, a sleigh dashed around the house. Theodora flew to answer the knock at the door, and there stood Mr. Lurgan and a big, bewhiskered, fur-coated fellow whom Theodora recognized as the stranger she had found on the trail. But – *was* he a stranger? There was something oddly familiar in those merry brown eyes. Theodora felt herself growing dizzy.

"Donald!" she gasped. "Oh, Donald!"

And then she was in the big fellow's arms, laughing and crying at the same time.

Donald it was indeed. And then followed half an hour during which everybody talked at once, and the turkey would have been burned to a crisp had it not been for the presence of mind of Mr. Lurgan who, being the least excited of them all, took it out of the oven, and set it on the back of the stove.

"To think that it was you last night, and that I never dreamed it," exclaimed Theodora. "Oh, Donald, if I hadn't gone to town!"

"I'd have frozen to death, I'm afraid," said Donald soberly. "I got into Spencer on the last train last night. I felt that I must come right out – I couldn't wait till morning. But there wasn't a team to be got for love or money – it was Christmas Eve and all the livery rigs were out. So I came on horse-back. Just by that bluff something frightened my horse, and he shied violently. I was half asleep and thinking of my little sister, and I went off like a shot. I suppose I struck my head against a tree. Anyway, I knew nothing more until I came to in

Mr. Lurgan's kitchen. I wasn't much hurt – feel none the worse of it except for a sore head and shoulder. But, oh, Gift o' God, how you have grown! I can't realize that you are the little sister I left four years ago. I suppose you have been thinking I was dead?"

"Yes, and, oh, Donald, where *have* you been?"

"Well, I went way up north with a prospecting party. We had a tough time the first year, I can tell you, and some of us never came back. We weren't in a country where post offices were lying round loose either, you see. Then at last, just as we were about giving up in despair, we struck it rich. I've brought a snug little pile home with me, and things are going to look up in this log house, Gift o' God. There'll be no more worrying for you dear people over mortgages."

"I'm so glad – for Auntie's sake," said Theodora, with shining eyes. "But, oh, Donald, it's best of all just to have you back. I'm so perfectly happy that I don't know what to do or say."

"Well, I think you might have dinner," said Jimmy in an injured tone. "The turkey's getting stone cold, and I'm most starving. I just can't stand it another minute."

So, with a laugh, they all sat down to the table and ate the merriest Christmas dinner the little log house had ever known.